THE COUNTESS INVENTION

LORDS AND UNDEFEATED LADIES BOOK 2

JUDITH LYNNE

Copyright © 2020 by Judith Lynne. 3rd Ed.

All rights reserved.

No part of this book may be reproduced in any form or by any electronic or mechanical means, including information storage and retrieval systems, without written permission from the author, except for the use of brief quotations in a book review.

This is a work of fiction. Names, characters, places, and incidents are either the product of the author's imagination or are used fictitiously, and any resemblance to actual persons living or dead, business establishments, events, or locales, is entirely coincidental.

Cover art by Melody Simmons

BOOKS BY JUDITH LYNNE

Lords and Undefeated Ladies

Not Like a Lady

The Countess Invention

What a Duchess Does

Crown of Hearts

He Stole the Lady (January 2022)

Cloaks and Countesses

The Caped Countess

The Clandestine Countess (July 2022)

PREFACE

Dear reader,

The events of *Not Like a Lady* took place in June of 1812, but its epilogue was set in December of 1813, fully eighteen months later. Many things occurred in those eighteen months, including the events of this novel, which begins in October of 1812. I hope you will therefore not be surprised at the appearance of many of our friends from *Not Like a Lady* within these pages.

Your obedient servant,
Judith Lynne

CHAPTER 1

The kitchen was controlled chaos.

"Does herself want tea?" Mrs. Orfill asked, pointing at the teapot.

Peg, the maid, shook her head no.

Mrs. Orfill nodded, sugared the porridge on the tray and added the napkin and silver spoon the mistress liked.

Her hands were calm, but her voice quavered a little. She ignored the shaking of her nerves. They all would. Everyone knew their livelihoods were on the line.

"If she don't want tea, she wants chocolate." Mrs. Orfill had filled the role of housekeeper as well as cook for a while, and she was the kind of person who used a little silver bowl to keep the butter cold, because she knew the mistress liked the butter cold.

* * *

OUTSIDE THE FRONT door it was quiet. A few people walking past on the little street saw Dr. Oliver Burke waiting at the townhouse front door.

A door on which he knocked at precisely eleven o'clock.

Gloves in one hand, he used the other to tuck the letter back into his coat pocket. Surely it wouldn't be necessary to show it. He had been invited, after all.

Dear Dr. Burke, I have a commission for an artificial leg that has given me some trouble.

He was struggling to remember the protocol for a visit to an actual colleague.

Perhaps he needed more actual friends, he thought to himself, not just lonely women.

Oliver considered himself a connoisseur of lonely women. Older ones who kept him on retainer as a physician, and younger ones, married or widowed, who did not.

The world was cruel to lonely women, and Oliver loved both conversation and women. Some days, it seemed that he had talked to every lonely woman in London.

His patients summoned him for tedious illnesses they could not shake, and even for company. Oliver didn't mind; his patients were, as a group, even more interesting than the younger married or widowed ones with whom he spent evenings, or nights. Sometimes, in fact, just talking. They were lonely, that was all.

You know I am not a medical man, and if I were, I doubt I could match your experience with such surgery.

There was of course yet another category of women, those that were quite young and still looking for a husband. Those seldom had any thought in their head other than husband-hunting. Avoiding their company was no hardship, and avoid it he did.

I feel confident I could produce a better designed result if I better understood the limb's reaction to amputation.

What he was missing was professional consultation. A collaborator. The inventor Mr. Cullen, with whom he'd been corresponding for months, seemed just the ticket.

* * *

Upstairs, the noise was all in Cass' head.

As the mistress of the house, Cass should have let Peg help her. But Peg didn't think this was going to work. And her old friend was a better housemaid than a ladies' maid.

Though perhaps a ladies' maid wasn't the right person to turn the mistress of the house into its master, either.

How hard could it be to be a man?

The small, narrow mirror only showed a few inches of her at a time, and they were always the wrong inches.

The suit fit well across the shoulders; Cass could be grateful today for the squareness of her shoulders. The coat dipped at the waist as it should, and skimmed past her hips, again very much as it would if a man were wearing it.

She'd wrapped her breasts snugly; the waistcoat and cravat would be fine. It was her hair, her blasted hair that would give her away.

For a woman, her hair was short. Cass didn't like a big weight on her head pulling her this way or that while she was trying to think. Last night she'd put in pin-curls, believing that she could arrange the curls to give the impression of a Brutus haircut, tousled at the top, with perhaps a few hairs at the side to impersonate sideburns.

She couldn't. They didn't. Pinned up at the nape of her neck, as far as she could tell in the glass, the back was fine, especially if she put on a hat, as she fully intended to do. The crown and the front, well…

Her hair didn't look like a young gentleman's; it looked like a schoolgirl's.

It was driving her mad.

Cass seized a pair of scissors, thinking to just cut the whole mass off, but in the end, she couldn't do it.

Why not? Vanity? What was the point of that? The face in the mirror was just her face, and had never inspired anyone to any observable fit of passion. Of feminine wiles, she knew she had none.

She wavered. Perhaps she ought to try the scissors. This *had* to work. Her home and everyone in it depended on this.

She couldn't. Aside from any remaining dregs of misplaced vanity, her grandmother would have hated it.

Cass folded her lips tight. She wished her grandmother could have simply left her this house, plain and simple; but women were not allowed to own property. Instead her grandmother had left her the *use* of the house.

But her father actually owned the house, and his conditions had to be met for her to stay in it.

Cass smoothed down the dark blue coat. If anything, Cass felt *more* appropriate dressed this way. It felt more right than the lavender half-mourning gown she'd put aside this morning. No matter that it was well more than a year since her grandmother had passed away, or that many did not long mourn their grandparents; Cass still missed her, every day.

She *had* to make this work to stay in her home. For such this was.

But her grandmother wouldn't have approved of cutting off her hair to do it.

She wouldn't have said anything. She would have had a disappointed, shocked look.

Cass could see it now, could see her silver-haired grandmother sitting quietly in her dark gown and pearls, perhaps knitting. No need to struggle with conversation; her grandmother preferred the quiet.

As did Cass.

* * *

Mrs. Orfill waved a hand at Peg. "Three minutes." She showed the same number of fingers. "Selene!"

The other maid, Selene, appeared around the corner, sailing gracefully in her starched white apron. "Yes, ma'am?"

"She's having chocolate. Likely she'll want an early luncheon or none at all. Better dust whatever you can in the library before she gets in there, because you won't get in there again today."

"Yes, ma'am," Selene nodded and disappeared.

"Mrs. Orfill, calm yourself," said Mr. Adams, the butler, as he arrived to take the tray. "Everyone knows what to do."

This was rich coming from him, as his eyes kept darting toward the front door, which the mistress had told him not to answer until she signaled she was ready.

"Of course, Mr. Adams, I know, I know," and the worthy woman slipped a few cheering pansy blooms onto the tray. "She's just been so worried, it makes me worry for her. Isn't there anything you can do to help her?"

Mr. Adams lifted the tray, but Peg, who was also his wife, shook her head and relieved him of it, disappearing up the stairs before he could object.

Mr. Adams helped himself to a cup of the tea the mistress hadn't wanted. "If this were not so alarming, it might be hilarious." He did not look like he found anything currently hilarious.

Mrs. Orfill clucked to herself. "She's borrowed your suit?"

He shrugged. "She has."

"Can't you do something?"

Mr. Adams looked worried, but shrugged again as he sipped more tea. "I've already loaned her my suit."

* * *

OLIVER HAD DECIDED as a boy that life was too short for self-denial. His medical studies had only confirmed the idea, and long before he'd gone off to the wars. A soldier feared that life was short; a physician knew it for certain.

The women with whom he spent his time were, as a category, intelligent. That was the type of conversation he liked, almost as much as he liked sharing a lady's bed.

In fact, talking was much safer than lovemaking. Talking avoided delicate questions about contagious diseases, or whether the lady would be shocked by the methods of contraception at his disposal. If a French letter would disgust her, talking could still turn the evening into a very pleasurable encounter.

And though no one would guess it from his spartan bachelor rooms, Oliver loved pleasure, and he loved women's pleasure even more than he loved his own.

Though he hadn't enjoyed himself much of late. Yes, his visit to Lady Hemsworth while her husband was out of town had been weeks ago—or had it really been months? He was working too much if he couldn't remember.

Were there no more lonely women in London? Oliver kept strict division between his patients and his *affaires*, but if he were this excited to meet a colleague, he needed other social interests.

That was why he was nervous. He enjoyed Cullen's correspondence on engineering the machinery used by the sailors and soldiers who returned to England shy a limb. Of all the pleasures Oliver enjoyed, even in anticipation, letters from Mr. Cullen were near the top of the list.

Cullen's observations were brusque and brief, but always correct. He had a delightful way of dispensing with local news or news abroad in a few crisp sentences, then moving on to state the mechanical problem he was trying to solve.

If this proposed date would be acceptable, I wonder if you would be willing to visit me at home.

Oliver would.

He looked again down the quiet street and tried not to wonder if he had the correct time. The fellow was expecting him, after all.

* * *

CASS HADN'T HEARD anything anything from downstairs but then she would not have. According to the clock, if Dr. Burke was timely, he was here.

She downed the rest of the cup of chocolate. She'd had a few spoonfuls of the porridge; Mrs. Orfill had so tempted her with the cold butter. She couldn't stomach more than that.

This was what she wanted. Mrs. Orfill's care. Her friends. This lovely little London townhouse. She would do whatever it took to hold on to it.

Had her grandmother been able to leave her the house outright, Cass might have managed to safely avoid all personal contact with the outside world.

But she couldn't. And her father, with his basket of questions about when she might be married, would only stay away if she kept this little house afloat without asking him for more funds.

And she *liked* the work she did. Every little step down that road had led to so many more that she'd lost track. This small project led to that one, this letter led to that one.

Now here she was, worrying over a commission on an artificial leg, which wasn't even the sort of thing in which she usually involved herself.

Worrying about it to the extent of not only corresponding with a surgeon who had done amputation in the war, but inviting him into her home.

She should have kept quiet. Limited her correspondence. Kept things under control.

Instead, she was preparing to be someone she was not.

How did she end up balancing her whole life on this peculiar meeting?

Cass winced. A peculiar meeting without her chaperone.

But how to explain to Dr. Burke that his correspondent Mr. Cullen required a chaperone, and hers often went missing?

Having Dr. Burke here was horrific, but surely it was better than venturing forth to meet with him in public? That might be permissible, for business; but she was not supposed to be *in* business.

Nor would it be possible to persuade Lady Inglemawr, if she could be found, to attend any discussion on the best way to build an artificial limb.

Not that Cass had asked.

This had to work because it had to work. If she could carry this off, she could have her home, and so could everyone in it. In here there was order, and predictability, and chocolate in the morning when she wished. In here it was safe. All she had to do was go downstairs and convince this Dr. Oliver Burke that she was the Mr. George Cullen she had pretended to be in writing.

Surely that was not an impossible task to undertake.

Cass tapped the hat onto her hair, then thought: of course, there would be no reason for her—for him—to be wearing a hat unless he were outside.

She'd need to slip down the back staircase, and come around the side, in order to come in the front door of her own home. Yes. It would work.

* * *

OLIVER WAS JUST WONDERING how long he ought to wait when a fellow in a dark coat and black felt topper came around the corner of the little crescent street and right up the steps to where Oliver stood.

"Dr. Burke," said the fellow, putting out a gloved hand and giving Oliver's a good shake. He didn't introduce himself, but he said, "So sorry, I'm just arriving myself. Let me show you in."

Before the man could touch the door knob, the door that had so firmly remained closed to Oliver was opened.

The butler made a half-aborted gesture, almost as if he were reaching to help his master up the steps, but then returned to stand straight.

"Sir," said the butler, giving the man in the hat a look that seemed sort of encouraging.

The fellow just touched the brim of his hat but didn't remove it. "We'll go right into the parlor, Adams," he said, and Oliver simply followed him in.

* * *

He watched the fellow remove his gloves, lay them on a sideboard. Oliver didn't care for the man's double row of brass buttons, reminiscent of military uniform. Fashionable, mused Oliver, but nonetheless he didn't care for the look.

"I'm so hoping you can give me some insight into this construction of the limb we have discussed in our letters," said the man Oliver was forced to presume was Mr. Cullen. "I feel confident that the articulation of the joints is superb, created with just the right range of motion to prevent hyper-extension. But the customer in question finds it painful, and I wish to give him better satisfaction on the commission."

The brim of the man's hat, still on, stayed a bit low, so Oliver couldn't see his eyes.

However, the rest of him, attired in the dark coat and fawn-colored breeches, was on complete display.

Leaving Oliver to wonder what it was about his medical reputation that would cause his host to think that Oliver would not notice that Mr. Cullen was a woman.

Oh, he'd met men soldiering who'd been born women, men who continued to be men when they went home from the front lines. If Mr. Cullen was truly Mr. Cullen, he was new to the task of showing himself as such.

Oliver decided to sit down.

"As I wrote to you, Mr. Cullen," Oliver said, leaning back and stretching his legs to cross his ankles, "I suspect you simply did not allow for the swelling during the day of the remaining part of the leg. No reason for you to know about it if you had no direct experience of it yourself. The attachment apparatus needs to allow for adjustment."

"I am hoping," said Cullen, inclining his head, "that you can give me ideas for more comfortable materials."

"I sent you some ideas about leather strapping options. Waist straps are commonly used."

"I am wondering whether lamb's leather straps might not be more appropriate."

Oliver's face showed his doubt. "I believe it will be too soft to support the weight of the artificial limb, unless you have found a way to make the rest of the materials magically light. Some straps can even go over the shoulder to support the weight."

"Lamb's leather would be gentle on the skin. Even though the customer has taken to wearing a double-layered linen lining sock for the thing, the straps and buckles cause him considerable contusion." Cullen still had not taken off his hat.

"The sock no doubt helps. The weight of the limb must be carefully supported, even for a limb amputated below the knee as you describe."

His host could not be persuaded to talk about weight. "It is most likely the buckles more than the leather causing the contusions. But as he walks with the limb using only a cane or two, I would not want to risk the limb separating from him altogether."

Oliver sat up straight, struck by a curious thought.

He stood and walked closer, to the desk.

He was talking about weight, while Mr. Cullen was still talking about materials.

Mr. Cullen was looking down at a pen holder, one ink-stained fingertip sliding the tiny device back and forth on the polished wood in between stacks of papers. Oliver could mostly see only the fingertip, and the top of Cullen's hat.

His host wasn't looking at Oliver.

And judging by this conversation, Oliver would bet that he wasn't hearing Oliver either.

Oliver walked away from Mr. Cullen to face the wall and examine the small group of placid paintings there. "The waist strap itself can dig into the flesh if not appropriately padded, but except on a very lean individual, it usually holds up quite well, especially for standing and walking. It should stay put."

Cullen's black hat nodded, as if the man concurred with Oliver's point. But what he said was, "I cannot expect you to be familiar with the construction work itself, doctor, but you have been kind enough to correspond with me about my questions, and I admit you are the sole hope I have of continuing to learn about the physiology of my customers. I am not a physician as you are, and I am not qualified to examine them as you are."

"I assume not," Oliver said, just a little softly, continuing his circuit around the room without moving closer.

As he expected, Cullen did not acknowledge Oliver's comment. Because he had not heard it.

Instead Mr. Cullen continued to nervously slide the penholder back and forth. "I do hope you can help me, Dr. Burke."

Oliver finally stepped back to the mahogany desk and leaned toward his host.

Cullen's hand froze.

Oliver picked up the slender hand, removing it from its repeated torture of the penholder, and held it in one of his. His other hand gently tilted Mr. Cullen's smooth chin upward. A chin that had never in its life known a razor.

He could finally see under the shadow of the brim of the hat. A pair of startled grey eyes framed with dark eyebrows fine as a bird's wing.

Oliver made sure to speak slowly where he—or she—could see his face.

"My friend Cullen," he said, "I do not wish to offend you if it is your choice to wear a gentleman's garb, though I do consider myself to have specific taste in clothing. But before we discuss this leg, I have a few other questions."

His host's mouth dropped open a little. Try as he might for the sake of his host, Oliver couldn't picture it as anything other than feminine. But he would try, if necessary, because he liked Cullen.

Oliver had a voice that was as deep as the ocean and he made an effort to pitch it as low as he could while still keeping it quiet so that no nosy servants could hear, if that was a concern. Perhaps the deeper pitch would help.

And Oliver said, "Why don't you tell me whether I should address you as sir or madam, tell me why you don't wish me to know that you are deaf, and then tell me where you have put the paper about strap construction that I sent you. I believe I can help you."

CHAPTER 2

He held just her fingertips in his hand, and his thumb stroked gently across her knuckles.

It was the most intimate sensation she'd ever felt.

It wasn't just that it sent tiny shocks up her arms into her body, as though she were waking up from a cold dream into a place of heat. It was also that his hand felt warm, and somehow familiar.

Apparently Dr. Burke had *no* interest in behaving appropriately.

Not that dressing in a man's suit and receiving him in her home was behaving appropriately.

Still, Cass felt like this situation was getting away from her.

Cass tugged her hand free from his touch, and pressed both her fists to her forehead as though preventing her head from exploding.

"I am Mr. Cullen," she said.

"I know," Oliver nodded agreeably, resting a hip on the edge of her desk. "We have just been discussing the artificial leg about which we have been corresponding for months. I didn't say you weren't Mr. Cullen. I said I was confused. I will address you however you like. I'm trying to point out, politely, that you seem in all ways other than your manner of dress to be a woman. You might be surprised to learn that in wartime one does sometimes find a fellow serving on the front

THE COUNTESS INVENTION

lines who has not begun life as such, so I am simply wondering if you truly wish for me to address you as Mister Cullen. Or, perhaps, if you would like some advice on how to make your outfit more convincing."

The worst. Cass had truly hoped that her subterfuge would not be a complete failure. And apparently it was a complete failure.

The man's calm was horrifying.

It was the combination of dressing like this and talking at the same time, she decided. Talking in person with new people was always disastrous. If only they had not had to converse. But then, if they had not had to converse, she could have kept up her convenient charade forever.

Certainly almost forever.

Her heart started pounding. This would require moving to her second most favorable plan, possibly her third.

Meeting in person had been an awful mistake. She couldn't make the same mistake with the Grantleys. Everything, everything could fall apart if her actual customers spread tales that she was not the Mr. Cullen she purported to be. No one would request her services and she would not have the funds to provide for this little household of hers.

But then she realized in the next second, Dr. Burke's knowledge of her secret wasn't the same as him *keeping* her secret.

Perhaps that was the key. Now that this man had her secret, perhaps he could be persuaded to help her keep it.

Just because he'd discovered one of her secrets—or two—didn't mean all was lost.

But then that depended on his kindness.

His letters; those had seemed kind. His carefully thought out and composed answers to her questions, his encouragement about her designs. No, she'd never met him before today—but didn't she know him, at least a little bit?

And hadn't he always been kind before?

She could try a bit of honesty, now that she was caught.

Ruthlessly she tamped down the sensation of embarrassment at her attempt at disguise. She'd certainly done her best at pretending to be Mister instead of Miss. Clearly, she had not done enough preparation.

Her habit was to stay quiet. To stay inside, to stay behind the door, the walls, the paper.

But what if, just this once, it would be more to her benefit to simply talk to him?

She said slowly, "Of course I felt you would not correspond with me on the matter at hand if I were a woman, so I simply signed myself otherwise, as I have been doing in this work these last two years. Then I needed to meet with you, and I thought I had better keep up the disguise."

Oliver nodded. "And no one told you that even in this garb, you do not appear masculine at all?"

Cass gave a small sound of distress. "I have struggled so much with this hair this morning, I cannot convey to you how vexing it has been. I knew it would give me away."

Oliver's expression remained placid. "Your hair."

He leaned in and removed her hat completely, revealing the mass of locks that she had wadded up beneath it.

He bent closely to examine the locks. "Yes, it is totally and only your hair that hints at your sex."

And his bending so close was a further difficulty, because unfortunately, Oliver Burke was distressingly beautiful.

So beautiful that Cass was having trouble looking straight at him. She just couldn't. Her eyes seemed to catch just the edge of his face and skittered away.

And he continued to display a regrettable lack of personal boundaries. Because the physician laid her borrowed hat on the desk and began plucking at her curls, freeing the ones on top that she had tried to arrange into a Brutus style and then crushed with the hat.

His own hair was very unfashionably long, pulled into a tie at the back of his neck like Cass' father had done when she was a child. It was thick and dark and streaked with bright bronze strands here and there. That wasn't the problem.

His face was the problem.

THE COUNTESS INVENTION

He was only inches away and Cass truly felt it would be as difficult to meet his eyes as to stare into the orb of the sun. Just the anticipation of trying felt nearly painful. Cass had a choice of looking at his face or his waistcoat, so she stuck with staring at the waistcoat.

For some reason, he was most determined to free her hair from its various bindings. His fingertips were moving around to the back of her neck and plucking out the hairpins she had placed there.

He apparently had *no* boundaries.

Cass ought to insist on some boundaries, if only for her own continued existence.

Then suddenly it was as though they had crossed some invisible threshold, and he was just there. Still far too close, far too personal, but it was possible to continue to live in his orbit.

Cass recognized the sensation from those few other men who had caught her attention and sighed, resigning herself to possibly months of stupid daydreaming about yet another man who barely knew she existed. She knew herself. She knew she was all too likely to be spinning tales to herself about whether or not he had meant more by it when he leaned close, or touched her arm.

She knew he did not mean *anything* by it, and it was all in her head. She hoped this time she could put more of a stop to her imagination. Nonetheless, it was easier to look at him now.

His angular jaw had a slightly golden tint, which deepened along his high cheekbones with just the slightest flush of red. Along with all this he had a high forehead, a nose that was strong, straight, and perfect, and lips that looked so soft and of such a deep color that the first word Cass brought to mind about them was *velvet*.

And his eyes—his eyes were neither blue nor green, but some sort of changeable color, framed with dark, long lashes that laid on his cheek when he looked downward. They were slightly heavy-lidded, a little sleepy looking. Between two dark heavy brows he had a sort of permanent worry-frown, the only flaw in a face that would have otherwise been far too perfect.

Those blue-green eyes now looked into hers.

"If you'll permit me," she heard him say, but he was already proceeding before she answered.

He'd finished freeing each of her curls from its bindings. Dr. Burke spread his large hands into her hair on each side of her head, raking his fingernails along her scalp and shaking her curls as he went. Then he did the same from the front of her scalp all the way back to the nape of her neck.

The sensation made Cass' skin prickle hot all over.

She wanted to make some sort of a sound deep in her throat.

It was an effort to stay silent.

"So lovely," he seemed to say to himself as he shook out her dark curls all over her head. But she heard it. His voice was so deep she could almost feel it reverberating in her chest.

She shivered.

He didn't seem to notice.

Oliver was caught up in the picture in front of him. He had never seen a picture quite like this. A Greek goddess of a woman, all long, strong limbs and flawless skin, in a gentleman's street clothes, surmounted by a crown of glossy dark curls.

Had *anyone* ever seen a picture quite like this? There was something so intriguing, not necessarily about the odd situation, but about her.

He only said, "Are these curls natural?"

"No." Cass hoped her voice sounded as normal to him as it did to her in her head. He was here to discuss business, after all. He didn't seem angry. Perhaps this was going well. It was so often hard to tell.

"Ah." Oliver greeted this news, too, with total equanimity. "It would be glorious too in its natural state."

He smiled.

And if he was beautiful before, the smile nearly made him impossible to see directly again. The smile was sweet and boyish and oddly naughty all at the same time.

He leaned closer. "So it's Miss Cullen then? Missus? What's your pleasure?"

And something tugged inside Cass, low inside, as if the idea of this man asking her to contemplate her pleasure was a bone-deep pull on her body.

"Miss Cullen. Cass—Miss Cassandra Cullen. Perhaps you could... sit over there," Cass gestured to one of the upholstered chairs.

* * *

Oliver tried not to look too delighted. He didn't know what his face showed but he felt as though he had won something, learning her first name. Her real first name.

She had such long, nimble hands. Even the way she pointed had a grace and a strength to it that drew the eye.

"But you will need to come with me so you can hear me, no?" he said, rising to his feet from his perch on her desk and offering her a hand with which to help her stand as well.

He didn't know why he had the urge to help her, other than perhaps habitual gallantry. She was as tall as he, with a slender figure that reminded him of statues of Diana he had seen abroad. The feminine curves of her were clear enough in that suit, but restrained, more mysterious than obvious. He had an urge to see her without the clothes at all.

But he hadn't come here today for those sorts of urges. He'd come here today because she was a person with whom he had corresponded about medical devices.

It was a peculiar intermingling of pleasures, mind and body, and it was new, and Oliver loved to discover a new type of pleasure.

Oliver felt like the walls between his tidy categories for women were in danger of crumbling.

Cass' dark, expressive eyebrows flew up as he gestured to the chairs, but she joined him and even moved her chair closer to his as she sat. Sat just like a lady in a drawing room, knees and feet together. It must be a bone-deep behavior.

"I can hear you at this distance," she said a bit shyly.

"But not well."

Cass shook her head.

"Is it more to one side or the other?" asked Oliver, leaning to one side as if to localize his voice but in fact just seeing her better in profile. Her face was as elegant as her figure, with a long aquiline nose that spoke to him of empresses. Or goddesses.

"We are here to discuss this leg, after all, not my ears," Cass said, shaking her head and giving him a quelling look.

Which only made him want to do something to get himself reprimanded. Perhaps even lectured. That look, on a beautiful woman with tumbled-down hair and in men's clothing—extraordinary.

But no, he could behave himself—he hoped—for the sake of a real friend. He and Cullen had been corresponding for months. He liked the fellow. He would still like the fellow even if he were a lady. Surely.

Oliver said, "No one has told you that you could not masquerade at all well as a man just by putting on a suit. I have no idea if anyone has similarly failed to examine your hearing."

Cass shook her head. "My hearing has been quite well examined. By the time my parents realized I had lost so much of it in the fevers I had as a child, they were nearly frantic. They had me examined by many physicians, most of them quite good in their field, I believe. The hearing was simply gone, and stayed gone."

Now that he was listening for it, he realized that the slight, very slight lisp to her voice was likely due to her hearing loss; there seemed to be parts of words she did not repeat because she did not hear them, such as their final sounds. It softened her words.

"Well, Miss Cullen, we have established how I should address you, and that you are somewhat deaf though not entirely, which you don't seem to want to discuss further. I will of course accede to your wishes. So perhaps we can move on to *why* you didn't wish me to know?"

At that, Cass just raised her hands and then let them fall, slumping backwards in her chair as if overwhelmed. It was the most ladylike sprawl Oliver had ever seen.

"I don't know what to tell you, Dr. Burke, I really do not. I was teaching at the school that I attended as a child, and I just drew a few things that the place needed. Little things like shelves, you understand. I drew them, and the apprentices in my father's cabinetry shop created them. And then one of the trustees told a friend of his that I would design something for the friend's home that he needed—he had a child who had lost both legs in an accident—and that was quite different and interesting, and then when that was completed I found myself with another customer, and then another. It turned so quickly from people I knew to people I had never seen, before I knew what was happening. And since the work is delivered from a shop in which my father has a business interest, the customers received their items from Mr. Cullen, and wrote back to the same person. So I used the name on my letters as well."

She let out a big sigh. "I never see most of my customers at any rate. They tell me what they need, I send them a drawing, they approve it, the piece is made and delivered to them. The manager of the cabinetry shop handles the payments and the delivery, as their shop makes most of the pieces."

Oliver nodded. "And then you decided to branch out into artificial limbs."

"This customer, Sir Michael, had purchased multiple carts that I make for gentlemen to use within the home. He liked them so much he asked me to make a saddle and a leg."

"A saddle?"

"Yes, and that needs work too, but it is the leg that bothers me."

Cass almost leaped from her chair and back to the desk, where several large sheets of foolscap were tossed among pencils and knives and shavings.

Oliver enjoyed watching this tumble-haired "Mr." Cullen scrabbling among the things on the desk.

She shoved a lock of hair behind her ear as she retrieved some printed sheets from under the foolscap. "There are many people making artificial legs in London these days." Cass handed him a worn copy of a journal that Oliver himself had not seen as she seated herself again.

"Where did you get this?"

She waved a hand again. "Oh, a friend of a friend." She pointed to the note in question. "This articulated joint—it is an extremely novel use of natural materials for the connections, and I wanted to try it. I included it in Sir Michael's commission, and he reports that movement of the ankle works well. It is the joining of the limb to his body that causes him pain."

She folded her hands together and held them tightly. "And he is coming here to discuss it."

"Ah." Now Oliver understood. "So this was merely the debut of your suit maneuver. If it worked on me, you would use it with this Sir Michael." He smiled despite himself. "And if it did not work? Because I can assure you, Miss Cullen, it did not work."

* * *

CASS BIT HER LIP. She had indeed had a secondary plan in mind, as well as a tertiary, and so on. That was how she worked.

She looked at him with what she hoped was perfect calm on her face. "If it did not work, I had hoped that you would pretend to be me."

"Did you indeed."

Cass counted herself lucky that Dr. Burke did not look angry. If anything, he looked delighted.

"I have a new idea," and he leaned closer. It was no hardship; he even *smelled* beautiful, like warm wool and beeswax-polished wood. Cass tried to mentally give herself a little shake to pay attention to what he was saying. He went on, "Why don't you be you, and I will simply join you."

Cass blinked.

"That is—"

She had to stop. Stop and think. This was how she got into trouble, by rushing.

She tried again; he was waiting patiently for her to finish her sentence.

Cass said, "They are not coming to see me."

"They are most definitely coming to see you."

"They are coming to see Mr. Cullen."

Oliver was not yielding his point. "As you told me just minutes ago, you are Mr. Cullen."

"No, I..." She had not anticipated having to explain this and she was surprised at how difficult it was to put into words. "They're expecting to meet someone with whom they can have a conversation."

The small frown between Oliver's brows deepened. "Are you and I not having a conversation right now?"

"Yes, but... They have someone in mind. Someone who is not me."

She didn't want to have to go into how badly some people behaved when she couldn't hear them; she couldn't explain it anyway. She had never understood the driver of the hansom cab who was so *angry* when she didn't understand his question, or the shopkeeper who shooed her out of the store if she didn't hear him address her. When he had so readily understood so many other things without her having to explain them, it was frustrating that Dr. Burke didn't understand the problem.

He *didn't* understand the problem. "I will be here with you, and as they have expressly *asked* to meet with you, I suspect they will be delighted to do so."

Cass could only insist again, "They don't want to speak with *me*."

"Miss Cullen." Oliver gestured to the papers all over her desk. "You are apparently corresponding with half of London, including physicians besides myself; at least one other physician, who has loaned you this journal. There appear to be many people who want to speak with you. To whom are they addressing those letters if not to you?"

Cass shook her head. "Two-thirds of the letters are just about the possibility of a commission, that is all."

"And they are writing to you for the work that you do so well. Who better to discuss your work than you?"

"It is not particularly difficult work. Making a piece of furniture shorter here, or adding wheels there." She *had* come up with a rather clever system of beads and wires for labeling doors for blind people, but she did not bring it up. That, too, was only beads and wires. "It is not work that requires genius."

Oliver's tiny frown deepened a little. "It does not matter that it is the work of a genius. It is work that they need, and it is work that you do well. Truly, who could possibly discuss it but you?"

He was being kind, but Cass could not risk her household on someone else's optimism. "In my experience, meeting in person does not go at all well."

Oliver felt as if he were treading on swampy ground. He asked gently, "Perhaps if your chaperone were to introduce you?"

Cass stopped herself from rolling her eyes. "Her ladyship will not be inclined to do so."

Oliver left the interesting problem of this invisible chaperone for later. "Then I will introduce you. And if you have been corresponding with Sir Michael as you have me, he has no more reason to be angry than I do, and no more reason to divulge your secret than I do. How have you harmed anyone?"

Oh, he was delightfully calm about all this.

Her mind clicked through all the unpleasant possibilities, but she couldn't deny that Dr. Burke had introduced the idea of at least a few pleasant possibilities. And while Cass despised the part of herself that all too easily read more into men's actions than was there, she nonetheless wanted another afternoon with the ridiculously good-looking Dr. Burke.

She could fantasize all night that Dr. Burke would come up with the right way to explain her to the Grantleys.

"Very well. It seems perhaps the most reasonable plan."

"Good." Oliver nodded. "It will be just fine, you'll see."

Cass wanted to assure him that it would *not* be fine. But sitting here in men's breeches, she felt that she was not in the best place to claim knowledge of how to behave in society.

She had not considered attending the meeting as simply herself.

He looked so confident. Cass wanted to feel that confident.

Perhaps it would work.

* * *

That settled, they finally turned their attention to the strapping mechanism for the artificial leg under discussion.

They were both startled when a maid with a thin, serious face and quick eyes appeared next to them where they sat beside the desk.

She looked back and forth between Cass and Oliver, appearing to be restraining a frown, before she curtsied toward Cass and made some lightning-fast gestures with her hand that meant nothing to Oliver.

Cass made a few equally quick gestures in return—more than a wave, certainly—and the maid disappeared.

Oliver thought to himself that it was odd that she'd had nothing to say.

"Has it been an hour already?" Cass leaned over the drawing Oliver was holding. Peg had appeared to remind her of the time unasked, and the reminder was not welcome. She also did not want Peg to give her *that look*.

"Has it?" Oliver sounded as surprised as she felt.

When she had tried going into society, in her debut season, many years ago, she had found that most men kept their distance and simply seemed to consider it her fault that she could not hear them. The ones who bothered to draw near tended to make her skin crawl. She never knew why, because she considered crawly skin a sufficient enough reason not to make their further acquaintance.

Oliver Burke did neither. He stayed within arm's length and with his voice, at that distance she could hear him quite well, missing only a few words here and there. If she were looking straight at him so that she could read his lips, she missed nearly nothing.

But looking straight at him for an extended period of time was probably not a good idea.

Cass had received less art instruction than ladies generally had. Her education, at the school for the deaf that had been founded just when she was a child, had focused more on practical matters than matters of entertaining. Even the rich students had not been expected to make a splash in society; they were expected only to get along among hearing people. Her drawing style she had learned from imitating the architectural books her father had had in his study, and her drawings were functional, not beautiful.

Now she felt that there had been aspects of her education that were lacking.

She wondered what type of artist could do justice to the curve of his cheek, the plane of his face where it became the line of his jaw. He was undeniably, unutterably masculine, and at the same time undeniably beautiful. Handsome would not be the correct word for him.

It was odd, she thought, that the most beautiful people had the most unremarkable features. It was something about the very regularity of the shape and organization of his face that somehow made it pleasing. She ought to study this more closely.

If he decided to dress as a woman, thought Cass with an inward smile of self-mortification, he would do a much better job than she had of dressing like a man. Though like herself, his figure would give her away. He was solidly built; though no taller than her, the shape of him underneath his coat made Cass confident that he could lift her with no trouble. Or move mountains, if necessary.

He was studying her drawing of a spiral ramp, apparently unconcerned with the passage of time. "This is quite lovely."

Cass smiled outwardly then, thinking that she must stop thinking the same thing about him.

"That worked quite well, for that customer," she said, uncurling the paper's corner. "I am proud of it."

"Did you go see it once it was built?"

"No. That would have been a bit difficult."

He tapped the drawing thoughtfully. "You ought to try it sometime, not just for the satisfaction of it, but to see how it is executed. You want to make sure the shop is building what you draw. And that it works."

Another simple, and useful, idea.

Oliver went on, "If nothing else, you ought to take the time to be proud of what you've done."

Cass shrugged. "As I said, there is no particular genius to it. Some people focus on how a person can go back to what they used to be able to do; I simply design options for going forward and doing what they wish to do now."

Oliver smiled. "Perhaps no particular genius, but a need, and you meet it."

There was another tap at the door, and a different maid, pretty and younger, entered the room a little slowly. "You asked for some refreshments, Miss Cullen."

"Oh! So I did. Thank you, Selene. Let me serve you something, Dr. Burke, you've been so kind. You've been here a long while, I'm sure you will want to be on your way soon, but before you go."

The maid's eyes stayed pointed straight ahead as she entered, looking neither left nor right. She handed Cass a basket with a little curtsey, then left the way she'd come, one hand trailing first along the edge of the divan, then the sideboard, then the doorframe, then she was gone.

Oliver let his hostess unpack a small plate of butter sandwiches and then one of cakes from the basket.

He touched the basket's smooth willow handle. "A practical way for a blind maid to deliver something."

"Yes, it is." She handed him a small plate and a napkin. "When you come by again tomorrow, to meet Sir Michael and his lady, you must stay for dinner."

"I would love to, but... do you not have a chaperone tucked away anywhere, Miss Cullen?"

She waved an airy hand again. "The Marchioness comes and goes as she pleases. She has a very full social schedule."

"I see." He didn't see. Having a full social schedule was not the job of chaperones. "Will she be joining us tomorrow?"

"Oh I hope..." Cass gave a little shake of her head. "I mean, of course she would not miss it. You will like her. Everyone does. But I find her exhausting. She has much to say and I cannot hear almost any of it." *And she's very pretty and you will not once look at me again once she is in the room,* Cass thought to herself, then immediately reminded herself not to be petty. That would be for the best, after all. And she liked her ladyship, she truly did. Sometimes it was a blessing that the exquisite little woman drew all eyes away from everyone else.

It was inconvenient that Cass enjoyed being seen by Oliver. He smiled at her and nodded at her and seemed to be listening to everything she said. It was so intoxicating that Cass could barely think. But it couldn't last, so she wouldn't worry about it.

"Well." Oliver ate the sandwich he was holding in two bites, then said when his mouth was free, "I look forward to returning. I assume that it will be incumbent upon me not to mention our first meeting."

Which Cass found thrilling, even given her dark thoughts about the Marchioness. He would not likely be back after tomorrow, but they would share a secret. He would keep her secret, she was sure of it.

And his help tomorrow would be invaluable.

"And you *will* assist me with the Grantleys' visit tomorrow?"

"Miss Cullen, I never abandon a lady in need."

* * *

As soon as he had left, Cass started up the stairs.

And found herself face to face with Peg. As though her childhood friend had been waiting there. Perhaps she'd felt Cass' step on the stairs?

Or perhaps Peg could simply predict Cass that easily.

This is what comes, Cass thought half-peevishly, of building a household from people one liked. Real gentry, the kind her grandmother had been, didn't go tip-toeing up the stairs worried about getting a scolding from a maid. This was absurd.

But as fast as her irritation had come, it melted. Peg's worried expression colored everything she said with her hands.

Are you all right? Did it go well?

Cass responded in the same manual language that they both had learned at the school for the deaf where she had been one of the rich students and Peg one of the poor ones.

You were right, he didn't believe that I am a man. It doesn't matter! He is going to help me. He will return tomorrow and it will be fine.

He will pretend to be you? Mr. Cullen?

Cass bit her lip. Dr. Burke had seemed adamantly against that option. *No, he offered to attend along with me. Me, Miss Cullen. It made sense when he said it.*

Peg's face made clear her sarcasm as she responded. *Oh, do tell me how he persuaded you with words.*

Cass put out a hand as if to stop Peg's sour attitude from proceeding. *Do you think I am so easily swayed by a man's beauty?*

Peg's expression said something about the persuasive power of Dr. Burke's looks, but what she said was, *You were going to convince him. Instead, he convinced you.*

Oh, I know. I am not good at talking to people, you know that. Cass covered her cheeks with both hands. She was trying to look stern, as she imagined a mistress of the household ought to look, but she knew she only looked as if she were stealing sweets.

Well, regardless. She was doing what she had to do. It was not her fault that Dr. Burke was not an everyday sort of attractive man.

Cass' hands launched into a flurry of expansion on her idea. *He understands what I need here. He offered to be here during the Grantleys' visit, as a physician, and that will be perfect. The whole outcome is exactly what we need. And then the Grantleys will go home and I will not take any more commissions of this sort of thing. We will stick to furniture and the like. And we will continue to contact customers through correspondence, as we do now, and if we keep expanding at the rate we are currently expanding, perhaps by next year we can open a manufactory at the school and be independent of my father's cabinetry business entirely. Independent!*

Peg shrugged, with a downward curve to her lips as she said *Yes. Certainly. Of course. And there are no other obstacles to this grand plan other than that the Grantleys are coming here in person tomorrow.*

A cold lump settled in Cass' stomach at the thought. It was so hard to talk to new people, and this was so dangerous...

Cass let out a huff of frustration. *Don't be small about this. You are my best friend! Be big! Encourage me!*

Aha. What am I encouraging, exactly?

Cass appeared to push away the sarcasm with a flick of her fingers. *You are an old married lady. This is why maids ought not to be married. Apparently old married ladies have evil minds.*

Do you truly not want him to return just for his company? Wasn't he a more pleasant gentleman than most you've met?

Very pleasant. But my concern is this household, not men. I cannot waver now.

Peg knew Cass' unfortunate history with mooning over men who turned out not to be seriously interested, at least to the point that she knew Cass' love affairs had largely been all in her own head.

She looked suspicious now about Cass' clear-headedness in this emergency situation.

Peg tossed up her hands, then went on talking. *You cannot take everything, everyone on to your shoulders. You cannot be responsible for us all.*

I can, because I am. Cass stepped forward to hug Peg, then moved past her to go change into the half-mourning dimity dress that she more usually wore.

Peg knew perfectly well how determined Cass was about this.

No, one visit with the baronet would not solve all of her problems. Whether the doctor with the gentle hands was there or not.

But it would help.

And Cass had gotten this far by tackling her problems one at a time.

CHAPTER 3

Had she been asked two days before, Cass would have pictured the visit of the Grantleys as a siege, with herself defending her home.

Instead... it felt like a siege, but with Dr. Burke defending as well.

Cass clasped her hands so they would not shake, and when she saw Adams heading for the door to answer what she knew had to be Dr. Burke's knock, she leaped up and followed along, not letting him out of her sight.

But just as Oliver had done the day before, the physician made it so easy. He merely bowed his head slightly, as if he were visiting an old friend, and gave Adams his hat and gloves.

Cass knew she was playing with fire. Aside from anything else—and there were other worries—she resolutely put out of her mind how vastly inappropriate it was to have an unmarried man paying a visit. As often as she told herself that having the Grantleys there along with the doctor was much safer than having him there alone with her, she knew that there were dangers to such meetings that she was no longer willing to risk. And some of those dangers might still be lurking.

But as soon as she saw him, she felt again those twin sensations from the day before: startlement at his good looks, and delight that he was here.

Even when his eyes swept her up and down, taking in her smooth hair pulled back with just a few curls to ornament it at the back and her half-mourning dress.

"A much less intriguing costume today, Miss Cullen," he said, gesturing that she should precede him into the hall as if it were his house instead of hers.

She laughed. "Sir Michael and his lady will be here directly. Please do join me in the library."

Oliver looked around.

"And your chaperone?"

Cass waved an airy hand. "She will be down directly."

This was not true, as the Marchioness was still not at home. Dangerous though it was, Cass was enjoying, for the moment, having no intentions of introducing her chaperone to the doctor before it was necessary.

So she hoped he would forget the missing chaperone. She wanted him to continue to be comfortable.

Indeed Cass was just welcoming him with a glass of claret when Adams announced the guests.

Lady Grantley was short, with pale golden frizzy hair escaping its bonds all over her head, and a sprinkling of sun spots over her nose and cheeks that bespoke a great deal of time outdoors.

Sir Michael swung after her on crutches, maneuvering himself between the furniture to stand behind his wife.

The Grantleys both had questioning looks on their faces as they stood there, looking at Cass and Oliver, and Cass felt welling within her the urge to blurt out her whole confusing *life*, hand waving and all, when Oliver smoothly took the conversational lead.

"Sir Michael Grantley, Lady Grantley, I am Dr. Oliver Burke, and I am so delighted to present to you Miss Cassandra Cullen. I understand that you have been customers of hers for some time through correspondence."

Sir Michael's keen eyes darted from place to place around the room, as if he expected someone named George to pop out from behind the door. But Lady Grantley's oddly pale blue eyes stayed on Cass.

Somehow Lady Grantley's look gave Cass back her voice. "I do apologize for the necessity of conducting business as Mr. Cullen, but I am truly very delighted to finally make your acquaintance."

Sir Michael still looked wary. "Well, Miss... Cullen, I am... delighted to finally meet you in person as well. Your equipment has been most helpful in resuming my life at Roseford since I returned from the war and inherited the baronetcy."

Cass' eyes widened. "I am so sorry. I did not realize that you had lost your father so recently."

"Indeed."

Lady Grantley's shrewd gaze finally broke into a smile as she appeared to make up her mind. "We are delighted to meet you, Miss Cullen."

Then she turned towards Oliver and her eyes were decidedly still appraising as they swept up *him*. "And you as well, Dr. Burke. You have assisted Miss Cullen in her work?"

"Only to consult on some small details of anatomy," Oliver assured her.

Now Sir Michael's piercing look was back, and aimed at Oliver, but Cass breathed a sigh of relief that at least the explanation was done, and there had been no explosions so far.

"Perhaps you would care to sit down?" asked Cass, a little faintly.

Sir Michael swung through the furniture and settled himself after he saw that his wife was comfortably ensconced in an embroidered chair.

Had Cass been there by herself, she was sure that explaining her identity would have been awkward, perhaps even dangerous if Sir Michael had a temper. She didn't feel she could have made the right explanations, and whatever he said back she would be unlikely to hear it all, and the whole interaction would have been disastrous.

Instead the most difficult part was done, and if she missed a few words in the general conversation now, it would be no large matter.

It was all so easy.

After some time and a glass of claret, even Sir Michael seemed to relax a bit, and Cass took the liberty of smiling at him as she offered him a second. He shook his head.

"More wine won't make me more relaxed about meeting with a woman about my artificial leg."

Cass's mouth dropped open. "Oh no, I didn't mean—"

"Sir Michael." Lady Grantley drew together her sandy eyebrows and gave him a glare that reminded Cass of an angry kitten. "Our hostess."

"My apologies, Miss Cullen," said the young baronet smoothly as if his wife upbraided him in public every day. Perhaps she did. "If you are looking for someone to be astonished, Miss Cullen, you will have to look beyond me." His lean muscled frame and bushy chestnut hair seemed to recall the Viking invasions of Britain. It was something in the way he swung himself about, Cass thought.

Sir Michael went on. "My wife exhausts my capacity for astonishment daily. So you see I will have none to spend."

"Fuff," said Lady Grantley succinctly. "We have brought the dratted leg with us, Dr. Burke; perhaps you would be interested in taking a look at its fit, and Miss Cullen and I can converse here. That would be efficient, would it not?"

Apparently it would. Adams appeared instantly with a paper-wrapped parcel that the guests had left with him, and showed Oliver and the baronet to an empty parlor almost immediately and closed the door behind them.

"So," said Michael immediately once the door had closed. "How are you in the house alone with Miss Cullen, hey? Consulting with her on anatomy? What do you mean by it, sir?"

Oliver suppressed a smile. The baronet was quite a few years younger than himself. "I happen to know you just met her for the first time today, so why the gallant concern?"

"I like Cullen, and my wife tells me that I am overprotective. Cullen's been good to me. The wheeled thing he sold me—she sold me," he corrected himself without missing a beat, "—it's made the house tolerable. I can't tell you what a difference. So I feel obliged to ask."

"I don't disagree with you, sir. In fact I am told that there is a marchioness supposed to be serving as a chaperone, but I have seen no sign of her either yesterday or today."

"Is she lying?"

Oliver shrugged one shoulder. "I doubt it. She's been very forthright with me."

Oliver thought "forthright" as a description for Cass might be pushing his luck; after all, they both knew she had masqueraded as a man in her letters. But he was steadfast. Keeping a lady's secrets was a familiar task for him.

Michael kept looking at Oliver as if he could see into the man's soul.

It went on a few seconds too long for Oliver, who didn't feel as though his soul would stand up to much of that kind of scrutiny.

"So you'll be keeping an eye on her, then?" Michael finally said.

Oliver didn't know this man; hell, he barely knew Miss Cullen. But something about the piercing gaze of the baronet made him want to answer honestly. "I ought to be staying far away from Miss Cullen, I'm afraid."

"Why?" barked Michael.

"I..." The urge to honesty didn't extend as far as explaining why his reputation would do Miss Cullen's reputation no good, and why he himself was not the kind of man who should be spending time with innocent unmarried young ladies.

For the first time, Oliver felt as though the problem wasn't just that unmarried young ladies always wanted to get married.

For the first time, Oliver felt that the problem was that he was in no way what Miss Cullen deserved in a husband.

"You were in the war," he said, his voice seeming to get a little stuck in his throat.

"Obviously." Michael waited for him to go on.

"You remember the surgeon who did this for you?" Oliver pointed at the leg that ended in a stump.

"Vaguely. He served on the ship. Don't recall his name."

Oliver swallowed. "I remember the face of every man I put under the knife on the battlefield."

Michael just sat, and the sound of the breathing of both men seemed loud in the very quiet room.

Oliver finally volunteered, "Oddly, I remember the ones who died better than the ones who lived."

"That doesn't strike me as all that odd."

"Most of them died."

Michael said nothing.

Oliver went on. "I remember their faces at night. When I'm trying to sleep. The blood, the screams—you remember."

Michael's face softened a little. "I was on a ship, soldier. Fortunately, not the same. But yes, I do remember those."

"I have not—adjusted to society since I returned. I was probably never fit company for ladies, and I'm certainly not now."

"Then stay away from them."

Some expression must have chased across Oliver's face.

He'd expected Sir Michael to ask about his position, or his background. He had not expected such a blunt order.

And Sir Michael startled him again when he added, "Are you the kind of man who is able to tell a lady no when she asks you for something?"

"In all honesty, Sir Michael, I am not." It was not the most damning of sentences, yet Oliver felt low saying it.

"Then stay away from them. Because there will always be that one lady that, even if you were good at saying no, will get you to agree to almost anything. And that lady out there, she looks persuasive."

That made Oliver narrow his eyes at the baronet. "Don't be absurd."

"I'm only telling the simple truth. You'd be amazed how being married amplifies your understanding of feminine expressions."

"You can't—I think you might be misunderstanding Miss Cullen because of her—"

Abruptly Oliver felt as though perhaps the secrets Miss Cullen wanted to protect, unkeepable though they may be, were not his to share. Her gender was not her only secret.

But after all, Sir Michael had met her, right here in her house. "She's deaf, certainly, deaf as a post, I can tell. Doesn't mean she can't think well of you."

Oliver was considering getting irritated. This fellow was too brash, and younger than himself, and presuming to give too much advice. "Nonetheless I think you are misunderstanding her," he said stiffly.

"She's pretty expressive," said Michael, finally picking up the apparatus of the artificial leg and getting to the business they were here for.

"Yes, her face, her hands...." Oliver had no good way of explaining what he thought he'd seen yesterday, when she'd moved her hands so quickly to one of the maids. "Look here, have you heard of deaf people speaking with their hands?"

"Are you asking me? You're the physician."

"Quite. I must do some research. It's not my field, I admit, and I don't know any specialists in any pertinent field that comes to mind."

Michael tilted his head a little. "If it's information you're after, I do have a man who might be able to help. My brother-in-law, in fact. He's here in the city handling some business affairs for me. He's the blazes when it comes to finding things out."

Oliver didn't bother to hide his surprise. "That is kind help, from someone who believes I ought to keep my distance from Miss Cullen."

Michael shrugged. "He is utterly trustworthy. If you need a hand, I'll give you his direction. It is ours as well."

"Yes, please do." Oliver understood the implied gentle threat. It was Miss Cullen whom Sir Michael respected, and wanted to help. He would rather his fellow help Oliver than have Oliver tripping all over the city possibly causing trouble for Miss Cullen.

Still, Oliver felt unaccountably pleased. He agreed with Michael that he ought to stay away from Miss Cullen. He also had every intention of finding out more about her.

* * *

"Miss Cullen, can we have a nice conversation if I pull my chair a bit closer?"

"What?" Cass startled a little. Her thoughts had wandered and she had not expected the little woman to want to talk to her. "I am out of practice in entertaining others with conversation, Lady Grantley. My apologies."

"I don't mean to put you to any trouble, Miss Cullen. It must be quite a lot of bother, conversing with people whom you cannot hear."

Cass' eyes opened wide, but Lady Grantley's smile was still simply friendly.

No one ever made mention of her deafness in company. Her father never mentioned it. Her task in company was to fit in, not to draw attention to her inability to hear.

Lady Grantley's smile faltered. "I apologize if I should not have mentioned it. I have an appalling lack of manners; I am afraid I have not had a lady's education. And my husband and I in our country home tend to ignore each other's bad manners rather than cultivating better, which is disgraceful of us. Please do forgive me."

Cass leaned forward in her rush to reassure Lady Grantley. "Please do not apologize! It is..." Realizing the truth as she said it, Cass said, "It is actually far more comfortable to have someone mention it than to pretend to ignore it but in reality simply to ignore me."

"You are kind. I have never met anyone particularly hard of hearing before and have no idea what the proper etiquette should be. Truly, the fault is all mine."

Cass finally smiled back at the little woman, whose tense posture and clasping hands were the very picture of concerned embarrassment. "I do not know general etiquette for such a situation, oddly enough, but for myself, I am not at all insulted."

"Oh good." Lady Grantley seemed ready to collapse back into her chair with relief. "Another dreadful social hurdle of manners passed. Do you know, I feel my entire life will consist of this unless I simply stay home and never leave. Which seems an appealing idea. You must call me Letty, my dear."

Cass' response was only a quizzical look.

"Letty, for Letitia. L E T T Y. Will that suit you?"

Cass just laughed at that. "I think it suits *you*, madam, very well. And you must call me Cassandra if you like, though my friends call me Cass."

"Do they? Lovely!" Letty clapped her small hands with delight. "Oh, I love making friends."

Cass stayed as she was, upright in her chair, hands folded in her lap, the picture of propriety; but the smile that flashed in response to Letty's outburst was genuine. "You are being very kind for all that we meet in these circumstances."

"What circumstances are those? Your kindness and generosity to my husband?"

"Oh no, L—Letty, that was a business transaction. I was very glad to have the work, believe me."

"And believe *me*, dear," said Letty, her smile turning into something more thoughtful and somehow older, "I do know how that feels. Aside from my sympathy with your business, I *am* grateful. Your devices have been immeasurably helpful to my husband."

"The carts," said Cass ruefully, "but not the saddle or the leg."

"Both have merits. It is worth experimenting, is it not? When there are so many soldiers returning from war who might need something similar."

It was exactly Cass' own feeling on the matter. "Letty, I cannot express how kind you have been today. Social experiences are usually so unpleasant."

"I cannot disagree, but..." Letty paused before going on, but then said decisively, "My husband says it is the people from whom the disagreeability begins that are at fault if a social situation is unpleasant, and that it is only my job to survive them."

"What, forever?"

"If I can! I intend to outlive every unpleasant person I meet by at least twenty years."

That made Cass laugh outright. It was a laugh that came from deep inside her, and she did not usually laugh in front of people.

In fact, she couldn't remember the last time she laughed.

That thought sobered her a little.

"In case you need me to elaborate," Letty added, "People should not be unpleasant to you, either."

"Oh, they are not unpleasant, exactly..." Cass thought back to her social debut and the season that had followed. All the events seemed to revolve around talking, or dancing, which was even worse, and she had not been someone with whom others had wanted to talk or dance. She wanted to tell Letty, too, how one step had let to another till she felt her position was so precariously balanced that one poke could bring it all tumbling down. "People are so difficult. That is partly why I waited so long to set a date to meet you in person. I wanted to meet you both, very much, but..." She couldn't think of a way to finish the sentence appropriately. But it put her in a terrible position to do it? But she worried that the Grantleys would destroy her necessary fiction? She did not want to be rude.

But again, Letty seemed to understand. "Friends do not gossip, Miss Cullen, and *that* my husband did not have to explain to me. I fully understood it already."

Cass just nodded.

"Forgive my intrusiveness, for we have just met, but we have such a short time to get to know one another. Have you other friends you trust?" There was a smile chasing around the corner of Letty's mouth. "Perhaps that appealing Dr. Burke?"

Before she thought, Cass said, "I think beautiful is the more apt word, Lady Grantley."

Then she dropped her eyes to her hands before forcing herself to meet her visitor's gaze again. It was apparent, she thought, that her thoughts were showing. What could she do about that?

Letty was still smiling. "Letty, please! Men get on their high horse, though, if you call them words that they don't feel are manly enough."

Cass didn't think Oliver would object. But then, he also had no right to object. She just shrugged. "My season was a long time ago, and my interactions with men are primarily through writing. I am no judge of what they do or do not like."

Letty nodded. "I have limited knowledge of men, period. I ought not to generalize from my knowledge of the few that I do know; and come to think of it, they are pretty individual after all." A dimple came and went in her cheek as she seemed to think of something extra-amusing. "But it is too personal to simply say that my husband bellows if I call him beautiful."

That made Cass laugh too. "I will consider it a sign of friendship, my lady."

"But you did not answer my question!"

Cass just shook her head. "I have long corresponded with Dr. Burke, but only recently met him, just as I have now met you. There are many others I correspond with, but personally..." She immediately thought of this house; Peg and her husband, and Selene, and Mrs. Orfill; they were her friends. But it would be too impossible to explain why her servants were the friends on whom she most counted. "I have a sponsor, Lady Inglemawr, who still takes an interest in me. And my father is very understanding of my desire to live here where my grandmother and I had our home together."

He was *not*, but Cass didn't feel able to explain all that, either.

"And others for whom you have done work, like my husband?"

"I seldom see anyone after a work is completed, my lady." For the first time, Cass felt it as something of a lack. Other than her father, who constantly reminded her that she was missing a husband, no one ever suggested to her that there was something she was missing, out there in the world beyond these doors. She suddenly remembered Dr. Burke asking her the day before if she had seen her favorite ramp actually built. "I avoid the difficulty of communication by staying at home."

"If that is what you like, that makes perfect sense." Letty looked around at the sunny yellow toile paper and the room appointed with rich dark furniture with every apparent convenience. "It is a lovely home. But then I have all the more reason to tell you while I have the opportunity. It has made a huge difference to my husband, and we both thank you. We owe you a debt."

Cass couldn't figure out where to put her hands. No one had ever complimented her so effusively before. No one had ever even mentioned the effect of her work.

"Thank you, Letty," she said softly, reaching over to squeeze one of Letty's hands in return.

Her hand seemed so large on top of Letty's tiny one, but Letty just patted it. "Isn't anyone ever pleasant to you, you sweet girl? You look like you are about to cry."

Cass decided to change the subject before she did cry. She never cried. It would be both unpleasant to see and a social faux pas.

She decided to laugh instead. She was quite a bit older than Lady Grantley, and it was funny to see the tiny woman being so motherly to Cass, who was also a good head taller. "Have another cake, Letty. My cook makes them brilliantly."

* * *

Was this how other people *lived*? It felt like a dream world, an unreal dream world where these delightful people came to her own house and said delightful things to her about her work and a beautiful man smiled at her and called her "Miss Cullen" as though he really meant to say "Cassandra."

Well, perhaps she was imagining that last bit.

Oliver Burke did smile attentively at her, and he sat close enough to her to breathe into her hair as he handed her drawings past her to Sir Michael Grantley. And he did it all while looking so breathtaking, that she could not help but read emotion into it. The emotion, she suspected, was all hers.

She'd been down *that* road before and she knew that she tended to imagine such things.

But oh, it was very pleasant to imagine that it was all just as real as it seemed.

Oliver made several suggestions about the attachment mechanisms of the leg which Sir Michael agreed to try. The baronet could afford to have another leg made up, he assured them, though he barely used the one he had. He would prefer to have a more comfortable leg on hand for those occasions when he wanted one.

"The manufactory where my items are made is in the city, sir," Cass assured him. "They will have something completed for you within a fortnight, I believe, and I'll have it sent straight to you at Roseford, shall I?"

The baronet agreed that it sounded ideal. "You may want to contact me first at the townhouse we have let for the time being. We may be there for a while, and even if we are not, my brother-in-law should be in residence and will know how to reach us."

Cass felt as if she floated through the rest of the afternoon.

And after Adams showed the Grantleys out, there was still Oliver, as she thought of him in her head, a solid figure of a man on her settee in her library and wearing that thoughtful expression on a face that ought to be registered as a weapon with the Crown.

"That was lovely," breathed Cass as she sank down in the chair across from him.

"Did you enjoy it?"

"They weren't angry at all. I didn't have to fight with my hair and I didn't have to even try to be Mr. Cullen. The new design will be so much better, and in combination with the ankle articulation, I think we have really made wonderful progress."

"Mmm." Oliver nodded as he downed the rest of the tea in his cup. "I've been thinking, there are some physicians who ought to know about your devices; they may get you more work. You do want more work?"

"Oh I do!" Sitting up straight, she nodded most emphatically.

"Good."

Relaxing again, Cass closed her eyes and almost swayed in place. "Everything is so perfect. I don't want this day to end."

"Will tomorrow be so awful?" Oliver asked her, his deep voice rumbling close by.

When she opened her eyes, he was just a touch away, that small concerned frown just marking the space between his brows, and looking as if he sincerely wanted to know the answer.

She had a very uncharacteristic urge to simply tell him her problems, all of her problems, and let him sort out which he might be able to help with. It would be such a relief.

She couldn't do that, of course. But it would be heavenly.

"Tomorrow will happen tomorrow," sighed Cass. She preferred to hope, after all. Why shouldn't it be a pleasant day tomorrow as well? She wouldn't have him, or anyone like him, but it would be a pleasant day. And as long as he left soon and didn't come back, she would have nothing but pleasant memories of her time with him.

Time that was over. "Well, I must be going too, and if you need me again, you do know how to reach me. Miss Cullen."

Oliver took her hand—she was so glad that he did it one more time—and this time, raised it to his lips.

His kiss brushed the back of her fingers, and it sent a shock through her. Cass felt like she had to hold herself particularly still or he would see it travel up through her body.

"Farewell, my friend," said Oliver, loud enough for her to hear, and then he was up, and bowing to her, and then he was gone.

Well. *That* would be worth remembering, right there.

Cass shook herself, then pinched her own arm, as hard as she could. She was not dreaming. It was so hard to tell.

She wished she could draw this day and keep it. It would so soon be gone.

She sighed. What did she have to be silly about? How many women had a chance to spend a day as satisfying as this one?

Women who had a man like that, something in the back of her head told her.

Well. That wouldn't be her, Cass thought to herself. She had enough problems without attempting an *affaire*. Her attempts in that area had already been disastrous before—at least she could avoid making *that* mistake again. No reason to continue down such a disappointing road.

No, she would simply remember his kindness and if another commission that required his help came across her desk, she would write to him.

Yes. That was what she would do.

She had supper ahead of her, a supper Mrs. Orfill would make exactly the way she liked it. Peg would have the bed made with fresh linens today, which she loved. Selene would arrange some of the late-blooming asters, which Mr. Adams would bring in here to brighten up the room. Everything here was just as she liked it, and she could continue to have it just as she liked it as long as she kept everything just as it was. These were the people who cared about her and the home that she loved. Heavens, even the Marchioness would be home at some point!

Cass put thoughts of the lovely-to-look-at Dr. Burke to the back of her mind, to take out and enjoy at some future time, like she did the silver spoons.

* * *

It was still early by the standards of the club when Oliver arrived there.

But he had already had himself a deep glass of gin, or perhaps it was two. So Oliver was already feeling a bit like he was floating, and rather divorced from the cares of the world, which was usually the sensation he went to the club to find.

And his most frequent drinking companion, Bradley Waite, was already there. Who noticed that Oliver had already downed a few.

"Hoy there, doctor fellow, what are you doing drinking without me?" Waite sprawled in his wide leather chair.

"I do a great many things without you, Waite, and that just makes most of them more pleasant," Oliver muttered as he dropped into the chair opposite.

"Such a bad mood already. I suggest you limit your intake until you can be a happier drunk."

"Then go away, because I shall be a very unhappy drunk tonight." Oliver's handwave attracted the eye of one of the staff, who nodded.

"Fair enough. Anything specific you intend to be unhappy about?"

Waite bent his head to his own glass of wine and inhaled the aroma before tasting it again. His cravat was loose as if he'd been lolling about in here for some time already. Oliver would bet that even if Waite managed to drag himself back outside, Waite would smell vehemently of cigar smoke.

Oliver didn't have to get closer to know that Waite would *not* smell of violet water. Or the creamy skin where a woman's long neck just met the dark of her hair.

Oliver congratulated himself on his restraint. He had not once bent closer to smell the nape of Cass' neck, even though it had been just in front of him all day. The scent of violet water, however, had haunted him all afternoon. Violet water and ink, from her fingertips. He could smell it now.

His friend looked puzzled. "Truly, Oliver, you do already look despondent enough to lay down under some wagon wheels. What on earth ails you, man?"

"Nothing." The glass had arrived. Oliver buried his face in it.

"Money? You don't have it but seldom need it. Your family? They're always a nightmare, so that doesn't change. Work? Consists primarily of holding hands with rich women, so what have you to complain about?"

Oliver's eyes shot a piercing black look Waite's way, then returned to his glass.

"Oh. Oho. Not a hand-holding woman? You can't be serious, Oliver. You've bedded half of London. Many of us have bets on when you'll bed the other half. You can't possibly be moon-eyed about some woman now."

"Shut up, Waite." Oliver raised his hand again. He wasn't done with this drink yet, but when he was, he wanted the next one ready.

"Does she *know* that you've slept your way across London?"

"There's no woman, and no, she doesn't know." Oliver realized somewhere in the back of his brain that those two sentences didn't go together, but the gin was helping to smooth over all the roiling waves in his mind, and he didn't bother to figure out what was wrong about what he was saying. "And anyway, I need the sleep."

"I know you do, old friend." Waite nodded quite as if he were sober. They had served in the same regiment, seen the same things. Neither of them slept soundly.

Oliver closed his eyes. Perhaps he would fall asleep in this chair. It would be wonderful if he did. He didn't often sleep at home; it was too quiet. And after all, lonely women deserved company too.

Just like he did.

He was beginning to suspect that he hated waking up in bed after bed. He was beginning to think that the word *company* was too complicated a word.

Cassandra Cullen deserved company, a tiny voice inside his head piped up. A good man's company.

Yes, yes she did.

Whether or not he was a good man—and he knew he was not—he *was* the one who'd spent the afternoon with her, catching himself staring at the flawless skin he could see at the neckline of her dress, at her wrists, catching himself wondering if it could possibly be that creamy and smooth all over. He was the one who'd helped her up out of the chair, watching her bright eyes dip down, then up to look into his, her wide mouth curve into a smile.

He was the one who'd helped her refine a design for an artificial leg, and their working together had been just as pleasurable a time as he had had in the company of any lady in the middle of the afternoon, or at night for that matter.

She was clearly sweet and had been brought up to be ladylike, men's suits notwithstanding. She didn't deserve to have him sitting here in his cups contemplating how long her legs had looked in that suit, and how they would feel wrapped around him if he could coax her into such a situation.

There would be no coaxing, of course, because Miss Cullen was not a lonely married woman *and* he was not her physician. No, that wasn't right. Oliver didn't sleep with his actual patients. The ladies who kept him on retainer were different from the ones who just wanted his company. The latter didn't need his medical attention; they just wanted his attention, period.

He was not actually a ... Whatever the word would be for a

gentleman who performed the same services as a ladybird, he was not one of those, right?

Oliver glared into his glass.

This line of thinking wasn't making him feel any better.

"She's not a patient, she's a lady." Some part of him heard how his words were starting to slur, but he ignored it.

Bradley Waite, his dark Brutus curls as badly in need of a wash as the rest of him, shook his head sadly. "No ladies," he said in all seriousness, taking another quaff of his drink.

No ladies, thought Oliver to himself. They were too dangerous. Absolutely no ladies.

CHAPTER 4

When Cass had received the note to visit her father for luncheon, it hadn't seemed like a trap.

Oddly fortuitous, seeing that she was spending yet another morning counting the commissions for the work she had scheduled, wondering if the household really needed as much beef as they currently ate, and writing yet another letter to one man who had absolutely refused to pay his outstanding bill.

It had been timely—at the very least, a meal she would not have to pay for!—but it hadn't seemed like a trap.

Her father had sent a carriage, which was usual and practical, and Cass did not dress except to put on a light woolen cape, which was also usual and practical. There was nothing about the arrangement that was unusual at all.

She saw two of her neighbors from the other end of her crescent street as she was climbing in, and she nodded, and that was usual too.

The woman—Lady Herbert? Did she recall that name correctly?—nodded to Cass and said something about the weather; Cass was not close enough to catch any of the sound and could barely read her lips at all. Cass just smiled and nodded back before she climbed into the carriage, and that, too, was usual.

She didn't hear the neighbors' comments as she drove away, which was also usual.

"Isn't that the heiress who hasn't married yet?" said Lady Hibbert as Cass' carriage pulled away.

Lord Hibbert, who had had absolutely no interest in heiresses since he had married one thirty years before, said only, "Is it?"

"What an interesting life she does seem to lead. She could have stopped to speak with me. I am not used to being ignored."

Lord Hibbert ignored his wife's complaining, and that was very usual too.

At the city home of William Cullen, Cass was shown to the dining room just as her father and his wife came in. She kissed them both and then sat at her usual place at the table, and there was nothing to fear in that.

She sat with Tobias, the oldest of her father's children with his second wife, on one side of her, and baby Grace on the other. Francis and Joseph, at in-between ages, seemed to prepare themselves for luncheon by chasing each other around the table. William Cullen balanced his insistence on dining at the long formal table with his indulgence of his sons' energy. Or perhaps the latter was simply a temporary nod to the inevitable.

Cass' father had firm and progressive ideas about family formation, and they did not include banishing children to nurseries. She quite liked her father's freedom with the children of his later years. She had seldom dined with her father, but then she hadn't had siblings, or, for many years, a mother.

She hoped that little Grace would enjoy this family tableau when she was old enough to understand how lucky she was.

Her stepmother, pretty as a china shepherdess as always in her old-fashioned ruffled gown, sat at one end of the table, and her father sat at the other. They seemed to be talking to each other about something. She couldn't hear a thing they said and didn't bother to try following their mouths as they spoke. If they had anything to tell her, they would.

Tobias loved seeing his older sister. At eleven, he enjoyed taking every opportunity to shout.

"I have a new boat!" he told her at top volume. "You must see it sail before you leave!"

Cass nodded, helping Grace to another bite of mashed turnip. She also adored feeding Grace. There were few people on earth more pleasant than babies who had not yet begun to talk. And Grace was a darling example, with dark swathes of hair on her head and two tiny perfect teeth.

The baby smiled, displaying both teeth and a great deal of mashed turnip.

The formal dining table was relatively long and there were servants on call everywhere, but Cass was able to indulge herself in feeding the baby and listening to Tobias shout. She only wished her father's ideas about his older daughter were as progressive.

Her father had waved a clenched fist about something, and Cass knew her stepmother was answering. If they were talking about her or to her, it would have to wait until later, as they very well knew.

"Is there anything else I can get you, Cass?" Her stepmother came close to kiss her cheek and speak as close as she could.

Her stepmother, whose name, Alfredetta, Cass still found rather startling, had always allowed Cass to choose whether to call her Mama, or Detta as her childhood friends had done. Cass enjoyed being able to call her Mama.

Detta was a little meek, to Cass' thinking, and she had never shed her taste for the fashions of the last century. Detta's voice was also a bit high for easy conversation. But they had spent years being part of the same family and Cass was quite accustomed to listening for it.

"I'm fine, Mama, I just need to see Tobias' boat before I go."

"Your father would like to speak with you for a few minutes," Detta said, and Cass could see the signs of strain at the corners of her stepmother's smile.

So. A trap.

When she settled herself in the chair in her father's library, she folded her hands quietly on her lap. Her father claimed he did not mind the manual language she had learned at school, but somehow when he saw her use it he became uneasy, and sometimes she used her hands to speak when she became excited. She would not become excited. She would restrain herself. She would be the model of restraint.

"Cassandra, I am extremely concerned."

"Try being restrained, Papa, I believe it is good for you."

William Cullen's sharp eyes narrowed. He had lost weight, Cass thought to herself. His face was too narrow, too bony without it.

He sat on the sofa near her, and she remembered how many years of conversations they had had there. He was a dear father, truly.

Cass had a feeling she would need to remember that for the next few minutes.

"I've overlooked your wellbeing, and it is entirely my fault."

"I'm quite well, Papa, so please do not feel guilty."

"I'm sorry to tell you that I've received a letter."

That made Cass' hair stand up along the back of her neck, and in a way that presaged nothing good.

"Surely you receive letters all the time without them being any great disaster."

"I've received a letter from one of your neighbors."

"Really?" Cass feigned bored interest. "Which one?"

"The letter says that the neighbor in question saw not one but two gentlemen go into your house on a morning just a few days ago. Apparently the Marchioness' carriage had left the day before and not returned, so the neighbor believes she was not in attendance. And then the next day, two gentlemen accompanied by a lady entered and spent most of the day."

"I'm sorry the neighbor didn't pay me a call. We made a lovely party of it and would have welcomed another."

"So you did have all these men traipsing in and out of your house."

"No, I did not!" Cass was not about to explain that one of the men she was accused of hosting was herself, but regardless... "There was no *traipsing*. Heavens, you make it sound as though a thoroughfare ran through the house."

"Did you have gentlemen callers without your chaperone there?"

"What?"

"Cassandra, I raised you, I know perfectly well when you are saying 'what' in order to give yourself time to figure out an answer to a direct question. Did you have gentlemen callers without your chaperone in attendance?"

"I had no callers, Papa."

"So who were these men, ghosts?"

Her father didn't have much of a temper but he was getting a bit red in the face. Cassandra wondered if she might suddenly be able to faint. Or perhaps set the carpet on fire.

She would never come in here again without the means of setting a fire.

"It was a customer for one of my designs, Papa, and his wife."

"And who were these other fellows?"

She was about to be *forced* to explain that one of the men witnessed by this wordy neighbor was herself.

Her father allowed her a great deal of leeway in many things, but Cass just had a feeling that he would not be amused by the idea of his oldest daughter on the streets of London in a man's suit.

Even if she had only been on the streets for a distance of perhaps thirty feet.

"Papa, I had a customer visit me. And a physician who has consulted with me on a commission for that customer. That is all. You ought to know me well enough to know that I am hardly entertaining flocks of gentleman callers at my home."

"Your mother must be spinning in her grave. Ladies of the *ton* do not conduct business. For that matter, gentlemen of the *ton* do not conduct business. She wanted you to marry an earl at least, to make up to her family for her great sin of marrying me. *Her* mother left you the residency of a London house to ensure it. Instead here you are conducting business with men traipsing in and out. What do you *expect* the neighbors to think?"

I expect the neighbors to keep their noses in their own houses, Cass thought but did not say.

Her father sighed heavily. He looked down at his hands, twisted the gold signet ring he wore on one finger. He looked old, Cass suddenly thought. Even though his hair was still dark and thick, his cheeks looked a bit hollow, and there were some new wrinkles around the corners of his eyes.

"Daughter," and he leaned forward and said it again so she would be sure to catch it, "Daughter, I promised your mother you would have the best education I could find. I never pressured you to take just any husband when you debuted. I wanted what your mama wanted for you, what your grandmother wanted for you, and they always said you shouldn't settle for anything less than an earl. I let the Marchioness sponsor you and continue to chaperone you because she let you do things as you like, but also because she said she was helping you to find a husband. Now I realize those two things were opposed. But my dear, I cannot ignore that you are still only twenty-six. The house your grandmother has left you was not intended to be a place where you stay inside for the rest of your life and moulder."

"I am confused, Papa. Do you want me to meet men or not?" Cass was sitting up ramrod straight. "Or is it only that you don't want me to meet them at the house?"

"Cassandra!"

"Nothing inappropriate happened, Papa," Cass insisted, with a sick feeling in her stomach as some part of her mind contemplated what might happen if her father ever came into the knowledge of everything she had done with the freedom she had enjoyed in recent years.

"Yes, it did." William Cullen's face looked if anything more haggard as he sat back against the sofa and regarded his daughter.

William Cullen considered his daughter to be the most brilliant woman he had ever met—talented and intelligent. He also thought with a father's prejudice that she was lovely, and he didn't mind that he had had no offers for her hand worth considering in her season or since. William considered it the fault of today's young men that they spoke of his daughter as haughty because she didn't laugh at jokes she couldn't hear. Clearly such young men had no taste.

But he felt old, and he was getting older. And he was beginning to

THE COUNTESS INVENTION

see his dreams for her slipping away. His dreams, and the dreams of his beloved wife who was gone, the beauty who had married him for love. He still felt he owed her that.

He'd thought that Cass felt that she owed that to her mother, and to her grandmother too, who'd had the same dreams.

Apparently the only one who didn't share those goals was Cass.

She knew perfectly well that it was beyond inappropriate to have men in the house and yet she had done it anyway. What was he to do with her?

"Very well. If you are so determined to conduct this type of business, you must find a husband who allows it."

"Papa! I—"

"I will not stand by and watch the destruction of your chances of a good marriage. Your mother made me promise, and nothing will make me go back on my word. I'll speak to the Marchioness immediately. She must know ways of re-introducing you into society, the right people, the right parties. You need a husband—nothing less than an earl!—and if he chooses to let you traipse in and out with men of business, fine, but those are discussions for a wife to have with her husband."

Cass opened her mouth again. Her father again cut off her speech.

"You know how to be a lady. You *are* a lady. Be true to that."

"I have never concealed from you that I was taking commissions to design furniture and the like for people who needed it."

"Yes, you described it as a very charitable endeavor conducted entirely through correspondence and totally suitable for a lady of distinction. But we both know that what you are actually doing is conducting *business* in order to earn the money to maintain your own household, because I would not pay for its upkeep."

"How else do you expect me to manage my household affairs?"

"I *expected* you to keep your grandmother's house closed until you were married, and then use it when you and your husband chose, like any reasonable married woman!" William's hands were both clenched and the red color of his face was alarming. "You continue to skirt around the edges of our agreements in order to do as you please but that is why I am being as clear as crystal now! Find a husband, Cass, immediately. At least an earl. That requires behaving as a lady should, and *that* requires no inappropriate visitors to your home. If your interest in helping others suffers for lack of customers, good. It cannot be your primary concern."

Cass' lips were folded together tight. "What a charmer you are, Papa. And I wonder what you would have done if my mother had followed those orders from *her* father."

He let out all the air inside him. "I should have missed a love that was sweeter than anything I expected to find in this lifetime," he told her frankly. "And are you in love?"

"No!"

"Good, then it won't cloud your thinking. Find a husband, Cass. Now."

* * *

Cass was still shaking with reaction when she arrived home.

Adams, upon opening the door, let out an involuntary *hmmph* of surprise. The mistress did not often look so rattled.

Hearing Adams, Selene turned toward the door from where she was dusting the vases that decorated the hallway.

"Is something wrong, miss? Are you quite well?"

"I'm fine," said Cass shortly, patting her shoulder as she moved past her and into the library.

Maybe she could lock the door and just stay in here forever, Cass thought a little wildly. She was reluctant to let go of the doorknob even once she had shut herself in.

If she could just hold this door shut forever, all would be well.

There was a plate of cakes near her favorite seat on the sofa. Cass went and picked them up. Ratafia cakes.

Blissfully Cass put an entire cake into her mouth and sank to the sofa, clutching the plate.

She *loved* Mrs. Orfill.

Staying in here gorging herself on sugary cakes was probably not going to solve her problem. Nonetheless, she was willing to give it a try.

Why couldn't her father be more reasonable? Yes, ladies married. Yes, her mother had wanted her to marry into the peerage. But *every* mother wanted her daughter to marry into the peerage. Why couldn't her father be happy with Cass' life? She was earning enough money to maintain the household, just as she'd said she could. She didn't need a husband to take care of her.

Her father had the most convenient tendency to ignore the fact that *he* had married for love. Which meant her *mother* had married for love.

In fact, she did not know for sure, because he was not a demonstrative man, but it seemed likely that he had married for love *twice*. At least, four children didn't seem to Cass like he hated his second wife.

If her father had discussed how to fall in love half as often as he had discussed art and architecture and manufacturing, she might be in a different position now.

But he didn't discuss love with her, and her mother hadn't before she died either. And her stepmother didn't, and neither did anyone at the school.

And the Marchioness who had sponsored her social debut had also had nothing to say on the subject.

Cass had turned to books, but they gave her an impression of love that was mostly alarming. People did awful and ridiculous and dangerous things for love, and more often than not, it ended badly. Worse, the mechanism of love was never revealed. Bodies, somewhat. Love, no.

Cass was left with the impression that love was something that spontaneously occurred in nature, like weeds springing from flagstones. At the same time, this spontaneous occurrence was invisible. She couldn't see it, couldn't describe it if she had to.

And her father's insistence that she get married had not featured any discussion of love either.

So she was left to assume that love was extremely important but did not apply to her.

This accorded with her experience. No one had ever had the least *tendresse* for Cass. The one or two good-looking fellows who had asked her to dance had soon drifted away. Perhaps she had failed to hear their proposals. She sighed.

She herself had not been entirely immune to the charms of men. Oh, she had watched them and occasionally, she had certainly dreamed. She had definitely dreamed of a few of them that she would like them to... well, to perform a husbandly service for her. She would adore having babies of her own. The books *had* been clear about the mechanisms of *that*. At least, reasonably clear. The prospect of doing *that* had at one time seemed a pleasant one.

Given her background on both the importance and invisibility of love, however, she had not been inclined to leave everything to chance.

And the experimental verification of the *processes* of love as she understood them had proven far less appealing than the prospect.

Oh, she had dreamed. She had spun long stories in her head of the lovely young men who would suddenly notice her and smile at her and somehow inexplicably fall in love with her. She'd definitely imagined.

And because she had to know how it would actually work before she committed to anything as final as marriage, she had, not once but twice, written an extremely forward note to invite for a visit a fellow about whom she had done a great deal of dreaming. A young man in whom she had felt she could have faith. And definitely, a young man whom she wanted to meet in much closer circumstances.

Perhaps the fault was hers, in that there were two young men who had so captured her imagination as to cause her to reach out to them. Perhaps she didn't understand love at all. Well, that was the reason for the experiments; she *didn't* understand it. She could only begin with the young men about whom she so vividly daydreamed for so long, young men who actually existed, and frankly, there had been several, though she did limit her daydreams to one young man at a time... until he disappointed her.

She had, not once but twice, engaged in behavior that young

ladies were *not* supposed to engage in, putting both a garden bench and a silk carpet by a fireplace to very illicit use. She had, not once but twice, found the entire endeavor far more trouble than it was worth: painful or boring, and entailing far too great a risk of discovery.

She had of course tried twice, because once was not a sufficient result to predict the future.

Cass was now, however, confident that the business was not for her.

Thinking back, she could not even understand her own actions in undertaking such a risk. Those young men, she felt certain, would never say anything; their behavior hardly reflected well on them. But she had put herself in appalling danger. She had put herself in danger of a pregnancy she could not explain, as well as put herself at the mercy of those men's whims. Looking back, she felt acutely that only after the fact had she realized what intimate danger there was of being hurt in many ways, and she was grateful she had ended up only disappointed.

The older she got, the more she could imagine much more dangerous outcomes from submitting so entirely to someone else's mercy.

She should not have been so foolish in the first place. Peg had told her stories of her life in the poorer neighborhoods of London, before she won her spot at the school for the deaf where they met. Cass had known the risks; she just hadn't believed them until she had gotten old enough to realize that her life was no different from any other woman's, not really.

It was far better to avoid the risks of such vulnerability. And if she did not need a husband for her livelihood or her bed, and she did not expect a husband to fall madly in love with her, why must her father make such a fuss about her having a husband at all?

Just the prospect of a husband stomping around the house and issuing orders about the way to arrange the furniture, or about the way she scattered her drawings over her desk, or even the way she was currently eating an entire plate of ratafia cakes, seemed miserable.

She could just picture him, a mean, glowering man who liked to use his cane in the house, an affectation Cass could not bear.

What might such a man do with the legal right to her home? To her bed?

In fact, picturing him now...

Picturing him now, Cass could see the imaginary scowling face of the dreaded evil unwanted husband turning into a much more pleasant one.

The man whose image came most quickly to her mind was, of course, Dr. Oliver Burke.

The poetic lines of his nose and jaw seemed permanently arranged in a slight frown, not a scowl, but he never seemed to be frowning *at her*. And those eyes...

Then she remembered his voice, so deep that it seemed to make the window-glass vibrate, saying, "I believe I can help you."

Cass took in a deep breath so fast she almost dropped the cakes.

He very well might.

CHAPTER 5

"Oh no, not you."

"Dr. Hunter, that is no way to greet a fellow physician, certainly not first thing in the morning."

"It's noon." The fiftyish man standing on the open hospital ward floor had bandages stuffed in one suit pocket and paper packets of medicine powder stuffed in the other. "I have no time today for your weekly pantomime where you show up here just to announce that you no longer do surgery, then inquire after every one of my surgery patients."

"I'm wounded." Oliver immediately began to examine the dressing on the man in the hospital bed, who had clearly had a below-the-knee amputation.

Dr. Hunter started muttering something about how if Dr. Burke were the one who was wounded, he himself ought to start claiming that he didn't do surgery, but Oliver ignored that too.

Instead he talked with the patient for a while, then smiled and said some reassuring things before taking one of the trays of bandages from Dr. Hunter's hands and walking with him across the ward.

"Seriously, Burke, I haven't time for your balderdash today. I have a stupid young lordling who got shot in some sort of a duel, and I have to remove his leg."

"I'm sorry, Hunter." Oliver often wished that the romantic young gentry who still occasionally indulged in dueling knew that if they survived, they might well lose a leg, or two, just from the loss of blood. "Would it help if I looked over your cases for you?"

Dr. Hunter's eyes in his plump cheeks narrowed as he took in Oliver's own slightly puffy face. "It annoys me that even recovering from whatever you drank last night, you'd have a steadier hand at surgery than I, and you claim you're not a surgeon."

Oliver didn't feel up to explaining how he saw his wartime service as a failed mission. He was happy to let Dr. Hunter think he was simply trying to separate himself from the lower-class activity of surgery.

"Your work is brilliant, as you know quite well. Just tell me if there's anywhere I can help, Hunter." He had appointments with some of the old ladies of London's gentry this afternoon, and those paid his bills, which were small. But he had to, he simply had to, be of some help somewhere along the way with someone who needed it.

Dr. Hunter sighed. "The little girl in the corner, I took a tumor off her back and I'm worried it's septic. Take a look, would you?"

Oliver nodded. "Of course."

"Of course." Dr. Hunter threw up his free hand, causing the paper packets of medicine in his pocket to rustle loudly. "Of course. Same old same old with you, my friend. It's nice to know you're consistent at least, I suppose."

* * *

THE SINKING sensation Oliver felt as he surveyed Lady Gadbury's chambers were certainly a change for him.

When did flattering invitations from lovely ladies begin to seem sordid?

"Lady Gadbury, I must decline."

"No, you mustn't decline, dear boy." She was fortyish, slender, with a graceful smile topped by an even more graceful twist of golden brown hair, embellished with feathers. She was very pleasant to look at and even more pleasant to be with. "You must say yes."

Oliver had some fond memories of reading with her in this very room, of drinking her madeira, and on a few occasions, of sharing her bed.

Why should he feel in need of a bath? She was everything he looked for in a companion, and clearly she was interested in his company.

She had roasted chestnuts waiting for him, which she knew he liked. She had a small harp ready, which she could play very pleasantly, but also a book from which to read to him, if he chose. She had prepared an evening for his pleasure, not hers.

Perhaps that was what held so little appeal. She understood him so little, really. It was the giving of pleasure Oliver enjoyed.

His smile was rueful. "I'm very flattered by your attentions, my lady, but I am not trying to be coy."

"You are not trying to be coy, that's true, you are in fact succeeding at being coy," and here Lady Gadbury tossed herself down upon the silk settee with a force that belied her elegant coiffure, maquillage, and gown.

"I do apologize. I..." Suddenly Oliver realized he had no real explanation as to why he was declining her invitation. It simply didn't appeal. *She* didn't appeal.

Did he truly need to find other amusement? Friends who were men, like Waite, seemed to be only entertained by much cheaper women, and drink.

Would it really be preferable to simply crawl inside a bottle?

"Truly, you are most kind, and I am ungrateful to decline the company of a hostess so gracious."

"You needn't sweet-talk me, man. If you're not going to stay, then go."

That startled Oliver, and he was immediately on his feet, gloves in hand. "Of course."

"No, I... never mind, Oliver, I should not visit my foul temper on you."

He sank into the embroidered chair opposite. "If I have caused it, I should bear it."

"No, not at all. Truly. I am simply... It is lonely here tonight and I enjoy your company as one enjoys boxes of sweets, indulgently. That puts no obligation on you."

Oliver took in her complexion with an eye more towards his profession. "Are you feeling quite well, Lady Gadbury? Are you eating as usual? Sleeping at night?"

She tossed him a sarcastic look, accompanied by an unladylike snort. "No worse than you, Oliver." Then she leaned over to pat him on his knee. "And if you won't call me Laura even when you are trying to diagnose me, then I am quite at arm's distance. Don't worry, I understand. Have you met some pretty young girl?"

Under the slight tinge of bitterness in her words, Lady Gadbury looked sincerely interested.

She really was a lovely woman. Oliver wished he had something to recommend, something he could do for her besides prescribe a visit to the country in order to rest.

So he wanted to be pleasant and to answer her question about meeting some pretty young girl. "I have not..."

But of course he had. Cass' face, with the fine grey eyes and the skin like cream, had leaped into his memory at the moment that he claimed he had not met any pretty young girls, as if his own mind wished to prove him wrong.

Cass wasn't just pretty, he told himself sternly. She was striking.

"I have met a young lady, madam, as one does in the course of a life in London, but she has no interest in me."

"Has she seen you, Oliver?"

He laughed. "She has."

"Then trust me, sir. She's interested in you."

* * *

HE SHOULD HAVE STAYED at Lady Gadbury's, Oliver told himself in the middle of the night.

He pulled at the sheet that was tangled around his waist. It was too warm in here. The housekeeper's son Tommy must have left a fire banked downstairs, because it was autumn; or this room had simply become too close.

Why the devil hadn't he stayed with Lady Gadbury? He could be lying in bed with her right now, surfeited on chestnuts and music, listening to her read him the latest novel.

Or listening to the way her breathing changed as she climbed toward the peak of pleasure.

She had been a diverting partner in bed, that he recalled well. She had been quite willing to let him try to discover for both of them whether or not she could reach that peak twice, or three times, or more.

Oliver considered it a failure of the medical field that the mechanisms of a woman's pleasure were so poorly documented. Clearly there were physiological differences. From what he could tell from army talk, men finished and stopped. From what he could tell from experimentation, women were not that way. At least, many women.

When he dreamed about the war, when he woke with the screams echoing in his head, he turned his thoughts to the most extreme opposite: a woman fainting with delight in his arms. The horrors of the world demanded a balance, and in London Oliver sought that balance. He wanted the women he bedded to be not just satisfied, but if possible completely destroyed by physical bliss. Then he could fall asleep not only satisfied in his body, but in his mind that he had perhaps put back into the world a little more of what the war had taken out.

If he no longer had a taste for women, Oliver very much worried that he *would* find himself crawling deeper and deeper into the bottle. Wine made him sleep but it did not let him stay asleep. Perhaps he would need to drink more gin.

He groaned, kicking off the bedding entirely and letting the air cool his skin a little. Perhaps he ought to pleasure himself to see if it would help him sleep. But at the moment that too felt somehow hollow. Like Lady Gadbury, it just didn't appeal.

He was a medical man. He knew the progression. He could try gin, and more gin, and then perhaps opium. And that often led to a sleep that was quite permanent.

It would kill his parents to lose another son.

Swinging his legs from the bed, Oliver wrapped the coverlet around himself and, with his pillow, lay down on the carpet.

Perhaps that would let him sleep.

* * *

THE NEXT MORNING, HE RECEIVED CASS' message that she urgently needed to see him, and it felt like the fulfillment of his bad moods. Oliver wasted no time in hurrying to her house.

It still surprised him to see the little crescent road transformed into a bit of bedlam. There were a few neighbors standing at the other end of the street, pretending not to look.

A carriage was waiting at the door of Cass' home. The house's environs were surrounded by an iron fence and a gate, all adorned with swooping curlicues and iron leaves. Greenery bloomed in and around the ironwork, giving the walk a little bit of a fairytale appearance, at least for the width of the house.

Footmen in livery were arrayed along the iron fence. They looked rather like bowling-pins, Oliver thought as he passed them, all standing straight and silent in their matching uniforms.

Adams opened the door for him before he knocked.

"Is Miss Cullen in?" asked Oliver, his tone conveying that, from the crowd in front, he rather expected the answer to be yes.

"Miss Cullen is in the library. The Duke of Talbourne is in the front parlor with her ladyship, the Marchioness of Inglemawr."

"It's a full house, isn't it, Adams."

"Indeed, sir."

"Perhaps you could show me in to see Miss Cullen for a moment, then put me in whatever room she sees fit to put me. Her message sounded urgent."

"Yes, sir."

It reassured Oliver more than he realized he needed when Cass saw him and her face lit up. She flew towards him, stopping just a foot short. Oliver was quite disappointed; he thought she might actually throw herself in his arms.

"Oh! Dr. Burke! You are here. So early. I should have specified in my message the time. Didn't I? Perhaps I didn't. This is too bad. I need to speak with you very urgently, and now the Duke is here, which I had forgotten, and I had promised him an item for his son, but the son does not even use a rolling chair any more so I don't know why he still needs new things, but it's less important than the reason I asked you to come. But I cannot ignore a duke."

Oliver could think of several reasons why a duke might just drop by, including the reason facing him now. "Aren't you ignoring him, Miss Cullen?"

"No no, I came in here for the drawing to show him even if it is unfinished. Her ladyship will keep him company."

Oliver watched her face closely. "Did he not come to see you as a personal visit?"

The dismissive noise she made seemed genuine. "I draft drawings of furniture. He is a duke of the realm and very highly placed in the government. He did not come to see me."

Oliver started to reach out to touch her for some reason, then stopped himself. Cass caught the movement out of the corner of her eye and looked at him.

He said, "Seeing you is more worthwhile than you may realize, Miss Cullen."

"Oh, I..." For a moment Cass forgot herself, lost in those eyes that drifted between blue and green, like a beckoning window on a great wide world.

They looked at each other.

Then Cass drew in a sharp breath. "It's, ah, it's, it's quite predictable, he drops by every few months, I can't understand it."

I can, thought Oliver to himself, but he stayed silent.

"At any rate, we must make him go away. Let me find this drawing. Will you go with me?"

"Anywhere you like."

That made Cass flash him a smile and she laid her hand on his chest, just for a moment, before turning back to the maelstrom of paper that was strewn on her desk.

Was he imagining it, or could he actually feel the warm imprint of her hand through all his clothes?

When Oliver followed her into the parlor, he took in as much of the scene as he could.

There was the Duke, a broad-shouldered, narrow-hipped man who was no longer young but who was aging well, to Oliver's visual inspection, and wearing a green coat with unfashionably loose trousers. He was not at all the silver and lace mannequin Oliver expected a duke to be.

Opposite him sat a small woman who gave Oliver the impression of looking like a firework. Her hair, organized in a becoming riot of curls, shone in every shade from golden to sunset red, and her gown was a robe *à la Turque* in stripes of blue-green and beige that set off the colors of her remarkable hair.

She was watching the Duke as though he might do something even more startling than pay a visit.

When Cass entered, the Duke stood, and the Marchioness with him.

"Your Grace." Cass curtsied very properly before sailing forward with the foolscap in her hand. "May I introduce Dr. Oliver Burke? Dr. Burke, may I present His Grace, the Duke of Talbourne? My apologies for making you wait, sir. This is the drawing of the table we discussed; I hope it is what you seek?"

The Duke's eyes flicked up and down to take in all of Cass, and then the same with Oliver, who had sketched a bow as he'd come in as well. "Miss Cullen. Dr. Burke, I am pleased to meet you." To Oliver, he

THE COUNTESS INVENTION

sounded anything but pleased. Impatient, perhaps even slightly dismissive, but not pleased.

The Duke's face was serious as he perused the drawing, which faded into nothing along the edges but outlined the table in question well.

His response sounded as carefully considered as his inspection of the drawing. "Yes. I don't expect my son to return to the use of his chair, but if he does, I want him to be able to work in comfort. The ability to change the height of the table as required is perfect."

"I hope Lady Inglemawr has been able to entertain you."

"Yes of course." Here the Duke gave a solemn nod to the sunset-haired lady, who inclined her head prettily in return. "Always a pleasure."

But he didn't seem to be looking at her ladyship with even the interest he showed for the desk, Oliver thought.

No, the Duke wasn't here to see the Marchioness. And he probably wasn't here for the table.

The thought rankled Oliver. If the Duke intended to offer for Miss Cullen, the man ought to do it. Coming to her house this way, even attended by a chaperone, only increased the danger for the young woman.

He could hardly scold a duke, though.

And in fact it was another half hour before His Grace finally took his leave, taking his footmen and his street-blocking carriage with him.

It felt as though the house had been occupied by troops and then just as suddenly abandoned.

"Well!" said Lady Inglemawr, giving herself a bit of a shake all over before rising to her feet. "I quite need some tea after that."

* * *

INTERESTINGLY TO OLIVER, Lady Inglemawr then disappeared into the depths of the house and did not return.

Which Cass ignored. Instead, she dashed for the door of the library and gestured vehemently for Oliver to follow her.

She scarcely had the library door closed behind him again before a river of words rushed forth.

"I am *so* grateful for your help, doctor, I really have nowhere else to turn. It is vital for me to continue to keep this household, not just for me but for everyone, well, except her ladyship, she doesn't need to live *here*, but my father has become so unreasonable and I—"

Oliver put out both hands in front of him in an easily understood gesture for *stop*.

She stopped.

Oliver regarded the closed door. Cass had closed it. The Marchioness had apparently gone straight to some other room without a care as to what Cass did.

This household *was* intriguing.

"Miss Cullen, please sit down and begin at the beginning."

Looking at him, Cass took in a deep breath. Then immediately, another inward breath.

"Let one of those breaths out. Sit. Begin at the beginning. Please."

Cass deflated. And sat. "Well I don't know how to start, now."

"Your father...?" Oliver prompted.

"Oh, my father. You see, he promised my mother before she died, *so* unreasonable, that I would marry back into the peerage. Because she married him, you see, and her family was so devastated, and I believe they gave him quite a hard time for quite a long time, but then my grandmother at least forgave him, I think, when I came along because she liked me very well. But in any event, my father promised her before she died—my mother, not my grandmother, although I think he might have said something similar to her before she passed away—and I thought you might help me."

"Marry back into the peerage." Oliver wanted to make sure he was hearing this correctly.

"Yes! That is what I just said. He has always said I need to marry at least an earl. My mother used to say it too, when I was little. I think she was, oh I don't know, talking sweetly to me? She loved to say things like that. At any rate he has said it for a long time but now it appears he *means* it. Which is awful. I don't want to get married and I don't know any earls and it is absurd. He will not let me go on as I am doing unless I am married. Which is just absurd. Am I not doing perfectly well now?"

"Other than your street being blocked by the carriages of random dukes, yes," agreed Oliver.

"So he is driving me simply to distraction. And I was sitting right here, at my wit's end, and nearly out of ratafia cakes, when it occurred to me. You!"

"Me *what*?"

"You have been *so* helpful. So kind. It occurred to me that as a physician, you must travel in many circles. You might know some earls! Do you know any?"

Oliver scrubbed a hand over his chin. "You wanted me to tell you if I know any earls?"

"Yes!"

"Forgive me if I sit for a moment." Oliver sank rather heavily into the settee next to her. "I had thought you were ill, Miss Cullen."

"Oh I am sorry! Why did you think so?"

"That's usually why people send urgent messages for physicians, miss."

"Yes, I see." Cass only looked a little abashed, and only for a moment. "I am sorry. I will be clearer in the next message. Only you see why I didn't want to write it out."

"If you had been able to write all that out I would be surprised," muttered Oliver, sinking back into his seat and regarding her with a mixture of relief and shock.

She wanted him to help her find someone to marry. An earl. Nothing less than an earl.

"Let me ask you something, purely for my own edification. Do you have any requirements of your own for this husband? Other than that he be an earl?"

"No, I don't want one in the first place, what is the use of specifications?"

"Mm." Oliver let his eyes roam to the far corners of the room before coming back to her. He felt like he would need something for his head soon. Perhaps he *had* had too much to drink last night. Or perhaps it was this conversation.

Cass went on. "I need one who will leave me alone, obviously."

That one seemed to push Oliver over some invisible cliff.

"Obviously? *Obviously?* There's nothing obvious about it, Miss Cullen. One doesn't usually acquire a husband for the sole purpose of having him leave you alone."

"Good, then, it's a good thing we have that requirement on the table."

Oliver began to worry about the quality of the liquor he'd consumed last night. Perhaps it had been adulterated.

He looked around. The room was not spinning and his eyesight seemed fine.

He looked back at Cass. Still sitting ramrod straight, hands folded together in her lap, face alight with serious concern.

"Very well. Very well. Suppose you wanted this earl husband. Isn't that the sort of thing your father should be arranging? You have had a season, have you not?"

Cass made a sort of an *umphh* noise and some of the animation went out of her face. "I was not a smashing success, Dr. Burke, as you may well imagine."

"I wouldn't imagine, but you apparently did not get married, for here you are."

"And it was so long ago. Almost a decade. There were no suitable offers, and society is torture, as far as I am concerned. So you see I don't know anyone!"

"What about the Marchioness? Surely this is a task she took on, as your sponsor?"

Cass rolled her eyes. "Her ladyship has many skills. I'm not sure matchmaking is among them. Don't tell anyone, but I think she enjoys living here in town with me and having her own social schedule."

Oliver was quite sure she did.

He still had an urge to massage his jaw, which was clenched for some reason.

But if he covered his mouth with his hand, she wouldn't be able to see his mouth as he talked. So he dropped the hand in what he hoped wasn't a too dramatic gesture.

"Miss Cullen," Oliver began in what he was sure was a very reasonable voice. "I would suggest giving the matter some time. Your father has been fine with your situation for some time, has he not? Whatever fancy has crossed his mind, he will be just as likely to forget it soon. Otherwise, how could you have been here so long already?"

"Well." Cass looked down at her hands before giving him a pleading look, as if asking him to understand what she was about to say. "Not long after my mother died, I started at a school that is not too far a trip from here, so I lived here with my grandmother for so much of that time. Then I was teaching, a little, at the school, and then my grandmother was ill, and so I stayed to care for her. To pass the time, I began drawing things that people from the school needed, as you know. And then my grandmother only passed away a little over a year ago. Her ladyship came to join me then, since she had launched my debut. It has been perfectly lovely and just as I would wish. But it is all quite recent, actually, and my father has not been in favor of this plan. And then..."

He waved one hand in a spiral as if to say *go on*.

"Ehmm... my father received a letter. About, erm, me. And you? In the... someone saw us in the street. And then the Grantleys the next day. And, hmm, they seemed to know her ladyship was not about."

"Aha. I see. So your father received a report that his unmarried daughter was entertaining all sorts of men alone. And he rightly objected."

Cass made a noise of distress. "Objected is one word for it."

Oliver could just picture it. He had little knowledge of fathers in general, but he could well imagine the reactions of this one.

"Well there's nothing for it, my friend. You're going to have to get married."

"I *know*! But I don't know anyone! Please, you must help me find someone who will make my father happy and then leave me alone."

"Alone." Oliver continued to find the idea appalling.

"Really! My grandmother left me the use of this house but my father refuses to pay for its upkeep. I must keep doing the work I am able to do in order to buy the food and the coal, and pay the staff. I cannot have a husband getting in the way of that."

"Wouldn't your husband pay for those things, if you were married?" It seemed eminently reasonable to Oliver.

Cass gave a little dissatisfied shake of her head. "I do not want him to do that! He would likely want to change everything around, change all the staff, and I can't have that."

Oliver had a dim idea that men usually did have their own staff about them when they set up a household. "I think you must resign yourself to that."

"Dr. Burke. I cannot. Do you not understand who we are? A deaf woman and her merry little band?" Cass looked like she could not decide whether to laugh or cry. "I cannot call Peg for you to meet as she does not have any hearing at all. Perhaps you have not really met Selene."

Retrieving a silver bell from among the mishmash of papers on her desk, Cass rang it vehemently.

Selene appeared almost immediately. "Yes, Miss Cullen?"

Cass went and stood next to her, by the settee.

"Selene, I am sorry to make so personal a request, and you must feel free to say no. But I would not want to speak for you. Would it be possible, would you mind terribly, telling Dr. Burke why you work here?"

The girl's straight back made her pose quite regal, and as she shifted restlessly for a moment Oliver thought that she would demure; but finally she said simply, "I need the money, miss."

Cass nodded, but then when Selene stopped, Cass said quietly, "Would you mind terribly telling him a little more?"

At that Selene froze, the cut of her golden-tinted profile giving Oliver the impression of a bronze statue. But then her smile came back, the live, sunny smile of a young woman, and she shrugged, as if shedding any embarrassment. "My father is dead, Dr. Burke, and my mother is infirm. There are few places willing to employ someone who is blind. Surely that is clear enough?"

"Thank you, Selene. I do apologize."

"Not at all, miss."

When the maid withdrew, Cass turned back to Oliver.

"So do you understand that she must earn her keep? I would also be happy to simply support her—Selene is actually a distant cousin of mine. It would be difficult, especially as her mother also needs the attention of doctors from time to time. But Selene refuses; she says she would rather work for me than anyone else, and would far rather work than do nothing; and she and her mother *would not eat* but for the money she earns."

Her expression serious, Cass went on. "My friend Peg could work in a factory—was trained, in fact, in weaving techniques at the school. There are only a few places she can work. She has always been entirely deaf and speaks only with the manual language. So she would have no choice but to work in the shop attached to the school, and the pay is very poor. Her parents are old and cannot work any more. She would have to live apart from her husband if she worked at the shop at the school; they have no place for married people. Between her parents and Mr. Adams' mother, they cannot all live on Mr. Adams' salary alone, and Peg hates being home alone all day anyway.

"Mrs. Orfill you have not met." Cass pressed a hand to her temple. "Mrs. Orfill is very sweet to me, very dear. She lost several fingers on her right hand in an accident with an oven. Her employer's response was to send her away. There is no shortage of staff in London; employers have their pick and don't hesitate to let someone go."

Cass' sweep of her arm encompassed her whole house. "This isn't just my own quirk of personality, doctor. These are *my* staff, I am responsible for this household, and I intend to maintain it."

Oliver nodded. Cass looked like a watchful lioness protecting her pack. And he understood. She was the ruler of this little household, and she needed that.

They all needed that.

Her extraordinary little kingdom was in extraordinary danger. At a moment like this, could he abandon her to her fate? To a husband that would *leave her alone?*

Leaning forward, Oliver clasped his hands and rested his forearms on his legs as though bracing himself.

"Here is a very terrible idea, miss. Would you like to marry me?"

CHAPTER 6

"That is a *dreadful* joke," Cass managed to whisper.

There Oliver sat, looking deadly serious.

"It is a terrible idea," he said again, "for several reasons. I don't—we will have to discuss them later; you would most probably prefer betrothal to me as a temporary measure to appease your father. But I assure you, it is no joke. You could marry me."

It was such an odd thing for him to say, was Cass' first thought, when he didn't love her.

But of course they hadn't been speaking of love at all, not through this entire conversation.

Nor did anyone of Cass' acquaintance consider love to be particularly related to her marriage prospects.

"I don't know where to begin." Her voice was very quiet now. "How does it solve my problem?"

"You wish to keep your house. You don't wish to lose your staff. I have nearly no staff and only a small place I have let. I don't mind your work—in fact I applaud it. And while I am not an earl... I am sorry to say, I will be."

Cass was having a hard time thinking straight. Beautiful men did not propose to her, and she had not expected anything of the sort from Oliver. "I didn't ask for your help to... I was not maneuvering for..."

"I know, of course I know. Don't trouble yourself on that score. You didn't know."

"You... are *going* to be an earl?"

"Someday."

Oliver did not want to talk about this, he truly did not. He felt sweat standing out on his forehead. Explaining his family was difficult enough under the best of circumstances. Explaining this was like performing surgery on himself.

Best to make it brief, like a battlefield amputation, Oliver thought.

"My older brother died," he said, quickly, loudly, to make sure he would not have to repeat it.

"Oh, I am sorry."

Both her hands caught up one of his. Her touch was cooling, somehow. Keeping him attached to the earth when his mind threatened to fly away from it.

"He stayed here, as the heir to a title ought to do. I wanted to serve, I had trained as a physician and was willing to serve as a surgeon; I thought I could be useful. When he grew ill, I was in France. He died. I am next in line for my father's title, which is Earl of Rawleigh."

"But you don't... you have a title you do not use? A courtesy title?"

"Lord Howiston." Oliver's jaw was definitely clenched now, and his teeth grated on one another. Lord Howiston was his brother Oscar.

"I see," said Cass gently. "You would rather not use his title."

"When I came home, I set up my practice using my mother's maiden name, which is one of mine as well. I was never Lord Howiston and I don't intend to be."

Cass closed her eyes. He looked so raw at this moment.

When she opened them she said, "So you have a family requirement that you also cannot escape."

"In a manner of speaking." Now that he had said it out loud, Oliver felt a little easier. It was easier to give her more details. "I have a younger brother who already has a son of his own. I feel no particular urge to provide further for the line. But I cannot escape inheriting it first, if I am alive when my father passes away."

A title had done his brother Oscar no good, thought Oliver with some bitterness, and it had done Oliver himself no good either. As far as he could tell, it hadn't done his father any favors, either.

Cass nodded. "Would your family welcome your marriage?"

Oliver snorted. "My lady, you cannot imagine how much jubilation there would be, if they were capable of anything like jubilation, which they are not."

This seemed like puzzling information; Cass was sure she had missed a word or two there, but decided to press on. "So you would truly be willing to marry me and leave me alone?"

At that Oliver just shook his head slowly, his eyes staying on her the whole time.

"If you marry me, Miss Cullen—and I am completely serious when I tell you it is a terrible idea—but *if* you marry me, I would be happy to combine my living with yours. And I would certainly *not* leave you alone."

* * *

CASS WAS GOING to need something stronger than ratafia cakes.

Unable to sit quietly on the couch any longer, she began to pace the length of the room.

"Dr. Burke... I am not prepared to take this conversation further in this direction."

"I feel the same way," he responded, knowing she was too far away to hear his actual words, only that he responded. Still, he felt they were of a mind on this.

Cass continued to pace, wringing her hands. She could *not* tell him... but if they were truly having this conversation?

She sat back down, just as suddenly. "This is awkward."

She stood back up again.

She wanted to run into the hallway, to find Peg. But what would Peg do for her?

She wanted her mother.

She wanted her *step*mother.

Anyone who would help her not have to say this.

It was excruciating, to have to explain this as a reason why he must *not* marry her.

Funny how she had not thought of this situation when she had done it.

"Dr. Burke, I must... confess something to you that I would... rather not confess, but if you are serious..."

"Don't I look serious?" Oliver spread his arms and tried to look harmless. "But truly, miss, you owe me no confessions."

"No, this is... this is something I would have to tell you... and if I don't you will think I am ungrateful to turn down your offer, which I am not, truly I am not!"

Oliver's stomach sank a little. She was going to turn down his offer?

He'd never proposed before and hadn't planned to do so today, and yet it didn't feel good to think she was going to turn him down.

"Wait... you have to confess something to me in order to explain *why* you must turn down my offer? And what would you be confessing to me if you accepted?"

Cass' eyes were on the ceiling, the floor, anywhere but him.

But she sat back down again.

"Enh, this is. Very well. The thing is... the thing is..."

Struck by a horrible thought, Oliver leaned his head a little closer. "Has someone—has some man—"

Cass squeezed her eyes shut tight, and nodded, a tight little nod.

"Miss Cullen." Oliver's voice was low. "That is not your fault."

"No, it is! I mean—you don't understand. Oh, this is unbearable. How can I explain."

Oliver asked gently, "Is it easier to go farther away when you tell me? Because I can still hear you."

"Yes. No! No, I would rather you were here."

Because she didn't want him to go away.

Which was an entirely different problem. She didn't have time for that problem *now*.

Still she kept her eyes shut tight.

"Very well." Oliver put both hands over his eyes. "Now I cannot see you, Miss Cullen, and you cannot see me. Does this not make it easier to say things you would rather not say but have to say?"

Cass opened her eyes.

There he was, a sturdy, mature man, sitting quite calmly on her couch, covering his eyes so he couldn't see her.

To make it a little easier on her.

Something washed through Cass at the sight of him. What a lovely man. Not just beautiful, but lovely.

She could imagine him playing hide and seek, just like this, as a little boy, with his lost brother.

And then her heart broke a little for him, and filled up with him a little too.

She leaned so closely that she could see the shadows of the beard he must not have shaved in his hurry to reach her this morning.

She whispered, "I am not a virgin."

After a few moments, Oliver nodded. "Go on. Tell me whatever you feel you must tell me."

"That's it. I am not a virgin. At all."

The adamant tone of the *at all* made Oliver want to smile, but he dared not. "And this was not without your agreement."

"This was at my own instigation."

Feeling it might be safe now to look, Oliver peered through his fingers at her. He blinked.

And blinked again.

"Bravo, Miss Cullen," was all he could think of to say.

She shook her head vehemently. "It is not just that I am not a virgin. I am not—Twice, Dr. Burke. Two different... experiments, if you will. It is not a pastime that suits me."

That made Oliver drop his hands altogether. "I want to accept your conclusions in all things, Miss Cullen, but I do find that hard to imagine."

In fact he could all too well imagine the opposite. He thought it would be a pastime that would suit her extremely well.

She let her shoulders fall in an emphatic shrug. "It is simply the case. I fully understand that people do such things in order to bear children, and if you wanted an heir—" here her eyes slid away again, "—we could discuss that. But to be subjected to that type of attention night after night—that would be exhausting to no purpose."

Oliver was mostly wondering whether or not the prime of English manhood had not been left on the battlefield after all. What limp-lilied excuse for a man—*two* of them, apparently—had left this poor woman with such an impression of what happened in bed?

"I think it is exhaustion to a very good purpose, miss, but that is just speaking for myself," he said absently, wondering what on earth could possess a man to arrive in the arms of a Diana like this and then fail her so.

"Because you have—yes, of course you have." Now she was twisting her fingers together again and studying the pattern in the carpet.

Which made Oliver feel like the lowest worm on earth. Because here was his—here was Miss Cullen absolutely agonizing over explaining her past history of *two entire men*.

This should be the moment when he explained the related reason why she should not want to marry him. And it was only one of the reasons. Lord, when she met his family she would run for Cornwall on her own two feet.

"I have," he said gravely. "But that is never the logistical difficulty for a man that presents itself to a young lady. You must have been very determined."

"It's just that there are so many books about it, Dr. Burke, so *many* books! It seemed as though it was something important, something I should know about, do you see my meaning? I've read those books, but I've also met so many married people who do not seem in the least bit happy, so I felt I had to investigate the, the heart of marriage as it were, and... my investigations came to nothing after all and I left it at that."

Her investigations came to nothing. That sounded to Oliver like a crime. "You got nothing from either encounter? No ill effects but... no pleasant ones either?"

Cass rolled her eyes at him. "Did I not just say I had read many books? I know that the little death is supposed to be this great reward of bad behavior. But nothing like that happened to me. I don't think I am built for it."

"You've never had this little death by yourself?"

That made her fix him with a look so pointed it could have cut him. "This is a very personal conversation, but surely there are limits to what can be discussed."

"I have never found that to be true."

"I have no intention of..." Then she threw her hands up in the air and half-muttered to herself. "A fine time to want a little dignity left, and you are a physician, *and* you won't rest until you know. Yes, some small effects, but nothing like the books. I cannot even imagine it to be something others would care so much about. There, does that answer your question?"

My God. Oliver was struck dumb.

As he sometimes did in moments of stress, he took refuge in the voice he used for his official medical opinion.

"You ought to know, Miss Cullen, that two poor experiences do not determine the remainder of one's physical existence. Indeed they determine nothing at all except that you had two poor experiences."

"Poor? Is that the word you used?"

"Trust me, my lady, they were poor." He paused. "But aside from that,"—*there was no 'aside from that', the woman had been sadly robbed and there were at least two men out there in dire need of a beating*, Oliver thought—"what I am wondering is, what had you planned to tell any other man who offered for your hand?"

Cass shrugged again. "As little as possible. What man wants to hear that his sweaty, oppressive weight is not welcome?" She shuddered a little. "I don't want to be *rude*. Plan A was to tell them nothing at all and hope they never wanted to consummate the marriage."

"Extremely unlikely, miss."

She went on. "If I did marry, I assumed it would be some very old man who just wanted me around to make sure he had soup, or something like that."

"Huh." Oliver could picture a few earls like that, but thought that even then Cass was underrating herself. The tiredest old lord would make an effort if Cass was the opportunity. "And plan B?"

"Plan B was not to get married. Actually, that was plan A. My father has not bothered me with this idea the whole year I've been in mourning. I thought perhaps he had moved on to other things."

"Very well, that's plan A and B; was there a C?"

"I suppose this is plan C." Cass waved her hands to take in the whole library. "I would have to explain that I would not make a good wife, and so since I assume the gentleman would have expectations of me—both that I am a virgin and that I would want to share his bed—I would have to make clear my side of the bargain. That I am not, and I would rather not."

"Aha." Oliver prided himself on grace under pressure, but this morning had him flummoxed. "So apparently neither of us thinks that the other one should marry us. Nonetheless, I believe that it is the only solution that presents itself?"

"I suppose." Cass felt both discouraged and exhausted. She had had such high hopes for Oliver's help. And now she supposed he was offering it; but in a form she could not take.

It would be foolish to marry him, even—or especially—given the way her insides had leaped when he had asked. And she was many things, but she was not a fool. Men wanted that activity, she was sure of that. And she wanted no part of it. When she'd engaged in it before, she'd never felt lonelier or more unlovely in her life.

Oliver was still on her settee, one arm along the back, regarding her with a contemplative look that she could not read. "What if your potential husband did not care that you are not a virgin, and felt he could convince you to want to share his bed?"

The thump her heart made in her chest was actually painful. She wasn't interested in hopes and squashed them. He didn't seem to grasp that she already knew the mysteries about which virgins were supposed to be so curious. She'd wanted those young men, she had. There was something in her that had pulled her toward them. But Cass didn't want to live ruled by those slight impulses when their results were so... frankly, unpleasant. Her freedom wasn't worth it. In fact, even within marriage, there was some part of her that felt her life depended on *avoiding* it.

In a drawing room or a ballroom, she was ignored, lonely, nothing. That seemed normal and she could bear it. To be ignored, lonely, *nothing* while being so intimately held in a man's arms—that was unbearable. Whatever her life was to be, she could not be that, not again.

She couldn't entirely rein in her imagination, of course; she had never been able to do so. She could *imagine* a world where her husband convinced her to want to be in his bed; she had *imagined* it before. She just already knew that the reality had nothing to do with the fantasy.

Yet Oliver wanted her to imagine it.

"I thought you said it would be a terrible idea for me to marry you?"

Oliver nodded. "Terrible."

He was moving slowly, slowly leaning toward her so that those decadent lips were getting closer and closer. Cass couldn't take her eyes off them, and she could feel his voice rumbling inside her.

As he very slowly leaned toward her he said, "You think about this terrible idea, and I will also think about it. And all we will promise each other, is that we will think about it. And to seal that promise..."

Then his lips touched hers and Cass drew in a sharp breath and she could feel the air moving between his mouth where he touched her and hers. It was the oddest sensation, being *that* close to someone.

Then his lips covered hers, and it stopped feeling odd.

He tasted better than ratafia cakes, sweet and dark and delicious. His lips moved so slowly along hers, she felt as though she waited years until they closed, plush and warm, around her own lower lip, and tugged, just a little.

She opened her mouth to taste him more and he made a sound she could feel. With the same sort of slowness he moved to slide just the tip of his nose along hers. How could something so small feel so intimate? How could she feel it down to the bottom of her toes?

Ever so slowly, his kiss seemed to melt her from the inside out. She never noticed when she leaned into his hand, where he cupped the side of her face so gently, or when her own hand sought out the line of his jaw and stroked it, just the way the curve of his lips stroked hers.

When she opened her eyes, she found that his own eyes were still closed. He had a very small smile on his face, a look that was happy.

Then he opened his eyes and looked into hers.

From just an inch away Oliver said, "There, we have promised to think about it."

"So we have," she whispered back.

That made his smile bigger.

Cass felt her heart thump again.

"What did we promise again?"

He took her hand and kissed her palm. That lit something else inside her, something heavy and warm. The room felt too close, but he was not close enough.

"We have promised to consider this very terrible idea," he reminded her.

"Yes." She remembered now.

"I will have to discuss it with my parents."

"Oh."

"I will not tell them your name yet, if you would rather I not."

"Don't. No, do. If you like."

"Very well. And you...?"

She needed to talk to Peg. Maybe the Marchioness. "Her ladyship might advise me on what to say to my father. But really, there is no point to getting his hopes up. I wouldn't make a—"

His lips caught hers again, stopping her from talking.

This time, he nipped her lower lip with his teeth.

When he drew back his expression had turned serious again. "You have plenty of good reasons not to marry me, Cassandra. Not enjoying it is not one of them."

She never blushed, yet she felt hot. Her skin felt hot.

Her eyes, following his movement as he stood, were huge and dark.

"Miss Cullen." And he bowed over her hand as if he had not just been taking the *most* exquisite liberties—with his mouth! On her settee!—and then he was gone.

After a long, long time, Cass felt that she must at least get up and go to see what Mrs. Orfill had in the way of spirits in the kitchen.

CHAPTER 7

*I*t would help nothing to delay the inevitable, thought Oliver upon leaving Cass' crescent street. He would have to travel immediately.

He would buy some meat pies for the journey and catch a mail coach, just as he was. Absently he patted his pockets. He ought to have sufficient money on him for the journey, and to return. He was even so interested in speed that he would trust his own skills for safety along the road, highwaymen though there may be.

He had no patients who could not wait a few days for his attendance, he thought, quickening his steps. Regardless, he would send a messenger to Dr. Hunter, and to his housekeeper to relay any messages from patients to that good doctor.

He told himself that he could wait until he returned to explain to Miss Cullen why she did not want him as a husband.

His family, miserable sods that they were, were enough reason for any young lady with even a modicum of sense to avoid joining the family.

He did not want to think about his drinking companion Waite's words at the club.

No average lady would want a husband who had slept with ladies throughout the *ton*, that was true. But Miss Cullen was far from average. She seemed to be a very unconventional thinker in several ways.

She might even understand that, truly, with... well... *many* of those women, he really had simply slept.

Like good food and wine, safe, warm, sweet sleep was a pleasure that Oliver treasured. Not enough time was spent on comfort in bed, Oliver often thought, and he meant it literally.

The happy glow of his memories dimmed considerably when it occurred to him that he might have traded those nights for a lifetime with a Greek goddess.

Not might have, he reminded himself sternly. Had. No doubt Miss Cullen would not have him, despite her dire need and his rash proposal.

At any rate he didn't have to explain himself to resolve the question. She *would* meet his parents, and that would put paid to any desire she might have to join his family.

Nonetheless, he set his feet on the path for the mail coach without really paying attention to what he was doing.

She was the first woman he had met whom he could imagine being his last.

* * *

LADY INGLEMAWR HAD EATEN every crumb of Mrs. Orfill's delicious supper, and was sitting staring at the candles in a way that told Cass that she was very far away.

Unfortunately, Cass needed her here.

"My lady, would you care for claret?"

The lady nodded. "Thank you, dear."

Cass rose and served her a ruby glass, taking the opportunity to sit nearer. She needed to have this conversation.

"My lady," she said again, "my father has reintroduced the idea of my marriage."

At that the marchioness' eyes widened. Cass thought she was paying attention now. "Has he."

JUDITH LYNNE

"I must ask—that is, he has asked me to ask, well, if you have any further plans for it?"

"What sort of plans?" Her words were vague but the look she sent Cass over the rim of her wineglass was as sharp as a knife.

"Any sort of, ah, goals? With regard to introducing me to eligible young men. Particularly, as you may recall, earls."

"Earls." She said it the way some other woman might have said *eels*. As though they were repellent and their worst qualities were contagious.

"Yes, my father still seems quite attached to the idea. I had thought that it might be a fancy that would fade for him as he grew older, but he has latched himself on to it more firmly than ever. I thought the younger babies had rendered him more jovial. How mistaken I have been."

"The world is not awash with earls that I can fill a pitcher with them and bring them here to the house, Cass," said the Marchioness with a tinge of reproval in her tone as she set her glass back down.

Cass was surprised to find she felt mostly relieved.

Lady Inglemawr studied her face. "You are not suddenly interested in marrying, are you?"

"Would it be very sudden? I have been approaching my spinsterhood for a long time. Perhaps it is here."

"That is foolish, you are a young woman yet. At least, I am not so very old, and if I am not..." Something seemed to take her attention very far away for a moment, and then she looked hard at Cass. "People talk as if marriage were the key to a lady's happiness. I can assure you it is not. A house, a position, these things are acquirable through marriage; happiness most definitely is not."

Before she could stop herself, Cass found her question rushing out of her mouth. "What about love?"

"What *about* it?"

"I mean..." Cass had the feeling even the question made her sound naive, and she did not want to sound naive, but the topic was *so* confusing. "I suppose love must play some part in marriage."

"Not in my experience."

And Lady Inglemawr sounded so sad, so bitter, as she said it, that Cass again felt that someone was on the verge of telling her something true.

So she pressed. "I do not want a husband, but I am so confused by the idea of love itself. It seems like it *ought* to be appealing, but..." Unwilling to delve into her own opinions about the topic, Cass desperately wanted Lady Inglemawr to explain it to her anyway. "The... act of... of marriage, of being married, seems as though it would be... more oppressive than appealing."

"The longer you hold that thought, the safer you will be." Lady Inglemawr's words clearly came straight from her heart, even though her eyes stayed fixed on the blood-red depths of her wine.

"Oh, I... I ought to make clear, I would be perfectly happy to continue on here as we have done."

At that Lady Inglemawr looked up. "Truly? You are not feeling your age and talking yourself into an eagerness for marriage?"

"No no, I do not... As I say, it does not *truly* appeal."

Lady Inglemawr's eyes narrowed. "You do not sound entirely convinced."

Cass tamped down her inner confusion and smiled with all the conviction she could muster. "I *do* know that I am long past any girlish fascination with supposedly romantic encounters, madam. As you say, marriage may bring with it the means to secure a home; you know I am doing all I can to avoid that trap."

"I do." The lady's mood lightened. "So then, this is not a matter of any urgency after all."

Cass felt that she had lost her target in this conversation. "My father is the one with the sense of urgency."

"And so he has always been. That is nothing new, is it?"

"Not strictly new, but you see—"

But Lady Inglemawr just patted Cass' hand. "He will calm down, just as he always does. This is one of those troubles that comes and goes, you know, my dear."

Cass did not feel that Lady Inglemawr quite understood the nature of her relationship with her father. "He would prefer you find me the husband that you discussed with him all those years ago."

"Yes, yes, I know." Her ladyship's tone was carefree. "So he always says. If you are unwilling, who am I to force you? Let your father stew, dear, he will come to his senses, he always does."

Perhaps she was right, thought Cass, though privately she had a sense that her father had reached the end of some sort of rope.

Her mother's old friend was exactly of Cass' own mind about the business.

Cass mostly felt just relieved.

Mostly.

Her ladyship was right. Why should she let her father push her into marriage now? Her reasons for avoiding it had not changed.

Nothing had changed, just because Dr. Burke had kissed her.

Not really.

* * *

For a long while after Cass had retired, Lady Inglemawr sat watching the candles burn lower and lower.

She could not stop thinking that Cass had seemed more curious than dismissive about this topic called "love".

When Adams came to inquire if she wanted anything else for the evening, Lady Inglemawr pursed her lips. "I was not aware that Miss Cullen entertained admirers in my absence, Mr. Adams."

Adams stood silently.

"Well?"

"I'm sorry, madam, did you ask a question?"

Well, thought Lady Inglemawr, that answered *that*.

It would not do for her, not at all, if Cass developed an actual interest in actual marriage.

"I have been remiss in my duties, apparently, but I must tell you that I will no longer be so. You know that gentlemen should never call on Miss Cullen in my absence; please instruct any callers that Miss Cullen is not at home."

That seemed to surprise even the phlegmatic Mr. Adams. "*Any* callers, madam?"

"Any callers, as you know there should be none. You do know the requirements of your position, do you not?"

"Yes, madam." Adams bowed before he withdrew.

* * *

Two days in a swaying mail carriage, hours in the back of a wagon hauling chickens, and miles of walking in the fresh mud of an autumn English roadway.

But it wasn't until Oliver came within sight of the entrance to Morland House that he felt tired.

He braced himself as he approached the door. Rather like a campaign, he thought to himself. Establish a position and hold it.

He'd already forgotten that he'd told Miss Cullen that marrying him would be a bad idea.

When Thompson opened the door, Oliver didn't wait for him to absorb the state of the clothing of the prodigal son.

"Are they at dinner, Thompson?"

"Indeed, my lord."

"Is my brother with them?"

"Mr. Evelyn is dining with his family in their apartments, my lord."

Of course he was. Victor wasn't stupid.

"I'm going straight in. You'd better bring me something to sit on."

Again at the door of the dining hall Oliver paused, and took a deep breath.

"Hello my lady!" he said cheerily, sweeping inside.

"Oliver!"

Thomasina Burke Evelyn, the Countess of Rawleigh, put both her bejeweled hands up in the air. "What a surprise this is! Why didn't you tell me you were coming? I know you didn't tell me, I would have remembered if you did. How long have you been traveling? Your shoes are filthy, dear, you don't want to wear those on the carpet in here. If I told you how much trouble we have been having keeping this carpet in order. I talk to the housekeeper about it daily, you know, and the maids don't seem to understand the state for which I am asking. They make an effort, you know, but it doesn't really show. Doesn't it look terrible to you? I know it was beautiful when it was made, you know that was a long time ago and carpets don't last forever but this one is special to me. My mother commissioned it, if you recall. Perhaps you don't recall. I know you don't keep track of information like that, but it's special to me, and I would like to see it kept well for the next family to live here. Whoever that might be."

Oliver wished that he had a timepiece available. How long had it taken his mother to travel from the original thought to Oliver's failings as an heir? And had she done it all in one breath?

"Good to see you, madam. My lord." Oliver kissed his mother on one dry cheek, and nodded at his father several yards away at his own place at the table.

"Oliver. Hm. Good." His father returned his attention to his soup.

"You didn't travel the whole distance from London in one day. That would be impossible. Though you certainly look as if you had done it. It is remarkable what the carriages can do nowadays. I certainly wish you had cleaned your shoes before you'd come to dinner, but of course I'm so glad that you've come. Are you hungry? There is a tomato salad coming out, I'm not very pleased with the tomatoes we have had this year but I suppose those are the best we can expect given the weather. It's surprising to have tomatoes this late in the year at any rate. Lady Bexley died from eating a tomato, did I tell you? It was astonishing. One day she was here, the next day she had died from eating a tomato. Well, not here, you know. That would have been horrible. Not that it wasn't horrible for her. She was eating at home, of course, her home, I don't mean ours, and the tomato choked her to death. Horrible. Unless I'm misremembering, and she was poisoned by the tomato. Is that how one would say it? If she was sensitive to them in some way? I used to have stomach aches from tomatoes myself, not bad ones, nothing that required the attention of a physician, but unpleasant, very uncomfortable. I stopped eating tomatoes, oh, forty years ago. I suppose if Lady Ashton had done the same she might be alive today. Or at least it is the case that when I die I won't choke to death. At least not on a tomato. That's why I always ask the kitchen to chop the cold dishes very small. I really can't eat them unless they are small bites, you know. I try to get your father to eat such things but he won't."

A footman appeared and spread a cloth on one of the dining room chairs. Another placed a bowl of soup identical to his father's before him.

"You aren't going to sit on my chairs in those clothes, are you, Oliver? Well I see you do intend to. Thank you, Bivens, for fetching a cover. How do you intend to dine this way, Oliver? Aren't you cold? No? Your clothes look damp from here but of course I don't see particularly well any more. I haven't been able to see very well for oh, perhaps the last ten years, isn't it?"

"I think you have some spectacles, madam," Oliver said reflexively. He knew she did. The same way he knew she was about to eat the tomato salad despite her claim that she never ate them.

It was indeed cold outside and dark as well. Oliver was famished from the trip as well as dirty.

He wished he was still on the road.

He downed the glass of wine and replaced it, knowing the footmen would keep it filled.

"I do have spectacles, of course, but you know I find them so uncomfortable. Maybe for other people they are comfortable, but for myself, I cannot stand them. You don't have spectacles, do you, Oliver? No of course you don't. You have always had excellent eyesight, ever since you were a very small boy. Do you remember when you were five and you came and told me that you had seen a robin's nest? And I could not see anything of the sort but apparently you were right. And that was, what, thirty feet off the ground? It was amazing. But then you were always an amazing child."

"Thank you, my lady."

"I am so glad to see you. I wish you had let me know that you were planning a visit. Do you have luggage? Of course you must have some luggage. Does Thompson know what to do with your things?

I'm sure you let him know. Your brother's family has taken over the east wing. We don't see him very often, actually. I wish we did. Sometimes the children have luncheon with me, and your father of course. They are getting so tall so fast. I told Victor that he needs to think more about their education than just the tutors he has engaged, but I don't think he has anything planned. Perhaps you and he will discuss it further. I think you should talk to him about educating the children. We never neglected your education, and you would not have been a physician without it. Not that your father and I ever dreamed that you would become a physician. I could not have imagined that you would spend so much time, years, really, in such close contact with people who are ill. I could not have done it. I don't know if it is good for you, really, spending so much time with sick people. But I know you always said that you wanted to do it, and then of course you did do it, and your education was a good foundation for the work you decided to take up even though your father did not want you to do it."

His father, Regan Evelyn, the sixth Earl of Rawleigh, put down his soup spoon. "Are you still doing that medical business, Oliver?"

"I am, sir, yes."

Oliver, belly still rumblingly empty, had finished his soup. He knew the next course would not be served until his father finished his.

He had better not try to fill up on wine.

*　*　*

OLIVER HAD JUST SETTLED into a hot bath, sighing his relief, when there came a knock at the door. "Come!"

His brother's face, wide and smiling with twinkling dark eyes, peered around the edge of the door. "Is it safe?"

"It's never safe. Good God, man, if you've ever loved me, ask someone to bring me up some more food. Don't our parents eat any more? And loan me some clothes, there's a good man."

"Will do."

Victor's head disappeared for only a few moments and then

returned to be followed by the rest of him taking up residence on a footstool while he watched Oliver sink farther down into the water.

"May I ask why you are at Morland, with no warning and no luggage?"

Oliver ducked and rinsed his hair, scrubbing at it before sitting up again and letting the water sluice down over his shoulders.

He had almost forgotten why he was here, so deadened had he been by the dinner table.

It was always that way.

"I might get married."

Victor let out a whoop. "Don't you *know*?"

"Not sure yet."

"Has the lady accepted you? Or has her father agreed?"

"Neither."

A low whistle. "I see what you mean. Doesn't look good for your side."

"Oh Christ." Oliver considered just sinking back down in the tub and trying to drown himself.

In London everything had seemed possible, despite the voice in the back of his head warning him that this would not go as he wished. Here, that doubting voice was everywhere. Echoing. Over the dinner table.

"Seriously, Oliver, do you intend to marry?"

Oliver glared at his brother. "You can shut up now."

Victor regarded his older brother, unshaven and exhausted, in the bath.

Something had sent Oliver flying on the road to a family home he didn't much care for. And it was probably something serious.

"I think that you intend *something*," Victor said slowly. "When you know what it is, will you tell me?"

"Why wouldn't I tell you? I just told you."

"We don't see you here often."

Oliver opened one eye and fixed it on his brother. "Apparently you *live* here and our mother is still complaining that she doesn't see you often. Don't you dare start on me."

"My wife feels strongly that everyone's sanity is best served when we keep a separate household from the parents."

"Mrs. Evelyn is a wise woman. I'll come see her and the children as soon as I can. And how is Viola? Any news from our sister?"

Victor's smile dimmed at the mention of their sister. "About the same. She wrote to me from Northfell; she doesn't sound exactly chipper, but she's well."

Oliver stopped himself from swearing again. "No one should live in this godforsaken house."

"But where would we live if we did not?" Victor's natural good spirits rose again. "Morland must have been a happy place at one point down through the echoing corridors of time. Perhaps it will be so again. Perhaps when you are the Earl."

"Don't."

"Why you refuse to talk about something that *will* come to pass is beyond me."

"Please."

Oliver looked tired and dispirited and while Victor wanted much more information and more time with his brother, he relented.

Victor said, "You know I'll help you. However I can."

"Thank you," said Oliver, and he meant it.

* * *

"Papa."

Cass approached her father's chair in front of the fireplace slowly. She had arranged a visit here at her father's home on her own terms for once, because she had plans. Multiple options for plans, of course.

Her father had a glass of spirits at hand, a pipe of rich, cherry-smelling tobacco, and was reading a letter by the light of the fire.

She wanted him mellow. She wanted to broach this subject gently.

And she had every intention of beginning in a sweet, daughterly way that he would appreciate.

Then he caught sight of her. "Cassandra. I wasn't expecting you this evening. Why didn't you come for dinner?"

It was a warm enough greeting, in its way, but then her father turned right back to his work.

It flicked something raw in her.

Cass walked around him and sat on a footstool on the far side of his chair, studying the way the firelight made shadows on his face, in his hair, and the smoke wreathed around him.

He looked calm, content, at home.

Wasn't that all she wanted?

Why shouldn't she have the same?

"Papa, I want to ask you to reconsider."

"Reconsider what?"

He was still skimming down the page of written figures in his hand.

Cass leaned just a little closer. "I want you to reconsider insisting on my marriage."

"What? What for? What now?"

"I don't think you realize, Papa, that to keep quiet house in the place Grandmama left to me, that is all that I want."

"All?" He was looking at her now, but she couldn't see his eyes in the shadows from the fire.

"It really is all that I want. I want to keep my little household together and I want to live my life. Quietly."

Her father stretched his neck from side to side, slowly. He laid his work in his lap.

He said, "Cassandra, you don't live quietly. That was just my point, the last time you visited here. You have guests, you have customers. You carry on *business.* You correspond with half of London. You live a life you simply cannot live as a single woman."

Cass felt herself start to frown, and stopped. Her grandmother had always said that ladies never frowned.

But she was wondering how to put into words what she wanted to say to him.

Inexplicably, she wanted to say it with her hands; but even if she had tried, he would not have understood.

"I do not go out, Papa. I have no society at all. I am conducting business in order to maintain the household because you said you did not wish to do so. Are you telling me that if I were willing to stop designing furniture you would let me live as I wish?"

"No. Not entirely, no."

Cass felt her hands fold into silent fists. "I am trying to follow all your rules, I truly am. I do not go out. I have no friends. I pay for my household bills. Why can you not be happy?"

William Cullen wished he could better see his daughter's face. She had her back to the firelight, or nearly, and she was in shadow for him.

He said, "I don't wish you to live your life alone."

Then he cleared his throat as if it had become thick, and picked up his sheet of figures again. "And I don't wish you to damage the reputation of my name, thank you. The children may yet wish to have a social life in the future that will depend on you not ruining my name."

Cass forced herself to unfold her fists. He had been so close to telling her something personal, something private. Then he brushed her off.

Like always.

But Cass couldn't let the topic go, not yet. "If you are so worried about my being alone, Papa, why do you not talk more with me?"

For the second time, the man was motionless for just a moment, as if taken aback by his own thoughts.

This time he bent his head and kept his eyes on the sheet of paper as he answered.

"You don't need me. I despise fathers who want to keep their daughters unmarried, as the king does. I want you to have a protector, and a home and children of your own."

"I would rather have someone to talk to, Papa."

William Cullen looked up—he had to. But he still couldn't see his daughter's eyes, and his own expression gave away almost nothing.

"So would I," he finally said, and this time there was no mistaking the thick catch in his voice.

"So—"

"Marriage is many things to different people, Cass. Don't give up on it yet. You are too young."

Cass drew a slow, shaky breath. There were thoughts crowding her mind about her precious mother, and her sweet stepmother, and what her father thought about marriage: questions she should have asked, or questions she ought not to ask but still wanted answered.

"If I at least consider marriage to an eligible man, will you let me be?"

"Hold on, hold on."

Her father tossed aside both pipe and paper as one of his sons came tearing through on some urgent childhood errand. He grabbed the boy by the collar. "Go get your mother for me, would you? This is urgent."

Cass rolled her eyes. "It is not certain yet, Papa. He has not asked for my hand."

Well, he did, she thought to herself, *but we have reached no agreement. We have only agreed to think about it.*

That made her think about the kiss with which they had sealed their bargain, and that made her feel just as full of questions and just as afraid of answers.

Cass steeled herself.

Her father was already waving his hands over his head in premature hurrahs.

"This is wonderful news! I—Wait. What do you mean he hasn't asked for your hand? Does he want to marry you or not?"

I'm not sure, thought Cass. "I'm not sure yet if I want to marry him."

"Balderdash! Cassandra, this is one of those things in which I will brook no more foolishness. You will get married. Is he—this *is* an earl, isn't it?"

"It's the heir to an earl, Papa." Here Cass made sure to lean closer to her father where he sat. "And I hope you are happy, because *if* I accept him, then that will be as close as I am going to get."

"So how did you meet him? Did Lady Inglemawr introduce you? Where is he from? Why hasn't he been to see me? How old is he?"

"Don't you want to ask about his teeth?"

"Cass, do not make a mistake here. This is good news. Do not convert it to something else. I must write to my solicitor. You will have a dowry, you know. It needn't be a lavish wedding. I mustn't—"

"Papa!"

"*What!*"

Cass folded her hands in front of her and leaned toward him. "If your heart is set on an earl—or this near inheritor—then you must *not* be premature. Can you not be pleased that I am at least considering venturing into society and finding a husband, whether or not it is this one?"

"Yes. Yes, I can."

Cass felt a sinking sensation of guilt looking at the relief on her father's face. This really concerned him. The man looked years younger only contemplating the possibility of his daughter's marriage.

"Why does this worry you so, Papa?"

"Why does it *not* worry *you*? I have oversheltered you, perhaps."

Cass pictured her grandmother sitting quietly in her parlor in the townhouse she called home, stitching something in her hands, her white-haired head bent over her work. Cass would a thousand times rather live that life than have some husband come in and upend her household and make her feel unloveable.

"There are worse fates than to live unmarried, Papa. Her ladyship my grandmother was very happy in her later years living with only me."

Her father just sat shaking his head at her. "Your grandmother had long before married and had her child. You are very precious to me, you are *my* child, and you are not deeply inclined to consider the effect of your actions. What would happen to you, and to the younger children if something happened to me?"

Alarm drove her to drop down and kneel next to him. "You are not ill?"

"No, I'm not ill, but I'm not young either. A man wants to have his affairs sorted out. At least, the right sort of man wants to have his affairs sorted out. I never fear your actions, daughter, but I fear for you." He patted her cheek. "Have a care for my wife, dear. Does it seem as if she would have an easy time managing my estate if I die?"

Cass admitted to herself that business did not seem like Detta's primary ability. It might not even be on the list.

"I have solicitors by the dozen but a man wants family to trust."

"Do you not trust me?"

"Of course I do, my darling. But that's exactly why I trust your judgment to marry someone who can help keep this family's livelihood together if something happens to me."

"This is too morbid a conversation, Papa, I won't have more of it." Cass stood up abruptly, smoothed down her father's lapels and shook her head quite firmly. "I expect better from you."

"I have expected the world of you, my dear, and look what you've done! An earl after all."

"Heir to an earl." Cass bit her lip. Her father wasn't being the least bit restrained in his excitement. When she thought about Oliver Burke, she felt any number of things all jumbled up together in her stomach. Her father seemed to feel nothing but happy.

She was the one who could wind up married to the man, she thought rather grumpily.

Her father appeared to have no qualms at all.

"In fact," he said, "Lady Inglemawr and I must consult. You have not been in society for some time. You need a trousseau."

"I thought a trousseau was for actual betrothals, Papa."

Her father rubbed his hands together in delight. "Sometimes one must work in anticipation of happy events, my dear."

CHAPTER 8

Lady Rawleigh had not taken the idea well.

Both her sons were walking with her in her gardens. Which meant sitting on a bench. Oliver had met older ladies with figures like his mother's, which was roughly the shape of a potato, who nonetheless marched all over their estates day and night. Lady Rawleigh did not care for exercise. Her slow movement to the bench that overlooked the puzzle garden was as far as she was inclined to go.

She was even less inclined to have a deaf daughter-in-law.

"When you say the girl is deaf... do you mean she is mute as well?"

A good night's sleep and a decent breakfast had restored a little of Oliver's optimism. Not much. He found it impossible to be entirely optimistic at Morland.

"She actually does have some hearing. And she's very intelligent. Very talented."

"I see." Lady Rawleigh did not look as though she lived in anticipation of discovering this unknown woman's talents.

She went on, "Would you... would your children be deaf as well?"

I haven't yet convinced her on the issue of what it would take to have children, Oliver wanted to say, but instead he said, "No, Mother.

She had fevers as a child that took her hearing. I believe that I would be able to prevent such a situation for a child of mine."

Lady Rawleigh looked troubled. "There are many duties of a countess, Oliver, many more duties than you realize. I do not see how a young lady so burdened would be able to undertake them all."

Oliver refrained from mentioning that he could not remember ever seeing his mother undertake any major effort. He was grateful to her at least that she forbore to use his title in addressing him, though his bitterer side suspected that it was only because it was as painful for her as it was for him to use Oscar's title to address anyone else.

"His lordship will agree if you ask him to do so, my lady," Oliver continued.

"But I do not! How can I ask him to agree to something so important when I am not at all sure that it is wise for you, my son?"

Oliver met his brother's eyes over his mother's head. It was time for the broadside.

"Madam," Victor said instantly, "Oliver has never before asked you to consider his marriage to any young lady at all. If you miss this chance, how many more years might it be before he finds another more suitable match?"

Oliver held as still as if enemy forces were approaching just out of his sight.

It was an underhanded maneuver, he knew. His mother had not begun bearing children until late in her life. She was now nearing seventy and she was feeling the weight of her age. His older brother had not married before he died, and his young sister was still unmarried as well. She enjoyed her grandchildren, but she had also always adored Oliver, whom she liked to say resembled her father more than any Earl of Rawleigh.

At least, she had liked to say that, before Oliver had become the next Earl of Rawleigh.

"I cannot, I cannot make such an important decision about this woman sight unseen. I do not know her, I do not know her family. Does anyone know her? I have never even heard her name before."

He was half-inclined to say straight out that if he chose to marry, there was nothing his mother could do to stop it. He was a grown man, and, yes, he was the next Earl of Rawleigh whether he resembled them or not.

But his whole family upbringing was organized around one simple truth that was hard to ignore: It's Best Not To Upset Her Ladyship.

Surely there was a way to turn this into the good news it ought to be and not get entangled in her forever-growing chains of complaints.

"She has had a season," Oliver added a bit desperately.

"And so have many young ladies. An heiress, you said? This could be appalling. One cannot put one's faith in families that are built on money."

Oliver pointedly did not look back at the crenellated towers and ivy-covered windows of Morland.

"No. No," said Lady Rawleigh, "this is too dangerous."

Oliver wanted to explain to his mother exactly what *dangerous* meant, illustrated with examples from the battlefield.

Victor caught his eye, shook his head.

"Madam," his brother said, "what might convince you of the lady's suitability?"

"Why, to meet her of course! And to see her behave in a way that would show me that she can take on the duties she would inherit. Yes, I would need to see her behave as a countess should."

"Sitting on this bench?" It was out of his mouth before Oliver could stop it.

Fortunately, his mother ignored him. "I had planned a house party this fall, and this will be an excellent opportunity. I will invite the young lady and her sponsor—Lady Inglemawr?—and we shall see."

Oliver felt the sky darkening, though the clouds had not moved.

This wasn't what he had hoped for at all.

* * *

HE HAD the same feeling when he found himself on Miss Cullen's doorstep, days later.

He had not lingered at Morland, though he had traveled back at a rather more sedate pace. Putting Miss Cullen through such a trial as his mother suggested rubbed Oliver the wrong way. Cass made him excited about possibilities. Morland only made him feel depressed. He had no interest in combining the two.

It had depressed him enough that his colleague Dr. Hunter remarked upon it when he stopped into the hospital as his first errand upon returning home.

"Yes, two old ladies sent me messages but funnily enough, when I showed up instead of you they decided their urgent problems could wait," Hunter had said grumpily. "Now go ahead and do your little song and dance, claiming you won't touch any more surgery, then checking out all my surgery cases."

Oliver had sighed. "I keep telling you. I had my fill of surgery abroad."

"You've got talented hands, for all you've lost the stomach for it, then. That fellow with the leg off above the knee and a finger gone as well, he was in last week. In absolutely fine fettle."

Oliver then just shook his head. Hunter had convinced him to do the surgery against his better judgment and it was as much luck as anything that the man was doing so well; above-the-knee amputations seldom survived. "I could tell you ten names of other men I tried to save with that same surgery who died."

Hunter had whipped back with, "Most army surgeons could tell me twenty. Don't look so downtrodden; I'm just giving you guff, lad. I know you're a big swell of some sort, hey? I heard that from the chief physician; surprised you come in here at all. I knew of a Scottish fellow who was a lord something, his father disowned him when he found out he was doing medicine."

"My father cut off the family money," Oliver had admitted, "but he dare not disown me, I'm his heir."

Hunter had whistled. "You don't say. And here I thought you were swimming in dosh."

"Only what I make, old fellow. So tell me which of my patients are awaiting my return, and I'll have a look at any surgery patient you like, and we'll call it even."

JUDITH LYNNE

And even after he'd visited his (largely perfectly fine) patients, Oliver was still waiting for the next thunder to roll. Well, he'd always felt that way since returning from the war, but this was an extra edge.

He *didn't* have much money. Young men set up households on less, in this day and age... but not much less.

And yet, he wasn't willing to give up on this marriage idea, either.

Unsure how to describe the situation to Cass, he was half-inclined to drag his feet.

And yet his feet had carried him here, to her house.

And he was still unsure of what to say, right up to the moment that Adams opened the door.

The butler's foreboding expression caused Oliver to become battle-ready in an instant. He almost unconsciously reached for a weapon. "What is it, Adams, what's happened?"

"Lady Inglemawr and Miss Cullen are not at home, sir," Adams said most properly, but his expression conveyed that there was more to the story. He was practically waggling his eyebrows in an attempt to convey more.

Oliver braced a hand against the painted white sill of the door. Cass was all right. Something else had gone wrong.

"Might I...?" He made a gesture as if to invite himself through the front door.

"I'm sorry, sir," and Adams' tone said he genuinely was, "but Lady Inglemawr is not at home and said to let you know she did not expect to be, today or tomorrow."

Which was to say, Lady Inglemawr had no intention of receiving him.

Or of allowing Cass to receive him.

Oliver felt his jaw clench.

"There is not even a fire in the parlor," Adams suggested as if it were new gossip. "One in the kitchen below, of course, but not here."

Oliver felt like Adams was sending him signals. If Cass was in trouble and Adams wanted him to visit the kitchen, he'd damn well visit the kitchen, Oliver thought.

Tipping his hat to Adams, Oliver went down the steps of the townhouse.

Then, as the upper door closed, he swerved around and went right down the stairs to the below-street-level entrance to the kitchen, where he didn't even bother to knock, just let himself in.

There was indeed a tidy fire. The low-ceilinged space was empty of other people.

Oliver had just begun to warm his hands—he hadn't even noticed the rain—when one of the maids he'd seen before came down the stairs and into the room, with Adams accompanying her.

She wasn't the blind one, so she must be the deaf one. Mrs. Adams.

And indeed her thin hands began to fly in the most extraordinary movements, some of them seeming as if they might make themselves apparent to him if only he could look more closely.

The urgency of her face, however, needed no translation.

"Miss Cullen is fine, Dr. Burke," said Adams, and Oliver let out a breath he hadn't been aware of holding. "It is only that, well..."

The woman's gestures became more frantic. She patted Adams' sleeve, as if urging him on.

"Feel free to translate freely, Adams," Oliver encouraged him.

"Lady Inglemawr says Miss Cullen is not at home, to you or anyone, until her ladyship informs me otherwise."

"Indeed." Following on the heels of his relief, the news that he was banned from Cass' company hit him in the stomach like a fist. "Well, I suppose I can be grateful that it isn't just me that Lady Inglemawr has suddenly decided to dislike..."

What an about-face this was.

But it seemed that Cass was all right.

The maid's gestures hadn't stopped.

Oliver prompted Adams, "Is there more?"

"My wife is concerned because Lady Inglemawr has taken Miss Cullen to select clothes for a trousseau, sir."

"That hardly seems dire." A trousseau? Had she decided to accept him? Or had some other proposal surfaced in the time he had been gone?

"Miss Cullen's father insisted on it, and Lady Inglemawr seems to have agreed reluctantly."

Adams continued speaking still watching his wife, who had worry, disdain, feminine disgust, and urgency written all over her face, even if Oliver did not understand the gestures she was making.

"My wife considers Lady Inglemawr's skills at selecting clothing to be dire when it comes to Miss Cullen, sir."

Oliver thought. He had only ever seen her in that lavender dimity dress... and in a man's suit.

"Lady Inglemawr seems well-turned-out," he said, searching the woman's face for more information.

The woman in front of him clearly could follow his expression.

Mrs. Adams rolled her eyes in an expression that reminded Oliver singularly of Cass.

Adams translated her hands' comment. "She seems to have terrible taste only where Miss Cullen's clothing is concerned, sir."

* * *

CASS WAS STANDING ALONE near the wall, twisting her hands in midair, awash in the susurrating sound of a sea of women's voices.

Lady Inglemawr had disappeared almost as soon as they had crossed the threshold of the shop, off to examine fabrics with one of the assistants who seemed to know her.

Cass was feeling less and less sanguine about her position against the wall as bevies of young ladies seem to pour in and out of the shop, all on some business that was apparent to them.

They were all shorter than Cass, all dressed in light, girlish hues, their outfits becomingly adorned with flowers here or ribbons there. On them, all the details went together in some sort of order that was apparent to them but not at all apparent to Cass.

The longer she studied them, though, the more it seemed she could ascertain the reason, at least from the principles of balanced design. This flower here drew more attention to the tiny waist of this young lady whose bosom was even more scant than her own. That flower there drew the eye to that girl's lovely neck and away from her generous hips.

Cass had always been more interested in the hard lines of buildings, furniture, and machinery than the soft lines of clothes. But she could see on display here the theory of dressing to draw attention to one's better features.

So what might hers be?

It was an intriguing question, but too nerve-wracking a place in which to think about it. Dress inspiration was everywhere, but these girls were all younger and smaller and Cass was sure they were far more socially successful. She felt as though she were a poison tree and that as soon as she was truly discovered, they would uproot her and perhaps burn her.

She wondered for a long while why she was even here. If Lady Inglemawr was selecting the fabrics in another area of the shop, was she herself not superfluous?

Perhaps she could simply walk quietly out the door and no one would notice.

She had her eyes on the door, in fact, watching for her chance, when through it she caught a glimpse of a surprisingly dark coat, swimming upstream against the tide of ladies.

The gentleman lifted his hat, returning smiles and nods all around, and the tide parted for him as if he were Moses.

Oliver.

Dr. Burke, she immediately corrected herself. Or Lord Howiston.

Inside her head, she enjoyed simply thinking of him as Oliver.

Cass moved toward the window of the shop. She could see him outside, looking at the shop door. Did he know she was here? Or was he here... to see someone else? To shop for someone else?

Through the window, she saw him lift his hat again, this time responding to the greeting of an elegant woman who stopped to speak to him as well.

His presence there had nothing to do with her.

Cass closed her eyes, turned back toward the dimmer interior of the shop.

Another one of her fantasies. In her head, she imagined that he was there for her, that he was *hers*. That was only in her head. He might well never speak to her again, for all she knew. Imagining what he would say, and what she would say back, and how that might escalate from there—this was a pattern she knew all too well.

She just had to remind herself that he didn't know anything about what went on in her head. Her imaginings were just hers.

She would have to deal with her fantasies herself.

She might be unsuited to the arts of love, but when she looked at Oliver she felt a burning desire to *possess*. Far more alluring than any hat or reticule, he was like a polished jewel she wanted to own. She wanted to *wear* him. She wanted him on her arm and all those ladies passing by seeing it.

She wanted to touch him, too, she was sure of that.

The memory of their kiss in her library made her knees go weak.

She wanted all these other ladies to know that he had kissed her. *Her.*

My goodness, thought Cass to herself, shaking her head and bending to pretend to examine some lace. He is the source of all the sins I've been warned about. Greed, pride. Gluttony.

That last might not make sense but she could not forget the taste of him on her lips.

Though she knew it was a pointless activity, Cass couldn't stop herself from imagining: *what if there were more kisses?*

* * *

OLIVER REGARDED the shop entrance with despair. He could no more enter that shop without drawing too much attention to his presence there for Miss Cullen than he could storm a battle line alone.

Casting his eye about for reinforcements, he saw, among the crush of women around him, Lady Gadbury.

She was looking exquisite in a pelisse of deep red trimmed with white fur. Her hat was a confection of the same red trimmed with lace and some sort of braid. She had excellent taste in clothing and she was right here.

And wonder of wonders, she nodded to him.

Oliver raised his hat to her, a smile on his lips. "Lady Gadbury."

She gave him a restrained smile, as was only proper, her retinue of servants pausing with her. "Dr. Burke."

"I wonder if I might be so bold as to request a small favor of you, Lady Gadbury."

That lady's eyes widened a little as she waved for him to walk with her. It would be terribly rude to keep her standing in the street, but Oliver kept his steps small, reluctant to draw too far away from the shop where he knew Cass was.

Lady Gadbury's head drew just close enough to his to share a few words nearly privately. "I am scarcely inclined to do you *favors* just now, Oliver."

He gave her a brilliant smile. "I know, and I do apologize again for my abrupt leave-taking. But I know you have a kind heart—of course you have, for what other reason would you have for keeping a lonely soldier company?"

She pressed her lips together, to keep from smiling outright, Oliver thought. "You overrate me and underrate yourself. What do you want?"

"There is a young lady in there who is about to be encased in a series of unflattering dresses, and I am hoping you will carry to her a message from me to the contrary."

Lady Gadbury turned to look thoughtfully at the door of the modiste's shop. "Madame Dudin is well known for creating flattering dresses, rather than the opposite; thus the popularity of her shop."

Oliver was reluctant to share all the details of Cass' peculiar home situation, but he felt that Lady Gadbury could be a good ally, if she would. "I believe her sponsor makes less than ideal choices."

"Who is her sponsor?"

"Lady Inglemawr."

"So? I know her. She is always dressed in flattering attire."

Oliver did not relent. "The young lady she is sponsoring is not."

"Are you that desperate to see a girl in a pretty dress, Oliver? Look around. London has thousands." Lady Gadbury waved an bored hand. The crush of women around him was there to prove her point.

"I just... I don't think the girl realizes how handsome she is. I would like for her... to enjoy her clothes."

That did sound like the Oliver she knew.

Laura Gadbury had taken up acquaintance with Oliver on the advice of a friend whose taste she trusted. It was the same friend who had also suggested that she try stuffed dates. For a lady whose days were primarily burdened with boredom, finding new treats was a constant and tiresome chore.

Oliver had been a lovely treat, but she was less attached to him than to the pelisse she wore. The pelisse fit her rather better. Oliver had always seemed a bit distant, even in the throes of passion. Or what had been her passion, she realized with more than a touch of chagrin. She wasn't sure she had ever really moved him at all.

Every lady who passed him on the street turned to look at him. Laura enjoyed thinking that they would envy her, had they but known that she had, however briefly, had his attention.

But it appeared that another woman had his attention now. And for all that she faced the loss of him with a certain amount of calm, knowing as she had from the beginning that it would come some day, it rankled her.

She wanted to see this young woman.

"I'll see what the modiste is about," she told Oliver briefly.

He bowed his thanks.

When she turned to go into the shop, she checked over her shoulder as she went through the door. Yes, he was still standing there, as if he were a little boy looking at a shop full of sweets that he could not have.

Well, that wasn't far off.

She realized as soon as she had gone inside that she had forgotten to ask Oliver for the girl's name.

But indeed there was only one real candidate for her errand obvious from the moment she entered the room.

It was a tall young woman with dark hair, restlessly moving up and down the interior wall without moving away from it. She was looking towards the depths of the shop as if waiting for someone, occasionally wringing her hands. She was the only person in the shop who was alone.

Lady Gadbury swept up to her with the confidence of a woman in a stunning red outfit.

"What a pleasure to meet you," she said, just inclining her head. "I am the Countess of Gadbury. I believe we have a mutual friend in common."

Cass recognized her as the woman to whom Oliver had been speaking outside. She curtsied. "I am Miss Cassandra Cullen. I am so pleased to make your acquaintance, Lady...?"

"Gadbury." Laura leaned closer and emphasized it more loudly. Was the girl stupid?

"Gabbery. It is a pleasure."

The girl was stupid. How odd. She wouldn't have thought that Oliver would be so vehemently interested in a stupid girl.

As Laura watched, the younger woman's eyes once again went over her shoulder towards the depths of the shop. "I would love to meet you under more sociable circumstances. My friend Lady Inglemawr seems to have been detained with Madame Dudin. Perhaps you know her? Lady Inglemawr, I mean?"

Laura did know Lady Inglemawr. "They must have much to discuss. Lady Inglemawr's wardrobe is stunning."

Miss Cullen's look then was wry. Perhaps she wasn't stupid. "Mine is not, and I do not have Lady Inglemawr's knack for fashion. I suspect that they are discussing my sad shortcomings and the difficulty of selecting new items for me."

Laura looked the girl up and down with more care. Tall, as Laura was herself; distressingly square in the shoulders, putting one more in mind of a stevedore than a ballroom, but with some slender curves to her figure nonetheless.

Laura could well imagine that if the girl did not have much of a bosom to display, Lady Inglemawr's inspiration regarding dress selection would be stretched past its limit.

The girl wore a much-washed dimity dress that did nothing for anyone. But its most disastrous feature was its perfectly normal girlish puffed sleeves. On Cass' shoulders, it made her look unnecessarily wide and blocky.

The gown offended Lady Gadbury's sense of fashion, even more than the loss of Oliver as an amusement offended her.

Laura pushed Cass toward one of the mirrors in the shop, gently, with her fingertips on one shoulder. It required quietly nudging past two other young ladies who were admiring one another in the glass; Lady Gadbury's press was inexorable, and the other women yielded.

She came up behind Cass and regarded her in the mirror, then pinched the puffy fold of a sleeve.

"You do not need more volume in the shoulders, my dear," she said, her head leaning close to Cass'. "Make sure the sleeves stay tight to your arms, you have seen the style, have you not?"

Cass nodded, eyes on Laura's face in the mirror, paying rapt attention.

"It is fashionable to have the dress short enough to show your slippers when you stand. Don't. It will make you look as if the dress is too short for you because you are so tall, and you do not need that. Make sure day dresses have a ruffle to soften your hem. And your evening gown should have something of the Grecian drape about it. Can you imagine what I mean?"

"Yes," Cass nodded. "I quite see what you mean."

Laura nodded as well. If she wore something that benefited her looks, she would be stunning. Up close, Laura could see that she had lovely skin and eyes.

And mobile, quick expressions. The girl was studying what she herself wore. When their eyes met again in the mirror, Laura had the impression that the girl wanted to ask her something about Oliver. Perhaps what type of clothes Oliver liked on a lady.

No, she wasn't stupid.

She must have seen them speaking together outside.

Laura felt suddenly more protective of Oliver than irritated with his spurning of her affections. She herself had a passing acquaintance with Oliver's mother, the Countess of Rawleigh. She would have to write to the woman to inquire about the state of her family. If this girl was planning to take advantage of Oliver's position in some way, Laura would have to see to it that it didn't happen. Laura was one of the few people in her social set who knew Oliver's family background. She flattered herself that he might be just a pretty plaything to her friends, but that she herself cared about what happened to him.

And a marriage was for life.

Nonetheless, she felt an equally strong urge to keep her promise to Oliver.

"Shall I speak to Madame Dudin?" she asked Miss Cullen while they still stood so close to the mirror.

"No," Cass said swiftly, "I believe I can manage from here."

CHAPTER 9

The thought of the club had given Oliver more of a sense of dread than anything else.

But he had nowhere else to go that evening. He'd left Cass in the hands of Lady Gadbury, and with the best of intentions, it had felt like a cowardly thing to do.

He should have stormed that castle of ribbons and buttons and done something for her. Something real.

Instead he'd left his—whatever Lady Gadbury was, to carry his message as if he were a damned schoolboy.

He'd rather have been talking to Cass, but Bradley Waite seemed to be the best he could do this evening.

What a comedown.

He stared into his gin. Even that had lost its flavor. Of course, it was his third glass. Perhaps his fourth.

"Whatever or whoever you're moping about, you might as well give it up as a bad job," Waite was telling him.

The man looked as disheveled as ever, hair darkened by shadows, red-rimmed eyes and only his gold signet ring winking in the light of the candelabras.

Oliver peered at him. "Why don't you ever go home?"

He'd never asked it before.

He didn't get the response he'd expected. "Oh no, the great Doctor Mope suddenly wants to know something about me."

"Why, Waite, is it such a secret?"

"Nothing about me is a secret, Oliver, nothing at all. All of London knows where I am, and that I am drunk. At almost any hour."

"But why? What are you doing here with yourself?"

"What are *you* doing here with yourself? Must I have some great plan to drink myself into oblivion just because that is your goal? That is your fifth drink since you arrived, you know."

Oliver's stomach roiled. He needed food, not more gin.

"I'm not trying to find oblivion," he told Waite, so sincerely that he believed it himself.

He wasn't. Or at least, for tonight, he wasn't.

"I am," said Waite, waving his hand to catch the eye of someone who would serve him more drink.

This was a tunnel that didn't have an end. Oliver had never seen it so clearly. Waite was not old, no more than he himself or a few years younger. But Waite had the swollen eyes and puffed skin of a man whose physical self was struggling to keep up with a spirit that was sinking fast.

"I've got to get out of here," Oliver said to himself more than anyone else.

* * *

It was a cold night and the fog rolled in drifts across the streets, as delicate and silent as a lady's footsteps.

Oliver found himself on Cass' street without any plan or forethought.

Even with a stomach full of gin and no food, Oliver's steps were sure. There was something in the back of his head that was telling him that this was a poor plan, arriving at Cass' house at night this way. But the front of his head, accustomed as it was to gin and poor ideas, ignored it.

He didn't bother to go to the front door. The house was dark; no one would be about, even if Lady Inglemawr would let him in. Which she would not.

No, there was still a glow. Downstairs.

Unerringly Oliver passed the front door and pushed on the iron gate that led to the steps downward to the servant's entrance.

The gate creaked open at his touch.

Emboldened by his luck, he decided to press on to see how far he could go.

Sadly, no farther; the servant's door was latched.

Oliver didn't give himself time enough to think even if he had been in the right frame of mind for it.

He knocked.

It was just a soft rapping; he didn't want to wake the house. Or at least some part of him didn't want to wake the house. The gin-and-bad-idea part of his brain wanted to howl outside the window till Cass came out and took him in like a found dog.

But there was still a part of him that knew that such a thing would not be dignified.

That part of him rapped softly, even though it was on the entrance to the kitchen in the middle of the night.

He waited, listening to his own breath, wondering if he could hear anything if he mashed his ear up against the door. He should try it.

He tried it.

The wood was rough and cold against his skin and he couldn't hear anything for what seemed like a long while. Maybe he would fall asleep against the door like this.

"Geddaway from the door, ye ruffian," he heard someone inside say.

Oliver put on his best old-blood accent, the one he remembered more from his professors at school than anyone at home. "I've come to see the lady of the house."

"Ye have not. The lady don't see you."

"I have. Please. I've come to see Miss Cullen. Please."

The voice inside seemed to relent. "What d'ye want with the miss."

"She is a friend of mine."

Silence, and there was a muffled clattering inside that Oliver couldn't decipher.

Then the door, miraculously, swept open.

He was standing inside the kitchen in the middle of the night, and a wide-hipped cook had raised a skillet against him as if it were a flintlock pistol.

She had soft jowls and fiercely bushy white eyebrows and she thrust out her jaw with a defiance that spoke to him of generals. "She is no friend of you."

"You know she is, or you would not have opened the door."

Oliver was having a hard time focusing both eyes at the same time, so he kept closing one and opening the other to peer at her. Same cook, same skillet pointed at him.

"That's not going to go off, you know," he said of the unfireable weapon.

The woman ignored his remark. "Miss Cullen isn't gonna see some street-sweeper at this time o' night."

"Nor should she," Oliver agreed. "But I can't help myself. I want to see her."

He was sure the woman facing off with him in the kitchen in the night was about to scream for the night watch, or perhaps simply take his head off with the cast iron of the skillet.

But Mrs. Orfill seemed to know something. Because she muttered to herself, "She's never so foolish."

But then she said, "*Don't* steal anything," and disappeared out the far door.

Before Oliver could really grasp what might be worth stealing there in the kitchen in the middle of the night, Cass was there.

She came straight up to him and felt his forehead as if he had a fever and said, "Dr. Burke, whatever are you doing here this time of night?"

Her fingers were cool and smooth and her voice soothed something inside him that had been churning. His eyes closed. Merciful saints, this was what he wanted.

He said, "Just visiting."

"Are you *drunk*?" Cass sounded more amused than appalled.

"Perhaps slightly."

"Mrs. Orfill, could you stir up a pot of tea for Dr. Burke?"

"'S not right," muttered that good woman, who had followed her mistress back to the kitchen, but she ladled some water out of a kettle and into a pot.

Oliver found himself sitting in a rough-hewn chair and leaning on a table spotted with flour and smelling of yeast.

It was warm in the kitchen, the soft orange glow of the banked fire making it mysterious and comfortable all at the same time, and Oliver could feel himself relax.

This was what he had wanted. He hadn't wanted more gin. He'd wanted this.

He wanted tea with Cass.

He wanted Cass.

"I don't want half of London. I want you," he told her as she leaned over him and poured tea into a cup in front of him.

Cass froze.

"You are drunk," she said, more accusingly now. "Have some tea, it will help. I hope. Mrs. Orfill, I've no idea what to do for a drunken gentleman."

"You do *nuthin* fer a drunken gennleman," said Mrs. Orfill in tones of vast disapproval. "It's too good for 'im by a long shot even ta let him sleep it off by the fire."

"Quite."

She sounded crisp as ever but she looked glad to see him. He could still tell when a woman was glad to see him. He was sure of that. He was pretty sure of that.

"What can we do to settle him... here, I suppose, Mrs. Orfill?" Cass asked, trusting that good woman to know such things.

Despite the cook's protestation of dark forebodings and the need to count the silver before letting such a reprobate stay unwatched in the kitchen, the cook shuffled off to find an unused quilt, so she said, and lock the windows and doors in case Oliver had any confederates about.

"She is probably wise," said Cass, seating herself across from Oliver. "I should throw you out."

"You should. Truly."

"Are you here because your friend Lady Gaberry turned you away?"

"What? Oh, Gadbury. Gadbury," he pronounced slowly, and loudly. Cass nodded. "You've met. That's good. Yes, she's fine." Then his brain caught up to his mouth and Oliver realized what she'd asked. "No no. I didn't... go there. I came here."

Cass' eyes stayed on him.

He had much to explain. This was intolerable. How could he explain how he had known Lady Gadbury well enough to speak to her in the street?

Cass rested her cheek on one fist. In the shadows of the banked fire he couldn't see her eyes. But he was sure she was looking at him. If nothing else, Oliver could usually rest assured that women at least looked at him.

He suddenly had a sense memory of the way she had looked at him when he'd sunk his hands into her hair, stroking and pulling at her curls to gently free the whole tangle and smooth it out. She'd looked startled, and there had been a spark of something else behind her eyes, he was nearly sure of it.

She couldn't be entirely unaffected by him, could she? It would be too cruel, if the one woman he craved more of was unaffected by his touch.

Oliver slid out of his chair.

"Here now, don't fall over!"

But he didn't. Instead he knelt before her, the cool flagstones digging in to his knees, and put out his hands to the only part of her he could reach, her feet.

She jumped as one of his hands found her foot under the hem of her gown, slid off the slipper she wore.

His thumbs stroked up from her heel and dug into the soft arch of her foot. The sound she let out, half a yelp of shock, half a groan of pleasure, made him immediately hard. Which he ignored.

When she spoke her voice was the same combination of alarmed and aroused. He could hear it. "Dr. Burke, you are not yourself."

"Oh, you think only you take pleasure in throwing propriety out the window?" muttered the man to himself as he kneaded her foot in both of his hands.

"There is flouting propriety and then there is setting fire to it," Cass told him, bending over as if to shoo him away from her foot.

But she didn't.

"You... you do know it is only me you are touching." Cass sounded as if because he was drunk, he was insensible.

His face flipped this time from relaxed to intense. He stopped moving till she looked up to meet his eyes. Only then he said, "I know exactly who you are."

Cass blinked. And blinked again. It was still difficult to look right at him when he looked this way. The frown pulled fires from his eyes.

She was only able to breathe when he looked back down to what his hands were doing to her foot.

He mumbled, "I can't stand the thought of you at Morland. The place is a huge mouldering graveyard of what happiness might have been. And yet. You've got to come."

"What? What are you talking about?"

"My mother is going to invite you to a house party. She wants to see how you behave like a countess."

Cass' muscles stiffened in Oliver's hands as if they'd been frozen to ice. "I doubt I have any ability to behave like a countess!"

"You have every ability to be a countess if you marry an earl."

Cass was quite positive that was *not* what Oliver's mother had in mind. "I must not go."

"You must go. You and Lady Inglemawr ought to have already received the invitation."

"Engh." The *frisson* of illicit pleasure Cass felt by having a drunken man secretly visiting her kitchen in the middle of the night dissipated.

"I am not marrying an earl. I have not agreed to marry anyone yet, even you."

The man whom she had absolutely not agreed to marry did not move from his position, kneeling on the floor, his hands traveling up from the sinful things they had been doing to the sole of her foot to caress the top of her foot. "It doesn't matter."

"I rather think it does."

"Not for you and me."

"*Especially* for you and me."

Oliver shook his head, giving Cass the impression that he was thinking about something else far away even as his hands cupped the back of her ankle.

The ankle had never struck Cass as any kind of a zone of inappropriate behavior on the body, not at any time in her life.

She had clearly been very wrong.

His hand was warm, and his fingers strong as he used them to shape the dome of the joint of her bones, there. In his hands her foot felt delicate, and special, as if it ought to fit in a princess' jeweled slipper.

Which she was sure it would not. Her foot was nearly as large as his.

But cradled in his hands it seemed small.

He smoothed his thumbs over the arch of her foot, and lifted it.

Cass had never in her life imagined the sensation of a man's warm lips, the skin around them slightly rough with unshaven beard, brushing the top of her foot.

But when she imagined ecstasy, she imagined something like the sensation that shot through her.

And it was only her *foot*.

His lips moved to the bend of her ankle. Then the first swell of her shin. The hem of her gown did not seem to bar him from moving further. Cass reflexively reached out and grabbed his head in both her hands.

Then Oliver looked up at her.

"I am mad to touch you. Are you not the least bit interested in letting me?"

Her mouth dropping open, Cass could only stare at him. She ought to send him away, or at least lock him here in the basement. This was madness.

"I think you are," said Oliver, smoothly coming up on his knees to reach behind her head and pull her down as if for a kiss.

He paused for a moment, as if waiting for her to tell him not to do this. Then another moment more.

And only when she opened her lips to his, there was his mouth tasting hers, claiming hers, reveling in hers, and if it was madness, it caught Cass up in a wave of the same insanity.

This wasn't the sweet slow seduction of their parlor promise.

His lips were moving with hers so perfectly that she felt herself fitting into him and following him naturally, her head tilting to accommodate him, her hands finding their own way up to caress his neck, his jaw, the roughness of his cheeks before she quite realized what was even happening.

"Oliver," she whispered against his mouth, and he just nodded. And kissed her again.

Oh my word, thought Cass, she could do this all night.

She had better not, thought another part of her brain, because unfortunately Mrs. Orfill would be back any second.

"Dr. Burke," and she couldn't stop herself from sounding breathless but at least she managed to remember how to address him. "You had better... we had better go to sleep."

At which he pulled himself far enough away from her that she could see his slumberous eyes banked with a fire that she did not understand, but which she very much suspected he could see reflected in her own.

"Is it... is it time to sleep?" he asked her with a lazy smile that melted into doubt, as he apparently remembered they were in a kitchen.

No she did *not* want to sleep. She was very much awake, and felt hot and urgent in a way that was unfamiliar but which did not feel much like sleeping.

Instead of lying to him she pulled herself upright. "Dr. Burke, I have shared too many of my secrets with you. That puts me in your hands. I am not married, and my father still very much hopes that I will be married. We have not at all settled that I ought to marry you. In fact, the strongest opponent of the idea seems to be you."

Cass was proud that she sounded pretty firm, pretty certain, she thought. Her voice was absolutely not wavering.

Her stomach was filled with butterflies, and her fingers felt empty from not touching him, but her voice sounded firm.

The beautiful Dr. Burke was swaying, very slightly, on his knees on her kitchen floor. He looked sure of nothing. That made her feel even more as though she were making the right decision to put a little space between them.

"I must trust you, Dr. Burke, you see I have no choice. Please be careful with that trust."

Oliver nodded, his expression serious, and then it turned sad.

"You'll come, you'll come to the damned house. Say you'll come."

Sad like a lost little boy, now, and she would no more have been able to refuse him than to turn him out of the house.

"If your mother invites me, of course I will go."

"It'll be miserable, it's always miserable there. But I want you to be there."

She wanted to ask him why. But she couldn't be sure of the reliability of the answer, not when he was so clearly this far into his cups. He seemed relatively lucid, but his behavior was very, very far removed from the man who had reassured her in her library.

Perhaps not so far removed from the man who had taken liberties with her hairpins, but that had been a unique occasion.

"Sleep some, Dr. Burke, and we will speak of this further later."

When Mrs. Orfill finally came, trailing an old quilt she'd found after her, Oliver was sitting on the floor, and Cass had fled.

CHAPTER 10

*I*n the morning he was gone.

Cass did not usually venture into the kitchen in the morning. She let Mrs. Orfill get on with the breakfast preparations as she liked.

But this morning Cass herself was in the kitchen, claiming to want tea and porridge but in fact drifting from corner to corner around the room as if she might find a physician happening to hide there.

"He's not sleeping under the fire irons," Mrs. Orfill told her with some acid to her tone after Cass had paced between the fire and the locked door for the third time.

"Who?" asked Mr. Adams, waiting to carry the mistress' tray upstairs to her room as usual.

"No one," said Cass, escaping up the stairwell after sending Mrs. Orfill a quelling look.

"Aye, a nobody," said Mrs. Orfill with a threatening wave of the spoon towards the fireplace, as if ruffian-like young men might come out of the bricks at any moment.

* * *

When Oliver had awakened on the floor of her kitchen, he'd felt a flush of embarrassment, stumbling out through the mews at the back of the house into the chilly rainy London morning before he'd even realized that there was no one awake to lock the door closed after him.

He'd never done *that* before.

So then he'd had to walk along her street until he saw signs of people stirring inside, until he could be sure that someone would be awake and fortify the kitchen as necessary.

He had so many things he wanted to tell her. He should have told her more about his family last night when he'd blurted out the invitation to Morland, which he remembered very well. He had not been lying when he told her that marrying him would be a terrible idea.

But armed with the memory of how it had felt, looking into her eyes, he was determined instead to hang on to her promise that she would be there.

He remembered the night perfectly; fortunately or unfortunately, drink did not impair his memory. He remembered the feel of her foot in his hands and the way she'd startled when he touched her. The way her lips had parted.

He dreamed of being able to have one of their comfortable talks in the library, or failing that, to visit her again in the kitchen. He knew that if he went back to the front door, he would be turned away by Lady Inglemawr's refusal.

Oliver needed help, and he needed it now.

* * *

It was a measure of the Grantleys' household that the butler who answered the door never even blinked at the sight of an unshaven man in disheveled gentlemen's clothing so early in the morning.

He did promise to see if Sir Michael or Lady Grantley was available. He did *not* show Oliver into one of the rooms.

Instead of the baronet or his lady, the person who came to greet

JUDITH LYNNE

Oliver at the door was a slender young man, a few years younger even than the baronet, with hair and eyes so dark as to seem coal black.

His expression wasn't warm, but he did bow.

"Anthony Hastings, Lady Grantley's brother."

"I am Dr... Dr. Oliver Burke, an acquaintance of the lady's and her husband's."

Mr. Hastings cocked his head. "Aren't you sure of your name?"

Oliver winced. "I am also Lord Howiston but I do not use the title."

This Mr. Hastings had a talent for not blinking.

After several moments, and then several moments more, during which Oliver began to feel even more uncomfortable than he had been to begin with, Hastings said, "Well, that is interesting. Do come in."

He showed Oliver to a small but cheerful parlor, in which the touches of Lady Grantley, Oliver thought, could be seen in the vases full of only brightly colored leaves, and what was apparently a fresh plate of cakes.

They smelled of cinnamon. Oliver's mouth watered. But Hastings didn't offer him any refreshment, so Oliver decided he was not yet so demeaned that he would ask.

Someone had also already placed a canvas drape on one of the chairs, as a silent reminder to Oliver of the state of his clothes. He desperately hoped his face was not as red as it probably ought to be. He sat on the chair.

That meant that for several moments the two men sat in silence in the parlor, smelling sugary cinnamon and not speaking.

Finally Oliver decided to break the silence.

"You have a knack for this, don't you?"

"For what?"

"Getting people to talk."

Hastings inclined his head. "It's actually all too easy. Disappointing, in fact, as they rarely have anything I want to hear."

Heaven help him, Oliver thought to himself, suppressing a sigh as well as the desire to roll his eyes the way Cass did.

Why had he even come here?

Because he'd wanted Lady Grantley to make him feel better.

He was going to have to develop better habits than using women as bandages, Oliver told himself sternly.

"Sir Michael told me you might be able to help me. I need to speak the manual language used at the asylum for the deaf in the south of the city, and I need it immediately."

Hastings said calmly, "Then go to the school and engage one of the teachers. That cannot be difficult."

"I can do so, but your brother-in-law told me you had a knack for finding things out. I would like to learn more about Miss Cullen's work there, as well as the manual method of speaking."

Hastings did not look like a *Hastings* to Oliver, and he still did not look interested. "I believe the traditional way is to speak to her."

"I would like to, but her chaperone has suddenly taken an interest in her job."

"Really." Finally, that seemed to be something Mr. Hastings found interesting enough to engage him. "Why is that?"

"I have no idea, and it's driving me mad to distraction. For months I have been able to correspond with the young lady, and several times met in her home for hours on end without interruption. Now, unreasonably, chaperonage everywhere."

Hastings' eyebrows both climbed on his forehead. "I hope you will forgive the directness, sir, but you look like the type of man who is the reason why chaperones were invented."

"No no, it's not like that at all. I've offered for the young lady."

"Again, forgive me, but I can easily imagine why the young lady and her family are not that interested in your proposal. I have no reason to facilitate it." Hastings folded his arms in front of him as he studied Oliver up and down. Oliver couldn't tell if the young man was simply puzzled by him, or judging him. Perhaps both. He had a very judgmental expression.

Hastings added, "I have no personal knowledge of these matters, but my understanding is that if the young lady accepts you, you'll have all the time to talk in the world."

"I don't think she'll accept me *unless* we have more time to talk."

"Thus the London social season. You must have attended parties where she was there as well? Does the young lady not dance?"

"The season is over and this cannot wait."

"This is a fascinating amount of urgency."

Oliver glared at the man. Dammit, he was a battle-tested surgeon and an heir to an earldom. He didn't need this sort of cheek from a stranger.

A blunt stranger. "Is she with child?" was Hastings' next question.

"No! We have not—Is your mind from the gutter, man?"

The man shrugged. "In a manner of speaking."

"Lift yourself up, Hastings. Miss Cullen is above your reproach."

Oliver's defense of the lady not present gave Hastings some sort of pause. He was genuinely puzzled by Oliver now, and beginning to look intrigued, perhaps despite himself.

"Sir, I have some ability with languages. I may look into this, but even if I do, you will likely need to take time to learn it, much as you would French or any other way of speaking. Have you any gift for languages?"

"Not really. I have studied French of course, and Latin. And I learned some Spanish on campaign."

"Not bad. You should have some idea of the task ahead then."

Oliver felt overflowing with impatience. "This will take forever!"

"Well, as my sister would say, best get started then. You may also be suffering from last night's drinking, or simply blind to the obvious, but if I may, I would recommend that you find out why this chaperone has suddenly decided to bar your entry. Not that she should not; she clearly should. But why did she not do it before? That is the only really interesting question that deserves investigation."

Oliver swallowed. He needed water, he was sure of that, though he was blessed—or cursed—by never having a headache even when he had drunk to excess. This annoying young man was undoubtedly right, which only made him more annoying. But his help would be, well, help, and Oliver needed help.

"If that help is amenable to you," Hastings offered as Oliver hesitated, "I'm happy to begin today. I can show you out before Sir Michael and Lady Grantley arise and proceed immediately."

"Good God, man, they have met me. I'm not so disreputable looking as you imply."

Hastings' black eyes were impassive.

"Oh for—very well. I'll go. And... and thank you, after all. I will owe you thanks."

As the fellow rose to escort Oliver out, the annoying man added, "It's not an intimacy, by the way, but I prefer to be addressed simply as Anthony."

* * *

Cullen, here are the drawings I intended to show you when we last met. These are of the printing press typesetting boxes for the boy who has lost a hand. I forgot to leave them with you; I should have. They are intended for your reference. I do not at all mind passing along your offer to the physician who spoke to me about it, and he will conclude the business with the man in question. Send your price along with your proposal and he will meet it, I am sure, as where else in the city can he find a solution as simply elegant as yours?

Regards,
Burke

FOLDED UP INSIDE THE DRAWING, which had this note scrawled in its corner, was another small paper folded very tight and sealed with knotted string.

Cass sliced it open eagerly.

My dear Cassandra.

I feel we still have much to discuss before we settle the question about which we both agreed to think. When you come and meet my family you will understand some, though not all, of my concerns. I ought to dissuade you, but I will not. I want you to come. I want you to see Morland and for Morland to see you. If you come to your senses and run the other way once you know all my concerns, I will not be able to blame you. But I suspect I will regret it more than you can ever know. I hope we will be able to speak more freely at Morland. I hope you make a safe and swift journey.

Yours,

Oliver

Cass clutched this second tiny note in her fist.

It was late; the boy Oliver had sent with the letter had brought it straight to the kitchen, and Mrs. Orfill had given it to Selene who had given it to Cass.

Cass put out the candle guttering at her elbow. She was not afraid of the shadows. She liked the noises the old house made as it cooled and settled around her in the night.

How had she come here, to be a prisoner in her own home? Letter-writing was better than sugar-cakes, to her. She could not assume all her correspondence was reaching her, as she still had not seen the invitation from Morland and Lady Inglemawr had not brought it up.

Slowly Cass mounted the stairs. She paused at the door to look inside the front parlor with its blue wallpaper hand-painted with bright birds. She could see her grandmother sitting right there in her favorite chair and smiling. Stitching.

Silently.

The picture in her mind was always of her grandmother sitting happily and silently in this house.

Was she ready to do that? To be that?

Lady Inglemawr's enforced isolation more than chafed. It was a sign of things to come. This was what her life could be like.

She had never wanted that.

Her grandmother had never been lonely, as far as Cass knew. Maybe her memories of her husband and her daughter gone before her had been all she wanted.

But Cass would be lonely.

She truly did not want a husband. She would have to find a way to convince Dr. Burke of that.

But she did not want to be alone here forever either.

THE COUNTESS INVENTION

If those were her only two options, then she was more right than she knew that she would need a husband who would marry her and leave her alone.

A married woman could not be kept shut up here in her own house.

Well, a house she had the right to live in.

Cass sighed a small, soundless sigh.

While she was looking into the shadowed front parlor a small voice inside her said, *perhaps...*

Perhaps what she needed was to go to Morland and be a social success.

Perhaps that *was* the best path to a husband. She had not attended a social event in years and Lady Inglemawr clearly did not intend to change that. She should go to Morland and be glittering and charming, and the other guests would remember her and invite her to other parties. She was sure that was how it was supposed to work.

She could be charming. She could. She had always been popular at the school, and even her students had liked her when she had tried her hand at teaching. She would be *extra* charming.

Or, more practically, perhaps she could figure out how charmingness worked, and apply it.

She would not go just to spend more time with the perplexing Dr. Burke. He was beautiful and he could do some wicked things with his hands and his lips, but he clearly drank more than she would ever have suspected, and he did not truly sound as if he wished to have a wife.

He would be there, of course, and she would have the opportunity to spend more time with him. There was a part of her that hoped that he had meant what he had written, in his letter, the hope that they would be able to talk more.

But that was just a hope. Hope was for lonely flowered wallpaper rooms. Cass would go to this house party not for hope, but to do what she actually wanted to do.

To make a social splash. To make friends. To make connections that could lead her to the type of freedom she really wanted.

Oh, she was definitely going.

Dr. Burke,

I've enclosed a rough sketch that conveys the idea of the track I mentioned when I saw you. The type box ought to slide freely back and forth on this and allow the boy to keep up with his cohorts. The materials and labor price estimates are included. Share with whomever you choose. I ought to be able to start the commission immediately, though it will have to conclude after some travel I must undertake soon.

Sincerely,
Geo. Cullen

And folded up inside the sketch, knotted with the same piece of string that had tied the note to her,

~~Dr. Burke~~, ~~Ol~~, I have been thinking as we agreed to do. I am still pressed under the weight of my concerns. I cannot say the same about your concerns as I do not know them yet. But I trust that you will share them with me when you have the chance. I do regret that recent developments here have made that impossible so far, but I expect we will be able to both satisfy our concerns at Morland. I so look forward to seeing you there.

Truly,
C.

She had wanted to sign "yours", but that seemed to belong to the fantasy Oliver, not the real one. She needed to know much more about the fellow, both the parlor version and the kitchen version, before she took any more liberties.

* * *

"I UNDERSTAND we have been invited to a house party by Lady Rawleigh," Cass said, attempting to sound casual, as she and Lady Inglemawr sat at supper the next evening.

Lady Inglemawr's head snapped up as though a bell had rung.

"How do you know that?"

"Why wouldn't I know?" Cass lifted one shoulder carelessly, as she had seen Lady Inglemawr do a thousand times. "I would be a poor hostess to you, Lady Inglemawr, if I expected you to handle all the mail alone."

Lady Inglemawr's blue eyes narrowed. She said, "I had not thought you wished to attend any more parties this year."

She had attended *no* parties this year, Cass thought acidly to herself, so it was rather annoying that Lady Inglemawr made it sound as though there had been dozens and her ladyship was merely wanting not to exhaust Cass.

Cass said, "I would not dream of putting you in the position of turning down an invitation from Lady Rawleigh. And you have been in such a social whirl for the last few weeks; I thought Morland might be a nice rest for you."

That put the ball back on her side of the court, Cass thought to herself.

Lady Inglemawr was still looking thoughtfully at Cass. Cass returned her gaze evenly and did not waver.

Lady Inglemawr was the one attending social functions, not Cass. If the lady wished to beg off, she would have to do it based on her own calendar, not Cass'. Something told Cass that Lady Inglemawr did not want her asking about her ladyship's social engagements. Something told Cass that Lady Inglemawr had not, in fact, been attending parties. Not public parties.

Cass was not ready to cut herself off from the outside world. Not at all.

And she would be damned before she would let Lady Inglemawr turn this house from a refuge to a prison.

That had never been their arrangement before, and she wasn't going to start now.

"Yes," Lady Inglemawr finally said, so softly that Cass saw more than heard it, but then she added, more loudly, "Yes, we should visit Morland, it will be a lovely time of year for it."

They finished Mrs. Orfill's delicious dinner in silence.

CHAPTER 11

*C*ass almost gasped out loud when Morland came into view as the coach neared its drive.

There were towers, and towers on the towers—she couldn't quite take it all in. Some Gothic revivalist architect had gone a bit mad. It wasn't a jumble of details, but it had frills, that was the only way she could think of it. She imagined how she might draw it, with these crenellations and those spires stabbing into the blue sky, the pointed arch of iron gates leading to the courtyard, and the dark mass of a smaller wing lurking in the background as if it didn't feel it had the right to step forward.

It was intimidating, forbidding, and yet somehow it gave Cass a sense of possibilities.

Her hands flew as her thoughts multiplied while the carriage drew closer and closer to the house. She could share them freely with Peg, sitting across from her, as Lady Inglemawr and her lady's maid Laurie would not understand.

It isn't as though I wish to be a lady of a fine manor. But I believe that if I were one, I could make the position worthwhile.

Peg shrugged a shoulder. *You don't have to. People in those positions, their job is to be the people, not do things.*

I could do things. I imagine Dr. Burke wouldn't be so miserable here if he associated some good benefit with the estate, rather than whatever dire past weighs him down so.

Is it just the loss of his brother? On that, Peg did look sympathetic. *Lots of men, lots of families are brought low by that one.*

I don't think so. Perhaps it is. I need to know him better.

Not as well as you need to know the other members of this party, if you intend to do it up right.

True enough. Cass glanced toward Lady Inglemawr, who was looking out her own window. *We have time. Let's go through it again.*

Once the invitation had been accepted, the Marchioness had provided Cass with the guest list, provided it almost gladly. Still, Cass had the feeling that the air was not clear between them.

Not that she had time to worry about it. She intended to make a good impression at this house party, if only to prove that she could. After her mortifying season, Cass associated nothing but misery with parties. Perhaps this one could be better.

Perhaps she wanted more than just to impress everyone.

Perhaps she wanted to impress Oliver.

Just perhaps.

Peg had been practicing the list with her for days. *There's Lady Gadbury*—Here Peg stopped and spelled out the full name to make sure Cass had the correct pronunciation. *The Earl and Countess of Rawleigh, of course, Mr. Victor Evelyn the doctor's younger brother, and Mrs. Evelyn—Dr. Burke said you might meet their children, they have two, a boy and a girl. His sister Viola is visiting in the north and will not be here. Other guests... a Lady Sherrin who is a friend of Lady Gadbury, I think, and some honorable Grantham Eliot, Marquess of Faircombe who's quite horse-mad and bringing his horse-mad daughter Charlotte with him. And Lady Charlotte's friend, a Miss Farsworth, Delina Farsworth. Might bring a son or two, apparently he has three, Grantham the second, Fredrick, and Geoffrey.*

Am I imagining things, Cass managed to make her expression dry, *or are there quite a few females at this event?*

The corner of Peg's mouth turned up in a smile. *You think the Countess wants to keep him distracted from you?*

Cass pursed her lips. It certainly did seem as though the Countess might have had that idea.

The only one she *knew* Oliver knew was Lady Gadbury.

Because she had seen them talking. And he had said her name so familiarly.

Well. She wouldn't borrow any trouble; she intended to see this weekend through and be simply a normal member of the party.

For once Cass felt equipped to be a fully-functioning member of a social affair. She was armed with wonderful gowns, for which she really must *thank* Lady Gadbury; she was also armed with information on the people whom she would be meeting, and with an invitation that had been extended to her, not just her father's money or Lady Inglemawr. This was a party where she was actually wanted. She fully intended to participate as one of the guests and make as much of a success of herself as she could.

I have always wondered if I could be a social success, you know, at parties and things, if I really had the chance. The right equipment, you know. The gowns and people's names and things like that.

Peg wrinkled her nose. *Why it's up to you to make nice to those people is beyond me. What makes them so great?*

Cass considered Peg's point seriously. It was a good point. *I am not sure they are so great. But I don't want to be small.*

That made Peg simply throw herself back into the coach's bench in shock. *You are great. You have always been great.*

Cass smiled a little as Peg clearly wanted her to do. Peg hadn't attended the balls during her season where she stood by the wall trying and failing to interact with others.

In her head, Cass pictured herself now almost as a warrior maiden on a charging horse. She meant it when she said she felt armed. She wanted to storm this party and emerge victorious, with Oliver and any other stray young men around following after her and waiting for her every word. She wanted to belong.

At the very least, she wanted not to be overlookable.

Never mind that she still wasn't quite sure what a social success ought to *be*, or how she was going to be one. She was sufficiently determined to try to leave her perfect little house with its predictable pleasures. It had become easier to leave, she mused, once Lady Inglemawr had turned it from a refuge into a bit of a prison.

Picturing her grandmother in her bird-and-flower parlor, Cass reminded herself that she at least wanted the *option* to have more people about if the notion struck her. Was it so odd for someone of her age not to want to spend the rest of her life without any excitement at all?

If she were ever going to master the art of interacting with people, this was her chance.

Cass was fully committed to the idea that she was going to meet these people, and have them meet her, on an equal footing, and leave this party without being mortally embarrassed.

If she could do that, it would be a triumph.

* * *

WHEN THEY ARRIVED, what seemed like a huge line of footmen greeted them.

The footmen helped Lady Inglemawr down from the hired carriage, and then Cass, then Peg and Laurie, her ladyship's maid. Lady Inglemawr and her maid were led inside; Peg stood waiting for Cass, a basket over her arm and a disapproving expression on her face and her hands folded together in front of her.

Cass couldn't stop herself from staring up at the towers of Morland; it took her some time before she could tear herself away from the way the windows were edged, and the way faux pillars stretched up the facade of the house for all three stories before ending in carvings that looked like doric capitals tucked just ender the edge of the room. Cass also made a point of taking in all the similar faces of all the footmen, several of whom were unloading their luggage from the carriage's roof.

Do not leave me alone yet, she said with her hands to Peg, who visibly snorted.

I'm not going anywhere, Peg said right back, *not until I know where I'm supposed to go. The likes of me could be sent to the gallows for turning up in the wrong place in a house like this.*

Cass thought Peg was exaggerating. She *hoped* Peg was exaggerating.

Once the footmen had all their luggage, she imagined, they would show her in.

A movement caught the corner of her eye and she froze almost mid-step, then turned to look.

One of the footmen had hands that were moving.

Just a moment, miss, he said, *her ladyship will not be down but the butler will show you to your rooms.*

Cass could not stop her broad smile. She nodded to the young man, who had the same short brown hair and sun-kissed face that all the young men had, but whose eyes were friendly. *Thank you.*

And sure enough, once the footmen carrying their luggage had arranged themselves behind her, a round man wearing a great many buttons appeared in the open doorway of Morland.

Cass presented herself, Peg falling in behind her. She knew she didn't need to curtsey to a butler. But the man looked so regal and so disapproving, she considered it.

"I'll show you to your rooms, Miss Cullen."

He turned before he finished speaking so she didn't catch all of it, but bolstered by the young footman's remark, Cass knew to follow him, and she did.

Once they and their luggage had been deposited in their chambers, Cass darted around, looking behind the velvet draperies, moving the carved gilt chairs, looking in the drawers of the tables and sideboards.

Peg just addressed herself to opening the trunks and organizing the wardrobe.

But this is beautiful! Cass burst out with excitement. *Oliver made it sound so miserable.*

Peg just shot her a look. Cass knew she shouldn't refer to him so familiarly, but after all, who would know?

Then remembering she had just met a footman who would know, Cass resolved to behave better.

Peg said, *A beautiful looking house doesn't mean it's a nice house.*

Well, Cass couldn't argue that one.

Once they'd both washed a bit and changed Cass' travel dress, Cass could not curb her desire to explore any longer.

I will return, she told Peg and ventured out into the hallway.

The footman standing there, not her newfound friend, said something; Cass just smiled and shook her head no. She wanted to explore, and build up a picture of Morland in her head.

She would treat it like a foreign city, as if she were visiting Paris or Rome, and she would learn it until she could draw a map of it.

There were several closed doors along the hallway where her room was, and Cass took a good look around, both to fix in her mind where she wanted to return, and not to open the other doors. It would make sense, she thought, if other houseguests were lodged along this wing.

Big doors, she thought to herself as she descended a gentle, wide staircase topped with a golden silk carpet. She would open only big doors.

* * *

THE CORRIDORS HAD SO many cunning little nooks in them, Cass felt as though she could spend a week simply exploring them.

Forget the people she might meet here. She could spend a month, a year drawing everything that interested her, inside and out.

The windows that opened on to the courtyard were multi-paned mullioned glorious testaments to some glazer's skill, and they gave the view outside a faceted, muted look, as if the simple courtyard's grass and sky was the heart of an antique jewel.

Cass leaned as close as she dared to the glass, until she almost felt its coolness against the skin of her face.

And then, when she turned away, she saw him.

Dr. Oliver Burke was standing in the hallway just a few paces away, the same mullioned sunlight falling on him, one hand half-raised as though he had been in the middle of some action when he caught sight of her and stopped.

He was looking at her the way that she was looking at Morland.

He was looking at her as if she were as surprising and lovely and miraculous as a clockwork butterfly. Or perhaps even as fantastic as a real one.

Cass felt her face light up, actually felt it. Her smile grew wide all on its own, and her feet started to move toward him.

She felt flooded with warm anticipation and delight.

And then her conscious brain thought, *Oh dear.*

CHAPTER 12

Oliver couldn't even remember how he had spent the last few hours of his life. He knew that the minutes had trickled away like sand, never to return and to be individually forgotten. His mother had asked him to accompany her to the gallery that contained paintings commissioned by the fourth Earl, who had been some sort of a connoisseur of art.

Oliver could not claim to share his ancestor's tastes.

He stood at his mother's side while she went on and on about a sale, or perhaps it was an acquisition, she was considering. It was clearly important to her, and Oliver wished for her sake that he could absorb more of the details, but they simply did not register.

Leaving the gallery he had stopped in the corridor, turning to help his mother up the stairs that led from there to the windowed hall that overlooked the courtyard.

And there he saw a slender beam of sunlight, in the form of a young woman with dark hair, leaning toward the glass as if ready to escape into the sky outside.

He knew without seeing her face that it was Cass.

And when she turned and saw him and her face lit up with an

excitement she could not hide, Oliver felt something answering leap inside of him.

There you are, he felt rather than thought, and though he had not known that he was filled with questions, at that moment, she seemed to be the answer to all of them.

He smiled at her because he could not help it.

And though he might be mistaken, it looked to him as though she smiled at him the same way.

The wandering of Oliver's mind down these pleasant paths of possibility was interrupted by his mother's inelegant throat-clearing at his elbow.

"My lady," he said, but looking at Cass, not his mother, so she could see his mouth, "may I introduce Miss Cassandra Cullen?"

And then he offered his hand. To Cass.

Knowing she was introduced, Cass had many split-second decisions to make. She decided to descend the two steps to join them where they stood before curtseying to Lady Rawleigh, and then she decided to look downward demurely as she should and risk missing something her ladyship might say, trusting Oliver to somehow repeat it if it were important.

Lady Rawleigh was several inches shorter than Oliver and also than Cass herself, and Cass wondered wildly for a moment if she was supposed to hunch over so as not to loom over the Countess.

Lady Rawleigh's eyes were rectangular copies of Oliver's, though less remarkable in color. They narrowed as she took in every aspect of Cass from the top of her simple twist of hair to the bottom of her light kid slippers.

Cass nearly held her breath, waiting for her ladyship to say something.

"I am so glad you are able to visit Morland," Lady Rawleigh finally said. "Lady Inglemawr is with you?"

"I believe she is refreshing herself after the carriage trip, and will be most eager to see you, Lady Rawleigh." Cass suppressed an urge to curtsey again. Lady Rawleigh was not tall but the overall effect of her jeweled hands and beaded gown was one of glassy, pointy authority.

"I hope so. I shall retire to the blue parlor," she said, looking up at her son.

"Very well, madam. I believe I shall show Miss Cullen the fourth earl's art gallery."

"But we have just spent half an hour in that gallery."

Oliver inclined his head to his mother as if to agree, but what he said was, "And Miss Cullen has not. Would you like to see it, Miss Cullen?"

Cass just nodded yes. She had no idea what gallery Oliver meant, but she was inclined to agree to anything he proposed.

Oh dear, she thought to herself again.

But she had no time to consider the depth of her self-deception in her reasons for coming here.

Oliver waved that she should precede him into the gallery, and just like that they had left Lady Rawleigh behind.

"Should we have waited for her to depart?" Cass whispered to Oliver once the footmen trailing her ladyship had disappeared.

"Most likely," Oliver shrugged. "Would you actually like to see some of the paintings? There is one of Morland's earliest tower that is supposedly quite good."

He didn't give a damn about the paintings. He was watching her. She darted from frame to frame, and then when she reached the doorway on the far side, she turned to look at him over her shoulder, then reached her hand back towards him, just as he had done moments ago towards her.

Was there a fairy tale about an enchanted golden statue, Oliver wondered as he got closer to her? Was the prince supposed to capture it? Bow before it?

What he wanted was a kiss.

Cass' smile faded as he leaned close and she could tell his intention.

"Shall I not?" asked Oliver, his voice thick in his throat.

"If you wish to kiss me..."

When she didn't finish the sentence, Oliver stopped.

Her lips had parted, and she was watching him.

He leaned in more closely still, and kissed her very softly on her temple, and felt the fluttering of her pulse just below the surface.

"Yes?" she said, arching one of those birdwing brows.

He couldn't decide if he was teasing her, or she was teasing him. Surely she must see how he was breathing hard; surely she must know.

The little smile playing about her lips said that she knew *something*. "Is it the dress?"

Oliver's hands went around her waist. She fit so perfectly into his hands. He wanted to pull her against him.

Instead, he only buried his nose in the spot behind her ear and closed his eyes.

They stood together that way for what seemed like a long time. Or maybe, thought Cass, it was just that time had also stopped, waiting to see what would happen next.

Finally pulling her more tightly against him, Oliver said very softly into her ear, "I do wish to kiss you."

"And will you?" she said just as softly.

"I don't want to kiss you the way I did before," he warned her, one of his hands sliding up her back to cradle her head.

"I think... that I might be willing for you to kiss me in any way at all," she admitted, pulling back to meet his eyes so he could see that she meant it.

Stifling a groan, Oliver pulled her that inch forward so his lips could meet hers.

Cass felt caught up in an Oliver-shaped whirlwind. One second he was standing there in front of her, his eyes boring into hers, the breadth of his chest rising and falling visibly as he seemed to fighting some internal fight; the next, she was wrapped up in him, caught up in him, as he crushed her body to his and seized possession of her mouth.

Their promise kiss had not been like this. That had been so slow that Cass could still remember every instant as if they had stretched out like leisurely weeks, remember every sensation, every tiny spot where he had touched her.

This was engulfing. She could only hold on, his arms wrapped around her, her hands gripping his shoulders as he pressed every inch of her into his body, which suddenly felt hard and implacable.

She fit herself into his arms, feeling herself soften in the heat that radiated from him. His mouth left where it had been plundering hers and traced along her jaw, her throat, tasting the beginning of the curve of her shoulder and then continuing to nip at her skin where it disappeared under the neckline of her gown. His arms around her waist held her tightly, but it felt more freeing than confining.

"Oliver," she whispered into his ear, surprised at how deep and throaty her own voice sounded.

He gripped her waist, tightly this time, and lifted her bodily to sit on the edge of a marble-topped credenza.

Cass felt breathless and hungry, light and heavy all at the same time, but she was not so disoriented that she did not notice herself being lifted and deposited on the furniture. When she opened her eyes she saw that he had his eyes still closed.

That plush, deeply flushed lower lip was slightly open. She *wanted* his mouth on her. Anywhere, everywhere. It looked all too possible, right at this very minute.

She had wanted that before and it had not gone at all the way she had imagined. He seemed to have gone somewhere else, his thoughts floating away after that kiss. Even as she had expected something like that, it was disappointing. At this moment, she was sure that she might have been anyone; his thoughts were not with *her*.

Nonetheless, that kiss had affected her. She felt her body wanting more.

But she was not ready to be ignored.

"Oliver?"

The uncertain note in her voice drew him back to himself.

When he looked at her again, he realized that he had stopped paying attention to her and to where they were.

He had her perched on the marble-topped piece, her arms dangerously mixing with the candlesticks and vases arranged there as she leaned slightly back, while his hand slid down her thigh preparing to tighten her leg against him.

The look she gave him was one he couldn't read. But she looked distant, and disappointed, and not at all happy to be where she was.

"Cassandra. My God. My apologies."

He hadn't moved.

The hand sliding down her skirt was in fact still drawing her leg around him. If he leaned only slightly forward, she would be feeling the shape at the front of his trousers very intimately.

Cass braced her hands, leaned ever so slightly back.

She just raised one eyebrow questioningly at him.

He couldn't read her expression, but he did know that the right thing to do was to at least move her off that table.

"Yes, of course, my apologies," Oliver said again, and this time he stepped back a few inches, putting out his hand to help her to stand.

They stood together, both catching their breath, but did not meet each other's eyes.

Cass was proud that her breathing sounded steady as she said, "Truly, is it the dress?"

Oliver's laugh was deep and loud as he finally took a big step back and looked more closely at her gown. On his first sight of her, his heart had sped up because it was *her*, not because of her clothes.

The gown was a sunny yellow, with ribbons tied around the high waist and trailing attractively. That was part of the reason why the sight of her had reminded him of a sunbeam, Oliver decided. Not the only reason.

"It is lovely." But as he stroked one hand along her neck to rest his thumb possessively against the line of her jaw, he said quietly, "It is not the dress."

"I am so gla—"

Before she could finish her sentence he kissed her again, thoroughly, as if he just had to.

CHAPTER 13

When she could breathe again she opened her eyes to look into his, just inches away. He didn't seem to want to move backwards at all.

He said, "It is not the dress."

Cass could not stop herself from stroking his temple, mirroring where he had kissed her. "You are unhappy here."

Yes! He wanted to shout. No one seemed to hear him. No one seemed to *listen*. She understood. Maybe she was starting to feel the gloom of this place too. He should put her in a carriage and get her away from here.

Despite his best intentions what came out of his mouth was, "No matter what they say, please stay."

"Are your parents so cruel?"

"No. I don't believe so. In their own way, they are not unkind, and ..." Oliver was searching for another description he could fairly apply.

"I am not delicate."

"Of course not."

"If you would prefer that I leave, just say so."

There was no way to explain. "I absolutely do not want you to leave."

Cass nodded, her lips folding firmly together. "Then at some point we must discuss further why we are both here. You keep insisting that I ought not to want to marry you. Why then did you want me to come?" They were nearly the same height and her eyes were calm as they looked levelly into his. "Why kiss me?"

Her and her short, simple questions. He ought to have an answer for her. He didn't. Or rather, he'd already given her all the answer he had.

Again his fingers plucked at one of her curls. Experimentally he plucked out a pin, just to see if he could make her hair move more freely. The curl stayed in its place when he wanted it to soften and melt into his hands.

He could just begin to explain his actions to himself.

When the dawn comes on a cloudy day, have you seen it? There is a bright blue light trying to shine through, and even though the clouds force the sky into looking more like midnight, you know the dawn is there, you know it survives. That is what I thought when I looked at you.

But he could not say that to her.

A dozen expressions chased themselves across Cass' face as she stared at him and he just stroked her face with his thumb, gaze level and serious.

Oliver said, "I wanted to see you. I want you near me. I want to touch you."

Cass blinked. He was quite... direct. Even knowing that the reality of it would not be as pleasant as she imagined, it *sounded* romantic; it sounded blissful.

But then discussions of bedding always *sounded* like that. Whatever money poets made, it must be measured by how many words they devoted to the glories of the bed.

"That is... is it flattering? I am not sure."

"Is it intriguing?"

He looked way too eager for compliments. "You look like a small boy who wants toys. I have little brothers, you know."

Oliver licked his lips. She couldn't help but watch. "Is that wrong?"

Against her will she felt a smile trying to escape; she ruthlessly tamped it down. "I am not here to cause you more difficulty, sir, but at some point very soon you are going to need to tell me if you wish to marry me or not. You have insisted I come to your family home as if you were serious about your proposal."

"I was. I *am*." Oliver had not been so certain till this moment, but now he felt certainty flood through him and turn to something durable and lasting.

"Then we are at the same impasse where we began. I do not wish to be a mattress for a man, and I cannot put it more bluntly."

"Then I must be just as blunt. You have formed an image of love-making that is a sad betrayal of only one tiny aspect of its possibilities. I could make love to you for weeks, months, and never burden you with the weight of my body."

Cass felt herself take in a quick shock of air; she couldn't stop it. Her skin tingled, at the crooks of her elbows and the backs of her knees. She prickled hot all over, and felt herself swell inside. Just from his words. Just from his *words*. She desperately wanted to find out if he was right.

"Cassandra. Tell me you did not enjoy those kisses."

She couldn't.

But he wasn't a one night experiment. He was proposing marriage, and once in, she would not be able to get out.

She had so many questions. She wanted to know what sort of actions *he* was picturing, and she wanted to know what he would do and what he would want in return. She wanted to know a great deal.

But that might be getting off the course of this conversation. Slightly.

So she said nothing.

"You must know that I would not offer to make it pleasurable if I could not assure you that it would be." Hoarsely he added, "You have only to put me to the test."

"I am..." At one time that was all she wanted from a man's bed. Though she had never actually tried it in a bed. Perhaps that had been her mistake? Oh, she could not distract herself with that now. "I do not... I am not sure that what you offer is what I want."

Oliver's tiny omnipresent frown deepened, but he nodded. "A husband who will be an earl. One who will keep your household as it is and leave complete control of the staff to you. One who is interested in your work. And one who very much wishes to *not* leave you alone. Most ladies seek fortunes and titles; those would be yours in due time, as you see." He gestured around him to the gilt splendors of the house. "Tell me what else you want."

"Is that what *you* want? You are the one who consistently insists that I do not want to marry you. Perhaps you can explain yourself."

Perhaps he could. He certainly should be able to. But then, he never had before. Waite and the other men he drank with, they never asked him hard questions like this.

Neither had the women he had bedded, Oliver realized belatedly. He had taken all of his dark moods to their beds, and they had never asked him anything.

"Perhaps I wanted you here so that you could see this miserable family and this miserable house... and this miserable man as closely as you care to, and then you could better decide."

Staying close enough to be able to hear him, she squeezed his hand reassuringly even as she said briskly, "I wonder if that is really what you need. I have rather a talent for this, if you'll permit me."

"Whatever you like, Miss Cullen."

"When I need to find out how to build something someone needs, I need to find out what they want to do and how they expect to do it, and then offer them some possibilities for how their goal *can* be done. So let me ask you this, Dr. Burke. What do you hope to accomplish here this weekend?"

"Survive."

One birdwing eyebrow arched. "Is that truly all?"

Oliver gave it a few moments' serious thought. "I would like you to meet my family, enjoy it, if that is even possible, and demonstrate to my mother how ridiculously narrow-minded her assumptions are. And I'd like to stay sober most of the time."

He made it sound so simple. At some point, he knew, someone in this house, most like his mother, would say or do something that would send Cass fleeing back to London.

Of course, then he would not have to find out if he was truly what she wanted.

He felt more and more that it would be too crushing to find out he was not.

Not that he felt unequal to the task of providing her pleasure. That he knew he could do. But she was reminding him, or teaching him, that there might be more to interactions between men and women and she might want things from him that he could not provide.

Like not running into his previous lovers all over London.

Let her think the most difficult part of this weekend would be the task of remaining sober.

Unaware of his thoughts, Cass looked pleased. "Bravo! Clear goals, clearly stated. How do you expect to do this?"

He sighed. "With a bottle of wine in each hand, but then the sober bit will not happen."

Again the arched eyebrow. "Indeed."

She was inexorable, giving no inch.

"So. I shall avoid double-fisted drinking, make sure my mother pays attention to your brilliance, and be however pleasant I must be to the guests to ensure that the party causes no rufflings among the fine people present."

"Excellent. I also wish to create no social rufflings, as you call them." Secretly she wanted to gloat over his compliment about her brilliance, but that would contradict her very ladylike exterior, and this was not the place and the time to forget to be ladylike.

"So, Miss Cullen, do you have any suggestions for devices that might help me accomplish my goals?"

She squeezed his hand again and her smile faded. "No, Dr. Burke. You have everything you need already."

His heart turned over in his chest. He could feel it. There was no physiological explanation for that sensation, and yet there it was.

Oliver sighed. "So we shall; so we must. We dine with his lordship and her ladyship and some of their guests this evening. The rest will arrive tomorrow, I believe, to stay through the week-end. There will be a hunt tomorrow afternoon and of course the party will dine together again. The whole thing will be the sort of deadly dull affair that causes people to stay in London all fall instead, preferring to choke in the coal fires. Do you truly expect to survive it?"

"Let me tell you whom I am prepared to meet." Quickly she rattled off the names of guests she knew.

Oliver added, "I have a friend, Bradley Waite, I've brought with me from the city, who will be with us as well. The Faircombe family won't join us till tomorrow, I believe."

"Do tell me about Mr. Waite. I don't want to have to guess how people are being introduced to me when I can't hear; best to be prepared."

"Bradley Waite is a waste of time." Oliver was not in a mood to mince words. "You are far more interesting."

Cass' heart thudded at the fresh new compliment, and again she thought, *Oh dear. Two* compliments far outweighed all her dreams of the young men she had fallen so desperately in love with at a distance. They had never really talked with her; she certainly couldn't remember them ever paying her even one compliment. This was awful.

She needed to stay clear-headed.

She intended to stick to her plan to be a social success this weekend at least. In fact, she had questions...

"Would you rather tell me more about how you know Lady Gadbury?"

"No, actually, I would not."

Well. That popped *that* little bubble of daydreams.

Cass shrugged. "Then show me your home. Show me this house."

Oliver looked around at the paintings collected by his forebears. "I am not sure this is my home."

Cass looked up at the moldings, the carved medallion decorating the ceiling. "If it has never been your home," she said slowly, "then it will be your home when you become the Earl. Will it not? And I would like to see it."

Oliver thought he hid his wince well when she brought up the idea of his inheriting, but he wanted to give her whatever she asked for.

Handing her out of the room, he asked the footmen still waiting there if they would ask Lady Inglemawr to join himself and Miss Cullen on a tour of Morland.

"There, propriety is sated," he said, settling her hand in the crook of his arm. "If she does not find us, that is no fault of ours."

"I do not think that is the way it is done," Cass shook her head.

"There are footmen absolutely everywhere. You will see. We shall barely be alone."

* * *

TRUE TO OLIVER'S WORD, there were indeed footmen everywhere. Cass did not see the young man she had met out front, but she was also paying more attention to her host than the staff. And to all the architectural and finishing details of the hall, which was rich in every direction.

It was all very beautiful and very formal. She was having a hard time believing that four small children had lived here; indeed, it was invisible that two children lived here now. She was trying to imagine a small version of Oliver roaming Morland.

"You must have *played*."

Oliver rubbed his chin. "Something like playing must have occurred, but I believe it was in the nursery during the appointed hours."

"You never played hide and seek in all these rooms? Never had pirates storm the steps? Sailed boats in a fountain?"

"There are three quite good fountains, one in the courtyard and two in the garden behind," Oliver confirmed. "I have never once sailed a boat in any of them. Why do boats come to your mind? Have you ever sailed?"

Cass nodded very seriously. "My brother Tobias has a new boat that he assures me is built for speed, not stability, and that is why it always tips over in the bathtub."

Oliver laughed. "I will not argue sailing points with an expert. I have never built a boat nor sailed one, though of course I sailed on one to fight abroad."

Cass' eyes grew large. "Was it very unpleasant?"

"Probably not as unpleasant as it would be if I were on Tobias' boat if it capsized. Too many men in a small space, and the unbelievably constant smell of seawater and rotting things caught in the planks. It was the voyage out. I was young and hopeful." Oliver shrugged.

"What about the voyage home?"

His voice grew almost too faint for her to hear. "I don't remember it."

Cass was trying to find a way to apologize for introducing sad topics when Oliver went on, still a bit quietly, as if he spoke more to himself than to her.

"Oscar carved boats. I'd forgotten that. He got a penknife for his birthday one year, I was so jealous. He did not stop carving for months. I don't know where he ever sailed them. If he ever sailed them."

Mouth dry, Cass closed her eyes and hoped she was doing the right thing to ask. "Is there a painting of him?"

As if realizing she was still there, Oliver looked up, surprised.

"Ah. No, not a painting, I do not believe so. But my sister Viola is a lovely artist; I wish she were here for you to meet. I believe she did some sketches of Oscar that were quite good."

"You should ask her for one. She is not here?"

"No, she is living with relatives farther north. Viola is... Actually, Viola is fine. When she is at Morland she is not well. Her mood sinks."

"Then it is very sensible for her to live elsewhere."

"Would we all were so sensible." Oliver's eyes warmed a little bit and crinkled at the corners. It was almost a smile. "Would you like to meet my brother Victor's family?"

Cass looked outside at the sinking sun. "Must we not attend dinner first?"

CHAPTER 14

*O*liver should not have escorted Miss Cullen down to the dining room. He did not care.

He would stay sober, and shave often, and his clothes, which were all the height of fashion, would stay clean and unwrinkled as best he could.

But he would not pretend not to know Miss Cullen, and he would not pretend that he was not interested in her.

Cass seemed completely calm, but Oliver could feel her tension in the hand she had tucked in the crook of his arm. He had waited while she changed, and he approved of the lavender gown; it was very becomingly cut and had a dainty lace overlay. It reminded him of her half-mourning while being nothing like it.

She wasn't gripping him like a chicken that needed to die, Cass assured herself, remembering how to look about herself and smile in company as they approached the drawing room which appeared to be filled with candles and people. She had quite properly taken his arm. She could do this, behave in a ladylike way. She had always at least been ladylike in company.

As she walked up to the line of footmen waiting in the hallway, a small furtive gesture of the hands of one of the young men caught her eye.

It was her friend from arrival. And he had said *hello*.

Cass stopped suddenly. Oliver stopped with her.

She could see exactly which young man it was. His hand had been at his waist, not in the right position, but she was sure he had said it. And she recognized his face.

Her father was always uncomfortable when he saw her using the manual language, and she knew Peg had had problems from time to time when she used it in public.

But there was no way she could simply pass that by.

She didn't approach the young man too closely, just asked him, *Are you deaf?*

My little brother, said the young man, without even appearing to look directly at her. He really did match all the rest of the young men with their short hair and their livery, his eyes still straight ahead, but the tiniest of smiles on his face.

She nodded, and when she moved, Oliver moved with her.

It had only been the smallest of exchanges, but as before, she felt better. It felt better.

The boy's younger brother must be at her school, the same school. They were not so very far from London. And her way of speaking with people was not so strange.

Cass had never before had such a rush of confidence from seeing just a little bit of the language she had *no* trouble using, in social situations or anywhere else.

She could do this.

Oliver patted her hand as, inside the dining room, they approached his mother.

Cass smiled serenely at the smaller woman, who nodded before turning back to Oliver for his introduction.

Cass wasn't fooled. Lady Rawleigh's sharp glance had taken in every aspect of Cass' appearance, but it made no difference to her. Cass had a faith in this gown, at least, that was unshakeable. And though it might have left some indelible mark upon her, Cass had faith that Oliver's kiss did not show.

She would figure out how to be charming to Lady Rawleigh.

As it turned out, Lady Rawleigh's voice was a bit too high for Cass to catch much more than an occasional word here and there, but it didn't seem to matter. Lady Rawleigh, once she began speaking, didn't seem to stop, and there didn't seem to be anything required of Cass but to nod occasionally and smile. Even as they progressed to the table and were seated. Lady Rawleigh's lips never stopped moving.

His lordship was even easier; the Earl of Rawleigh said nothing at all. It surprised her a bit that a man of his age had such a fashionable manner of dress, wearing Brummel's dark coat, though in a deep blue, and breeches, rather than the multicolored finery of his youth.

Apparently Oliver came by his interest in clothes naturally.

But the Earl took his seat and said nothing to anyone that Cass could tell during the entire meal.

If charming the Earl and Countess could consist of simply existing in the same room with them, Cass felt she had the process mastered.

Oliver was seated on the opposite side of the table in the dining room. It mattered not at all, because she could barely see him through the candles and decorations that marched down the center of the table, which was many feet wide.

She didn't want to appear to stare at the glittering candelabras, the art on the walls, or even the shimmering wallpaper.

Lady Inglemawr was much too far away at the table to hear, and besides she seemed to be, as she so often was these days, thinking about something else entirely. She seemed to speak a few times to Mr. Waite, who was between her and Cass, but was otherwise quiet. Which suited Lady Rawleigh's dinnertime conversation style.

Cass simply sat, on one side of Lady Rawleigh herself, with Oliver's friend Mr. Waite on her other side. That man seemed far more discomfited by Lady Rawleigh's never-ending stream of words; Cass was grateful she couldn't hear it.

She ate what was put in front of her, and occasionally tried to produce a facial response that was appropriate to whatever Lady Rawleigh was saying, based on Mr. Waite's reactions.

Cass was calm. This was simple, eating dinner. There was really so little for her to do.

She could just see enough of Oliver's face to frankly keep from being utterly bored. As long as the vague noise of others' voices, primarily Lady Rawleigh's, kept washing over her, Cass just kept nodding. Occasionally she smiled. She could tell that Oliver was occasionally glancing her way, and that the small frown between his brows was deep with some sort of worry.

And then she saw, as time went on, Oliver's face flushing darker and darker red.

He was taking a restrained amount of wine. His flush wasn't from drink. What ailed him? Cass would feel foolish asking a physician if he was quite well, but she couldn't think what else she would do if he continued to turn this mottled shade of red.

At some point during the third course, Cass realized that what was wrong with Oliver was that he was *laughing*.

Actually laughing.

He was sitting in his seat, laughing so hard that she could see him go crooked in his chair. He appeared to be trying to stay upright. He didn't seem to have the least ability to hide that he was practically crying with laughter, but he also didn't seem to care.

Cass couldn't hear it but she could see it. She saw him dab away the tears in his eyes.

Cass had no idea what *that* was about, but she knew when someone was laughing *at her*, and this wasn't it. When Cass glanced toward Mr. Waite, she found that he too had noticed Oliver's laughter and certainly didn't share it, but he did not seem concerned.

Lady Rawleigh didn't stop talking and Lord Rawleigh didn't start, so Cass decided to assume that things were going well unless or until Oliver actually fell out of his chair.

* * *

OLIVER'S HAND as it captured hers leaving the dining hall was warm.

He still had something like tears lurking in the corner of his eyes as he grinned at her and escorted her from the room.

"Are you quite well?" she hissed at him. She saw Lord Rawleigh cast a glance their way as he left the dining room himself, and he looked disapproving.

She could feel the chuckles still bubbling up in Oliver.

"I am very well. Completely. I've never in my life seen anyone more suited to my mother at conversation. You just smiled and nodded and let her go on and on."

"I couldn't hear anything she said!" Cass half-exclaimed, looking around to make sure no one else would hear her.

"I know!" He shook again with suppressed laughter. "Perfection! Utter perfection!"

Cass just shook her head. "You are quite strange."

Bradley Waite came near and leaned close to both Cass and Oliver. "I say, Burke, you didn't let me in for what an amazement your mother is."

"Waite, I'm not even sure why you are here. Did I actually invite you?"

"I don't remember. I might have simply followed you here to get some fresh air and a new supply of liquor."

"That sounds plausible." Oliver had noticed that Waite's consumption of wine over dinner had been as restrained as his own. Getting out of London had been good for his friend. Good for both of them. "Will you hunt with the party tomorrow?"

"I may just do that."

"Good heavens, I was joking. Can you ride?"

Waite just laughed. "I ride very well, Dr. Burke. Do not judge all the rest of us by your shortcomings."

Cass was close enough to both men to hear almost every word. Oliver seemed relaxed with his friend in a way that he was not anywhere else. She liked it. She made sure to smile at Mr. Waite. "I do apologize for the dullness of my dinner conversation."

He smiled back. "Never say so. My God, I never heard anyone talk so much in my life. And all of it an endless fusillade of complaints. I feel sticky. I could not believe your tact in ignoring all the various lists of your shortcomings, Oliver. And each one delivered tied up in a ribbon of compliments. Extraordinary. I have never heard anything like it."

Cass' smile faltered. Apparently she had missed quite a lot.

Oliver breathed in deeply, and slowly let it out. "A lifetime of practice, my good fellow."

"Remarkable. And your brother lives with his family here?"

Waite's tone made it sound like an unwise proposition.

Oliver reassured him, "Mr. Evelyn's apartments are in that far wing, and they visit my parents only occasionally."

"Glad to hear that. Imagine small children having to sit through that. And you, Miss Cullen, did you not find it wearing?"

The man's interest seemed to be genuine and after all, there was no point in trying to hide what she could not hide. "I am quite deaf to almost everything more than an arm's reach away, Mr. Waite, so I could not hear it. I find myself grateful."

"And here I thought I would be able to adopt the secret of your universal calm. I am disappointed."

He put on such a look of mock sadness that he made Cass laugh. "I have no such secrets to share. I believe the secret to a good sturdy sense of calm is to sleep well and live with few regrets."

The tall young man's eyes regarded her with more attention, and some admiration. "That is a secret worth knowing, Miss Cullen, thank you."

Lady Inglemawr had disappeared again. Oliver took her absence in stride. "Miss Cullen, let us go and visit my brother's family."

Waite looked perfectly happy to be left behind. "I believe I will begin pursuing Miss Cullen's excellent advice, and retire. Evening, Burke."

CHAPTER 15

By the time they reached the wing reserved for the use of the small family, the children were long abed, as Oliver's sister-in-law explained.

Cass was delighted to find that Victor was a squarer-jawed, younger version of Lord Rawleigh, sporting a very unfashionable beard that Cass couldn't help but think would look splendid on Oliver too.

"We have little society and even less reason to cater to it," he said when he saw Cass noticing it.

"I cannot believe her ladyship would stand for that."

The humor had gone from Oliver's voice, but his brother only grinned as he responded, "I shave before I see her, certainly."

And Oliver's sister-in-law Mrs. Evelyn introduced herself to Cass with a hug and a simple "My name is Ginnie," and went from there to showing Cass to a comfortable seat on the settee and plying her with madeira. She settled quite close to Cass on the couch herself, which Cass thought was her natural friendliness; Oliver moved a chair closer, and upon seeing this, without asking, Victor followed suit.

Cass immediately liked the young couple's warmth, and liked it even more when she realized that neither of the young Evelyns addressed Oliver using his title.

Oliver downed half his glass before launching into a retelling that Cass mostly followed about how the dinner downstairs had progressed. His good humor came back, and the affair seemed to have permanently affected him; he could not describe Cass' blissful ignorance of his mother's flood of words without chuckling.

Victor looked like he was ready to be just as amused as Oliver, but Ginnie's graceful forehead was wrinkled with frowns.

"Do not be too delighted, Dr. Burke. Your mother will have noticed that Miss Cullen could not understand her, I promise you."

"Oh, I don't think it matters much. She has never shown much interest in whether any of us is listening to her," said Oliver carelessly.

"Trust me, she cares. She remembers when someone does not give her their undivided attention, and she comes back to the grudge, I assure you."

Victor looked concerned. "Has something happened between you and my mother, madam?"

Ginnie did not look as if she were willing to confirm or deny the possibility. "Be careful," was all she said to Cass, and Cass believed her.

Cass didn't want to make her more uncomfortable—she barely knew her—but she couldn't help one tiny further probe. "Do you have any other advice?"

Ginnie shook her head, this time smiling. "Other than to avoid living here? No."

"Madam!" said Victor, his good-natured face now outright astonished. "I had no idea you did not care for living at Morland."

"There is something about it." She didn't quite shiver, but her shoulders tensed. "It is as if nothing ever truly happy could happen here."

"But it did. You gave me two beautiful children and I am unspeakably happy here with you, and them." Victor beamed with the look of a happy young father. Cass would have been willing to wager that he played with his children every day.

And that made Ginnie's face break out in a lovely smile that transformed her from slightly pretty to very lovely. It made Cass smile too. Ginnie inclined her head toward her husband. "I stand corrected, of course."

Victor reached out to take her hand. Cass tried to look away from the private look they gave one another, but it was loving and long and almost impossible to avoid.

When Victor turned from his wife to Oliver his usually jovial features turned a bit somber. "Have you received a letter from Viola? She is coming here, you know. Not this weekend. But apparently in the spring. Has she written you?"

"No, how is she?" Oliver sat up at the mention of his sister.

"Not ill. Just the same as usual."

"Viola feels about this house just as I do," Ginnie half-muttered into her glass of madeira.

"My very dear!" Victor sounded even more astonished this time.

"Oh, don't harass her, Victor, this house is a mouldering pile of bricks that never did anyone any good." Oliver moved as if to down the rest of his glass, then seemed to second-think himself and only sipped it.

Cass looked around. "But it is beautiful."

Ginnie shrugged. "Cold."

"Well." Victor looked simply taken aback. "Apparently we should be investigating other living arrangements."

"We wished the Earl and Countess to know the children... as Oliver has no heir and... Oscar did not either." Ginnie looked uncomfortable bringing up the topic, but Oliver just nodded.

"True, plus I have no independent income," said Victor as though it didn't bother him terribly much. A true aristocrat, thought Cass. How different from her father's position, and how much like her grandmother's family. "I am not intrepid like my brother here, traveling to Edinburgh to study and become a physician, then going off to war."

"War contributed nothing to my pocket, or anything else, I assure you," Oliver said.

* * *

JUDITH LYNNE

UPON LEAVING THE EVELYNS' apartments, Oliver tucked her hand back into the crook of his arm proprietarily, leaving the footmen who waited outside to follow them.

"What on earth has happened to Lady Inglemawr?" Oliver asked as if inquiring about the weather.

Cass threw her free hand into the air. "She seems to be quite absorbed by something. She said nearly nothing during the entire day in the carriage. It is remarkable."

"Convenient for me."

"Is this the lord of the manor carrying off the unsuspecting lady? Is that what they do here?"

Oliver frowned rather than smiling at her attempted humor. "Probably. Despicable forebears. That must be why the place feels this way. It is not that old—my grandfather built this part of it—but it bears the weight of a long line of despicable forebears."

"Let it go, Oliver." She squeezed his arm a little. "You are talking yourself into your mope."

"Quite right."

After a bit more walking and a few more turns, she was not surprised to find them in a library.

The footmen waited at the door again as Cass preceded him into the space that seemed to soar upwards, all of it lined with shelves.

"Oh my," breathed Cass, taking in the leather bindings in waves of different shades of browns and reds. The little collection of books her mother had left her would be swamped in a place like this!

"Not your library, but I hoped you would like it."

"All our best conversations happen in libraries," she told him with a smile as she turned up the lamp that was still burning in the room.

Oliver watched her cross to the settee to sit near him again, close enough to hear him. He could look at her all night. He could look at her forever.

He was staring at her for so long that Cass wondered what she'd done wrong. "Yes?"

Tentatively he raised his hands and moved them.

Cass was watching his face and almost missed that he was trying to copy the hand motions she had made earlier. *Are you deaf?*

Eyes wide, she made the motion for *no*.

"No, I'm not completely deaf." She repeated the motion for *deaf*, slowly. "I am very hard of hearing, though."

Then she asked him, *Are you deaf?*

No, he motioned back, and even that tiny conversation gave her a sort of a thrill.

He said, "I want to learn to talk this way, and the fellow I consulted said I should ask you."

"Why? I mean, why should you want to learn?"

"I don't think I quite know. I just know that I want to talk to you more than I've ever wanted to talk to anyone, I think. And I want to hear you."

Cass' expression was a combination of puzzled, amused, and a little crestfallen as she motioned back to him, *If I talk this way, you will see, not hear.*

Then she said it out loud. "That is seeing me, not hearing me."

"Not so. It is you talking. That is what interests me."

Carried away by the certainty, the solidity of his request, Cass could not help but answer, *True, this is the way I talk.*

"Tell me what that means."

She showed him more words, and she could not have described even to herself the particular pleasure she took in watching his hands, more and more familiar every moment, shaping the words.

When she thought of it again, the smell of the candle wax burning lower reached her, and she realized she had spent hours teaching him the motions for this word or phrase, or that one.

"It's an extraordinary invention," mused Oliver. She had just shown him how to move his hands to indicate *doctor*. "How did it come about?"

"Some of the instructors studied in Scotland, like you, at Mr. Braidwood's school for the deaf there. They brought the manual method to London with them. At the school, deaf children come from all over, and wherever there are deaf people, they talk with their hands. At the school the words are shared, and we all end up speaking the same language."

"Do all the instructors speak this way too?"

Cass couldn't tear her eyes away from his hands. They looked so strong, and so gentle. What made hands look gentle? She wondered. "Many of them. In fact that is partly why the headmaster engages some of them. He says it is faster and more efficient to hire good graduates who already know how to use the manual method of communication."

"That makes sense. And all the instruction is this way?"

"Oh no." Cass couldn't help a half-smile at the thought of the way her friend Peg had complained about her oral method instruction. "The entirely deaf students are also taught to speak out loud."

"How can they, when they have never heard speech?"

"It's very laborious and difficult, and it can be unpleasant." Cass put the picture of Peg sticking her tongue out at the teacher out of her mind. "I began with hearing and never lost it entirely so I only had lessons in pronunciation."

"I would like to say they must have had remarkable teachers as well as remarkable pupils, but I suspect I am going almost entirely on your example, and I doubt there are any others like you."

"On the contrary. There are many students like me, and like everyone else. Students come from rich homes as well as poor ones, country and city families, even titled families. There are only so many places at the school, so they hold a lottery. Even so, the place is always stuffed to the rafters with more pupils than it expects to hold."

"Ah. A ripe environment for the development of students who get the odd idea that they can do as they like."

"Perhaps." Cass' smile stayed subdued. "Did students of medicine in the north not run wild when they had the opportunity?"

"Some," Oliver admitted, "but only those who were not interested in completing the degree in as brief a period of time as possible. One could stay and drink and carouse, but not do those things and finish. And I was not so delighted with Edinburgh's weather that I wanted to study for more years."

I understand, Cass said, and Oliver's eyes lit up with excitement that he had understood her, too.

He was so sweet like this, so charming.

Over the hours they had drawn close to one another, facing each other on the settee, each one with a knee drawn up onto the couch and so close that there was nearly no room for her knee against his.

Unsure how she felt about this situation, Cass said very quietly, since they were so close, "I would wager that you are sitting there imagining how to convince me to do something far more inappropriate with you on this couch."

She could see his expressions, each one as they crossed his face: disbelief, chagrin, and finally, surprising her, sadness. "I have only been thinking how much I enjoy this. I have made no seduction plans."

"Is not this how women are seduced?"

Oliver looked around the darkened room in the late night. "It is," he admitted, "but while I had hoped for the privacy, I had not intended to take *complete* advantage of it."

"No?" Reaching out, Cass used just one fingertip to touch the tiny frown in between his eyebrows that came and went. She stroked the sweep of one of his thick, dark brows, and when his bright eyes closed she felt pleased as well as emboldened.

She used the same fingertip to trace the bone of his cheek, then his jaw. Then she touched the ridge that led down the side of his neck, from just below one ear to where his skin disappeared beneath his neckcloth.

Impatient with its barrier to her investigations, Cass' fingers tugged at the knot in the cloth, the cool linen coming free in her hands so she could let it fall open.

As the fabric slid around his neck and away, baring the way his pulse was speeding up to her eyes, Oliver's eyes opened again and his gaze met hers.

"It would seem," and then he cleared his throat so he could continue, "it would seem that *you* have been sitting here thinking of ways to convince me to do something far more inappropriate with you on this couch."

Oh no. Had she lost her mind? Was this what happened when daydreams and reality came too close to one another? She had resolved to never be the least bit forward again, and here she was *undressing* him.

She was still trying to figure out how to flee the situation when Oliver added, "I have not been planning a seduction," he said, his fingers once again moving up to remove one of her hairpins, as if he could not help his attraction to the things, "but I am not averse to participating in one."

No. No, no, no. This was not where she could go, not again. She *would* not. When had her daydreaming mind turned into her lawless wandering fingers?

When they had kissed in the gallery she had felt just as alone as she expected to feel. That she had not wanted. This sense of sweet closeness to Oliver, she wanted this very much.

But she would not let it carry her away. She needed to at least to control herself. She might yet have some remaining shreds of her self-respect.

Cass shook her head, sliding away from him.

Casting about for some desperate shelter for her own embarrassment, her tone turned cool. "Very nice, how you make it my idea. Very clever."

Then a thought struck her. Her eyes opened wide. "*Very* clever. You... you have done this before."

CHAPTER 16

Oliver swallowed. "I told you that I had, Miss Cullen."

"*How often?*"

This was the moment Oliver had been putting off. Now that it was here, he wasn't ready.

He had no answer.

But something in his expression must have told her. Told her enough.

"So this is... what you do. You do this? A soft couch, a late fire, and there you are, having another woman?"

Oliver shook his head. "I believe there are still footmen awaiting us outside that open door, so this is hardly conducive to that level of seduction."

"What level of seduction would you say applies in this situation, Dr. Burke?"

He did not reply.

"I do see. This is ... this is how you treat women. How many women?" When he still didn't answer, she asked a bit brokenly, "*All* women?"

"No!" His denial was explosive, even as he kept his voice too low to attract any servants still remaining in the hall. He would be damned if he would go check. "Not all women, of course not."

"Lady Gadbury?"

That took the wind out of him more than slightly. "Well, yes."

He met her eyes.

She was—she could not think of the word. Angry? Of a sort. It was a curious mix of disappointment and cynicism along with it, if anger it was.

He didn't look guilty *or* angry, and she was not at all sure what she was supposed to do with this.

"I do not know the part I am to play." Cass was sitting straight now, feet on the floor and her hands clasped in her lap. "What do your women usually do?"

"It's not—They aren't—"

She waited for him to finish a sentence.

He could not.

"So." Cass swept one graceful hand in a small circle, indicating the whole room. "Have you had other women here?"

"What, here at Morland or in this room?"

Cass felt her jaw drop. "How many women have you seduced?"

"I do not keep a tally of women I have seduced, Miss Cullen. Nor do I count the ones who have seduced me."

"Lady Gadbury seduced you, I suppose."

"As a matter of fact, she did."

"And how many others?"

Leaning forward on his knees as he had when he had suggested that they marry, Oliver scrubbed both of his hands across his cheeks. When he looked at her again he looked old and tired.

"I did tell you, Miss Cullen, that marrying me would be a terrible idea."

The blunt reality of his expression crumbled something inside her. A dream was dashed wherein Cass could have worn, shown, *possessed* the bewitching Dr. Burke like a jewel. What pleasure could she take in gloating over her decoration in front of other women, knowing how likely it was that they had already worn it?

THE COUNTESS INVENTION

"But I am left to fill in the details, Dr. Burke. If I am understanding you correctly, your wife would not be able to visit a shop in London without tripping over one of your *affaires*."

"Oh come now!"

"Or did you limit your attentions to the ladies of the *ton*?"

"I rather did." Oliver sighed and dug his fingers into his own hair, freeing it from its bond.

Consciously or unconsciously, that was a move that was both unfair and illustrative. With his slightly tousled hair falling free over his shoulders, Oliver in the low firelight looked unutterably beautiful to Cass, like some alluring devil who had just climbed out of a bed.

Which apparently he had.

"So your wife would not be able to attend a society function without finding herself facing your *amours*. All of whom would know every intimate detail about you. All of whom would be imagining your hands on their skin, your taste—"

"Stop! They are not past loves. I didn't..." Flinging himself up off the couch, Oliver began to pace the carpet in front of her. "It was done as easily as pouring wine into a glass and then down my throat."

Cass felt her heart pounding now, but this time with an icy bitterness that seemed to chill her from the inside out. She was glad for it. It made it easier to look at him, made her glad to know what he was like. "Well, I do feel honored then, I suppose. After all, you have lost hours of valuable seduction time just now with me, learning language that will be unlikely to help you seduce more women. Unless you have your eye set on Peg, though if you do, I have to warn you she loves her husband."

"Don't." He didn't meet her eyes. "I... I thought I needed them."

"I hope it made you happier then, for a little while." Her clipped cold tone made it sound as though she wished for anything but. "If you had to take comfort, you took it."

"I didn't take. I promise."

He looked back up at her then, shaking his head. She didn't see, she didn't see at all.

"I swear I gave every one of those women more than I received. I swear it."

"What, money? Treating them like that, that is supposed to be a benefit? Your precious time? I promise you, sir, there is no amount of money that repays one for the sensation of being a hollow receptacle for a man's lust, and no amount of time taken that a woman would not have spent almost any other way."

Oliver just kept shaking his head. "I swear to you that was not what I did."

"You can keep your words to yourself and avoid being forsworn." The memory of the way he had seemed to drift away even as he was kissing her in the art gallery gave her a cold shiver. "You planned to do the same with me right now, didn't you?"

Cass didn't know why she felt so chilled, and Oliver didn't know why she had forgotten that it was she who had untied his neckcloth.

The same cloth that dangled loose around his neck right now.

He pulled it free, showed it to her, dangled it from his fingers. "Miss Cullen," he said, low but loud enough to reach her, "*I* was not planning a seduction."

At that Cass could not sit still a moment longer. She *threw* herself from the settee, intending to dash for the door.

"We are talking about very different things." Loud enough to reach her. He was still so close.

Wishing that she did not want to, Cass looked back at him, his body outlined in the orange glow of the fire.

"Miss Cullen," and Oliver moved close, so close that no one could possibly hear the words except for they two alone, "This is a time to tell me the truth if ever there was one."

That felt like a low blow. Cass had an urge to run. But he knew the truths she had not told anyone else, and she couldn't deny that. She could see it in his eyes, that he knew, he knew every time she had told him something that *wasn't* true, and he still trusted her to tell him the truth now.

She could *feel* his voice as he went on, "I think you should tell me what gave you such a low opinion of love."

"It isn't love!" She spit it out. Fine, if he wanted to hear it, she would say it. "There was nothing of love about it. I dreamed about him for months, *months*, writing long pages in my diary about his hair and his eyes and just everything, all on the basis of a few polite smiles and bows. When I invited him to my home he was shocked. When I propositioned him, even more so. But apparently a man doesn't turn down a free opportunity to bed a girl, and so he did. I don't think we had more than twenty words of conversation between us. It was a bit painful, so fortunately it was over quickly. The earaches I'd had as a child were more unpleasant. But I might truly as well have been asleep. He took his pleasure and climbed off and said he had to be leaving. That was the extent to which he touched me. He never even looked me in the eye.

"The second one was kinder. He was young, younger than I, and nervous. He smiled at me, at least, and his smiles were a little warmer than just polite. The castles I built on those smiles. I was sure that he was devoted to me, ready to carry me off to elope if need be to have me. Instead he was so excited when I kissed him that he nearly spent then. We could have saved the next ten minutes if he had. When he left he looked truly disappointed that I had accommodated him. Apparently women who truly love men do *not* engage in such activity with them. With a worldview like that, it honestly horrifies me that the world continues to be peopled.

"I know the truth the books lie about. I know what you did. Don't you believe for one minute that those women wanted that. I cannot believe any woman wants to feel so... so worthless."

As if the word had taken the last of her energy Cass sank back on the couch, lifting a shaking hand to her forehead.

She tried to catch her breath, wondering where all that bitter anger had come from. She had not felt angry at the time, and she would have said she had not felt angry since. She would have been wrong. She did feel angry, and it had just come flooding out.

In front of Oliver Burke.

He still had the orange glow of the firelight behind him, and he was not looking at her. He was standing and staring at the floor, his hair loose around his shoulders, his neckcloth gone and his collar unfastened, and she could swear she could see a muscle jumping in his clenched jaw.

"What are *you* angry about?" Cass asked without stopping to think. "At least my *affaires* do not number in the hundreds."

"Neither do mine." His response was curt. "I am angry because you were so poorly treated."

She shook her head. "I told you—"

"Please. Please do not insist again that you were not. I will go mad. That is what poor treatment *means*, Cassandra. You should never feel worthless."

He was standing over her now.

Warily she looked up at him. "That seems to be what the act entails."

"You spent more time trying to find attachment materials for an artificial leg."

Cass gasped. "How dare you!"

"I am only telling the truth when I say, as I have said many times, that I wish to accept your conclusions in all things. But this... misapprehension of yours is going too far. You must either accept the knowledge I have gained through greater experience, or you must continue to experiment."

"Your greater knowledge is not an attractive quality right now, Dr. Burke." She narrowed her eyes at him.

Oliver seemed to shrug that off. "Yet there it is. I know what you so disliked. Why do you not attempt to fix it? Like a rolling cart for a man with one leg?"

Cass opened her mouth to contradict him, then snapped it shut. Why *hadn't* she pursued a way to fix it? Isn't that what she did?

Not that she was one-legged. "I am not one-legged."

"I do not believe you are."

"In matters of pleasure."

"Cassandra." With the glow behind him she could barely see his eyes, but in the shadows they seemed to glitter. "I have never said that you were."

"So what..." She was having trouble working this new thought into her worldview. "What do you think I need in terms of a... ramp, or a rolling cart?"

"I do not think you need a ramp. I think that you need a much better lover."

"You."

"At the risk of being accused again of seduction... yes. Me."

Cass felt some of the air go out of her. "I like you too much to put you in that position."

At that, Oliver dropped to his knees just in front of her, his face unavoidably close to hers. She could see that his eyes looked like vast, churning oceans of emotion and he was looking at her. Only her.

He said, "I am willing."

Cass couldn't look at the raw emotion on his face. She covered her face with both hands and tried to even out her breathing.

When she looked out between her fingers, he was still there.

"Let me show you what you *don't* want."

"*How?*"

"Oh, I know what it is." Roughly Oliver pulled at his shirt buttons, baring more of his chest. She had expected it to have more hair. The more of his skin she could see peeking through the opening of the shirt, the more bare she felt herself.

Tossing his cufflinks on the floor, Oliver rolled up his shirtsleeves as well, exposing the corded muscles of his forearms and the slightly darker hair there.

Turning his head to the side he spread his arms, offering himself, nearly motionless. "This is what you don't want," he said.

Cass felt a little dizzy. The breadth of his chest, his arms, the strength of his neck, they practically screamed for her touch.

Before she had made any real decision, she found her fingers slipping through his open shirt to caress the skin of his chest.

Except for the tiniest clenching of muscles she knew he was using to keep still, Oliver remained motionless, his eyes on the floor.

Her hand curved around the base of his throat, toyed with the hair that fell down over the cool linen of his shirt.

He stayed still.

Delicately she let her fingertips trail up along the back of his hand. Nothing.

Boldly, Cass slid her fingers into the waistband of his trousers, pulling the rest of the shirt free there. The solid mass of his body felt hot to her touch.

But he did not move.

Moment by moment, Cass felt her own excitement trailing away, like the last of a wave on the beach. Her heart slowed, her breath came more calmly.

He stayed still, even though his arms were trembling with the effort.

Cass sat back.

"Who would want this?" Oliver rasped. "What kind of connection can two people have if nothing passes between them?"

"I could still..." Cass stopped, confused.

"You could still do anything you liked with my body. But you might as well be alone."

Surging up off the floor, Oliver wrapped his arms around Cass' waist, pulling her to the edge of the settee and fitting his body between her knees. Spreading his hands into her hair on both sides of her head, he said into her ear, "On the other hand, what if we speak? What if I tell you how I wish to kiss every inch of you from the tips of your toes to the tops of your ears?" One of his hands fitted itself to her waist, began sliding up her body as if he counted each one of her ribs. It stopped just cradling her breast. "What if I tell you how I wish to make love to you with my hands, with my mouth, with all of my body until you cry out for release? What if you tell me how it feels when I touch you here—"

Gently, one of Oliver's thumbs brushed her nipple.

Cass shook, nearly falling forward into his arms.

His voice was still there, breathing into her ear; his lips brushed her earlobe as he spoke. "Tell me. What else shall I do?"

She didn't know but she would bet her life that he did.

"You mean it is only that we did not speak."

"I very much mean it is that you did not speak. Without telling, without listening, it is indeed a hollow way to spend one's time."

"Words are not my strength, sir."

"I disagree. But even if that were so—" Oliver brushed her nipple again, never taking his eyes off hers. The intimacy of him watching her shiver made her insides hot all over again. "Even if you never said a word, Cassandra, you and I would have much to say to each other."

She could feel herself melting into this couch, into his arms, soon, all too soon, perhaps on to the floor. This demonstration had gone far enough, at least for her sanity. "I concede your point."

Oliver went still all over, then reluctantly, slowly, took his hands from her hair, her face, her body.

Sitting back on his heels, he looked up at her.

Cass smoothed one trembling hand over her hair, but she kept her eyes on the walls. "Surely that is enough of a demonstration of your understanding of a woman's needs."

"For this room, for now," and Oliver glanced meaningfully toward the door.

"You think we will *continue* this later?"

"Miss Cullen, you now have all the reasons why you should *not* marry me. I believe more strongly than I ever have that you *should*. I can make my case more convincing at any time."

Why did that sound equal parts dangerous and enticing?

She took a deep breath. "I think without a map of your former flames, so that I could plan my routes through London accordingly, I cannot make a proper decision."

That made Oliver chuckle. Cass was relieved by how much it broke the tension in the room. She was exhausted.

Heavens, was that the sky lightening in the distance through that window?

Oliver shook his head. "I cannot provide you with such a map, but I can promise, or rather I would promise, that all its landmarks would be only of historical interest. My future attention would be all yours."

My future attention would be all yours. When Oliver had first suggested the idea of marriage, Cass had only felt disappointed. The promise that his future attention would be all hers, on the other hand, sounded glorious.

But she said, "That sounds like quite a game of chance, for a woman to decide that now you have had your fill of other women and can promise future fidelity."

"I have already decided it." Oliver looked at her for a moment in thought, then reached over to the floor to pick up his cuff-links and slide them in a pocket.

Just that small thing kept Cass on a knife's edge at the thought of committing to him so entirely. The way his body moved, and the firm swell of muscle she could see through his open shirt as he did, almost made her mouth water. But the casual way he retrieved his belongings from where he had tossed them in undressing made her think that he must have done this many, many times before.

He said, "At least all our secrets are laid bare between us. You have only to pursue my proposal, or not."

He too looked over at the windows lining the wall of the library and saw where a sliver of yellow light was appearing over the horizon. "We haven't stayed here all night, have we?"

Cass just threw her hands up in the air. "I have no more contradiction in me, Dr. Burke. It appears that we have."

CHAPTER 17

Safely returned to her chambers, Cass was wondering how she would get out of this dress by herself when she caught sight of a lumpy form underneath a coverlet on the settee.

Oliver had silently escorted her here and bowed as they parted. He was gone. She didn't know what *this* was.

She still didn't know what she was thinking or feeling, the insides of her head were so jumbled up, but the lumpy coverlet stopped her thoughts cold.

Approaching it, she poked it.

It moved.

Cass was still deciding whether to yank it off or run when a hand appeared.

Then two.

Cass' jaw dropped open. *What are you doing here?*

Peg did not look like she wanted to report on the entire story. *I needed a place to sleep.*

Why aren't you in the servants' quarters?

They aren't open.

Cass shook her head a little. *How could they not be open? The house is filled with staff.*

Peg made several faces, blowing out her cheeks, looking up and down and all around without meeting Cass' eyes, but Cass simply asked again.

How could they not be open?

They don't seem to be open to me.

Cass' blood literally ran cold. She felt the chill under her skin, freezing her.

Why? She was not letting this go.

Peg just shrugged. She yawned and straightened her legs. She had slept curled up on the settee, in her clothes.

Seems that the housekeeper didn't like the look of me. One of the footmen offered to find me a warm spot in the stables but I don't know him! I thought I'd simply better stay here.

Didn't like the look of you. Cass' eyes took in every aspect of Peg's clothes, from her spotless cap to her stockings, rumpled though she now was.

Don't make me say it, all right? She didn't want a deaf girl in the servants' quarters. You know it gives some people the willies.

As much of the willies as it gives me knowing you might have slept in the stables? This is appalling treatment of a guest.

Let it go, Cass, Peg said with a warning look. *We're not here to cause trouble for a countess.*

We're not here to be abused by one, either. Cass gave Peg a measuring look. *And you said it was the housekeeper who didn't like the look of you.*

Peg's motionlessness told Cass everything she needed to know.

Taking a deep breath, Cass looked around the room.

The first dim light of an autumn day was creeping into the room. She needed to change out of this evening gown, then she needed to sleep, at least a little. Then she would deal with her hostess.

Turning back she said, *Why didn't you at least sleep in the bed?*

Blinking, Peg said, *I don't know.*

They both laughed.

I thought you might be back at any moment.

Then Peg's eyes got large.

Say, where were you all night?

I need some sleep, was all Cass said as she bent to slide off her slippers, having no intention of divulging any further details to Peg.

Cass wanted a little more time to think over the evening. The night.

Dr. Burke had made many persuasive arguments. Were they merely the arguments of an accomplished rake? Or could she trust the feeling she had that he had crossed some bridge with her? Perhaps *for* her?

* * *

"My lord, Lady Sherrin isn't feeling well and wonders if you'd attend her."

Scrubbing a hand over his face, Oliver glared with one eye at the sunlight streaming in through the many-cornered window panes. Then at the man inside his chamber door. Then back at the sunlight.

Had he really left Miss Cullen at her own chamber door just a few hours ago?

It was so unlike him.

And he so wanted to see her again. For as long as she would have him.

"I am sorry to disturb you, my lord," said the footman with nearly a suitable level of apology, Oliver thought, for rattling a man rudely awake after a few hours' sleep.

Well, more than a few, he had to admit as he dressed and scraped back his hair. By the light, it was noon, or nearly.

He had just barely been introduced to Lady Sherrin, but she'd seemed healthy enough. A friend of Lady Gadbury's, about the same age and from the same part of London.

When she called "come in" to Oliver's knock, he realized he should have checked with Lady Gadbury before so naively presenting himself here.

Or a solicitor, or perhaps a bishop or something.

"My lady," he said, bowing slightly to the woman seated inside, who was wearing a fine white nightrail consisting mostly of lace, with a wrapper of even more transparent lace thrown over it. "I was given to understand that you were urgently unwell."

"Only mildly, Dr. Burke. Or should I say Lord Howiston? How have I never heard your title before Lady Gadbury informed me?" The lady's dark hair lay loose around her shoulders; her eyes dipped down then back up to look coyly at him. She had a lush figure and he could see nearly all of it.

Oliver was not in the mood for whatever this was.

"Because we do not know each other, Lady Sherrin. Dr. Burke is fine."

Rather than take the chair she offered, he strode to her and abruptly took her wrist, began taking her pulse.

In half a minute he retreated to a safe five paces away.

"You seem in good color, Lady Sherrin," Oliver said, "with a strong pulse, no labor in your breathing. What causes you to send for me?"

That lady seemed taken aback by his abruptness, opening and closing her mouth several times before managing to squeak out, "I'm terribly lonely, Dr. Burke."

Wonderful. Fantastic. Perfect. This was what he needed to make this house party complete.

"Lady Sherrin," Oliver exaggerated each syllable to put a very clear verbal distance between them, "did someone put you up to this?"

"No! I don't know what you mean by put up. Lady Gadbury did say that... that... that you were no longer her... well, that you were in need of new female company. Tired. Of her, I mean."

"So charming. Lady Sherrin." Oliver bowed again. "You are a lovely woman and I thank you for the compliment. I am not in need of new female company. Nor do I ask old friends to find company for me."

"Oh, she didn't—! I mean." This grown woman was stammering, a blush climbing to her hairline and both hands pulling the lace tightly closed as her rejection progressed. "She didn't tell me to do anything. She did say that you would likely be amenable."

"Did she. Flattering." Oliver was considering feeling angry as well as affronted. "I'm not that amenable."

"Well, you could hardly expect me to know that," said Lady Sherrin, finally snapping a little as she tried to press the lace nightrail higher around her neck. "That is not what I have heard."

"Excuse me?"

"In London, doctor. My understanding is that you're entirely amenable." She shrugged a shoulder. "To anyone."

It was the careless little shrug that knocked the breath out of him a little, that shrug as much as the "anyone".

"Well then." He was having a bit of trouble drawing enough breath to speak loudly. "Please do me a favor, Lady Sherrin, and correct that misapprehension in any future conversations you have about the topic." His glare, however, was forceful, and icy. "To anyone."

"I will, sir," she said faintly, although she was already speaking to his retreating back.

Except that he stopped just beyond her doorway.

Lady Sherrin could see out past the outline of his shoulder to where Cassandra Cullen, in a very becoming pale blue day dress, was standing in the hallway, staring at Oliver.

CHAPTER 18

"Dr. Burke," Cass nodded to him.

Oliver's eyes grew wide with sheer panic.

He had dreamt about her, literally dreamt about the scent of her skin, and here she was seeing him coming out of Lady Sherrin's room like this.

Oliver half-turned to see if Lady Sherrin and her cleavage and her damned lacy nightrail were visible from the hallway.

They were.

Muttering curses he had only ever heard, and used, in the army, Oliver pulled Lady Sherrin's door shut.

"Good morning," said Cass, and was that something of a smile playing about the corners of her mouth?

Oliver stepped close. "I hope you understand that Lady Sherrin called upon me purely as a medical man this morning."

"I see. What time was that? And what have you been doing since then? Since it is nearly noon now."

"Miss Cullen..." groaned Oliver.

"Will she survive, do you think?" The smile was definitely being suppressed.

Oliver's eyes narrowed. "You're toying with me."

"And enjoying it."

Oliver let out a huge sigh.

Cass wasn't ready to quit. "Does this happen to you often, losing several hours in the company of a suddenly very healthy lady patient?"

Oliver's mouth immediately shaped to say "no", then he remembered the last summons of Lady Gadbury, back in London. Well, she hadn't claimed to be ill. At least, he'd known perfectly well that she wasn't.

When he didn't immediately say the "no", though, Cass' lurking smile slipped away a little.

"The occasional misunderstanding happens for any number of reasons," Oliver said, leaning close to make sure she could hear him. "May I accompany you to luncheon?"

"I am looking for Lady Rawleigh, actually," said Cass, looking a little uncertainly back toward Lady Sherrin's door though surely she must know Lady Rawleigh would not be in there.

"You can look all you like but I doubt you will see her for a while yet," Oliver assured her, taking her hand again and tucking it into the crook of his arm to show her the way.

* * *

THE LOOK on Oliver's face when he saw her coming out of Lady Sherrin's room had mostly been hilarious.

He was so obviously caught, and doing nothing. Leaving. The lady was sitting right in the room, clearly inappropriately attired, but also sitting upright, hardly lying ravished on the bed.

But the more Cass thought about it the less it amused her. Oliver was clearly annoyed about something, and she thought back to their discussion about their previous *amours*.

Not loves. Bedding, she thought as crudely as she could put it to herself. He had referred to making love, but not to any feelings, for anyone. He had admitted to bedding women, just as she had admitted to bedding men.

Perhaps it was just reflexive for him. Perhaps he just did it out of habit.

She wished that he had brought up the topic of love at least once.

She had to put it out of her mind. Turning it over and over again in her head wouldn't change it either way.

Oliver was greeting someone. "Ah, Lord Faircombe. How nice of you to visit us, and I see you've brought your son. Only one this time?"

The luncheon room seemed filled with broad shoulders and blond hair.

"Just the one," boomed the big man as he rose and bowed to Oliver. "Grantham's taking care of some business for me in the city, but Frederick may be here later. Geoffrey just rode over with us. He hasn't anything to do," said the Marquess with a careless flick of his hand.

Young Geoffrey blushed a little which was a bit out of place on someone who had so clearly inherited his father's shoulders. "Thank you," he said in a restrained way to Oliver, bowing to him as well. "And you recall my sister, Lady Charlotte."

"Lady Charlotte! No! I remember you being very small indeed," said Oliver with a slight smile, as that young lady also rose and curtseyed to him.

Lady Charlotte was as tall and athletic as the rest of her family, though with golden brown hair rather than Geoffrey's paler color.

Oliver's smile seemed to hit her rather like a bullet. If the young lady had had anything to say by way of greeting, it had been knocked cleanly out of her head by his smile.

Cass considered rolling her eyes, but she was determined to make a success of herself this weekend. "Lady Charlotte," she said, curtseying most properly to Charlotte Eliot, Lord Faircombe's daughter.

"Yes, this is Miss Cassandra Cullen, from London," said Oliver, rather proudly presenting Cass.

Lady Charlotte seemed to be taking all of Cass' measurements with her eyes, Cass thought. Perhaps to fit her for a coffin.

But Cass just turned and took the hand of the last occupant of the room, almost so small as to be missed. "And you must be Miss Delina Farsworth."

The young lady dimpled visibly. "So nice to be known," she said, and the smile reached her eyes and was warm.

"And Lady Inglemawr!" Cass was surprised to see her there, bottle-green sarcenet dress in perfect order, as was her riot of Titian curls.

Lady Inglemawr seemed to flush slightly but she just waved her knife at the table. "Do eat," she said ungraciously, as if forestalling further conversation about where she had been since they arrived at Morland yesterday afternoon.

The available dishes were laid out on a sideboard, and by the time she had selected herself something, Cass had turned to the table to find that Lady Charlotte was setting a filled plate on the table at a seat next to her own and gesturing for Oliver to sit.

That gentleman cast Cass an apologetic look, but he took the young lady's invitation.

Leaving Cass to take a seat next to the young blond giant.

"Does Lord Howiston enjoy horseriding?" Geoffrey asked her as she sat.

He had the voice of a strapping young country lad, and from a distance easily measured in inches, she had no trouble hearing him at all.

"Lord Howiston. Oh, Dr. Burke. Not that I am aware, but we do not know each other well. Has Lady Rawleigh been here?"

"Not at all." The young man sounded definite. "Well, if Lord Howiston doesn't care for horses, my sister will give up on him soon enough, don't worry."

Cass turned to look at the young man calmly opening an egg.

"Why should I worry?"

The look Geoffrey turned to her was one very different from what one might expect to see on a lumbering country lad, and quite at odds, too, with the dismissive way his father had introduced him. Geoffrey was bright, and Geoffrey had seen the way Oliver had looked at her.

And he must have seen Cass look back at Oliver.

"My sister," the young man said, softly enough not to carry far but still loud enough to hear, if only barely loud enough for Cass, "my sister still thinks for some reason that she is just about to locate the

JUDITH LYNNE

perfect husband. It hasn't happened in five years and it won't happen now. She gets excited when we are invited to a new place, that is all. And I believe she is impressed by Morland."

Cass looked around at the papered walls and polished walnut. "Morland is impressive."

Geoffrey shrugged, which was a serious business in one so broad. Lord Faircombe and Lady Charlotte began a conversation about breeding hunting horses, trying very hard between them to draw Oliver into it.

Good luck with that, Cass thought.

* * *

CASS HAD LEFT before Oliver could extract himself from the hunting conversation.

"And will you be shooting today? Pheasant?" He was speaking to the Faircombe father and daughter but his eyes followed Cass. Miss Farsworth rose along with Cass, and spoke to her, and the two left together.

"Of course pheasant," Lord Faircombe said while still masticating a bit of porridge. "Charlotte doesn't care for killing foxes."

"Do you not, Lady Charlotte?" Oliver was surprised enough to ask the question.

"I don't," she said, almost biting it out. "They don't deserve it."

Well, there was some grudge there Lady Charlotte was holding about fox hunting, but Oliver wasn't interested enough to begin a whole conversation about it.

He was about to excuse himself and follow Cass—there was something about her expression as she'd sat and talked to Geoffrey that had bothered him—when a footman interrupted him with a card. "My lord."

So Oliver had to excuse himself from the table anyway, just to head to the downstairs parlor rather than follow Cass as he would have liked.

"Mr. Hastings. What an unexpected pleasure."

The sour look on Hastings' face made it clear that this visit was anything but a pleasure. "Mail coaches, Dr. Burke. Mail. Coaches."

"You must have been in a hurry. Have we offered you any refreshment? Please," he said, turning to the footman, "bring any number of hot and cold refreshments here to Mr. Hastings. And his friend."

The footman bowed and withdrew.

"So, introduce me."

Anthony seemed at least somewhat mollified by Oliver's businesslike approach. "This is David Castle, of the Institute for the Deaf in London."

The young man accompanying Anthony Hastings looked barely old enough to be out of the schoolroom himself. He was a sunny looking lad, with blue eyes and short gold hair, too short to be fashionable. Oliver wondered if he were a teacher or a student.

Are you deaf? Oliver asked him.

Mr. Castle's eyes lit up as if by candles.

No, he said in return, *but I am a teacher and have learned some of the manual language, from Miss Cullen in fact.*

"I apologize, I mostly understood only the *no,*" said Oliver.

"Miss Cullen is an excellent teacher," David Castle told him, still with the same broad grin.

"Indeed she must be," remarked Anthony thoughtfully. "So you took my advice and asked her what you wanted to know."

"Somewhat."

"Meaning?"

"We only spoke a few days ago, man, there hasn't been time to discuss everything I would like."

Anthony's eyebrows raised. "How much do you need to discuss?"

Oliver wasn't about to tell this annoying whippersnapper that there was a good deal to discuss.

"Mr. Hastings. I can only assume you have traveled here with such urgency for an important reason."

"Indeed. One was to bring you Mr. Castle as a teacher, which you may not need, clearly." Anthony didn't seem particularly disturbed by the uselessness of that errand. He shook out one of his wet gloves.

"The other was to bring you the answer to the more urgent question we discussed."

"What? Oh. Oh yes." Belatedly, Oliver remembered the question of Lady Inglemawr's sudden interest in chaperoning Cass, and vehemently. "And Mr. Castle should stay for this?"

Anthony was unperturbed. "Mr. Castle is the crux of the answer."

The young man shook his golden head. "I happen to *know* the answer, that is all."

Oliver stared at him. And stared some more.

And finally said, "Well, what is it?"

The young man jumped in his chair.

"Oh! Ah. Lady Inglemawr, uh, has a lover."

Oliver just looked at Anthony.

Who shrugged. "It is always the most obvious answer."

Desperately hoping this was nothing to do with Cass' father, or anything that would hurt her, Oliver prodded again. "The Duke of Talbourne, I suppose? Out with it, man!"

"No, actually." The young man looked to Hastings, whose expression was impassive, before he finally brought himself to go on. "Actually, it's one of the Duke of Talbourne's... footmen."

Oliver gaped.

He was going to do something about his open mouth, he really had had too little sleep.

"A footman. You are serious."

David Castle just nodded, his blue eyes somber. "Deadly serious. It is a lad named Phineas Sayre, and it has been going on for at least a year."

Oliver blinked. "I can't take a name like Phineas Sayre seriously."

"You do not have to." Anthony had rested his hands on top of one another across his knee, his wet glove dangling from his fingertips. "I followed up and confirmed. Nearly no one knows."

"How do *you* know?" Oliver prodded David.

"Lady Inglemawr has accompanied Miss Cullen to the Institute several times. They use a hired carriage, but I noticed that there was the same footman with them at least twice. Lady Inglemawr disappeared soon after arriving, and when Miss Cullen asked me to find her, I found... them... in a... well, in an... embrace. In a laundry closet."

Anthony didn't pause to let them all consider the implications of a laundry closet. "There are a few people assuming that the Duke of Talbourne is having an *affaire* with Lady Inglemawr, and absolutely *no* one cares about that except a few people who are hoping to use it against Talbourne. But it's definitely this Phineas lad she's going to see."

Oliver shook his head, squeezing his eyes shut; he didn't want to know. "How much of a lad?"

Anthony looked like he wanted to take pity on Oliver. "He's at least twenty."

"Good God." Oliver liked to think himself unshakeable but found that he could still be surprised. "She's at least forty."

Anthony shrugged, and if there were some inclination to smile somewhere inside the dour young man, it seemed to be fighting to get out. "There are many who would say, well done her. And many who would say, well done him."

"This is appalling. This will do horrendous damage to Miss Cullen's reputation if it gets out."

Anthony leveled a glance at Oliver for that one. They both knew that Miss Cullen's reputation was in at least as much damage from Oliver as from anyone else.

Oliver frowned. "You know what I mean."

Mr. Castle, sweet young man that he was, seemed more concerned about Miss Cullen than anything else. "What can I do to help? Miss Cullen has never been anything but nice to me."

That made Oliver perk up his ears. "How nice?"

"Settle, doctor," Anthony cut him off. "I have interviewed the fair young Mr. Castle already. You have nothing to fear from that quarter."

And unaccountably, the young man actually blushed. Apparently even being accused of romantic involvement with Miss Cullen was too much for his delicate constitution.

Oliver shook himself. Morland made him melancholy and he

needed more time with Cass and less time on ridiculous business like this.

But Anthony Hastings had clearly gone to quite a bit of trouble to tell him this.

And he truly did need to know it.

"So I suppose when she disappears, she has a way to spend some time somewhere with her light o' love."

Anthony nodded. "They have a few rooms," and he named the neighborhood. "She doesn't come out for days."

"Impressive," muttered Oliver.

David blushed again.

"Mr. Castle, forgive this indelicate conversation. Anthony, I don't know what to do about this. Lady Inglemawr has until lately been a most liberal chaperone. Obviously if Miss Cullen is married, she loses her opportunity to stay in Miss Cullen's house yet disappear with someone else's footman every so often. This does seem to explain my sudden expulsion from the house. Does His Grace know about this?"

Anthony shook his head. "To the best of my knowledge, he does not."

Oliver was coming to feel that Anthony's knowledge seemed like a solid foundation on which to bet. "So His Grace still comes to visit for some other reason?"

That also interested Anthony. The man was like a bloodhound for gossip. "How often does he visit? Is he also courting Miss Cullen?"

David Castle's eyes lit up. "You are courting Miss Cullen?"

Heaven save him from innocent young men. "As best I can," Oliver admitted. "Nonetheless. The problem I was mentioning was that Lady Inglemawr has a clear reason to be opposed to her marrying at all. No wonder I was turned out of the house."

"You were turned out of the house?"

"Are you a relative of Anthony's?" Oliver quelled young Mr. Castle with one more glare before turning back to Anthony himself. "I'm going to have to tell Lady Inglemawr that I know."

Anthony didn't argue, just said, "A cornered mouse will kill a snake."

Oliver nodded. "Would you like to stay for this godforsaken house party?"

"I wouldn't miss it," enthused David like a small child.

Anthony shook the wet glove again. "I intend to bathe and become quite, quite dry before I venture outdoors again. If attending a house party accomplishes that, I may do so."

"Thank you." Then before his guests could think he was thanking them for accepting his invitation—though the way Anthony said it made it seem as though he were indeed granting Oliver a favor by accepting—Oliver added, "Thank you for all of this."

"It is not much. Don't forget, Mr. Castle is your present."

"If you would like to learn more of the manual language, sir," added the young man quickly.

"I would. I am hoping still that Miss Cullen will deign to give me a little more instruction."

CHAPTER 19

Cass made sure to make a deep, deep curtsey and let Lady Rawleigh begin speaking first.

That courtesy proved a challenge, as it was several minutes before she ascertained a break in the flow of words, which had all been about carpets, as near as she could tell.

"Lady Rawleigh, I wanted to ask about my maid."

"Yes, Miss Cullen?"

Lady Rawleigh already looked annoyed at the change of topic, the ruffles edging the front of her gown seeming to bristle, so Cass pressed on as quickly as she could.

"My maid was not given quarters last night."

"What's that?"

"Quarters. A room. For my maid."

"I do not even know what that means."

Cass began to wonder which of them was hard of hearing.

"My maid presented herself downstairs last evening but was told there was no space for her in the servants' quarters. Her choice was to spend the night in the stables or stay in my chamber with me."

"Yes, what of it?"

Cass was confused. "Is there a shortage of rooms at Morland, my lady?"

"Of course not! What a preposterous idea." Now the ruffles were bristling all over Lady Rawleigh's gown, and trembling with indignation. "Morland is quite large, as you can see for yourself."

"Why turn away a maid for lodging, then?"

"We are not a lodging house, Miss Cullen," and Lady Rawleigh's tone got even frostier.

Cass was watching her lips very, very carefully and standing as close as she felt she could dare. She still missed a word here and there, but this was making even less sense to her than that explained.

"Of course not," and Cass felt it would be wise to bob her head again in a small curtsey. "I'm only wondering why a room could not be found for my maid."

"Do you have any idea of the expense of these house parties, young woman? People descend from all over as soon as you open your doors —two more men from London this morning, and I assure you that was not at my invitation! And everyone has horses that must be fed and stabled, and the men who look after them, maids, hairdressers, coachmen—I expect gardeners will be next. Lady Tratterton brought her cook with her last year, can you imagine? As if my home could not provide her with decent food! What an insult. And every—"

"Excuse me, Lady Rawleigh, I did not know," said Cass quietly. Luncheon had been undercooked toast and overcooked eggs and porridge. Cass did not know Lady Tratterton but applauded her initiative. "So there were other staff who could not be housed last night?"

Lady Rawleigh's eyes glittered in her round face and she stood up from her chair. Which hardly made a difference in her height, but conveyed a certain menace nonetheless.

"Miss Cullen," she bit out. "I am not accustomed to interruptions."

"Of course not. My sincere apologies," said Cass, bobbing her head again. It was clear enough that the Countess was not accustomed to interruptions. "You must be so busy, hosting such a large party. I only wanted to take my small problem away and not bother you anymore."

The idea of not being bothered any more seemed to appeal to Lady

Rawleigh enough. "Very well, you may go."

Ugh. Cass knew she had been dismissed. But her question hadn't been answered at all.

Perhaps if she tried a different approach.

"If you did not know of the mistake last evening, my lady, perhaps you will direct me to the person in your household who could repair it for me. Your housekeeper, perhaps?"

Lady Rawleigh waved a hand and was clearly past ready to return to the teacup waiting next to her chair. "My housekeeper let me know that there was no space and I quite agreed with her."

Now beyond confused, Cass asked the only question that still occurred to her to ask. "Why?"

"It upsets the staff to put sick people in among them, and I cannot have my staff complaining. We are all put to our limits this week-end."

Cass refrained from mentioning that the only difficult limit that appeared to be facing Lady Rawleigh at the moment was the teacup that still awaited her ladyship's attention.

"My maid is not sick, your ladyship. I am sorry for the misunderstanding."

"Well, she is not well, is she? Cannot talk, and staring at everyone all the time. Like you are staring at me. It is distressing at the very least."

Cass at this moment had no intention of taking her eyes off Lady Rawleigh. She needed to make sure she had every word correct.

"I do apologize," she said, not meaning it at all. "So you and your housekeeper took it upon yourselves to banish my maid from the house."

"Not at all. What an idea, young woman! And what a tone. The girl is welcome to stay in your chamber, if you insist on having her here." And now Lady Rawleigh's eyes glittered as hard and sharp as her diamonds. "As are you."

"Yes, I see," said Cass with a careless calm that she did not feel. She was shaking all over, she was so angry; she hoped it did not show. "Well, you are clearly very busy. I am sorry to interrupt you."

Lady Rawleigh's eyes narrowed. "I do not like sarcasm either, young woman."

"That *is* a shame, Lady Rawleigh," Cass said with a great deal of fake sympathy, and curtsied one more time, deeply, before she withdrew.

* * *

CASS WAS SO angry her hands were shaking still as she explained the situation to Peg, back in her chambers.

Peg, to her surprise, was mostly just philosophical.

It's not the first time something like this has happened to me, Peg said. *You've got your father and your money to make sure it doesn't happen to you.*

But it is happening to me, Cass thought, but didn't say it.

Instead she said, *It is beyond rude. I don't even know words for what to call it.*

Peg shrugged. She looked a bit thin and frail in her clothes, thought Cass. Cass could imagine her, on the streets of London as a child, with people shouting at her just because she couldn't understand them. She knew all that and worse had happened to Peg as a child, and perhaps this wasn't as bad as that.

But it wasn't better.

She does not like me, that is one thing. But to take that out on you!

Peg just shook her head. *Don't you believe it. She's just like that. She's not thinking of you, or me, or anyone.*

Cass wasn't so sure about that.

Of course you must stay here till we leave, she said firmly, making sure Peg understood.

I understand. It's a big bed. It's fine. Peg gave her a sly look. *If indeed you will be sharing it with me at all. Or are you going to be out all night again tonight?*

Cass just shook her head, frowning.

Peg laughed but gave Cass a pointed look as well. *You're in a lot more danger than I am, old friend.*

Cass wanted to argue about that, but then from the corner of her eye she caught some sort of commotion outside.

A wagon was pulling up the drive to Morland, followed by several riders on horses.

Now what, Cass motioned, exasperated. *I'll be back*, she added before heading downstairs to look.

* * *

"The hunting party needs a medical man, my lord," said the footman apologetically.

Oliver didn't question it, just rolled from his bed where he was attempting to catch up on a little more sleep but had been kept awake by wondering what to do about Lady Inglemawr and her lover.

Running down the stairs and out the front door without his coat, he was confronted with the sight of...

Lady Charlotte Eliot lying in the back of a wagon.

Her midnight blue riding habit was just pulled up slightly so that he could see her well-turned calves disappearing into her fetching little boots.

"Oh for the love of—"

"I am so glad you are here, my lord," Lady Charlotte said demurely, her thick dark lashes fluttering against her cheek. "I am in such pain."

"So am I," announced her friend Delina with open annoyance, and Oliver reached up to help Delina hop down from the wagon where she had been riding with Charlotte.

Geoffrey too wore a look of mostly disgust as he strode up to the wagon. "My sister was unhorsed and turned an ankle badly when she landed. Is that right, Charlotte?"

"True," and again Charlotte looked downward demurely. If she was in pain, it was very fetchingly arranged pain.

Delina just folded her lips with disapproval.

Charlotte held out her hands. "I cannot walk," she said, quietly, but piteously. "Perhaps you could carry me in?"

She was very clearly and directly addressing Oliver, and everyone knew it.

"Of course," said Geoffrey cheerfully, reaching into the wagon and effortlessly hoisting his sister into his arms.

"Thank you," said Charlotte between her teeth, and Oliver thought he saw Charlotte pinch her brother.

Rather hard.

"I shall follow you," Oliver said, moving out of the way so Geoffrey could carry Charlotte in.

"I say," said his friend Bradley Waite, coming up behind him. "I thought you said no ladies."

"Not that one," Oliver confirmed quietly. Her brother seemed to be handling her well enough for the moment. At least she hadn't enrolled him in her scheme. "Where's Lord Faircombe?"

Waite snorted. "When there are still pheasant to be shot? You think he would stop for a daughter's turned ankle?"

"You look surprisingly well," Oliver told him, suddenly realizing that for the first time in years, Waite didn't look either drunk or hung over from being drunk.

"I like the country air," Waite shrugged. "But then I'm in no danger. If you get out of this weekend unbetrothed, it will be because you are heavily armed. I suggest pistols."

"Not that one," was all Oliver said as he went inside to check on his so-called patient.

Of course who should he see coming down the stairs as he went in, but Cass.

"Is everyone well?" she said with genuine concern.

Inwardly sighing, he gestured that she might accompany him if she wished. When she drew close enough he added, "Nothing serious. Lady Charlotte may have turned an ankle."

Cass' concern turned to amusement in a heartbeat. "Oh dear. Was she wearing a lace nightrail when it happened?"

Behind them Waite burst out laughing, and he didn't stop when Oliver turned to give him a cutting look.

"Let's all attend Lady Charlotte," Cass said, managing to keep a nearly-serious look on her face as she gestured down the hallway to both gentlemen.

Oliver very, very, *very* badly wanted to kiss her.

CHAPTER 20

Cass expected to begin dressing when she returned to her chamber. Peg was in a tizzy over what to do with her hair.

Instead, she got quite a pleasant surprise in her sitting-room.

"Why David!" she exclaimed, putting out both hands.

As he grasped them warmly, she caught sight of a thin dark fellow lurking in the corner. "I mean, Mr. Castle," she said immediately.

David laughed and, freeing his hands, said, *What a pleasure to see you again!*

It was so good to see one more familiar, friendly face that Cass felt herself in danger of overflowing with emotion.

The presence of the stranger helped.

Introduce me to your friend?

"Miss Cullen," David Castle said out loud, "this is Mr. Anthony Hastings. I've only accompanied him up here on an errand."

"Very kindly too," said the thin man, and coming forward, bowed low over Cass' hand. She could easily imagine him wearing a sword at his side for some reason. The smile reached his eyes, and Cass returned it.

Mr. Hastings went on, "We had conducted some business with Dr.

Burke previously, and are taking advantage of the hospitality of Morland before we head home."

"Such as it is," Cass said dryly before she could stop herself.

Anthony Hastings' dark eyes crinkled again.

"But you must stay for this evening! Meet the rest of the party. At least after dinner. You must."

"I have nothing to wear and am not accustomed to such titled company," David said immediately. "No, thank you."

"I believe I will," said Anthony, surprising her. "We have a mutual acquaintance, Miss Cullen, in Lady Grantley, my sister, and her husband Sir Michael Grantley."

"That is wonderful! I wish they were here themselves."

"They are very fond of you, miss, and I know they will be interested in a full report on the proceedings."

Cass paused, then said delicately, "So you know how we know each other?"

"Indeed, miss, and if I did not Mr. Castle would have enlightened me on the trip up here. He had very few topics of conversation other than your inventiveness and the things you have built for the benefactors of the Institute."

Rolling her eyes just slightly, Cass turned over her shoulder to cast an admonishing look at David. "Please stop praising me! My father has not given up the idea of my marrying into the gentry, and he would be so disappointed if word travelled about what I do."

"Never a word." David mimicked locking his mouth with a key. "In fact, even more reason for me not to join the party tonight, as keeping secrets is not my best quality."

Anthony added nothing to that, only watching David closely as he hugged Cass.

Cass added, "I imagine you are the unexpected guests arrived from London just this morning. And you have rooms assigned to you."

"Yes—is it so surprising?"

Cass just shook her head.

Ringing a bell, she waited until a footman appeared in her door, and beckoned him closer.

"These gentlemen have rooms, do they not?"

"Yes miss," the footman affirmed.

Of course they did. Cass clamped a tight lid on the bitterness that threatened to show on her face. "There is a footman I spoke to last night, just outside the dining hall; I want to make sure Mr. Castle gets to meet him."

The footman hesitated.

"What is it?" asked Cass.

The footman could not have been eighteen years old; he was young, his livery sat uneasily upon his rather scrawny frame, and he was clearly deciding what he could and could not say. Cass could practically see the gears turning in his head.

"What?" This time she demanded her answer.

"That was Reggie, miss," said the young footman, "he was the one what spoke to you last night. He was let go today, miss."

Cass froze.

"What?" she said again.

She made him repeat it, slowly and loudly, so she could make sure she didn't have a word wrong.

"Why was he turned away from his post?"

The young footman was even more reluctant to report this. "It's as much as my own post is worth, miss."

"Answer her, young man, we will sort it out," said Anthony, appearing immediately over her shoulder.

"Her ladyship saw him break rank last night and... do something with you. He's not supposed to move except on an errand and he's not supposed to talk with the guests."

"He spoke to you?" Anthony directed the question at Cass.

"Yes," she said faintly. "Yes he did."

Looking back into the room, her eyes met the shocked blue eyes of David Castle.

I spoke to him, she said, unable to keep the pain out of her expression.

What, with your hands? David looked surprised.

Yes. He has a brother at the school, a little brother. I never even found out the boy's name. I wanted to ask him, I wanted to talk more with him. He was a friendly face when—I needed a friendly face so badly and he was there. It meant the world to me right then.

David Castle's boyish face hardened into surprisingly harsh lines.

Anthony was questioning the footman further. What was his name? What was the full name of the footman who had been let go? What was the name of the head of staff who had given him notice? Anthony seemed to have a method for interrogation once he got started.

Cass interrupted him with only one question of her own. "Did her ladyship know?"

This lad, who called himself Fred, clearly wished he had given up this conversation long ago, but there was no way of ducking out of it now, not with three London people staring at him and the young lady pushing him.

"Her ladyship insists on having final say in any staff being hired or fired," Fred admitted.

Cass nodded.

Something in her spine tightened. She could feel herself drawing up. Perhaps this was what men felt like, she thought, before they began a fistfight.

She said, "Mr. Hastings, I could use more staff at my home in London, and my father is always looking for good men at his many business concerns. Could I entreat you to arrange to find the young man who has been let go and escort him to London for further employment, please?"

"London!" said the young footman reverently.

She looked his way and smiled at his open excitement. "Would you like to go too?"

"Would I! I got four sisters at home and only me for support—I could send 'em so much—I mean I could send *them* so much money if I earned London wages!"

"Let us see what we can do, then. Mr. Hastings?"

"It would be a genuine pleasure to help, Miss Cullen," said that man, bowing so low again that again she could swear she could see where there ought to be a sword at his side.

The footman added, "No one's happy about Reggie being turned out, miss."

Both Cass and Anthony turned to him sharply.

"What do you mean?" she urged.

"Well, you can imagine there's a lot of the staff who don't find Lady Rawleigh all that charming, if you know what I mean," said the young fellow. "She lets go plenty of people every so often, so there's always lots of us who are new, and no one exactly loves being here. Some of us—I include myself as I've worked here several months, miss—some of us are just hoping, y'know, for the day when Dr. Burke, when his lordship I mean, becomes the Earl."

"Yes," and Cass nodded her head thoughtfully, "I can well imagine that you are."

Another young man in livery appeared at the door. He seemed confused by the presence of a footman already in the room, and he bobbed his head.

"Mrs. Evelyn sends her respects to Miss Cullen, and would like to know if she would like to visit the children before dinner."

Cass' eyes lit up and she immediately sought out David's face.

He was laughing. *You ought to visit the children!* He'd seen her often enough at the school with the little ones; he knew how much she enjoyed them, the smaller the better.

Peg poked David's arm from behind, finally getting his attention. *I want you to explain to me what all is going on, but if there's wee ones involved I know she will be running off directly. Stay here and keep me company.*

David nodded. *I'm not dining with the Earl and Countess.*

"I'll stay here," he added out loud for Anthony's benefit.

Anthony nodded. "If I miss the dinner, trust me, I will see you afterward, Miss Cullen."

* * *

THE COUNTESS INVENTION

THE VERY SMALL lad who was third in line for the earldom of Rawleigh stood clutching his mother's skirts and refused to take his fingers out of his mouth.

He pulled his dark brows together in a tiny scowl and shook his head very firmly *no*, managing to keep his fingers in his mouth through the whole performance.

"This is what we get day in and day out now, refusal," said his mother, but her tone was fond as she rested her hand on her son's small head.

"He manages to make it charming," Cass laughed. Clearly the boy was related to Oliver.

Ginnie shrugged. "He has his talents, after all." She looked up. "And do you want to see the baby?"

"I would like nothing better," Cass assured her.

Ginnie went on tiptoe over to the crib but as soon as she got there started laughing out loud.

"You tricky thing, you are supposed to be sleeping," Ginnie chided her daughter very softly, and the baby just laughed.

"She ought to be asleep?" Cass bent over the crib next to the baby's mother, wiggling her fingers at the giggling little cherub.

"She is developing many new little games."

Ginnie lifted the baby into her arms, shaking her head at the nursery maid who stepped forward.

Cass cooed. "I would say you are the sweetest baby, but my little sister Grace in London might hear about it and she would never forgive me."

Ginnie chuckled. "I might not say that she is the sweetest. Maybe the brightest."

"Very bright. Can you say mama? Mama?" Cass remembered with each of her younger siblings that nothing had delighted her stepmother more than the first time her child said *mama*.

The baby just blinked and smiled her wide, toothless, happy baby smile.

Cass made the hand motion for *mama*. "Mama?" Then she made it again.

Ginnie gasped when the baby brought her hands together, mimicking at least the placement of Cass' hands.

"She is not deaf, is she?" Ginnie asked, squeezing the baby till the little one's face began to screw up in consternation at being held so tight.

"Of course not! Anyone can speak with their hands; she might be able to make the speaking motions before she can make speaking sounds."

"Is that unusual?"

Cass thought back. Few babies made their way to the school; it was for school-age children. But she had definitely seen small toddlers speaking, ones who had deaf parents. "I do not think so."

Ginnie relaxed her grip on the baby, and Cass marveled again at how nerve-wracking people seemed to find the manual language.

Rather than bringing up the topic of Lady Rawleigh's actions, Cass said, "Your husband is far more comfortable here at Morland than is Dr. Burke."

Ginnie just shook her head. "I think he is simply able to brush it off in a way that the others cannot. Oscar could not. Viola cannot bear it either. That is why she is living with relatives in the north. She cannot abide the place."

"But you can?"

Ginnie's smile was small and tight. "A married woman has few choices when it comes to living arrangements."

That Cass understood.

Still she asked, "Will you be able to convince Mr. Evelyn to move your family elsewhere?"

Ginnie chewed her lip even as she rocked the baby. "We might discuss it. We are living here by the grace of his lordship and her ladyship, of course."

"Of course."

Cass felt as though she might, in some small way, be starting to understand why Oliver spoke of Morland the way he did. It was not just the house, or his parents, or the general somber mien of the place.

It was something it did to the people inside. It certainly seemed to be pinching Ginnie. Perhaps it had affected Lady Rawleigh too.

Or perhaps Lady Rawleigh had always been like that. If so, it seemed that through decades of her living here, her glum self-centeredness had seeped out into the stones of the place.

It would be awful to leave here and never see this toothless baby smile again, Cass thought, wiggling her fingers again at the baby until she giggled.

But it would be worse to have to stay.

CHAPTER 21

"I cannot speak with you now, I am sorry to say; I must dress for dinner," said Lady Inglemawr upon Oliver's entry to her sitting room.

He had bowed from the door, and the good lady was seated at a small table with a book and no sign of rising. But it was still her first speech upon seeing him.

She was not going to make this easy.

Better to do it quickly, Oliver thought, like tearing away a bandage that adhered to the wound.

"I shall not stay long, though I do hope to speak to you briefly alone."

He turned his head and addressed the footman who had shown him in. "That means I would like you to leave, Mr. Sayre."

The young man was wearing what looked at first glance like Rawleigh livery, but Oliver was familiar enough with the real thing that he noticed the difference in the texture of the wool.

The young man's profile, as finely sculpted as if it had come from a painting on a Greek vase, froze for only an instant. Then he moved as if to push Oliver out.

"Never mind," said Lady Inglemawr, waving her hand, and Sayre stopped immediately. He looked to her for his next instruction.

She gave it. "Just give us a few minutes, would you please? I will be fine."

Sayre looked Oliver up and down. "I will be right outside if my lady needs assistance."

"Yes, yes, thank you."

When the door closed behind him, Oliver took a few moments to seat himself in the chair opposite Lady Inglemawr.

As the silence stretched out, she snapped at him. "Yes, I suppose you are coming to throw my peccadilloes in my face. You of all people."

"I am not one to throw anything in anyone's face."

"Nor should you! The very idea. Someone like you who's been in every bed in London, coming here to throw my shortcomings up to me. Me!"

"Lady Inglemawr, perhaps I should say something before you fill in both sides of the conversation. I have no stones to throw at you. Though I have not been in every bed in London."

"Oh please!" the Marchioness huffed. "I have friends, you know. Friends all over London. They all know about you. Women talk, you know."

A chill chased down Oliver's spine.

Nonetheless he tried to go on. "Lady Inglemawr. You must realize I know who Phineas Sayre is. Ingenious to have him accompany you here; you are bold. But I must also tell you that you cannot use Miss Cullen as a shield for your comings and goings. If she wishes to marry, you must let her."

"Marry you. Pheh." Lady Inglemawr was still incensed, puffing one of her curls away with the force of her disdain. "Miss Cullen is a lady, a well-bred lady, Dr. Burke. Or Lord Howiston, whatever you prefer. Whatever I call you, you aren't fit to touch her shoe."

"Again, I am not one to argue with you on anything on that score. Miss Cullen is indeed a far better person than I am."

At that, Lady Inglemawr seemed to bring herself into the room for the first time, looking directly at him instead of at her long-held worries and fears.

She said, "Then why are you here?"

"Because I do want to court Miss Cullen. And I cannot do that if you bar me from the premises. You cannot bar me."

A little curl came to her lip that Oliver did not like. "Clearly I can, as I have."

Oliver sighed. He had thought she might be reasonable. She was not.

"Very well, since we must both dress for dinner let me be brief."

He leaned forward till his face was only an arm's breadth from hers.

He said, "You are right, Lady Inglemawr. I am a terrible man. I have no compunction about reporting Mr. Sayre's behavior to the Duke. I have no compunction about spreading the news about *you* throughout London. As you say, I have access to the ears of many, many women who would love nothing more than to hear exciting gossip about Lady Inglemawr, that fashionable widow known to all the *ton*."

She paled.

"You want to continue your *affaire* at the cost of any possibility of a private life for Miss Cullen. I am telling you that won't do. How you arrange your life is entirely up to you, as long as you do nothing to bar Miss Cullen from appropriate social interaction with eligible men."

"Like you!"

"Like *anyone*."

"Oh please! As if your motives here are so pure. I do not just know of your reputation distantly, Dr. Burke. I know several ladies who have sobbed their hearts out to me after you abandoned them. *Sobbed*."

This completely blindsided Oliver. "I *beg* your pardon?"

"As if you do not know the number of broken hearts you have left all over town. Well, you probably do not. Perhaps you do not count them. You do not wish to collect them? Just scatter them in your wake?"

"My lady." Oliver braced himself in the chair with both hands on its heavy wooden arms. "I have never promised a lady anything other than a brief time to spend together. I have never told a woman that I loved her."

At that Lady Inglemawr outright laughed. Laughed loudly and bitterly, not caring if Mr. Sayre or anyone else heard her through the walls or the doors. "What every rakehell young man says. As if bedding a woman contained no promise."

The door opened and Phineas Sayre bowed in the door again. "Is all well, my lady?" he said in low tones that would not carry.

"Phineas." Lady Inglemawr's relief at the young man's reappearance was palpable. "Dr. Burke was just leaving. Please show him out."

Oliver did not look as if he intended to rise. "Lady Inglemawr—"

"I will make sure Miss Cullen has an appropriate social schedule if she wishes to meet eligible men. Does that suit you?" Her question was brusque and not at all delivered in a conciliatory tone.

"Appropriate meaning—"

"Whatever she wants. Whatever *she* wants." Lady Inglemawr waved a hand and her Mr. Sayre opened the door wide. "Good evening, Dr. Burke, I am sure we will see each other later."

* * *

OLIVER PACED the hallway waiting for Cass to appear so that he could accompany her into the dining room.

He didn't care how his mother had seated them. There was no one here who didn't know that he was interested in Miss Cullen. If he'd ever had any skill at hiding his interest, it was certainly not a skill he had now.

The ridiculous comings and goings of the members of the house party had kept them apart nearly the entire day. He wanted Cass to know that he supported her, that he was there if she needed anything.

He was so busy pacing that he didn't hear her coming down the stairs.

Her hand appeared on his forearm, and when he looked up she was there.

Rather than hide her face in a girlish fall of curls, the dark swirl of her hair was pulled back simply, even starkly, from the bones of her face, revealing all the perfect smoothness of her skin. The birdwing eyebrows were lifted, the gray eyes sparkling.

And her figure was draped in some sort of Eastern style that made Oliver think of Cleopatra.

The neckline, trimmed with tiny glass beads, caught on one shoulder and dipped to the other side, just managing to cover both breasts. It would have been shockingly revealing without the tissue-thin linen chemise underneath, which actually covered her entire decolleté and down to her wrists but which seemed to disappear from only a few steps away. The glittering sweep of the neckline was echoed in the way the fabric caught at her side and seemed to fall, baring the long line of her hip down to her feet.

It was not an appropriate dress for an unmarried woman.

It was a glorious dress on his Cassandra.

He motioned, *You are...* but he didn't have the word so he finished out loud. "Beautiful."

She motioned. *Beautiful. You are beautiful too.* Her eyes admired the dark cut of his coat over his shoulders, and seemed to linger over his face.

If Oliver had ever had a blush in him, it was rising in his face now.

She looked thoughtful.

"Does something trouble you?" he asked.

"A few things. Nothing in particular. However... You asked me to consider the terrible idea of marrying you."

"I did." Oliver's heart thumped in his chest.

"It might be terrible for you to marry me as well."

"Not possible."

"Nonetheless." She shrugged one perfect shoulder. Oliver's hand literally itched with the urge to caress her there. She said, "You will see what you are asking for tonight, I think."

* * *

Dinner was bearable, if only just. Lord Faircombe was seated on one side of Cass, and he spent the entire meal holding forth to Lady Rawleigh about horses. She caught a word of it here and there. This amused Cass in a tired way, for she knew that Lady Rawleigh preferred to do the lecturing than be lectured to, and she also suspected that Lady Rawleigh didn't give a fig about horses.

On her other side Geoffrey was actually good company, but he was subdued.

He kept looking across the table toward his sister on one end and Delina Farsworth on the other.

Cass smiled a little, imagining his reasoning. "Are you attached enough to Miss Farsworth, Mr. Eliot, that you would be sad to see her go?"

For it was clear that Miss Farsworth had not patched up her bad feelings after Lady Charlotte's turned-ankle performance of the afternoon, as Cass thought of it. The little china-doll young lady was refusing to even look at Lady Charlotte, instead spending her time chatting with, of all people, the Bradley Waite fellow Oliver had brought with him from London.

Cass thought Geoffrey Eliot might be a bit jealous of the older, clearly more sophisticated Mr. Waite, especially now that Miss Farsworth's attention was fully on him.

But Geoffrey just shook his head.

"If Delina and Charlotte don't make up, I don't know what's going to happen to Charlotte. She doesn't know what to do with herself half the time as it is. If Delina leaves us, she will run mad."

Cass thought that faking a turned ankle to get Oliver's medical attention already qualified the young lady as silly, at least, though not mad. "Is she so changeable?"

"She thinks she is," said Geoffrey soberly, looking at the way his sister was fluttering her eyelashes at Oliver. "But she is not."

This was too mysterious for Cass and didn't make for much entertaining conversation. Geoffrey had nothing further to share on the topic of young ladies he knew, or ones he didn't know, and that exhausted her ability to think of dinner conversation.

JUDITH LYNNE

Perhaps she should have read more books in school, Cass thought a little wildly. Or perhaps, like her father's study, this was a room in which she ought only to come if she brought the means of setting a fire.

But Geoffrey took pity on her eventually. "You do not have to be entertaining, Miss Cullen. You are pleasant, which I actually much prefer."

And the kindness of his smile as he said this made Cass believe it.

Lady Inglemawr, opposite Lord Faircombe on the other side of the Countess, was also quiet, ignoring Anthony Hastings next to her, which seemed to suit that gentleman just fine.

And at the opposite end of the table the earl had clearly clustered his children around him, having Oliver on one side of him and his daughter-in-law on the other.

Cass was pointedly set in a position neither part of the visiting peers on one end, nor part of the family on the other.

Aside from anything there was to eat—which was surprisingly little—Cass was distracted throughout dinner by her desire to throw her silverware to the floor and demand justice from Lady Rawleigh for Peg and for the dismissed footman.

Something of her desire to shout must have shown in her face, because Oliver kept sending her inquiring looks, but that only redoubled Lady Charlotte's efforts to keep Oliver's eyes on *her*.

Lady Sherrin across the table occasionally spoke to Mr Hastings on her left, but otherwise was quiet. Cass might have imagined some chagrin in her expression every time she looked Cass' way, which only served to make Cass more uneasy about whatever had transpired between the woman and Oliver this morning. Why would she still look so abashed, if nothing had happened?

It was a trying meal that had nothing to do with eating and Cass was relieved to get to the end of it.

In a terrible breach of protocol, Oliver came around the table as they arose and took her hand, tucking it into the crook of his arm just as he did when they were alone. Cass felt herself draw a deep breath, as if she had been holding it, and let it out again.

Leaning closer he said so that she could hear, "You need prove nothing to my mother."

But that, far from relaxing Cass, just snapped something into place inside her.

No. She did *not* need to prove anything to his mother. If anything, Lady Rawleigh owed Cass an explanation or two.

But Cass would be damned if she would leave this house without showing Lady Rawleigh exactly how she could serve as the Countess of Rawleigh, should she choose to do so.

Oliver was leading her down the hall, and once again Cass saw those approaching, intimidating doors, with the large room beyond glowing with candles, the golden light shining off the floor, the windows, the gilt picture frames.

This time, there was no friendly face among the footmen, no one to tell her *hello* and give her that friendly boost before she went in.

At least Oliver was with her, though he was so wound up himself it felt as though he was a million miles away. Being at Morland definitely distracted him.

She was alone.

Except, no, she wasn't.

Was that a pair of eyes turned her way?

Cass spotted the footman from earlier, the young lad. She hadn't even gotten his name. He was looking straight at her without moving a muscle, and then he nodded. Just one small tiny nod.

He was there for her.

And when she looked past him, she could see another pair of eyes, and another, breaking the smooth line of footmen that seemed to go on forever. Looking at her.

Across the hall there were two more pairs of eyes. No, three. Four, actually.

Looking at her.

Giving her a little nod.

As if to say for all the world, *we are with you, miss.*

She breathed again.

Not only could she do this, she *would* do this.

And when she crossed the threshold into the room, she saw all the guests scattered around among the lights of the candles as if in a tableau, each one caught by the light in a moment of motion.

Why did they come here?

Why put themselves through the difficult trip, the awkward interactions, Lady Rawleigh's terrible table?

They were lonely.

They were all lonely, Cass realized. Or at least bored. They wanted comfort and amusement and company. That was why they came to Morland.

It was not their fault that Morland had little in the way of comfort to offer.

They wanted something from Morland that the house was not designed to provide, at least not as it was. As a device for amusement and human interaction, Morland would not be enough on its own.

She would have to provide a smoother operation.

They were all just moving parts, Cass realized, the candlelight glow reflecting from their glasses and their hair and the polished floor.

If this party was a device, it was her job to figure out how best to make it go.

She could do that.

CHAPTER 22

Tonight Cass was a Greek goddess impossible to miss.

Oliver preferred having her alone to himself, but surely now no one could miss what he saw in her. Her tall, elegant figure draped in shimmering sparkle, her hair and skin glowing in the light, she was a painting in motion.

There was something different about her expression. Some edge of determination that he had not seen there before.

And she was talking with people here and there, but she was talking to the footmen much more.

Oliver could never resist watching her, but tonight he couldn't take his eyes away from her.

She raised a finger, and a footman appeared next to her instantly. She leaned close to speak to him quietly.

"Mr. Waite needs to drink more slowly. Please bring him some tea in a tumbler next no matter what he requests."

The footman didn't even nod, just inclined his head the tiniest amount and disappeared.

Oliver moved a little closer.

Cass had smiled at Geoffrey. "What does Miss Farsworth enjoy for entertainment, Mr. Eliot?"

The white-blond young Viking of a man smiled at Cass. "She loves to dance, Miss Cullen."

"Excellent!" Cass lifted a hand and another footman appeared. "Ask Lady Rawleigh if she would mind if we began the dancing in a few minutes, then tell the musicians to take their places."

Oliver noticed there was no option for them to delay dancing if Lady Rawleigh did *not* want it.

"Mr. Eliot, have you met Lady Sherrin? Lady Sherrin, Mr. Eliot is so interested in the social whirl of London. He has never been."

Geoffrey looked surprised—perhaps he had never said anything to Cass about London, but that seemed immaterial to Lady Sherrin, who began reporting on the events of the past social season, and the lady somewhat lost her sheepish look when Cass' eyes turned her way.

Oliver followed Cass' progress around the room with amazement. Sometimes she asked what the person wanted, sometimes simply supplied it. With a lift of her finger and darting footmen coming and going, Lord Faircombe had brandy but Lord Rawleigh had sherry, both exactly as they preferred.

Lady Gadbury promised to sing if Lady Charlotte would play the piano, and as it turned out Charlotte was rather good. It seemed to mollify the young lady a little, and when Lady Gadbury's song was over several people called to Charlotte for another, which made her flush with something that must have been like happiness.

Lady Gadbury retired to listen to Lady Rawleigh, which didn't seem to tax either lady. Cass kept an eye on them as she introduced Ginnie and Victor to Anthony Hastings.

"Is this an awful party?" Cass asked Anthony sincerely, truly wanting the young man's opinion.

"I've been to far worse," said Anthony, sipping his claret.

When the dancing began, Oliver danced with Delina Farsworth twice, then Lady Gadbury, then Lady Sherrin, before gracing Lady Charlotte with a dance.

No one mentioned her erstwhile turned ankle.

The young lady seemed a bit chagrined as they began but seemed to enjoy being swirled through the steps of the simple polonaise they shared.

When it was over, Oliver gallantly showed her to a seat.

Cass had to pause in her work to take in the way Oliver's coat tightened over his back when he bowed.

She appreciated that he did not ask her to dance; she could not really hear the music, not well enough to do as the other ladies did, and she did not want to put her efforts on display.

It was still a curious sensation, to watch other women enjoying him, even to this very limited extent.

Was she able, she wondered, to put aside how much other women had enjoyed him?

And while she could not hear it, she knew that the other women present who had their eye on him felt shockingly free to tell him so.

Like Lady Charlotte.

"Is it tiresome, being beautiful?" Charlotte exclaimed just as Oliver was about to fetch her a glass.

"Excuse me?" Oliver was startled enough to turn back and stare at her.

"Is it tiresome? You are so extremely beautiful, perhaps it is tiresome having silly young ladies fall at your feet all day."

Oliver found himself looking more thoughtfully at Lady Charlotte than he had yet done through the whole party. He couldn't truthfully say that he was not aware of his looks, nor could he truthfully deny that there had recently been some silly young ladies.

"You have not been tiresome, Lady Charlotte," he said, giving her a smile.

"I do not—you must understand I do not usually behave so shamelessly."

"If you behaved shamelessly, I am sure it would be rude of me to notice it," and Oliver bowed.

But his words didn't seem to have the effect he expected.

For Charlotte just scowled. "Yes, that is what we must all do all day, be polite and not notice what others are actually saying and doing."

"Is it?"

She continued to scowl into her crystal glass as she sipped. "I prefer horses," she responded briefly.

Oliver looked around. "I prefer people."

"Do you? That is so odd to me."

"I do. Now of course you know that I know little about horses. But even when a person cannot speak, there is something deep in his eyes that reaches out to you and lets you know when he is happy, or suffering, or needs your help. There is a connection there."

Lady Charlotte seemed to consider this seriously.

"I feel that way with horses," she said.

"And perhaps your friend Miss Farsworth?" Oliver prodded.

Charlotte looked Delina's way and this time her scowl was more petulant. "When she is not busy judging me."

"Ah, Lady Charlotte, it is our oldest friends who know us best, and that is not always easy, is it."

Charlotte seemed to be fighting a smile as she looked back up at him. "If you are kind as well as beautiful, you honestly must just expect ladies to throw themselves at you day and night."

Oliver had to laugh.

* * *

Cass might have thought about being jealous of Oliver laughing at Lady Charlotte's side, but she really didn't have time.

If he was laughing, that would contribute to the general gaiety of the party, and that was all to the good.

Lady Sherrin and Geoffrey seemed to have run out of conversation but that was fine; she suggested to Geoffrey that he ask Miss Farsworth to dance, and that sent Bradley Waite over to entertain Lady Sherrin for a while.

Lady Gadbury had clearly reached her fill of Lady Rawleigh, so she suggested to Ginnie that she show Lady Gadbury the paintings and let Anthony and Victor try to get Lord Faircombe to say anything about anything other than horses, or perhaps let Lord Rawleigh say something.

Cass had never yet seen Lord Rawleigh say anything.

When Oliver delivered Lady Charlotte to Mr. Waite for a turn on the dance floor, Cass appeared next to him.

"Lady Sherrin is considering a game of whist. Perhaps you can advise her," Cass said quietly.

Oliver met her eyes. "You haven't the slightest qualm about pairing me off with these women, have you."

The muscle in Cass' jaw ticked; Oliver had seen it in men but never in a woman.

"Your mother does not expect me to do it, so I will." Cass looked over to where Lady Rawleigh sat alone on a velvet settee.

"My mother looks lonely," Oliver mused out loud.

Cass looked at his mother for a long, long moment, and Oliver couldn't read her expression.

Lifting a hand, Cass said to the footman who appeared, "Lady Rawleigh would like another glass of sherry."

The man bowed his head and disappeared.

"What did you do to the footmen?" Oliver wondered.

Cass just smiled thinly. "If you would prefer a game for two, Lady Sherrin knows backgammon."

"I'll bet she does," Oliver said, but Cass was already gone.

CHAPTER 23

The dinner had been light, and the drinks were being absorbed all too readily. Cass noticed the problem.

With a few words, Cass had some plates of thinly sliced cold beef put out, along with oranges, some cubed cold beets in a vinegar dressing, and some spiced butter sandwiches.

The food seemed to revive everyone's spirits, and before long there was laughter and music in every corner of Morland's old ballroom, making it ring.

Lady Rawleigh was in her third glass of sherry and looking rather grim when Lady Sherrin pulled her into a game of whist. The Countess seemed to enjoy it, and won five pounds from Mr. Waite, which embarrassed him enormously and delighted her to the same amount.

Like everyone else, Oliver followed Cass' suggestions and circulated among the party for the rest of the evening, enjoying himself tremendously, feeling even the black mood he always felt inside this hall lifting somewhat, as if Cass had indeed brought that dawn light to Morland's clouds.

He noticed that Cass did not suggest that he dance with Lady Gadbury again, however.

That lady spoke only briefly to him from time to time, playing cards with his mother and his sister-in-law and winning some money from Lady Inglemawr as well, which made her look quite satisfied with herself.

Oliver drank some brandy with his father and felt like even that taciturn fellow must admit that Cass had transformed Morland into someplace warm and happy.

Happy.

He wished his brother Oscar were here to see this, he truly did.

But if Morland were only to be a happy place for one night, he was glad that he himself was there to witness it.

* * *

Lady Rawleigh seemed to tire first.

"I will retire with you, madam," said Lady Gadbury, gathering the folds of her skirt in one hand.

Immediately Cass was there, curtseying first to Lady Gadbury, and then a deep formal curtsey to Lady Rawleigh.

When she stood, she met Lady Rawleigh's eyes directly, and Lady Gadbury could not read her steely expression.

"Have you had words with that girl?" Lady Gadbury asked under her breath as she walked Lady Rawleigh down the hall, followed by footmen with candelabras.

"Of course not," Lady Rawleigh snapped. "As if I would stoop so low. The girl is common along with all her other defects."

"I am sorry to hear that. As I told you, I believe your son has developed a fascination for this girl," murmured Lady Gadbury.

"It is of no import."

Lady Gadbury knew perfectly well that Oliver lived without any financial support from the estate. "It is of import if he does something rash."

"He will do nothing of the kind."

"Forgive me, I did not intend to contradict you, madam." Lady Gadbury bowed her head with deference toward the other Countess, for all Lady Rawleigh stood a full head shorter and more. "Young men do take notions and it is sometimes very difficult to dissuade them."

"You may think that because my son has been permitted to take up a profession, and to serve in the army, that he has run wild. That is not so. In fact," and here she snapped her fingers so that a footman jumped forward. "Inform his lordship that I must speak with him immediately."

The footman bowed crisply despite the late hour, and dashed away.

"No more problems this evening, Lady Gadbury. Please do accompany me to my chambers. You must have some amusing news of London fashions you have not yet shared."

Lady Gadbury, whose stock of news about London fashions had already been exhausted this week-end by the Countess, searched with one part of her mind for something else to say, and with another, worried that she had tipped the scales too far by speaking to Lady Rawleigh of her concerns for Oliver's well-being.

* * *

Lord Rawleigh bid goodnight to the party and withdrew, and Lord Faircombe shortly after that, apparently exhausted by chasing pheasants.

Without their hosts, the party had officially ended, but several friendly conversations, and a few games of cards, had sprung up around the room, and the company seemed inclined to linger.

Oliver came up behind Cass as she surveyed the room, bumped her arm very slightly with his own so that she would know he was there.

When she turned to face him he couldn't hide his surprise. "You look very tired, Miss Cullen."

But she just smiled, a satisfied little smile. "It has been a long evening, Dr. Burke."

He nodded. Leaning even closer he said, "It may be the first time in a hundred years or longer that anyone has enjoyed themselves at Morland. And it is due to you."

Cass nodded, her eyes till taking in the little tableaus of people talking here and there by the light of lowering candles. "Yes, it is." Her smile slipped only slightly. "And I have been a social success after all."

"I daresay you have."

"Yet nothing has changed. No one has talked to *me* all evening."

"No? But look here."

Just as Oliver drew her attention to it, Bradley Waite approached them, bowing to Cass. "Miss Cullen. Thank you for a lovely evening."

"Our host and hostess have retired, Mr. Waite, but I am sure Dr. Burke receives your thanks on their behalf," she said most properly.

Waite reached out to take her hand and kissed the back of it. "I know whom I should thank, Miss Cullen."

With another nod, he departed.

"He looks ten years younger and free of demons for the first time since I can remember," Oliver told Cass quietly. "Lady Charlotte and Miss Farsworth appear to have mended their disagreement. Lady Sherrin actually looks like she is enjoying Geoffrey Eliot's company."

"Geoffrey Eliot is much wiser than anyone realizes," Cass said back just as quietly.

That startled Oliver again. But he went on. "And Anthony Hastings is enjoying himself, unless I am mistaken, and I don't believe that man enjoys anything."

"Mr. Hastings has done some good deeds this evening and deserves to enjoy himself." Cass nodded as if to emphasize her point.

"I feel as though I have missed many important conversations, Miss Cullen. Indeed, if you are not the social center of this gathering, then no one is."

She turned to smile at him over her shoulder. "Perhaps you are, Dr. Burke."

"I am at best ornamental."

Cass just shook her head, and seemed to take it for a joke.

But Oliver meant it entirely.

He added, "You had nothing to prove to my mother, you know.

Or me."

"I had something to prove to myself."

"Miss Cullen."

"Yes?"

"You must realize by now that you are equal to any of life's challenges."

She focused on him, really looked at him.

"Where is your chamber, Dr. Burke?"

His dancing eyes showed the edges of a real smile. "That is not the sort of question a proper young lady asks."

"I believe in my decision-making this evening, sir. And it is only a question. Who knows what may come of it?"

Still with laughing eyes, he leaned even closer. "The family wing on the west side, on the second floor. The door has an appalling set of carved cherubs over it. I will not be held responsible for them."

"I understand." And her own eyes twinkled a little as he bowed, and withdrew.

Cass looked at one of the footmen, still awake and upright at this late hour. Instantly he was at her side.

"What is your name?"

"Jeremy, Miss Cullen."

"Jeremy, please extend my thanks to all the footmen, and those in the kitchen who gave us such an excellent cold table on such short notice. I apologize that I do not know everyone's name to thank them individually."

"Of course, ma'am." The young man flashed a grin, only for an instant, then seemed to remember his uniform. "It has been our pleasure, our genuine pleasure."

"The pleasure is all the guests', Jeremy, but for tonight, that is good work enough."

She sighed, looking out over the remainder of the guests again. She was tired.

It had not been the sort of social success she had dreamed of as a girl.

It had been better.

CHAPTER 24

Peg was primarily delighted that Cass returned with all the hairpins she had had when she left. Cass brushed out her own hair, sitting in her linen chemise on the small upholstered bench at the foot of the bed, while Peg fussed with the gown.

Peg put it down to comment, *It isn't appropriate for an unmarried woman.*

Cass shrugged one shoulder. *Who will know?*

All those people downstairs know.

My father doesn't know, and London doesn't know. Cass could not bring herself to regret anything tonight.

Peg looked worriedly at her. *You look peculiar.*

You look peculiar, Cass shot back. *I am exhausted. Please, I beg you, go to sleep.*

* * *

PEG UNTIED the strings of her stays, but Cass still felt too unsettled to undress.

It's beyond late.

Go ahead and sleep. Cass didn't remind Peg that she was well used to doing without the services of a lady's maid.

I don't like to... but I can't keep my eyes open for another minute. What hours these fancy people keep!

Cass kept on turning over in her mind all the things she had said and done at the party that evening, wondering if there had been a better possible pairing for cards, or dancing, or music.

She wondered if she could have ordered a better menu if she had reviewed the kitchen first, or if it were better to trust it to the cook.

She wondered if Oliver would have preferred to dance more with Lady Gadbury, and wondered why he had not asked her to dance again. Was it only because Cass was watching?

The longer she sat, listening to Peg's breath evening out as her friend fell asleep, and watching the light of the moon travel across the embossed ceiling, the more Cass wondered, not what everyone else would have liked for their amusement, but what Oliver would have liked.

He had done everything she suggested, and she could remember the turquoise color of his eyes as they smiled at her, at the end of the evening.

She would not have heard the music.

But she wished she had danced with him.

* * *

CASS REFUSED to tiptoe through the hallways.

She did, however, step very, very quietly.

She would just visit the family wing, she told herself. She would see the way the windows were set on the second floor, and she would see the state of the staircase, and she would investigate these apparently appalling cherubs that decorated Oliver's door.

Cass could just imagine herself, drinking in the details—what must such carvings be made of?—and then smiling enigmatically at the doctor's door before walking away. Perhaps she would just lay a hand on its panels.

She found the door easily enough and without tripping over any footmen, for once.

The cherubs *were* ugly, and Cass stared at them for what felt like a long, long time.

Even as she knocked softly on the door, she felt torn.

When Oliver stood there, his shoulders looking more than ever able to lift the earth, looking at her, she still felt as though she had not made up her mind.

Then his slight frown turned to that sunny, open face, and Cass felt quite certain.

He said, "Are you addicted to bad ideas, Miss Cullen?"

She just smiled as she made the motion for *no*. "I believe I am addicted to dreaming that it will all turn out well."

There was a low fire in the room, and it was warm inside. Oliver surveyed her dress. It was the lavender half-mourning she had worn the day they met in person.

He lifted an eyebrow at it, then at her, which looked very, very wicked.

She laughed out loud. "Is it the dress?" She twirled for him.

"It would never be that dress."

Then in two steps he was there, and he had her in his arms, and he was kissing her and she was laughing and Cass realized that kissing and laughing went perfectly together.

Oliver was chuckling too as he buried his hands in her hair. "No hairpins for me to play with."

"You are sadly deprived."

"You walked the hallway like this?" He smoothed the dark wave of her hair over her shoulder.

In response she did the same, pulling his own bronze-finished tumble of hair forward. "Did you? Our hair is about the same length."

His smile faded a little as he met her eyes. "Do you really want this?"

"Dr. Burke, you offered."

Lady Inglemawr's insults were playing over and over in his head. "I have learned that I may not be as gentle with women's hearts as I thought I had been."

Cass' nose wrinkled a little, but she just shook her head. "As you yourself have told me many times, I am not your past *affaires*. I am the person who promised to consider your proposal of marriage."

"I don't..." Oliver wanted to find the right words. This was one heart he *must not* wound. "I thought I left this loveless pile of bricks behind me when I went out into the world. I may have taken it along with me, inside. Apparently I have not recognized love when it was directed at me. And I certainly do not know how to give it."

That tallied with Cass' understanding of the world. "I did not ask you to love me, sir. I came here for my pleasure."

Oliver still looked uncertain. Or something. Something was pulling that frown back into his face.

That made Cass uncertain. "Are you not sure? You said I could put you to the test."

"And I never meant anything more." Here Oliver's arms tightened around Cass till she could not breathe. The pounding of her heart made breathing even harder.

"Wait, wait."

Oliver released her immediately, but Cass just lifted her arms. "This dress will be gone faster if you help."

He grinned again as he swept his hands up her body, stripping the lavender dimity off, and then in the next moment she was swept up in his arms and carried to his bed.

The embroidered coverlet and smooth linen sheets had already been turned back as if he had been just about to lay there. Cass stroked the sheet thoughtfully. "I wonder if my mistake has been never trying this in a bed."

"Cassandra, you are killing me."

She looked up to where he still stood, leaning over her, looking at her, truly, the way she imagined a starving man looked at a feast.

"Well, you may kill me back," she said, lifting her arms to him.

He groaned. It was a groan from deep inside him, she could hear that.

THE COUNTESS INVENTION

With a powerful move of his arm, he shoved all the heavy coverlets from the bed to the floor before laying down beside her.

"What did you do that for?"

"You don't like to feel smothered. I want to give you room to breathe."

She wanted to explain that she sometimes forgot to breathe when he was touching her, when his hands smoothed up the fabric of the stays to cup her breasts. "It is too quick to touch you like this," he said, nosing at the neckline of her chemise, "but I feel as though we have spent months building to this point."

"Months? Even when you were writing letters to Mr. Cullen?"

"I liked you before I met you, Cassandra, and it has only built every second that I've known more about you."

She couldn't stop a little moan when his hand closed over her breast, adding, "I don't *feel* as though you need to go slowly. But then I am not the expert."

"I am not an expert either."

"Don't annoy me *now*."

"Cassandra, I have never done this before. You and I are here together right now, like this, and I need *you* to tell me how *you* feel and what *you* want. That has never happened before."

"Oh." She considered asking him how many such encounters it would take before he became an expert, but that seemed petty, and she wanted to let petty go right now. She wanted to let go of everything but him.

"Then you should kiss me," she told him, and for the first time, let herself get lost in his kiss.

She loved feeling the muscles swell in his arms as he stroked her. When she gripped his arm, she felt him tense, and then relax in her hands. "Feeling you move is intoxicating."

"Then you must understand why I like it too."

"Should I take off my petticoat?"

"You should do whatever you like." His mouth was traveling to the lobe of her ear, which he teased with soft kisses before taking it in his mouth.

When she gasped aloud, she felt him chuckle.

She couldn't stay quiet. "How on earth would anyone ever suspect an ear would be capable of *that?*"

"Someone discovered it long ago." He nuzzled the curve of her ear even as his arms tightened around her, rolling her closer to him.

She fell into his arms so easily, so naturally.

"I like feeling your voice in your chest." It felt like an admission, as if she had been keeping it another secret.

"I can help with that," and Oliver managed to get himself out of his own shirt, tossing it away from the bed, and laying back down so that she could run her hands over him unimpeded.

His skin was so soft, so warm, and the dusting of hair that fell along the muscles there was so very masculine, that it begged Cass to investigate it just by existing.

Cass felt like she had asked for, and gotten, a gift. It made her smile, it made her bolder. "I would rather have the petticoat off."

"Then lose the thing. We can throw it in the fire if you want."

"Are you always so extreme in these matters?" Cass unbuttoned the petticoat, and wiggled out of it. Oliver pitched it after his shirt.

"Yes." His arms closed around her again.

She was leaning over him now. "I like this. I like having you spread out before me."

"I think it will be my turn soon."

His lips, his hands roamed everywhere, and Cass was a good mimic of a good model; she followed his lead.

When her hand slid down over his chest to the smooth belly below, then over his hip to squeeze him towards her, she was rewarded with a deep groan she could feel in her chest as well as hear.

"If you set that tone, my lady, you will find it comes back to you."

"I like to believe things will all work out," she reminded him softly, nipping the end of his nose with her teeth.

With a great heave, Cass found herself somehow turned around with her back to him sitting on his hips, leaning forward while he untied her stays the rest of the way.

The sensation of Oliver's hands worshipping the curve of her back made her head fall forward. It was easy to wrap her arms around his knees, crush herself into the muscles of his bent legs.

All too soon, Oliver had tugged the chemise up too, and she helped him slide it over her head.

She could feel his fingers following the lines left by the strings on the stays.

"Are they unattractive?" Cass turned over her shoulder to look at him.

"No," said Oliver hoarsely, "though I prefer your skin smooth and unmarked."

Her hair glowed against that smooth, creamy expanse of nearly flawless skin. She was truly as if a statue of a goddess had come to life and he was being given divine favors.

"I like seeing you better." She bit her lip.

Oliver helped her shift again, so that they faced each other, her exquisite thighs on either side of his hips. He resisted the deep-seated urge to thrust upward against her. If he had never done anything worthwhile in his life, he was going to pleasure this woman tonight, and her pleasure would be his.

He smoothed a fingertip across the bitten lip.

"You act as if I wanted your words kept inside. Give me all you have."

His Cassandra gave him a big, dazzling, wicked smile, and relaxed full-length against his body.

He moaned deep in his chest, knowing she would feel it. "I can now die happy."

"I like you happy."

Gently, he circled her delicate wrists to place those graceful hands he loved to watch against the carved headboard of the bed. "I like you happy," he rasped before he turned his attention to the smooth, mouth-sized breasts with their eager nipples that were now displayed before him.

He let her squirm for what felt like forever as he caressed undersides of each breast, kissing the sensitive skin there, and teased each nipple with his lips, his tongue, brushes of his rough cheek.

Even through the fabric of his trousers, which were restraining him almost painfully, he could feel her getting warmer. The thought of how slick she would be for him came close to derailing his goals, but Oliver called on his last reserves of determination even as one of her hands drifted down to tangle in his hair.

"I can't... I cannot..."

"Tell me."

"I can't do this much longer."

"You *can*," he told her with certainty, "but what do you *want*?"

"I can't. It is... it is almost torment. I am so..."

"Tell me again how the peak of pleasure is nothing so great that poets should be writing about it."

He could see her glare down at him, and he knew she could feel him chuckle.

"This is not... This is unbearable. Does this go *on*?"

"As long as you wish, but I think you do not wish it to go on?"

"I can't *stand* it."

"Tell me." He reached up to take her arms, close them around him, bury his head in her softness. Careful not to lie on her, he rolled her down beside him, kissing her all the way.

"Tell me more about how it feels," he said against her lips as his hand slid down over the softness of her belly, then up one of her thighs.

She moaned and her legs parted in invitation to that wandering hand.

"What are you smiling about now?" she demanded as his hand drew closer to the curls that she could feel had grown wet with his attention.

"This," he said, and slid his fingers through the soft lips parting for him there.

The shock of his touch, insanely intimate, rocked through her and made her back arch. The sound of her indrawn breath was enough to almost echo in the room.

"I forgot to tell you," Oliver said, once again nuzzling her now nearly painfully hard nipples, "sound *can* travel through these walls. So you might wish to try to be quiet."

"Are you joking?" Cass panted, her eyes dark as she looked at him with amazement. "I mean, are you honestly trying to make me laugh?"

"No." His answer sounded very reasonable as his hand did it again.

Cass' body arched again, and the sound she let out was almost a soft keening sound.

"You are not quiet," Oliver observed smugly as his hands, his fingers moved again and again, and Cass put her own hand over her mouth to muffle the noise she could not help making.

"I think I am," she managed to get out as a full sentence before his deft fingers slid *inside* her.

"You should not be quiet," and Oliver's mouth came over her own, not to silence the sounds, but to take them for her.

Cass felt her whole body contracting to a hot awareness of that spot where he was touching her. It felt too hot, and slick, and she could feel her own muscles, muscles she'd never been aware of before, clutching at his long, strong fingers even as her hands clutched at his shoulders.

And then his thumb pressed down and she felt herself explode from the inside out.

She could not stop the sound she made, though Oliver muffled it for her, and she could not stop the way her body, out of her control, shook against the protective wall of his body.

When she managed to open her eyes again, he was there, smiling at her, from just inches away. Watching her. Waiting for her.

With her.

"Are you ready to do that again?" Oliver murmured against her ear.

"What? What are you talking about?" Cass fought to take a deep breath. She was trembling all over and his words did not make sense.

"Again, Cassandra? Would you like to do that again?"

"I don't understand."

"Just tell me yes or no. Would you like that again?"

The world was short of air. But Oliver's eyes held her and she gave the answer she wanted to give. "Yes."

Immediately his fingers dipped deeper inside her. She could feel him find a spot that was a reach for him, and the heel of his hand pressing against her made her grind against him. She did not think about it, she just did it.

Oliver moaned his approval and lay closer to her, pulling her body into his with one of his strong arms.

His mouth kept moving, and she clutched at his head, mostly to keep from drowning, she thought, but her attention was focused on the hot deep center where he was pressing and pressing in circles, and something heavy was gathering inside her belly, something momentous and big.

"Are you well?" she could hear Oliver murmur against her ear, and she nodded. She was fine. She thought she was fine. She might explode into a million pieces, but she was fine.

Then Oliver's warmth left her—she missed it immediately—as he shifted to sit upright on the bed, pulling her thighs into his lap.

"Is this comfortable?" He was still watching her face.

Cass wanted to say that it was not, in its way—it was terribly undignified and open and she could never have imagined a man between her thighs *this* way, holding her and touching her and watching her all at the same time—but it was, and she had to nod.

"Good."

And with both his hands available Oliver did something, one hand stroking her, small tiny sensations of his thumb, which had just enough roughness that she knew it was *him*, at the base of some part of her that felt swollen and sensitive and desperate, and his other hand still pressing those small circles deep *inside* her that felt wholly different, a growing hot heaviness like a banked fire leaping back into flames, flames that licked down her legs to her toes and up her body to spread out to her fingertips, and Cass felt like she might catch fire at any moment but she wanted to die this way.

When the peak came again it was less of a surprise, but when it hit, it still felt to Cass like she was falling off a cliff, but this time on fire.

And he was holding her.

The pleasure came in waves that radiated out from the center of her, going and going until she felt that they might never stop.

They might *never* stop.

Something caught inside Cass, something deep in her body, from her clenched toes to her fists tangled in the sheets, and she could feel the sweat trickling down her spine, she truly was on fire, but the pleasure only receded, it didn't go away, and Cass knew, she knew that if she chased it there would be more.

She managed to lift her head and meet Oliver's eyes, which were blue flames and fixed on her.

And she managed to gasp out, "Go on."

Oliver only nodded, but he shifted down to where he could still use his hands, her thighs spread open over his shoulders, and also could bring his mouth to that urgent, fiery center.

As his lips closed over the aching swollen sensitive spot that he had been caressing, he sucked. And his fingers inside her pressed into the what felt like the core of her being. Pressed *hard*.

This peak grabbed Cass and carried her up into the center of a thunder and lightning storm from which there was no way out. She could not see or hear, though she knew she had her hands pressed to her own mouth to keep her screams muffled. She felt herself gush hot liquid over Oliver's hands, and felt only amazement that her body could do that, could do *this*. Surely this would kill her.

She collapsed back on the bed.

Slowly, slowly she seemed to come back to earth, come back to awareness.

She came back to an awareness of Oliver, looking peaceful, stroking his hands along her thighs, patting her belly, and saw that he was instantly aware that she was back with him.

He had never taken his eyes off her for a second.

"More?" he asked.

Cass could feel laughter bubbling inside her, but she was too wrung out to do it justice. She felt simultaneously light enough to float off the earth, and also sweaty and damp and slightly sore and thoroughly, thoroughly sated.

"I think it would kill me."

"It would not, but you might need a rest, I think."

Oliver shifted so he could lay perilously close to the edge of the bed, and pulled her into his arms.

He kissed her, gently, on the forehead, even as his arms held her tight.

"A rest. You *think*." Cass sighed shakily into his chest. "No one could do that twice in a lifetime. Why are you balancing on the edge?"

"To give you a place to lie with me that is dry."

She ought to be embarrassed but she just felt awed. "Do you do this *every time*?"

"I told you, Cassandra," and he kissed her forehead again, the edge of her hair, her eyelids, gently, one at a time. "I have never done this before."

That wasn't what she meant, but she did not want to argue. With anyone. Ever again.

"You are so exquisitely beautiful," Oliver whispered into her ear as he held her close.

She considered not feeling beautiful. She felt sweaty and shaky and extremely vulnerable.

She believed him.

But the whole thing seemed impossible.

"I am grateful, *very* grateful, that you find all *that* beautiful."

Very gently, Oliver held her even tighter, and rolled them so that she was sprawled against him. "That is what the poets themselves long for and seldom get to see."

Hands still shaking, she traced his jaw, his nose, his forehead with her fingertips. "I think they mostly wrote about—" Then she gasped. "What about you?"

"I'm right here." Oliver kissed the palm of the hand she had against his cheek.

"I mean—with all the—what about you?"

"I got to see what the poets dream about."

Cass couldn't stop her smile. But she was insistent. "But your pleasure, do you not need...?"

"You mean this?" With a flex of his hips he pressed his still trouser-clad front against her belly. She could feel the hard length of him there. "It is fine."

"Fine? *Fine?*"

Oliver laughed. Why had she never imagined a beautiful man laughing in her arms this way? "It is a little achy, and very, very hard, as you can tell."

"But don't you... won't you...?"

"Were we not testing whether *you* would enjoy it?"

"Well, I did!" Cass was aghast. "That does not mean you cannot. Do you not... can you do *that?*"

"Oh my darling." His arms around her back tightened again, and Cass tucked that word away in her heart for later contemplation. "I don't believe so. That kind of pleasure seems to be the gift of women, and those who help them seek it out and find it."

"Well that just sounds defeatist." She reveled in the feeling of Oliver snorting into her neck. She went on, "But you must, you must be able to achieve the peak, surely."

"That was not the task, my lady."

"For heaven's sake! That is not—"

Rather than talking more, Cass managed to push herself upright.

Oliver looked warily at the goddess sitting between his feet. "What are you doing now?"

"What do you think?" She had his trousers unbuttoned; the feeling of setting himself free was a massive relief.

"That was not my goal tonight."

"Well, it might be mine, did you ever think of that?"

Wiggling off him so that she might better wrestle his trousers down, Cass nearly fell off the bed. Oliver caught her with both hands around her shoulders.

"Thank you," she told him most sincerely. "I am still shaky."

"What do you—"

But then she had him freed, most of him, and Oliver had to gasp himself, unable to stop himself thrusting into the slender hand she had closed around his length.

JUDITH LYNNE

"God," he choked as she stroked him, his hands automatically reaching for something to steady himself. He only found the headboard behind him again; he laid his hands against it, trying to keep from letting himself go.

"That looks *lovely*," Cass nearly purred with satisfaction, and the sight of her smile, her glossy dark hair still damp from her pleasure and tumbling over her shoulders, brought him from eager to ready to shoot in mere seconds.

"I am glad that you—" But he did not get to finish a comment that sounded suitably sophisticated for this moment, or any comment at all, because the soft skin of her palm twisted over the tip of him as she shifted her hand and stroked again.

Oliver groaned and could not stop the motion of his hips as his body strained toward her, exploding with his release, before he collapsed onto the mattress himself.

"Hah," said Cass, looking extremely pleased and also, he could tell, wondering what to do about the streaks of evidence of his pleasure that now fell across his belly and chest.

"Give me a moment. We can clean up a little."

"Take all the time you like," said Cass, wrapping her arms around one of his bent legs to lay her cheek against his knee.

And Oliver envied the poets. Because they had the practice to use words to describe someone like this glorious woman made of joy and sweetness and the feeling of having her here with him.

It went way beyond lucky.

He could only smile at her.

"It may take me a minute," he warned her.

"Hah!" she said again. "I still doubt I can walk."

He wanted to hold her again, tightly.

He wanted to hold her forever.

Still catching his breath, he said, "Would now be a good time to ask you to marry me again?"

Cass just shook her head slowly, a serene smile spreading across her face like warm sunshine. "Asking me now would be taking advantage of my disorientation."

"I disoriented you. I feel I should benefit from it."

"Tomorrow," she had said, as he swung his legs around and sat upright next to her. "Tomorrow will be soon enough for serious discussions. I do not feel serious now."

"And I accept your conclusions in all things," Oliver said, stealing another kiss because he could.

CHAPTER 25

"Lord Howiston."

Someone was calling Oscar? Why would they do that?

"Lord Howiston. I do beg your pardon, your lordship."

Oliver blinked his eyes hard. Some lad in livery was hovering over him sounding apologetic and, based on the angle of the sun, he had had entirely too few hours of sleep. Again.

He slapped his hand against the mattress at his side. Cass. Where was she?

Then he remembered. He had bundled her up in that dress and her shawl and kissed her lips that were still flushed from their lovemaking and she had gone back to her own chambers.

He had wanted to walk with her, but she shook her head no as well as made the motion for *no*.

"If I am out wandering the hallways in the small hours, I am peculiar. But if you are with me? What am I then? No."

And she'd kissed him, and he had used all his remaining strength not to drag her back to his bed.

And now it was—what the hell time was it?—and this fellow was standing over him.

"What?"

"His lordship requires your presence, sir."

"Who?" Oliver wasn't getting more cooperative. "Faircombe? What for? Tell me he has turned his ankle horse-riding, I dare you."

"Lord Rawleigh, sir."

His *father*?

What could his father want with him?

* * *

OLIVER SELDOM SAW his father at any time of day, so perhaps it should not have surprised him to see the older man dressed and clean-shaven.

His father sported a long queue, like Oliver's own, having long ago given up the powdered wigs of his younger days.

It made Oliver consider the similarities between them rather than the differences his mother always delighted in pointing out.

"Sir." His father avoided calling him by his title but couldn't seem to bring himself to use Oliver's first name either.

"Your lordship," and Oliver inclined his head.

His father's eyes, still clear and missing nothing, flicked over Oliver's disheveled hair and dark shadow of unshaved beard. "Still so meticulous with your toilet."

"It is the second morning I have been awakened for an emergency of some kind, sir." Oliver swallowed the apology he wanted to give reflexively. He would not apologize for being summoned at this hour.

"I did not want this matter to grow any older. Lady Rawleigh tells me that you have expressed an interest in marriage to this Miss Cullen."

"It is more than an interest."

"It is less than an interest. It is nonexistent."

Very well, if that was how the old man wanted it. "I assure you, sir, it is more than an interest. It is a plan."

"Is there an agreement between you two?"

Oliver wanted to say yes. He had it on the tip of his tongue. But he did not want to say yes to that question until Cass said yes to his.

"I take it from your silence that there is no agreement. That only gives us the benefit of avoiding solicitors. Best not to add breach of promise to your other accomplishments."

Rather than getting angry, Oliver felt utterly calm. He was of age. His father could no more stop his marriage to Cass than he could have stopped Oliver's medical studies, or his service in the wars. "If you recall, sir, I have a long record of taking the action I choose to take."

"When you affect only yourself, sir, I have no quarrel with you. But in this matter I will be obeyed, because this is a matter of the title."

Oliver only shrugged. "You cannot prevent my inheritance of the title, no matter how much it pains you."

The Earl's eyes now turned as hard as granite. "No, I cannot. And that gives me a pain I do not expect you to understand, as you will never feel it. The line of title says who we are to Britain and also what Britain is to us, not that you have ever felt the weight of that."

"Britain means so much to me that I sailed abroad to fight for her, your lordship. I have stood ankle-deep in blood for her. What comparable passion do you have?" Oliver snapped, more puzzled than angry by his father's incomprehensible standards.

"I had sons for her. And I will not give up this responsibility because of your sudden desire to cloak your insatiable need for the opposite sex in the institution of marriage."

"I beg your pardon?"

"Sir, I receive reports on you from time to time. I have no illusions about you and I have little interest. I do not care how many women you bed. But you will not marry and ruin the unbroken line of this title."

"Sir." It was early, Oliver had slept little for the entire week-end, and while his father's obstruction was something he expected, this speech was making no sense. "Perhaps you have forgotten that marriage *gives* legitimacy to any children of union between men and women? I can assure you that I have no other illegitimate children, and only my legitimate heirs, should there be any, would inherit the title you now hold."

"You will have no legitimate heirs, as you are no legitimate heir of mine."

"*What?*"

"I think I have explained myself."

Oliver looked at his father's ramrod-straight back, so similar to his own. His father had never been close with him, but he had always felt a type of respect for the man.

"I don't... I don't think you intend to say what you are saying."

"I'm old, sir, not senile." His father had his hands clasped behind his back, legs braced.

But the look on his face... Oliver knew regret when he saw it.

"Your lordship, *why?*"

Lord Rawleigh sighed. It was the heavy, tired sigh of an old, old man. "I've never understood you, Oliver, but I have been proud of you in my own way. You have never been at all the son of an earl, with your studies and your profession and your travels to fight. It never bothered me; I had Oscar." And now his father looked every day of his age. "But Oscar is gone and you are my heir. And I can stomach your philandering and your trade and your mingling with the poor and sick, but I cannot stomach knowingly breaking this family's custody of this earldom.

"I don't care if you have children. Have as many as you like. But not within marriage. Because I will not see the title go to a child of yours. Victor or his son will be your heir, and that is final."

Oliver just spread his hands. "The threat of my marriage brought this dilemma home to you?"

"Of course."

But the way his father's eyes dipped when he said it set a bell ringing at the back of Oscar's mind.

He advanced toward his father, slowly.

Step by step, he thought through this impossible problem out loud.

"Your wife, my mother, undoubtedly told you of my conversation with her on the subject of marriage when I was last here. You could have summoned me at any point in the intervening weeks, or even written me your ultimatum. You did not tell me this until now because you did not think this until now."

Another step. "Your objection is not to Miss Cullen, because again, you would have told me yesterday, or even the night before if you thought ill of the young lady. You don't dislike her; you barely notice other people, isn't that right, your lordship."

And another step. "You have acknowledged me as your son through my entire life, even as you cut off my funds, through medical school, through the army. You knew, apparently, the life I was leading in London and you had no objection."

And one more. He was practically nose to nose with his father. And this was his father, the man whom he had called father for his entire life no matter what. His voice was softer now, he was so close.

Oliver said, "You have only decided this morning to tell me that you will not allow me to marry. I believe you when you say that the only thing that moves you is the inheritance of this title. It is the only thing I have ever seen you care about, that is certain. So what has so moved you to the certainty this morning that I am *not* your son?"

He looked into his father's eyes. "Why now, father?"

The Earl only looked away.

"The only person I can think of who would be able to persuade you of any suspicions you might have had about my ancestry, is your wife."

"I forbid you to bother your mother with this," the earl said immediately, one fist clenching in midair.

Oliver looked at it. And him.

"My mother has decided to confirm for you these suspicions of yours. And we both know it is not because of me. She dislikes Miss Cullen."

"I cannot permit you to marry at all," Lord Rawleigh looked as though something were tearing apart inside him.

"Since I am only willing to marry Miss Cullen, your blanket refusal covers her as well."

Now Oliver leaned forward, and his voice was solid and sure. "But you have never controlled me, sir, and you will not now. I am of age

THE COUNTESS INVENTION

and the young lady is of age and even you cannot force the entire Church of England to refuse to marry us. I assure you, we *will* be married. So organize your life around that realization."

Oliver spun on the heel of his boot and made for the door.

"I *can* compel you, Lord Howiston."

"You have no levers left, sir. What can you forbid me? Money?" Oliver let out a grunt of dismissal, continuing to walk to the door.

"I cannot forbid you anything but I can cut off your brother and sister."

Oliver stopped.

Turned back.

His eyes fixed on the Earl. "You are serious."

"Deadly."

"You would not turn out your son and his family. And her ladyship my mother would not turn out her only daughter."

"This is my decision, not hers. And I assure you. To keep you from introducing bastardy into this line? I would turn Victor out in a heartbeat."

"Your small grandchildren. The mother of your grandchildren. You know they have no money, and no means of making any."

"The title will come to them with the estate, the houses, the money, the lands, at the proper time."

"And until that time, *how shall they eat?*"

"It will not come to that, sir, because you will not force it to come to that."

Oliver just stared at his father.

"You do not have the money to house them," Lord Rawleigh went on, "as you and I both know. Even your Miss Cullen's funds along with yours would not be sufficient, not for schooling and the other things I know you want those children to have. And Miss Cullen's father will not support you if you marry his daughter against his will only to bring her the stain of marrying a bastard son."

"You will not tell him."

"There is nothing I would not do to protect this line."

"Why?" Oliver kept asking because he truly did not understand.

Maybe he would never understand. "Why do this? This title has never brought you any joy. *Nothing* has ever brought you any joy. Your marriage, this house, your joyless life, these are your problems, not mine. And I never wanted this title, the title has choked the life out of you probably since the moment you were born and it was a millstone around my brother's neck and now you fashion it into a noose to choke me too. Why?"

"I cannot explain duty to you, sir. I cannot explain what it is to believe in your duty and do what your destiny demands no matter the cost to you personally. I apparently failed to raise you to understand that."

"Thank God for that," and Oliver left the room.

* * *

When Cass awoke, it was both because the sun was in her eyes and because Peg was poking her in the ribs.

There is no breakfast as such here, right? But there is luncheon and you want to be ready for it, said Peg, referring to the late repast that served as both the early meal and the midday meal for the party-goers, who tended to rise late. *There's a bath and time to wash your hair if you hurry.*

Cass suppressed the grin she felt wanting to spread all over her face. Peg would notice and Peg was not stupid. *Thank you, I will bathe immediately!*

And she did, glad to have a tub to sink into and glad for Peg's assistance with washing her hair. If she tossed it enough it should dry quickly and let Peg dress it for the day.

She wished she had the morning to herself, to mull over the party, and the night before. All of the night before. Mull it over and over again, if she could.

She could not believe that such a thing had happened to *her*.

She was more willing to believe that fairy kidnappings were real, and that she would now be forced to live for a hundred years underground, than to believe that Oliver Burke had made love to her, much less that he had made love like *that*.

Cass felt light as a feather, she felt beautiful, she felt like she was glowing. She felt a little sore here and there but that just made her smile a small, secret smile that no one would understand but Oliver.

Oliver! She desperately wanted to see him.

If a tiny shred of doubt remained in her mind about the wisdom of marrying him, she was ready to set fire to that shred of doubt. He had not spoken any words of love; she did not care. She had not expected any such thing and if she still secretly longed for it, at least a little, she had *no* intention of wasting another moment worrying about *that*. She adored him, they suited each other, and she could no longer claim any objections to sharing his bed. In fact the opposite.

She adored him.

Oh dear.

Cass stopped mid-motion as she reached for her soap.

She *adored* him.

She had never expected anyone to love her.

It had never occurred to her that she might be the one to fall in love.

Well, all the better.

Right?

This would work out because it had to.

The sweet glow she felt in her body down to her bones started to fade as she wondered what would happen if he continued his habit of lovers all over London once they were married.

No, he wouldn't do that. She trusted him.

She wasn't sure why, but down to her bones, she *did* trust him.

She had felt mostly sympathetic for him facing the transparent traps of Lady Sherrin and Lady Charlotte. She could see the problem; he was not only beautiful to her, he was objectively beautiful, and women wanted him.

Well, not *him*; they didn't even know him. But they wanted something *from* him. Or to wear him, she thought a little wryly.

Cass could not explain it, but from the day he had come to the house and been so kind about her attempt at deception, she had felt that if nothing else, she could trust him.

Now she knew that there was a great deal more to him.

But she trusted him just the same.

Her smile came back. Cass fought to keep it down to a reasonable size. It was going to be tough work. Unfortunately a Morland houseparty did not lend itself to her kissing Oliver whenever she pleased.

That was going to be difficult.

CHAPTER 26

Oliver was proud of the way he marched away from his father's study. He was a little surprised at his own ability to keep his feet under him. He felt as though he had been shot.

He could imagine, dimly, a future time when he would have the luxury of anger, maybe even hate. While he had no illusions about his mother, he had never dreamed that she would be capable of this.

Without realizing it, he found that his feet had taken him across the length of Morland and down to the guest wing where the house-party was housed.

He could not tell Cass. He needed time to figure out what to do.

He had to talk to *someone*.

Oliver found himself rapping at Lady Gadbury's door before he had even realized that that was where he was.

Her lady's maid greeted him with an irritable scowl, which shifted to surprise to see him standing there.

"Who is it at this hour, Matilda?"

"It is... Dr. Burke, madam," said the maid, opening the door wider for Oliver.

Lady Gadbury was seated at a bench before a dressing table, her nightrail clinging to her with the dampness of a morning ablution and her hair, still thick and shining, was flowing down her back.

She looked even more surprised than her maid.

"Oliver? What on earth? I cannot call it a pleasure because it is an imposition to call on a woman in her chambers. But we are after all in your home, so I must forgive you."

Oliver felt the beginning of an ache at the base of his skull as he considered correcting her about what was or was not his home. "Laura, I'm flummoxed."

"What on earth? Come sit down, man, and tell me about it."

He dropped into a chair. From where he sat he could see her rubbing scented oil into the skin of her arms, her decolleté. At one time he would have enjoyed it. Now he didn't care.

"My father has forbidden me to marry Miss Cullen."

"Well, that *is* for the best, isn't it?"

Oliver gaped at her.

"What?" Laura Gadbury took up her hairbrush, began to run it through her hair. "You don't want to be saddled with a woman like that, and goodness knows you would tire of her too soon to even make a good showing of it. Why would you want to be married anyway, with your tastes?"

"My *tastes* are for Miss Cullen, as you well know." Oliver felt his jaw clench, sending the throbbing in his head spreading through his skull.

"That is only today, Oliver. You know better than anyone how your tastes do change. Let's leave aside the topic of what she does or does not offer you." Lady Gadbury noted how the muscles in Oliver's jaw were tensed, and she kept half an eye on him while pretending to see only her own hairbrush. "What do you offer her? A future title? A life of penury—in the trades—until you inherit? The pleasure of meeting the women you've bedded all over town, and the knowledge that the number will keep growing?"

"Why do you assume that?"

"Why do you *not* assume it?"

Oliver's head was still spinning, from his father's accusations, from his mother's betrayal, and now this. "I cannot explain myself, but I can assure you that having found the woman for me I will be true to her."

"What a notion! All women are 'for you', Oliver, in case you hadn't noticed."

Oliver felt an unaccustomed streak of ugliness cross paths with his usually calm temper and decided to make a foray into the outer world. "Laura," he said evenly, "you yourself are evidence of my choosiness, not the opposite. But if you are feeling old, or unattractive, please mark down only your own social worth. It does not affect my selectivity at all."

She stopped in the motion of raising the hairbrush. And turned to face him directly.

"That was unkind and unjust."

"Ungallant, certainly. But largely just." Oliver pushed himself up out of the chair. "Why do I keep seeking out women to soothe my feelings at my lowest moments? It never serves my purpose. My apologies, Lady Gadbury, I had been thinking of you as a friend."

"Don't leave angry, Oliver, my word. I have known your mother longer than I have known you. I think you give her remarkably little credit for understanding her own son and what he needs."

"Madam, I give her no credit at all."

Opening her door, Oliver walked out.

Only to come face to face with Cass in the hallway.

* * *

Cass caught the image in the flash of an eye, but it was burned into her mind and it would not be leaving her any time soon.

Oliver, still unshaven and tousle-haired, coming out Lady Gadbury's door. That lady clearly dressing in the background, her hair down, her nightrail just tossed on.

Cass' hands had probably tangled his hair that way, she thought wildly. Please, let those tangles be from her own hands.

She was going to start carrying a bow and arrows. She was going to start carrying a *pistol*. The neverending parade of women trying to take Oliver from her stretched out before her like a long weary road.

But then she caught Oliver's face.

He didn't look like a boy with his hand caught in someone else's pocket. He looked startled to see her, then glad, she wasn't misreading that, he clearly looked very glad.

Then a sadness settled over him and did not leave.

"Miss Cullen," he said, bowing to her. "May I escort you downstairs?"

"Of course," she said, and smiled at him.

And when she put her arm on his, she could feel the current flowing between them.

* * *

HE COULD FEEL through her hand, her heat, her affection, her *love*.

Christ, it was torture.

She was going to forgive him. She was going to forgive him *again*. Not Lady Sherrin, or Lady Charlotte, or even the most dreaded Lady Gadbury was going to shake her faith in him.

He could not bear to explain the horror of his family's actions.

He could fight his mother. He couldn't fight his mother, his father, and the opinion of everyone who had ever known him. Apparently they knew things about him that he did not know himself.

And he couldn't turn his young brother, with his sweet wife and tiny children, into homeless vagabonds. Nor could he provide for them.

His family had him trapped—the title had him trapped—and he would never be free.

And his only comfort was that he could keep it from ensnaring her too.

If he explained his parents' actions, she would forgive him again, because she loved him. He knew that now. She had already forgiven him yet another visit to Lady Gadbury that was far from appropriate. If Oliver wanted Cass to leave him, he would have to do something unforgivable.

Which might kill him.

Because he loved her too.

CHAPTER 27

Oliver separated from Cass at the table, where a number of the other guests were still gathered, though largely only lingering with their tea.

Lady Sherrin and Bradley Waite sat with Geoffrey Eliot and his sister. Lord Faircombe and Miss Farsworth were not in attendance, nor were their hosts or Lady Gadbury. But Lady Inglemawr was there, as well as Anthony Hastings, and young David Castle sat with him.

Oliver surveyed the situation like a site for surgery. He would have to make quick cuts. The shorter the work, the less the agony.

Too many people had seen him show favor to Miss Cullen. If he did not marry her, her reputation would suffer a blow from which it would not recover. Apparently all of London knew of *his* reputation, for all he thought he had been unnoticed. And apparently there were women all over London with very poor opinions of him, which he had not known either. There could be traps set by many of them for Miss Cullen everywhere if he did not cut ties completely.

More importantly, she would never have a chance to marry anyone of any standing at all if society had any inkling that she returned his regard. No one would believe that she was still untouched if her name became linked with his. The fact that she was *not* was immaterial. If she wanted to marry anyone else, she must continue to appear above the attentions of a man like Oliver.

He had to find a way to cut ties such that she would completely, irrevocably drop him, cut him, never speak to him again, or she would be tainted by association with him and never have a family of her own.

The thought of his Cassandra marrying someone else felt like it could stop his heart.

But he could not bear, could *not* bear, the thought of Cass spending the rest of her life alone. She deserved so much more than that. She deserved everything he could not give her and so much more.

He watched Cass apply herself to a cup of tea. A sweet, secret smile lurked around the corner of her eyes that she clearly could not entirely suppress. She had never looked more beautiful. She looked like a woman who had been made love to.

Why had he not believed himself when he told her it would be a terrible idea to marry him?

Why had he not realized sooner that he loved her?

Oliver wished he could believe that the night they had spent together would be worth the pain he was about to cause her.

But he was not so self-serving as to believe that.

Lady Gadbury arrived and took a seat next to Lady Charlotte.

"Lady Gadbury. You will be staying for the week," Oliver said, clearing his throat a little.

"Yes, London is quite dead for the year now, and I will keep Lady Rawleigh company."

"And is Lord Faircombe staying for more shooting as well?" Oliver was watching his timing. Cass was standing and walking over to the sideboard to survey the repast.

Geoffrey answered, "My father intends to stay for a full two weeks, and I will keep him company unless my sister wishes to return home."

"I have not decided," Charlotte added shortly.

Cass was passing just behind Oliver's chair. His pulse pounded in his ears and he thought he might be sick.

"And you, Miss Cullen, I suppose you must return home to attend to business."

Oliver could smell Cass' violet water. He knew she was standing right behind him. He knew she could hear him.

Everyone could hear him. A pin falling to the floor would have been quite audible, the room was so silent.

"Whatever do you mean by business?" Charlotte asked immediately.

"I am sure he refers to an inheritance or something similar to which Miss Cullen must attend," said Geoffrey, frowning at his sister.

"No, in fact Miss Cullen builds very clever devices for people with arms and legs off, that sort of thing." Oliver did not know how he was managing to sound so nonchalant. "All over the country. Of course she has a pen name as *Mister* Cullen. Managing to support your household well enough, aren't you, Miss Cullen?"

Oliver turned in his chair to look.

She was looking straight at him.

The plate of toast in her hand was about to fall.

"Can I help you with that, miss?" Oliver asked her solicitously, reaching for it.

"No," she said, her voice only a shade above a silent breath.

"Of course," and he turned back to his own soft-boiled egg, which there was no chance he could eat.

"How mysterious!" Lady Sherrin sounded delighted. "You have not told us anything of this exciting adventure!"

Ladies who had adventures did not marry peers, Oliver thought to himself.

But even as he opened his mouth to correct her, Anthony Hastings had leaned forward to set down his own cup of tea, with rather more force than tea usually required.

"On the contrary, Lady Sherrin, business is hardly an adventure. My sister Lady Grantley is the primary party organizing horse training at Roseford Manor, and I believe her work is gaining some recognition in interested circles."

"Or notoriety," commented Charlotte into her teacup.

"I do apologize, Lady Charlotte, I must have mumbled. Recognition was the word I used."

His hard black stare stayed on Charlotte until she narrowed her eyes at him, causing Geoffrey to frown at his sister again.

Anthony sat back in his chair. "Adventure is not a word that one applies to a young lady."

"Nor is business," said Lady Gadbury, applying butter to her toast in a slow, deliberate way.

Oliver was still sitting half-turned in his chair, unable to take his eyes off of Cass'.

It was the last tie between them.

She cut it.

Turning back toward the sideboard she handed her plate to a footman. Without another word she left the room.

Someone help her, thought Oliver, hoping the desperate screaming in his head would reach someone, anyone, who would go to Cass because he could not.

Anthony Hastings rose from the table. "I believe I have some business to attend to myself," and he bowed to all assembled. "Are you also finished eating, Mr. Castle?"

"Absolutely," and the grim tone and look of the golden-haired lad had locked his usually sunny expression into something old and hard.

Oliver looked at his plate and stayed in his chair. For Cass to have any chance at the love of a good man, Oliver must never speak to her again.

It was over for him now.

* * *

ANTHONY AND DAVID both caught sight of Cass as she started for the stairs.

She tripped on her hem on the first step, nearly going down headlong.

"Miss Cullen," and Anthony seemed to have a way of magically transporting himself to her side, he moved so fast.

He had her supported by her arms before she fell, but she would not look him in the face.

"Miss Cullen," and the usually resourceful Anthony Hastings seemed to be at a loss and looking around for help when David reached their side.

The young man's hands flew quickly. *Tell us how to help.*

"I don't know how you can help. I don't think it can be helped," Cass said faintly.

She looked colorless and pale.

"Please do not faint," said Anthony, shaking both her hands in his till she finally met his eyes.

He wished she hadn't.

"I must leave."

"Don't. Gossip spreads like fire in a paper factory if you don't put out the flame immediately."

"You do not understand. He did that deliberately." Cass was shaking her head, looking down again at her hands. "And Lady Sherrin, Lady Charlotte... Lady Gadbury alone would have been enough."

Tearing her hands away from him Cass started to mount the stairs. She gathered her skirt in one hand and climbed. With each step she seemed to be moving faster.

"Let us help you."

"Find me a carriage." Her voice wasn't faint now. The carriage Lady Inglemawr had let would not return for them for two days; she could not wait that long.

"You don't want to travel in the mail carriages." David sounded firm.

"Someone in this godforsaken pile of rocks must be willing to loan me a carriage."

Unmannerly though it was, Anthony was following her up the stairs, David beside him. Anthony leaned toward the other young man. "See if Geoffrey Eliot can do something."

David Castle ran back down the stairs the way they had come in an instant.

Anthony found he had nearly to run to keep up with Miss Cullen as she strode down the corridor. Her legs were long and she was not moving sedately now.

When she flew into the chamber, she startled Peg so much that that woman dropped the clothes brush she was wielding.

We are leaving immediately. Cass' face brooked no discussion.

Peg looked toward Anthony but he had no way of explaining to her, even if he could have used his hands to do it.

What dress do you want to travel in? Peg's question seemed a bit diffident. Cass' face was hard, her jaw set, and she looked very unfamiliar to Peg.

My old one, of course, said Cass with the briefest of glances.

* * *

GEOFFREY HANDED her into the Faircombe coach. "Please tell me if there is anything I can do."

"Do not berate your sister," said Cass without looking at him. "She will only be one of the many."

"We are all sorry to see you go so abruptly, Miss Cullen." Geoffrey looked as if he would like something—or someone—to pummel right about now.

Cass didn't care.

"Mr. Hastings and Mr. Castle will attend us back to London," she said just as shortly as she was saying everything right now.

Lady Inglemawr was already ensconced inside, and Geoffrey handed up her maid and Peg after Cass, then stood back to let the other gentlemen in as well.

"It is my pleasure, Miss Cullen. I only wish I could do more."

Her expression was blank as she only said, "Goodbye."

CHAPTER 28

Lady Inglemawr held the broadsheet by the very edges, trying not to actually touch it. She sighed. "I suppose 'Clockwork Heiress' is better than 'Clockwork Lightskirt'."

Then, hearing Cass' step on the stairs, Lady Inglemawr tossed the entire thing into the fireplace.

When Cass entered the room, Lady Inglemawr was standing on one side of the room, Adams on the other, and a suspicious looking shred of rough paper was just dangling out the side of the fire grate.

"Adams, I do want the papers."

Adams set the tray down. "There is something amiss with the delivery today, Miss."

Cass just sighed. "Did you burn them?"

Adams said nothing.

"If someone has burned them, send someone to fetch more. I told you, I want to see my usual papers, every day."

He bowed and withdrew and left Cass with her tea and Lady Inglemawr looking worried.

* * *

The townhouse had always been quiet, but now it was the quiet found in ruins after a storm.

There had been letters waiting for her when she returned home. She had not answered them. The pile grew a little larger every day.

But you should respond, before any gossip reaches any of your customers. Peg's encouragement was at odds with her dubious expression.

Cass simply could not bring herself to do it.

The idea of signing herself again as Mister George Cullen felt repellent. She had had no idea how much the secret had weighed on her until she was free of it. Now that it was out and the possibilities it had protected were gone, she could not bring herself to try to go back under its shelter. The idea of any *more* secrets also galled her.

In her head, it was not quiet. In her head, she screamed epithets at herself almost by the second, cursing herself for a fool in every possible way. She had been a fool to trust him, she should have known that from the first. She had been a fool tenfold to love him.

Her instincts meant nothing. She'd *known* that. The closed door of this house was her only protection, and she had opened it. She blamed herself.

Though she blamed him too, him with his damned beautiful eyes and that plush lower lip and the way he had made her feel. She blamed his kisses, and his hands, and that deep voice that she could still feel vibrating under her fingertips.

There is a note from your father, Peg added hesitantly. *He wishes you to visit him. He says he will send the carriage tomorrow.*

He can come here if he wants to see me, Cass tossed out carelessly.

He... never does, Peg seemed to feel Cass needed reminding.

He can start. Sighing, Cass stared at the pile of letters. What was the purpose of answering them when their writers would not be responding again? Nonetheless, writing a letter might feel good. *I would be covered with ink if I tried to finish answering those.*

Peg said nothing. That truth was self-evident.

Was she trying to talk herself out of letter-writing, or into it?

On second thought, Cass went on, *send out for a hansom cab. And tell Lady Inglemawr that we are going out.*

JUDITH LYNNE

* * *

THIS TIME when Cass entered Madame Dudin's, it was as if all the other young girls were as a mist. She neither cared to differentiate any individuals among them, nor did she try.

"Please fetch Madame Dudin," she said to the first assistant she encountered.

"I will be happy to help you in a moment," said the girl, not even looking at Cass' face.

"Miss," said Cass, moving so that she stood directly in the girl's path. "I do apologize for the inconvenience, but I need to see Madame Dudin. The sooner my business is concluded, the sooner I can leave."

Something in the edge on her expression seemed to spook the girl. The assistant looked to Lady Inglemawr for confirmation. But that woman, her hair twisted up and pinned in what seemed to be a hasty crown and her gown looking suspiciously like a plain blue cotton day dress, just shrugged. No one could tell Cass anything any more.

In a few moments, Madame Dudin, with a high bosom and even higher irritation, appeared in the middle of the shop.

"Madame, if you please..." Whatever speech she had planned trailed away when she caught sight of Cass' face.

"I do apologize for interrupting, madame, but I only wish to spend a few minutes. I need three dresses of a plain black poplin, cut to fit me with the measurements you already have. No ruffles, and I do not care about the style."

"The young lady does not care about the style!" Madame Dudin drew herself up to her full height, a good six inches shorter than Cass, and puffed out her cheeks as if Cass had cheerfully suggested that they all set themselves on fire.

"I do not. I want deep pockets on both sides, for pencils and those sorts of things, and the color must not show stains from ink."

"*Black!*"

"No ink stains. Is that sufficiently clear, madame?"

"Black." The color was paining her. "Would linen not do just as well? It is very *durable*." The modiste said it as though it referred to a particularly distasteful crime. Cass just nodded.

"Yes. No ruffles, no lace, no beading. Black. Thank you so much. Do let me know when I should come in for a fitting."

And Cass strode out with Lady Inglemawr trailing behind just as they had come in.

* * *

"Is this what you will do everywhere, now? Simply march in and demand things?"

Cass just shrugged one shoulder. "When one has lost everything important, everything else becomes extremely simple."

"I wish I could do that." Lady Inglemawr said it very softly.

"Please speak up."

"I wish I could do that!"

That roused Cass into something like surprise. "Why would you want to do something like that?"

Lady Inglemawr's eyes were down, and she was tugging on the buttons of her gloves as though she were going to tear them off. "I suppose... that man told you about my own problems."

"He did not." She bit it out.

"Ah. I supposed he had... well..." Lady Inglemawr now clearly wished she had never said anything.

Cass sank back into her own seat. She could not, after all, find much energy within herself to care.

But then Lady Inglemawr let out an explosive, *"They..."*

Cass only raised an eyebrow.

"I was an idiot to be thrilled by my marriage. He was rich and titled and that was all I cared about. I never asked if he was cruel. I bore his temper and his fist for fifteen years before he died. *That* was the happiest day of my life."

The pain in Lady Inglemawr's voice broke through the shell of silence Cass felt all around her. She leaned closer to catch every word and closed one of her hands over the other woman's, stilling her tearing at her gloves.

"No one cared about *that*. He was only what they expected him to be, and so was I. I was the Marchioness, no one cared about *me*, only that I did what the Marchioness must do. And when I did find love, I... I couldn't *tell* anyone, no one would understand, no friends."

Cass just patted her hands. "They are not friends."

Lady Inglemawr let out a strangled laugh. "Oh I know, dear, I have always known. That is not what I am saying at all. What I am trying to tell you is that... if love matters to you at all, marrying an earl was never going to make you happy."

Cass squeezed Lady Inglemawr's small hands together one more time before letting go. "I had never dreamed of falling in love, Lady Inglemawr. It is a great surprise to me, but yes, love matters to me a great deal. I knew nothing about it, and as it turns out, it is the end of happiness, not the source of it."

Lady Inglemawr looked as if she wished to argue, but could not.

* * *

WHEN THE HIBBERTS saw Lady Inglemawr and then Cass descending from the hansom cab, Lady Hibbert became so excited that she tugged at Lord Hibbert's watch chain. That gentleman grabbed his pocket watch and forestalled a terrible accident.

"I told you that was her, sir, the heiress on our very street."

Lord Hibbert squinted. "Looks like the same girl to me."

"That is what I am telling you. That young woman, our neighbor. That is the Clockwork Heiress that drawing in the paper was showing."

"What, the one of a woman with a winding handle coming out of her back and wearing a man's jacket?"

"Yes! I know you saw that paper this morning, I showed it to you!"

"I thought that was some new fashion."

"No, that is the Clockwork Heiress! She invents things in the house and sells them all over the country!"

"Not really." Lord Hibbert seemed to start following what his wife was saying. "A merchant? In the Viscountess' home? You must be mistaken."

"I told you that must be her!"

"On what basis do you assume this, madame?"

"Oh, you know, the writers for those papers make up little puzzles you can solve to guess names and such if you know who the people are."

"If you know who the people are, can't see much point to making more of a mystery about it." He watched the two women disappear into the townhouse. "I don't like the idea of a woman making money on our street. Isn't seemly. This neighborhood is of the highest quality, after all."

"But I am sure the Viscountess must have left the house to her in some fashion, sir, else she would not be here at all."

"She ought to have some other home to go to, and go to it," harrumphed Lord Hibbert.

CHAPTER 29

No one could persuade her not to read the papers, but Mrs. Orfill did beg her not to keep them.

Lady Inglemawr suggested that she burn them.

"The poison opinions of the *ton* do enough damage without treasuring them like they were gold," said Lady Inglemawr, with enough acid in her tone and for once sufficiently loudly that she was *very* easy to hear.

She made her impression. Cass burned them.

It was three more days before her father arrived.

She received him in the library, and she simply let him rail while she looked at him.

"You look tired, Papa."

"Did you not hear a single thing I just said?"

"No."

"Cass." Her father leaned forward as if to test the temperature of her forehead. She pushed aside the touch of his hand with her own, just shook her head no.

And sat there.

"Cass, you do not seem to understand that there is no rescue for this."

"I know very well. When I have to close these doors, I will require you to find places for my staff. They are my friends."

William Cullen looked around the room with puzzlement, though there was no one else in it. "What do you mean, friends?" Clearly he had never heard the words *staff* and *friends* used interchangeably.

Cass just shook her head and smiled for a moment. It faded away.

Her father went on. "Anyway, that is not my concern. You will never marry a peer, but you should still marry. I have not given up the hope for you to have your own life."

"What, a banker, Papa? A butcher? I thought of my life as this home and the work that I did. You are undoubtedly thinking in terms of social role, so what do you think I should reach for next?"

"I... I will admit I did not expect to find you like this."

"Like what?"

"So... so limp and unresisting! You do not seem like yourself."

"Do I not? And how would you describe me, Papa? You have never seen a single thing that I have created. You have never met one person that I helped. Why is that?"

Her father looked astonished. "My promise to your mother regarded your marriage. Your whole *life*. I have never wavered from that."

"My life, as it turns out, consists of this." Rising with something of her customary energy, Cass grabbed several of her foolscap drawings in one hand, tossed them to the couch where he sat. Her father picked them up, rifled through them. Cass went on, "It could have been enough. I would have been *happy*. Why you could not leave well enough alone I will never know."

"I promised your mother!"

"It is curious to me, Papa," Cass said slowly as she sank back into her seat, "that *this* is what you continually recall of my mother. What I remember was how regretful she was about my loss of my hearing. What I remember was that she blamed you for it. I remember you arguing about it. Do you not remember any of that?"

Her father stayed silent.

"I remember your relief when you finally sent me to that school.

And I remember the other children telling me how their brothers and sisters and parents learned something of the manual language we all used, so that they could talk. But you never did, did you."

Cass clasped her hands in front of her, sitting straight upright, with her knees just as close as they had ever been. It was exactly the way she had always sat, but a new tone to her voice made everything different as she said, "Why did you never want to really talk with me, Papa?"

William Cullen could not meet his daughter's eyes.

"It must have been hard for you, losing your wife without her forgiveness, her understanding. It must have been hard for you having me about the house, staring at you all the time, trying to figure out what was happening and reminding me of your failures to her, and to me."

Cass reached out and tapped on his knee, as she would to get the attention of someone who could not hear.

When he finally looked up she said, "Those are your regrets, Papa, not mine. Stop holding my dead mother over me and go home and tell your wife you love her. Because I suspect you do, and that you never tell her so."

The older man's eyes sparkled with something that looked suspiciously like tears. "I cannot just leave you here, like this."

"Have you not left me here like this for a long time?"

"I have... many failings as a father for which to apologize."

"I am sorry, Papa, I sounded waspish." The words seemed sincere but still devoid of emotion.

William Cullen wiped his eyes. "We ought to... talk about the further disposition of the house. Later. When you are stronger."

She could see the tears sliding down his cheeks now, and she wished that she could wipe them away, but it felt to her as though even that small motion called for her to feel anything other than empty, and she did not.

Cass did reach over to repossess her drawings. She flipped through them herself, slowly. They soothed something inside of her. They were nothing brilliant, but they were clever, and they were *hers*. "You know where I am, Papa, and I will still be just as out of society as I have always been. I hope you let your younger children learn from my mistakes. Perhaps you will be able to give them a bit more room to breathe. And please, go home."

* * *

As the weather grew colder and the house even more damp from the unforgiving rain, the chill crept inside and seemed to settle and harden.

Cass wondered, on some of the long gray monotonous mornings, if perhaps the house might solidify into one large cube of ice, and if it did, would they all be preserved in it.

Then the first letter came.

"Open it!" Lady Inglemawr sounded uncharacteristically excited.

Cass just sat there at the table, looking at the letter on the tray Adams was holding as if she had never seen a letter before.

"Of course," she said faintly, taking up a knife from the table to slice it open.

She didn't notice how many people were looking at her as she skimmed the page, or that they were all holding their breath.

"It is from Lord Swithin," she said, sounding puzzled. "He wants to know if I have made any progress on the commission about which he wrote to me. Do I have a letter here from Lord Swithin?"

"There are so many letters you did not open," Selene said with the slightest touch of reproval in her tone as she pretended to focus on dusting, while Adams only said, "I will check, Miss Cullen."

"We should make a game of it. A ratafia cake for every letter you open," Selene suggested, pausing with her hands resting on the blue-figured vase.

Cass rewarded her with a slight smile and an audible "Ha ha" before adding, "He says that he knows I have had a difficult time of it but wishes to hear from me soon." The look she gave the paper was puzzled as she read it again. Perhaps she had read it wrong.

"Here is Lord Swithin's previous letter, miss," said Adams, returning and offering another little bundle of words on his tray.

This one too, sliced open and read, made Cass' brows pull together in confusion. "An entire house! His mother is taking possession of the dowager cottage on his estate and he wishes me to outfit it for her comfort. She has arthritis in all her joints and even opening a door pains her."

"She is getting a dowager cottage. Surely she'll have servants to do most things for her." Despite her tart words, Lady Inglemawr's voice practically twinkled with the excitement of something pleasant happening in the house.

"I suppose," Cass half-whispered.

After she had read both letters through twice, she looked up. Lady Inglemawr, Adams, and Selene all awaited her next breath, and Mrs. Orfill was peeping around the corner from the hallway.

"I suppose only Peg has actual work to do today. This cannot... He cannot be serious."

"Why not? He does not want to marry you. He wants you to outfit his dowager cottage," said Selene with perfect practicality.

"Hmm."

Cass left the letters on her desk but the next day there was another one. Two days after that, another. And then the next day, there were three.

Peg dusted the books in the library, surreptitiously organizing those of Cass' papers that had somehow travelled around the room in the past few weeks, landing here and there in sad disarray.

Cass showed her the three letters. *They all want me to do more commissions for them.*

Why shouldn't they? You did work for them before.

Not all; this one is new—and a bishop!

Perhaps, said Peg, coming to stand next to her by her desk, *perhaps they need you more than they need to shun you.*

Cass just shook her head a little. *And this one—this is the physician who loaned me the journal on artificial limb materials. I thought he must* want it back, and he does, but he asks if I want to see a paper he has gotten from Scotland on the subject.

Peg looked over the small pile of now-opened letters. *I expect you do.*

Cass threw up her hands, then said, *I don't understand.*

Peg stuck out her lower lip thoughtfully. *I know nothing about lord people or any other kind of high types of people, but I do know they didn't invite you to a party or anything like that, did they? They're just picking up their business with you where they left off.*

That is true. Most of them don't even mention the horrid papers. Here Cass looked rueful. *Except this fellow who has addressed his letter to the most esteemed Clockwork Heiress. I think he thinks he is funny.*

You can be grateful that one isn't inviting you to any social events.

Cass spent the rest of the day wondering what was happening, and what she should do. It wasn't that she enjoyed floating around the house feeling sad and empty; that was simply what had happened, and she hadn't had the energy to figure out what else *to* do. All the roads to the future had seemed closed.

But here were doors opening that she hadn't expected.

Was there a reason to go through them?

Was there a reason *not* to?

Then in the evening post came a short note from a direction she knew well: Roseford Manor.

> *My dear Miss Cullen,* Letty Grantley wrote in a slapdash hand, *you must visit Roseford Manor for a Christmas holiday. We get little news of society here in our little village, but my brother has painted a picture that appalls me, and the newspapers we do take are equally horrid. London must be awful right now. Roseford will be at least warm and friendly, and there is good bread and applesauce and a great number of horses. What else could one want for a holiday? Our cook may attempt to roast a goose. It may be disastrous. You do not want to miss it. Please do say you will come. Write to me to say so and I will have rooms prepared for you and yours.*
>
> *Most eagerly,*
> *Letty Grantley*

Cass put aside the question of correspondence to address the more pressing, and unexpectedly pleasant, question of Christmas.

Sailing into the parlor, she found Lady Inglemawr at her needlepoint by the fire.

She suddenly realized that Lady Inglemawr had not left her a day since she returned.

"My lady," she said with an attempt at something like a smile, "what would you say to spending Christmas in the country?"

The Marchioness could have responded that no one traveled at this time of year. Instead she looked up and saw Cass' face wearing a human expression for the first time in weeks. Anything other than blank sadness was a welcome change.

So what she said was, "Shall I hire a carriage?"

CHAPTER 30

The night before their departure, Lady Inglemawr asked quite out of the blue, "Would you be willing... that is, would you let me assume the household bills for this house?"

"What... why would you ask that, my lady? I really mean, why has it occurred to you?"

Lady Inglemawr sank into the chair next to Cass'. "I did not... Well. I have let other rooms in town, and if I let them go I would have the funds to support this townhouse entirely. I did not... It would have been unwise of me to put you in the position of... living under the same roof with... my behavior has not—"

"Please, my lady, we must reach the end of the thought even if it kills us."

The exquisite little Titian-haired beauty actually squirmed in her seat. "My... lover would have to see me here and that... would be bad for your social situation."

Cass nodded, sighing a little. "Which is destroyed."

"No it is not! Miss Cullen, those letters you are receiving show that you are unmasked as a woman of business and perhaps beneath the *ton*, but you are not branded a lightskirt. If someone were to observe the comings and goings of... my friend, you might be in a worse position indeed. My solution is not a good solution if you still wish to marry."

"I see." Cass smiled a little. It felt stiff and unfamiliar on her face. "Let us think about it. We will have time on the trip."

Cass did not have to think about the possibility of getting married one day; that was impossible. She felt as though she had only really had a heart for a very short time, but she had given it away, so unwisely, and there was no way of getting it back now.

Oliver had disappeared. Not only had he not presented himself to explain, as she had hoped he would the first few nights that she was home, but he had disappeared. Delina Farsworth wrote to her and told her that no one at Morland knew his whereabouts, and Bradley Waite, who had accompanied the Eliots back to the Faircombe estate, sent a brief note asking if she had any news, which implied that he had none.

Whatever mistakes she had made and wherever he had gone, he had taken her heart, and the idea of marrying anyone else was absurdity.

She dreamed about him, that open, boyish smile that he seemed to give only to her, and she screamed about him in her head when she imagined how many women he truly had seduced with that smile. And she reminded herself over and over that she had been wrong, so wrong. All the mistakes had been hers to make, and she had made them.

But Cass did not want to refuse Lady Inglemawr's offer outright. It would mollify her father and Lady Inglemawr both to think that marriage was something she might still one day consider. And it was reassuring somehow, finding that Lady Inglemawr was a friend after all.

* * *

Letty was alternating between scowling and poking at her recalcitrant ball of tangled yarn, daydreaming about the kisses she would steal from her husband under the kissing ball, and wondering aloud

THE COUNTESS INVENTION

what they could do to keep her soon-to-arrive visitor Miss Cullen entertained.

Mrs. Peterborough, her husband's oldest family friend, sat on the couch as well, stitching linen napkins with an impeccable hemstitch and stalwartly not pointing out the poor quality of Letty's knitting.

When the maid Sarah appeared in the door, apparently breathing hard from her hurry, Letty was ready for a new amusement. Sarah curtsied. "There is a carriage coming up the drive, ma'am."

"What fun this will be. We should have visitors more often!"

Then Letty's festivity disappeared when she finally saw her guest step through the door.

"But Miss Cullen, you should have come sooner!"

Miss Cullen had been slender before but now looked like a graceful shadow made of bones. Her dark sweep of a gown gave no relief to the eye as it reached almost to the floor, its unbroken drop making a startling contrast to her face and hands, which had faded from cream to stone in their color.

Miss Cullen did smile, though it instantly dissolved. Still, it had been there. "I am quite well, Lady Grantley, I hope you are as well."

Letty decided then and there that Miss Cullen, however intelligent she may be, was no judge of her own wellbeing, and Letty acted accordingly.

"Sarah, we must have hot baths for our guests tonight as well as the warming pans, and would you send someone to the stables to let Anthony know Miss Cullen is here? And Griggs, would you ask the cook for some fresh tea and any sandwiches or such like that she can serve immediately? And be sure to ask her for the jelly. You have a sweet tooth, if I remember correctly, Miss Cullen, do you not?"

"Yes," Cass was startled into saying, adding, "But I am not hungry, please do not take any pains on my behalf."

This Letty ignored entirely. "Sir Michael will want to know our guests are here when you return from the kitchen, Griggs. But jelly. And ask her to boil an egg, please. But send the bread and tea first."

"Ma'am," said the old butler, bowing smartly, and withdrew immediately.

"And you must be Lady Inglemawr," Letty addressed the other woman, who wore a dazzling bottle-green traveling coat and a becoming riot of red-gold curls in her hair. "Would you like to go to your chamber?"

"Quite."

Letty waved to a footman, who leaped forward to lead Lady Inglemawr away.

"I just want to sit quietly," murmured Cass.

* * *

THE OLD WOMAN sewing on the settee in the parlor had thick, gnarled joints in her fingers and more wrinkles on her face than Cass had ever seen on anyone.

She greeted Cass politely enough when Letty introduced her as Mrs. Peterborough, but then said, blessedly, nothing.

Cass ate some of what Letty had brought to her, but found it soothing to simply sit and watch Mrs. Peterborough sew.

When finally the older woman looked up and said quite bluntly, "Who is that mourning dress for, young woman?". Cass felt sufficiently calm that she just answered with the first thought that came to her head.

"Myself, I suppose."

"Hmm." Mrs. Peterborough went on stitching.

After a few minutes she said, "I never had the luxury of mourning for myself."

Cass didn't mind; the old woman's comment didn't seem personal, somehow. It seemed as simple an observation as whether or not it was raining.

And then after a few more minutes Mrs. Peterborough added, "But then, I never felt like I had a reason."

Cass watched her fingers nimbly working the tiny silvery needle.

Finally Cass said, "It's also terribly practical. Ink stains do not show."

"Ah," said Mrs. Peterborough.

CHAPTER 31

Almost against her will, Cass found herself eating more at Roseford. Which made no sense, as the food wasn't made by her beloved Mrs. Orfill. If anything, the Grantley's cook was a slightly cranky woman who did not like Letty Grantley's constant forays into her kitchen. But the food was fresh and good, and the Grantley's table included a surprising array of things that had grown, either in the soil of Roseford Manor itself, or in its forest.

Sir Michael and Anthony Hastings both seemed to be making an effort to be charming and amusing at mealtimes, and Cass found herself occasionally genuinely laughing.

She had forgotten how to do that, but at Roseford it just seemed to happen.

And for some reason Lady Inglemawr went on an absolute tear, learning everything there was to learn about cooking and housekeeping from Letty herself.

Cass had brought both Peg and Ira Adams with her, leaving Mrs. Orfill in charge of the house. Selene also had had to stay in town, as her mother was bedridden in the servants' quarters on the fourth floor. William Cullen, in a fit of remorse, sent over a few footmen to ensure their safety, including wide-eyed Reggie and Fred who had both been relocated from Morland with Anthony's assistance.

Cass did not know whether or not it had been a good idea to speak her mind to her father, but Detta was sending her regular notes now, signed with very sincere love that Cass welcomed all the more for its familiarity, and filled with a determination to keep a close eye on Mr. Cullen, which was new.

Cass hoped this was something of a holiday for the Adams', as there were no formal social occasions at Roseford and little for them to do. Laurie, Lady Inglemawr's very fashionable young maid, sniffed disdainfully at the ecstatic way Lady Inglemawr learned to make a pie crust or core a cabbage; but the maid seemed to quite enjoy showing Sarah new hairstyles. And how to hide it when one burnt off one's curls with a too-energetic application of a hot iron.

"Are you glad you came?"

"You know I am." Cass was winding yarn for Letty in the drawing room. She saw no reason for Letty to learn to knit, but the younger woman seemed determined to learn it, and was also very bad at it for some reason. Cass felt compelled to help in any way she could.

"And how long will we have the pleasure of your visit?"

Cass smiled. "Have I worn out my welcome?"

Letty just looked at Cass' smile thoughtfully. "When you walked in my front door, I thought you had forgotten how to do that."

The smile faded.

"Are you well?" Letty prompted, more quietly but still loud enough that Cass would hear.

Cass only shook her head. "How can I trust any decision I make ever again? I was so very wrong about him, so entirely wrong. How can I ask anyone to trust me with any decisions ever again? My desk at home has a stack of letters from people who still want me to design things for them. How *can* I ask them to trust me with money for my work? Or worse, with the welfare of their family?"

Letty nodded, and frowned her fierce-kitten frown. "Miss Cullen, you know the leg you made for Sir Michael had serious problems. So did the saddle."

"I recall."

"Still, you improved the leg tremendously. It is quite comfortable for at least several hours now, you know that. And though Sir Michael has mastered the balance of going without, he sometimes needs the use of that saddle. He would be delighted to explain both its benefits and its drawbacks to you."

Letty poked at her yarn with visible annoyance, then went on. "You have never promised anyone perfection, Miss Cullen, nor has anyone expected it of you. You have promised them help. And that is why they still want your work."

Cass slumped a little in her chair, as if exhausted by the need to remain upright. "I want to crawl into a box, have it nailed shut, and dropped into the English Channel."

Letty shook her head. "I don't think you do. That is those horrid scandal papers talking."

"I do not care about them as much as you might think. Their arrows have no sting; they are wide of the target. Clockwork Heiress? I have never built anything from clockworks."

"So what stings?"

"*I* know how I failed myself. I know I believed things I should not believe. I know how foolish I have been."

Blowing out a vehement sigh, Letty laid down her recalcitrant knitting. "Miss Cullen. If a woman is fooled by a man who sets out to seduce her, I know whom I would blame."

Cass could not explain to Letty how wrong her description was; she did not want to think about the ways in which it was right. She could only let out the thoughts that had been swirling repeatedly in her head for weeks. "He must have planned to drop me like that all along. What else explains it? A whim? He certainly did it purposefully. I *cannot* stop thinking about the fact that he did it purposefully. I never saw any streak of cruelty in him, and I must have convinced myself to overlook it, the streak is so broad."

"How would you know why he did what he did if you did not speak to him?"

Cass reared away as if she had been offered a live spider. "I do not wish to speak to him!"

"Nor do I recommend it," Letty amended hastily.

"I do not know where he is! I do not *wish* to know where he is! I hope *he* was nailed into a box and dropped in the English Channel and is on his way to the archipelagoes on the other side of the earth!"

"Quite! Quite! I only mean, you must not torture yourself wondering what you cannot know. We don't know why he did what he did; we may never know. Anthony says that there is some gossip in London wondering where he is, but nothing like the coals that were heaped upon you. Your names are not connected in the gossip rags and he seems to have dropped off the world, indeed. Best to leave it behind you and move on."

"I am telling you, I know that he had a cruel streak that I mistook!"

Letty nodded. "Of course. Of course. I can only say that when I met him he did not strike me as unkind. And believe me, I have long, long experience of a man who never uttered a speech that told the truth. But whatever reason he had, it is behind you, that is all."

"Yes," said Cass, her animation sinking away as she turned her attention back to the yarn.

CHAPTER 32

Mrs. Orfill was so glad when the rest of the household came home that she cooked a ham.

Cass wanted to scold her—she was not that sure they could afford ham—but she could not. Mrs Orfill had also baked stacks of ratafia cakes, and apparently that was the price of Cass' silence.

Cass just smiled to herself, opening another letter at her desk with her small silver knife. Then she caught herself at it.

She still had friends in the world, friends who made the days worthwhile.

And she still had customers.

She couldn't muster up her old energy, but she could smile.

Perhaps that was something to build on.

* * *

WEEK AFTER WEEK, Cass darted around the house, writing, reading, drawing, and talking out loud to anyone who would listen about the commissions that were requested.

Sometimes even to people who would not listen.

I am doing the ironing, Peg motioned to her slowly, as if Cass had lost her ability to reason.

Quite, but I am wondering if a wooden beam could be balanced on a fulcrum made of wood to lift someone who cannot lift themselves. Or would the fulcrum need to be of a more durable material?

I don't know what that is and I can't pay attention to you and iron at the same time. Go bother Selene.

Cass bit her lip. *Selene told me to bother you, she is helping Mrs. Orfill with the pot scouring.*

Go bother Ira.

Ira just nods and pretends to listen.

Peg smiled to herself. *That is true.*

Cass didn't really mind. She went off to write down her speculations and figure out a correspondent with whom to share them.

* * *

EVERY DAY WAS EASIER when nothing came to remind her of him.

It wasn't *easy*. Just a little easier.

She did correspond with a few other physicians, and for the most part their letters had the same businesslike, direct tone of their letters before. She loved their devotion to their patients, but it was hard to open their letters. They only drew her attention to the correspondent she no longer had.

When a letter came from the direction of a Mr. Bradley Waite, Cass looked at it a long, long time before opening it. She had just begun to believe it was possible to take a deep breath again. If her heart would never heal, at least it was beating. What was the point of talking further?

Eventually she opened it, telling herself that it was best to have it done and over with, her fingers shaking as she slid in the small knife.

Miss Cullen,
    I cannot recommend leaving London highly enough. At least for me, it has perhaps saved my life. Where I had before felt nothing but the gray weight on

THE COUNTESS INVENTION

me of every new day, I now find myself leaping up in the morning, ready to discover the world.

I tell you this not to celebrate, though I feel like celebrating, but to send you a story of change. I am haunted by the way you looked leaving that last meal at Morland.

I have for a long time felt that life was a dull, heavy thing, and it is a shock to me to find that I was wrong. In my gratitude, as I feel that I have escaped from under that which weighed me down, I write to tell you that I hope that you too have already returned to your more energetic self. I feel I may hope so, as youth often has a type of buoyancy that comes to the rescue at times like these. But I know, all too well, that often it does not.

I have not heard from our mutual friend the doctor since we parted. But I hope you will forgive the intimacy when I tell you that it was he who always maintained to me that helping others gave his life a purpose when nothing else did. Whatever he has become and wherever he is, I choose to believe that his conviction in those moments at least was right. There is balm in living in the world rather than withdrawing from it, if one can withstand its knocks at all. And you, Miss Cullen, are certainly capable of anything to which you put your mind. I am convinced of it.

I hope this letter finds you well. Whether it does or does not, if there is anything I can do that would prove the service of a friend, please write to tell me so. A letter sent here should follow me to my new direction if and when I leave.

Your servant,
B. Waite

Cass let the letter fall into the most recent pile on her desk. It looked harmless there, like the leaf of a tree among many other leaves, indistinguishable.

She had only casual memories of the letter's writer, but his words stirred up thoughts and feelings she did not want. She had plans to make for her work; she had no more plans to love. Mr. Waite did not seem to understand that, for there was an undercurrent to his words that made her think that he still hoped his friend would somehow re-emerge. And that she would care.

JUDITH LYNNE

She wondered where Oliver was only in those moments when she felt desperate to ask him the questions that had cut her so often that their wounds refused to close. She wanted to know why, more than anything else, *why*. She wanted to know why he had done it, but more, she wanted to know why he bothered to take an interest in someone like her in the first place only to drop them *that* way. He had had so many other beautiful women to choose from, she was sure of that. Why offer his help and then take it away like that? Why offer *himself*?

Pressing her hand on the top of the pile of letters, Cass crushed them into a tiny flat stack. There, it was all smaller.

She was no genius at organizing her own materials, and when a day or so later the letter disappeared from its stack, Cass never even noticed.

* * *

When Lord Swithin invited Cass to see the work that was in progress on the dowager cottage, Cass dashed up three floors of the house to show it to Lady Inglemawr even as she dressed.

"He cannot understand that I am a woman," Cass said, her excitement drowning out her surprise.

"I believe he has convinced himself that you are married. See, this is addressed to Mrs. Cullen."

"Well, then I have used all the possible salutations," muttered Cass. "But can we do it?"

"It is a much longer journey." Lady Inglemawr dug at the edges of the paper in her hand with her fingernail as she thought. "Several days farther north. It will be very uncomfortable. It could even be dangerous."

Cass flicked that concern away with a wave of her hand. "If it is dangerous, you must stay here. I will be well enough on my own."

"Why do such ideas even cross your *mind*? Of course I must go with you." Lady Inglemawr looked at the color rising in Cass' face for the first time in too long a time. "We must find a way to make it work."

Later in the parlor, however, Lady Inglemawr confided the request for the trip to Mr. Adams.

"It is many times the distance of the brief trip to Roseford," she said quietly. "I do not wish to unduly burden you, Mr. Adams, but I do wonder what you would think of such a trip."

Adams looked highly uncomfortable at being drawn into a conversation with a marchioness at all. But he understood her dilemma; of the people in the house, he was perhaps her only option for a sounding-board.

"Is your concern what others will think, madam?"

"Actually, no. If I attend, I believe that will raise no questions, not that any are being raised; Miss Cullen is not attending social functions now. I am more concerned with such a long trip at this time of year. There will be ice and snow, and the coaches may not run with regularity."

"Perhaps you should consult with Mr. Cullen, madam, Miss Cullen's father."

"Mr. Cullen is not happy with me, Adams, and I suspect that if Miss Cullen raises this idea with him he will quash it."

"You prefer Miss Cullen to make her own decision, madam?"

"Just so."

"Then I have no other thoughts to add, madam," said Adams with his fatalistic air.

"Of course. Of course. My apologies."

She kept turning it over in her mind even once she was alone again. The trip *was* dangerous. Cass, who had traveled little, did not seem to realize how dangerous. The London papers, proud of boasting of the speed of this company's coaches or that one, also held notices of bounties offered on the heads of highwaymen who robbed the coaches. This far into winter, she knew there would be fewer carriages to rob; she doubted that coincided with fewer robbers to do the robbing.

Even a simple accident with the carriage could be deadly in truly bad weather.

If Cass was going to do this—and Lady Inglemawr suspected she *needed* to do it—it would fall to Lady Inglemawr to take her position seriously and take steps to ensure their safety.

Lady Inglemawr did not consider herself a strategist. Her personal life had already required from her all she felt she had to give towards the ends of subterfuge and scheming. Nonetheless, for Cass, whose heart she had failed to protect, she would stretch her capabilities to the utmost.

* * *

"We will be faster and lighter for the trip with only three of us," Cass reminded Lady Inglemawr as she pulled on her gloves on the day of their departure. Cass had decided that her own toilet did not require even the appearance of a lady's maid, and Peg could stay comfortably at home with her husband.

When the hired carriage was loaded with their luggage, and Laurie her ladyship's maid stowed inside, one of the footmen was just about to help Cass inside as well when she caught a good look at his face.

He had his hat pulled down toward his eyes, but Cass knew she had seen those broad shoulders and that profile before.

"Sir," she said, leaning slightly toward him, "you assisted us when we took a hired carriage to Morland as well, I believe."

The young man, for such he was, as she could see when he moved the hat slightly up on his forehead, blushed quite profusely, but nodded. "I did, miss."

"Have we been introduced?"

The young man stood quite straight. "Phineas Sayre, Miss Cullen."

"Are you employed by the carriage company?"

"Miss Cullen," Lady Inglemawr said, suddenly appearing at her side, "I believe we must begin this journey or we will never finish."

Cass looked toward her ladyship with a raised, questioning eyebrow, then back at the strapping young man. Then both her eyebrows flew up as she looked back at her friend.

"*Oh*," she said.

Lady Inglemawr, with a slight flush coloring her cheeks as well, nodded and sounded a little flustered as she said, "Shall we go in?"

Inside the carriage, Cass wanted to ask many, many questions.

And it must have shown on her face because Lady Inglemawr just shook her head. "Don't, please."

Cass cast a glance at the maid. "Oh, of course."

That just made Lady Inglemawr blush harder. "Not for Laurie's sake. She, ah, they have met."

The maid gave Cass a look that simply seemed very French.

"It is just that I prefer to have my private life private," Lady Inglemawr murmured, sufficiently softly that Cass just barely managed to hear it.

Well, so do I, thought Cass, but we don't always get what we want.

But it was perhaps because she had not been able to keep her private life private that Cass did not interrogate Lady Inglemawr further. If anyone knew what a dizzying hurricane love could be, Cass did.

But perhaps because she was not pressed, Lady Inglemawr did offer one more elaboration. "The older I grow, the more I believe that secrets are to be valued according to what they protect or harm."

Cass wanted to ask more about exactly what secrets they were discussing, and whether Lady Inglemawr felt they were secrets to protect or secrets to harm, but Lady Inglemawr only looked out the window in a firm signal that she had nothing further to say.

CHAPTER 33

Cass tried not to think of his name any more, but "he" had been right about her seeing her own work completed, Cass thought as she watched snow fall outside the post-chaise.

Four days in the farther north and Cass felt almost herself. At least, when talking about her work. Lord Swithin had looked a bit nonplussed when Cass had started waving her hands with excitement, but he had still been very glad she was there. He called her Mrs. Cullen the entire time, and she did not correct him. Her name did not matter. The lovely work did.

It had been wonderful, seeing in person how the wood and metal were shaped to make something new, and Cass had been able to make several small adjustments in the nick of time. Both the cabinetmaker and the ironmonger had patiently explained more to her about their materials, and she had learned so much so quickly.

For larger work, she mused, a trip like this was well worth it.

Cass closed the curtains, both sides and front, shutting out her view of the swaying wide back of the driver seated on one of their two horses, as well as her view of the countryside.

That made the little cabin dark, but it was cold, and none of the three women inside wanted it any colder, even wrapped up as they were. The trip was long, with frequent stops for fresh horses and long nights at cold inns; and the way the chill stung her fingertips just seemed to make the trip longer.

She looked over at her seatmates, Lady Inglemawr next to her and Laurie against the far wall. The close quarters helped generate a little warmth. The other two women looked dozy and bored, and just as happy to have the curtains closed as not.

Cass sighed silently to herself. During the day she did everything just as she ought. What was inside her, fortunately, did not show. She might seem fine, but she knew she was still hollow. She was a chimney built not around air but around a core of hard loneliness and regret. Few feelings stayed in her; it was as though they floated up and away, as though she was no longer built to hold them at all.

Feelings were beyond her capabilities.

Here in the dark, what she remembered most was not the feelings of his lips or his hands, but the feelings of peace and happiness she had felt near him from the very first day they met. He seemed to have taken the happiness with him to wherever he had gone. But in the dark, she did feel peace. It was a relief that her ability to feel peace, at least, had come back.

Cass closed her eyes. It was balm to her soul, truly a healing balm sinking into a place inside her soul that had been dry and painful, to remember Lord Swithin's obvious and sincere gratitude. Still, Cass could not help but wonder how she could improve the design of the sloped floor she had added to the place where his new wing joined his old. It had needed something for his mother to hold, and the railing was easy enough to add in an attractive way. Still she was not satisfied, as the railing had hurt his mother's hands.

Abruptly, Lady Inglemawr *screamed*, and all the little carriage's inhabitants were thrown about by the vehicle's sudden, swaying, violent shudder to a halt.

In a blur of time and motion, Cass found herself, disoriented, on the post-chaise floor.

Realizing where she was, the question also immediately leaped to her mind: why had Lady Inglemawr screamed *before* the carriage stopped?

It took Cass what seemed like interminably long moments to claw her way out from the pile of women and women's skirts.

The hood of her cloak had fallen back and her bare head felt the chill. Cass fought to open the carriage's door handle. Lady Inglemawr was clutching at her skirts, trying to hold her back, hold her down, but Cass did not even notice.

She threw open the carriage door. Startled by another scream from behind her just as she did, she stumbled and fell out of the door into the snow.

Scrambling up to her hands and knees, Cass saw, just yards away, a man sitting on a horse. He was pointing the long barrel of a pistol straight at her.

The universe became a crystal moment of the weapon's muzzle pointing straight at her, the pinpricks of ice melting against her fingers, and her breath sawing in and out of her chest.

She could hear Lady Inglemawr still making noise behind her. Without taking her eyes off the gun barrel, Cass slowly rose to her feet, carefully reached behind her, and closed the carriage door, providing at least that thin barrier between the highwayman and her fellow travelers.

It was nearly impossible to tear her eyes from the pistol. But she had to know what was happening.

Darting her eyes to her left, Cass could see the coach's driver slumped on his horse, his coat drenched a deep, dark red. His fingertips hung limply from his arm dangled over the snow, and from them dripped blood.

And sprawled atop the carriage itself was Oliver.

He had his arm raised and a deadly looking pistol aimed right back at the highwayman.

It couldn't be him. Cass blinked, and blinked again. She was afraid to rub her eyes. If Oliver couldn't be real, then why was the highwayman real? Because there was no mistaking that the highwayman had his gun pointed at her. He was terrifyingly real, from his three-cornered hat to the hooves of his horse shifting in the snow, and he was threatening her with death.

Oliver was shouting something. She could see the tension drawn in every line of his body as he held his weapon rock-steady.

Daring to glance to her other side, Cass saw Phineas Sayre just a few paces away, also standing in the snow.

The young man was watching the highwayman as well. He had both hands spread at his sides. Cass wondered if he too was about to produce a pistol.

The horse of the highwayman stomped impatiently in the snow. Its breath made a small white cloud.

She couldn't see the man's eyes clearly, but she knew they were on her.

Whatever Oliver was shouting, the highwayman stood fast.

Then the horse shifted, or perhaps it was the highwayman.

And both guns fired at what seemed like nearly the same time.

Cass could hear the reports, faint pops accompanied by muzzle flashes of the weapons. The highwayman fell backwards in his saddle. She could see him pulling himself upright even as the horse shied, then he swayed sickly as he turned and galloped away.

All was still in the small snowy clearing for a moment.

Oliver launched himself off the carriage and in the next second he was right there.

He spun Cass in place so he could keep looking down the road where the highwayman had gone. With one hand he kept a pistol aimed down that road; he was running the other over her hair, her clothes, everywhere.

"Are you hit? Are you hurt?"

She had never heard him bark that way, louder than the gun report had sounded to her.

"No, I—I'm not hurt."

That seemed to settle him slightly. He met her eyes, only for the barest fraction of a second, and laid his seeking hand against her cheek.

Then he was pulling the spent pistol from his waistband and

JUDITH LYNNE

handing it to her. She juggled it for a moment; the barrel was hot. "Can you load a gun?"

"No."

"Get into the carriage. Sayre! Is her ladyship well? Laurie?"

Just steps away, Lady Inglemawr was caught up in the arms of the broad-shouldered young man who seemed to be favoring tightly holding the lady rather than examining her for injuries.

Cass still had not moved.

Rather than yanking her to get her to move, Oliver grasped Cass around the waist and pulled her up and into him, taking the three steps to the other couple while carrying her like a child.

It was absurd, they were nearly the same height. But Cass had definitely *been moved*.

Without conscious thought, her own fingers moved over his hair, tightly braided for once, his still not-quite-shaven jaw. It was Oliver. He was real. He was *here*.

"What are you doing here?" she whispered.

"I am sorry but we must move. Sayre, if her ladyship is well we must get the ladies into the carriage. I need your help to move the driver; he's done for."

Laurie was sitting on the step to the carriage, one hand pressing to her head. Oliver dropped Cass to examine the swelling bump on the maid's head, then gently helped her back into the carriage.

He turned to Lady Inglemawr.

"I will not, I cannot ride without you next to me!" that lady cried out, clinging to Sayre's coat lapels.

Cass felt a burst of sympathetic feeling choking her but unlike her ladyship, Cass could not let it out. The distance between herself and Oliver seemed like a gulf cutting down to the core of the earth.

But when Oliver's eyes turned pleadingly to her, she understood that he needed her to show Lady Inglemawr what must be done.

Cass handed his empty pistol back to him. He shoved it through his belt.

"Let us settle ourselves inside," she told Lady Inglemawr, gently peeling one of her friend's hands away from the erstwhile footman. "I will sit with you. We must leave in case that fellow had friends, unless I am much mistaken."

"Exactly so, Miss Cullen. Permit me?"

Permitted or not, Cass felt both of Oliver's hands around her waist, bodily lifting her into the carriage, where she scrambled to sit. Oliver picked his loaded pistol back up from the tiny carriage step. In the next moment Lady Inglemawr had likewise been helped inside and it seemed like only moments before Oliver was tossing their smaller luggage in with them.

Cass was attempting to stack the bags under their feet when the older woman gripped her by the hand and clung. "Is this our end? Did you see the awful *blood*? That poor driver, that poor man!"

Laurie slumped against the seat back, still holding her head. Cass shifted as if to reach around Lady Inglemawr to check on her, but Laurie shook her head. "I am fine, mademoiselle, but so tired."

All three ladies heard the thud of Lady Inglemawr's trunk being loaded into the footman's seat in back, and then the gruesome thump of something heavy shoved into the luggage rack in front.

Cass sat back and was actually perfectly happy to let Lady Inglemawr lean into her. Her ladyship had tears running down her face and dripping into her collar, and she could not stop talking, but none of her words penetrated Cass' stunned silence.

The carriage jerked back into motion.

Where had Oliver come from?

"Did you know he was there?"

Lady Inglemawr's flood of unheard words stopped. "What, that awful gunman?"

"Dr. Burke."

Now Lady Inglemawr was quite silent.

Cass turned in her seat, barely stopped herself from shaking the smaller woman. *"Did you know he was there?"*

Cass did not know what her own face looked like but judging from the look on Lady Inglemawr's face, Cass' expression must be something awful.

Cass' hand twisted at the throat of Lady Inglemawr's cloak.

"Phineas, I sent Phineas," gasped Lady Inglemawr. "You were determined to go, you *needed* it, and I am not so clever that I can invent new stratagems daily. It has been *so* helpful to let Phineas serve as a footman when I travel. I asked the doctor to do it, I asked him to serve as a footman for the journey, and he agreed. Practically before it was out of my mouth. All it took was for him to absent himself whenever we alighted. And you have paid no attention."

He had been with them *the entire way*? He had ridden with them all those miles north, and started back, and she had never even known he was outside the carriage, only a few feet away?

"How on *earth* did you know where to find him?" Cass had taken Lady Inglemawr with her, very properly, the day she had visited the dwelling from which Oliver used to send her letters. He had not been there, and the young man who was there had a young wife, her sister, and her ailing mother living with him. That young man had no knowledge of any servants who might have worked for the previous tenant.

Cass remembered how resigned she had felt in the cab going home. She had not expected to find any answers, and she had not. Where had Lady Inglemawr?

"His friend, I saw his friend's letter in the pile on your desk and I thought the man *must* have an idea, and I wrote to him. He had had no word, but he remembered the name of a hospital where Dr. Burke had sometimes worked, and when I visited, he was there. It took some swallowing of my pride to ask anything of him given how he spoke to me last, and how he treated you. But I felt it was the only way, and I am so glad, so glad! What would have happened to my Phineas if Dr. Burke were not here? Phineas is a complete stranger to gun battles! Heaven help us!"

Cass could tell by the way Oliver had held himself, the look in his eye, that Oliver was *not* a stranger to gun battles.

But he was *here*.

The carriage rattled along, and Cass opened a side curtain. She did not want to see who was driving in the murdered man's place, Oliver or Phineas. The snow outside coating everything with white and giving the whole scene an otherworldly feeling. Cass might have thought she was dreaming this, but for Lady Inglemawr's tears, Laurie's pale face opposite, and the clear memory of that first moment of seeing Oliver there, right there on the bench of the carriage.

It seemed like only moments but must have been the better part of hours before they pulled to a halt on the side of the road.

Oliver threw open the door. He surveyed all three women in an instant, then said, "Lady Inglemawr, Mr. Sayre wishes to speak with you."

Oliver handed the lady down from the carriage, then climbed in himself.

Cass could not stop staring at him.

Oliver seemed almost reflexively to find the spot where Cass' blood pulsed at the base of her throat, to study something about her eyes, feel the temperature of her face. Knowing the other ways he could touch, Cass could feel the way he had focused on her as a patient. Then Oliver turned his attention to Laurie.

He was examining her eyes closely just as he had looked at Cass' when Cass said, "You will not speak to me, will you."

"Miss Cullen," said Oliver, a little thickly as if something was caught in his chest, "this young lady has an injury that needs my attention."

Throwing open the door to the carriage herself for the second time that day, Cass stepped out, this time managing to reach the ground on her feet.

Only a few paces away there stood Lady Inglemawr, once again clasped in the arms of the broad-shouldered Mr. Sayre.

Her head was against his chest and, in contrast to her weeping through their most recent riding, now her face was calm, albeit marked with the traces of her tears. Her arms were wrapped around his waist, holding him tight as well. And his eyes were closed as he rested his cheek against her bright hair.

"I see," Cass breathed to herself. Their emotion toward one another was palpable, obvious, and beautiful.

Oliver climbed out of the carriage behind her. "Sayre," he called without formality. "I must take the women to the inn ahead. Are you going or not?"

"We will not be going," said Lady Inglemawr, answering for him.

Truly, she looked completely composed now. In fact, she looked happy.

Cass shook her head in disbelief. "What do you mean?"

"My dear, we are leaving for America. We have been discussing it. Why not now? You can tell people we were shot in the attack."

"And have them looking for that brigand for crimes he did not commit?" Cass was aghast.

"What, three murders instead of one?" Phineas Sayre's voice was pitched higher than Oliver's but was quite loud enough to carry. He seemed caught up in the moment, practically exultant. "Let him hang."

He turned to Oliver.

"Let us take one of the horses and you take the other."

"How far ahead is the inn?"

Sayre surveyed the road around him. "Truly, not far. Less than two miles."

"But what will you do for money?" Cass was unable to comprehend what her friend was saying. Sail? For America? To live in an uncivilized new country?

But Lady Inglemawr too was almost glowing. "I have nine hundred pounds in my travel trunk."

"*What?*"

"What??" Oliver echoed Cass' uncontrolled shout.

Lady Inglemawr only nodded. "We have been discussing what might be a good moment for us to disappear."

"But your income from your husband's estate must be much more!"

"Most of the Marquess' money went to his heir. I have saved everything I could for years to reach this point, and I would happily forgo any more to have a husband I love."

Oliver just looked at the young man. "You can travel with her far enough to book passage? You cannot go to London."

Sayre just nodded. "We will need clothing for her to go unnoticed, but yes."

The young man's jaw was square and set. He did indeed look as if he had studied this situation for a long, long time and was ready to take the plunge.

Cass could not stop shaking her head *no*. "You cannot, cannot leave everyone—"

"Only you, my dear. Aside from Laurie, there is no one to miss me, and no one I will miss but you."

"But you cannot—honestly—this... very young man?" Cass knew she was floundering but words had left her.

Lady Inglemawr laughed out loud. "Mr. Sayre is twenty-three. I am thirty-eight. Not so impossible. I believe we would love each other if the difference in our ages were forty years instead of fifteen." She turned in his arms to face Cass, lean close enough to be heard. Sayre, unwilling to let her go, kept his arms tight around her, her back warmed by his chest. "We have loved each other long enough to know that we will never be happy without each other. And we cannot truly have each other here. I would rather begin an entirely new life in a new land than live with the finger-pointing and the lawsuits from my husband's heir and the viciousness of the petty gossip."

"But it fades fast!"

Lady Inglemawr loosed herself from Sayre's arms to hug Cass, only for a moment. "It faded for you. You have far more true friends than I had, and where you do not have true friends, you have faithful customers. Britain loves its shopkeepers, in its own way."

"Can you take both women on one horse?" Sayre's question was addressed to Oliver, the younger man casting a dubious eye on the still-falling snow. "One horse will not pull the carriage; you'll have to leave it with its unfortunate driver here."

"Of course," said Oliver, "I will come up with some explanation for the missing bodies and horse. We must go gently, for the young lady's head. But it is not far. You have much farther. You will be well?"

"I think we will be just fine." And here for the first time Sayre's features opened into a wide grin, and he looked very ready to sail into the wide world with his lady love and stake his claim on his own new life.

"How much ammunition have you?" Oliver offered Sayre his empty pistol; after a pause, Sayre took it.

"I believe I have enough."

"To fit this bore?"

"I believe so."

"Help me tear some of this tackle. It must look as though the horse broke loose."

Cass watched Oliver produce a pocket-knife and slice half-way through several of the straps, then pulled them apart the rest of the way. "Will that work?"

Oliver's hands left shredded edges; he kept his eyes on his work. "Generally speaking, miss, people hear what they expect to hear."

Emerging from the post-chaise, Lady Inglemawr now had a bright smile on her tear-streaked face. "Laurie has offered me nearly all her things in exchange for the pick of what I leave behind! See, was that not easy?"

"And perhaps her valise," Sayre suggested.

Lady Inglemawr waved an acknowledgement as she began to pull at the luggage packed just behind the horses.

By the time Oliver had the horses separated, the Marchioness reappeared, quite transformed. She looked ten years younger, her sunset-gold braids stuffed under a practical woolen hat and her clothes exchanged for a maid's sturdy cotton and linen.

Cass thought her ladyship might at least sigh a little as she patted her fur-hemmed cloak, now tucked in over Laurie in the carriage seat, but the woman looked nothing but glad.

"I have everything," she said, winking at Cass, and then laughing out loud. "I truly have everything."

Cass watched as Sayre helped her ladyship—Lady Inglemawr—her friend up on the horse's saddle. She sat sideways, gripping the tack a little awkwardly, but she looked ready for anything.

"But will you write? Under what name?" called Cass as they started away, and she stifled an irrational urge to run after them in the snow.

Lady Inglemawr looked over her shoulder. "It will be a letter from Mary, just plain Mary. You'll know."

Cass could feel her jaw hanging open, as her tongue was growing cold.

But she did not close it until Oliver's hand fell on her shoulder.

"I hope you can ride," he said grimly when she swung round to face him. "Laurie is injured and we must get her warm, and the horse has no tack for riders. I thought we had better give them the saddle, but perhaps I made a mistake."

"I will do well enough."

In truth she was not a good rider, and it was all she could do to stay atop the swaying sloped back of the carriage horse, which did not care for Oliver leading it on foot, and keep hold of Laurie before her. Oliver had buckled a strap around the two of them to keep them together, which was uncomfortably tight but helped to keep them warm. Oliver walked beside them, pushing occasionally on Cass' knees or Laurie's to keep them from sliding off.

The walk was difficult enough that it kept her from shouting at the back of Oliver's head to demand some explanation, any explanation.

He plodded next to them and offered none. She could not see, from her perch on the horse above him, the tears running down his face.

CHAPTER 34

The sight of them trailing into the courtyard of the inn was surprising enough that some of the other travellers came out to meet them.

In a few words Oliver told them of being accosted by the highwayman and that they had had to leave their murdered driver with the carriage—along with two other traveling companions about whose location Oliver was more vague. They'd wounded the thief in the process of cutting loose a horse, and when the cut tackle had finally given way, that horse had run off, he said.

"What about that thief?" Cass heard a gruff demand.

"I doubt he'll survive," said Oliver with a shrug. "I hit him solidly in the arm, likely shattering the bone; even if he can find good care, he's likely finished."

Cass had never heard Oliver sound so casual about anyone's pain. The set of his mouth and something at the corner of his eyes told her that he thought, or felt, more that he did not say.

Quickly Oliver organized the men to take Laurie inside and to find someone to bring her broth or weak tea, and to put her by the fire. He would follow.

It must have been that unaccustomed note of command to his

voice, because they did as he said, leaving him to half-carry Cass inside and up the tiny staircase to the room one of them had described as the best and the last available.

Oliver inspected the room briefly, checking the windows and making sure it had no other occupants and that it had a small fire of its own, before turning to Cass, who stood in the middle of the room just watching him, aghast.

"Miss Cullen," he said in that deep voice that could speak quietly and still reach her, and turned to go.

"*How dare you.*"

Oliver turned back. "Miss?"

"How *dare* you save my life and leave me here—what, without any explanation? What are you *doing* here? Where have you been? Have you not thought of me once?"

From where she stood, even in the dim light of the low-roofed little room, she could see his chest rising and falling, fast. She did not know if that was the exertion of getting her safely here, or something else.

"Every moment," he said, and turned to leave again without looking at her.

"Then *why?*"

She had no other question.

He gave no answer.

When one of his feet lifted again to move toward the door, Cass snapped.

She reached him instantly and hauled him around by one arm.

"You *coward.*" She barely had control of her voice; it was somewhere between a shout and a scream. She suspected it travelled. She didn't care. "You tell me you loved me at least a little, or admit that you are a liar. Or tell me why you bothered to seduce me at all."

"*I love you.*"

He grabbed her tight, pulled her against him so hard she could barely breathe.

"My God, I love you more than I can put into words. You can feel it, can't you? Can't you tell? Don't you *see* it? Because I have never been able to hide it."

His lips were on her forehead, her cheek, tenderly kissing even her eyelids, brushing lightly across her open lips even as his arms crushed her to him.

He was drowning her in rich, hot sensation. She clung to him. She *wanted* to drown.

He seemed to be muttering to himself as much as to her, "I didn't know until it was too late. Too late. I should never have subjected you to those people, to that place. It was a dream to pretend I could have all this, with you. It was all my fault."

"Oliver," she breathed into his kiss, "Oliver, you must tell me *why.*"

He was pulling her off her feet.

Reluctantly, he set her down.

"I must attend to Laurie. Her head has been badly jarred. I have seen soldiers develop injuries that way that never left them. The inn has travelers but it is not very full; I can ask a responsible barmaid to watch her for a while. If she sleeps, we must make sure she also wakes."

Again he tried to go.

Cass' hand shot out and grabbed him by the arm.

As if compelled by her grip, Oliver added, "Then I will return to you."

"You will? But…"

"I have told them I must make sure my wife is well settled. It is the least of the tales we are telling."

* * *

When he returned to the room it was dark out, and even dimmer in the room, but the little fireplace crackled yellow and Cass was still awake.

She felt she would never sleep again.

"Did they bring you any food?" was all Oliver asked as he came into the room, settled himself in the one low chair, and sighed as he stretched out his legs. "I think I have aged ten years today."

"They did. Did you eat?"

"No."

Wordlessly Cass thickly spread a piece of the bread still on the table with butter, and brought it to him. When he had wolfed that down in what seemed like two bites, she brought him the rest of her stew.

"Why didn't you finish it?"

"I couldn't."

Deliberately he chewed and swallowed. "I saw you before you went to Roseford. You should not get that thin again."

"Where did you see me?"

"On the street."

"I almost never..." Cass trailed off. "How did you know when I would be out?"

Oliver did not answer.

"Oliver, if you will not tell me why you threw away my trust, would you at least tell me where you have been?"

He winced at the first part of the sentence, but only said, "Working."

"Your apartments were abandoned."

"How did you... When were you there?"

Cass just folded her arms and kept her mouth closed.

He got the message. If he was going to stay quiet, so was she.

He put the now completely empty bowl on the floor.

Leaning forward on his knees as she had seen him do before, Oliver started to move his hands.

I didn't know how to explain to you. I still do not know how to talk to you. I thought I knew but I do not.

Cass' gasp filled the room.

Kneeling in front of him, Cass leaned into the space between his knees, between his hands. She touched them the way he touched her: desperately longing, caressing, holding.

"You went on learning."

He nodded.

"Mr. Castle taught you?"

"Mr. Castle," and here Oliver leaned back a little, "offered to cut out my intestines and braid them into ropes. Fortunately I was able to find a teacher at the institute who had not yet formed such a low opinion of me."

Cass leaned her own arms on Oliver's thighs, felt the muscles move under her touch.

He wouldn't meet her eyes.

She reached up and touched his chin, moving his eyes into the light, and had a sudden sense that they had been here before. *He* had touched her this way, unmasking her, on the first day they met.

"Oliver, the day we met you saw me with all my flaws. I had lied to you, made a foolish pretense at being someone else, dove into ridiculous ideas without thinking them through. I broke too many rules and did it gracelessly. But you never made me feel anything other than..." How could she say it? "You always made me feel somehow special. Well, perhaps you make all women feel that way. But you did it for me. You offered me help. It was a gift. I began falling in love with you the moment you offered to help me, did you know?"

His eyes were red; perhaps that was why he didn't want her to see them. And unshed tears still overwhelmed their barriers and defied all his defenses to slide down his cheeks.

"I want you so badly I can feel it, an actual ache I feel inside me, from my teeth to my toes. But that is not all I want of you. I want..." Here Cass swallowed. "I *wanted* you to love me and to *let me love you*. The only way I know to love someone is the way you taught me. Won't you let me help you? If... You say you love me, but did you love me then? *How* could you love me and do what you did? *Why did you not let me help you in return?* You truly must tell me, or my doubt of myself will drive me mad. I do not want to spend the rest of my life hating myself for trusting you, and so dry and scarred inside that I cannot even cry."

Oliver's hands covered his face, hiding whatever was happening behind them. Then he scrubbed them up and into his hair, which, wild as ever, was pulling free from its ties and forming thick bronze waves around his face.

"Whereas I cannot stop crying," she heard his muffled words behind his hands.

He surprised Cass when he leaned forward and shoved his face into the crook of her neck, breathed deep.

His hands caught her under her armpits and pulled her up off her knees, into his arms again, hard against him like he had held her just a little while before.

But this time he added broken words.

"I cannot help anyone. I cannot avoid hurting people. All I... when I got back from the war all I wanted was *not* to hurt people. You can't imagine how a man screams when you cut into him alive. And they died, so many of them died... just like that driver today, I could not save him, the bullet cut him so near to the heart, I had no way of saving him and the kindest thing to do was to let him die of the blood loss quickly more than slowly. I could not *help him.*

"I thought I was giving women pleasure, and came to find out that I was only hurting them too, in a different way. I'm... a disease, there's something wrong with me. You cannot imagine my—"

But then the flow of words chopped off.

Oliver dug his face harder into her neck, brushing his cheek, his chin against her throat till she was sure the marks would show. But she did not want him to stop.

"I can imagine your parents," she said quietly into his ear. "I met them."

"No, you don't—"

When again he fell silent, Cass grabbed his head with both hands to lift it, and shake it.

"You are not a disease, Oliver. I am sure you broke hearts, perhaps too many. And you could not save those patients. But I would rather be with you, a man who tries, than any other man in the world."

The faintest ghost of something softer touched his eyes then, and before she could lose ground, Cass pressed her advantage.

"You did what you did for some reason. You made love to me like I was the last woman on earth just the night before, and then the next day you plunged a knife into my heart. You have to tell me why."

"I made love to you like you were the last woman on earth, because to me you are the only woman on earth. I will miss you every day of my life."

How could he grab her heart and squeeze it like this with only his words?

"Oliver. My darling man, my beautiful man. Do you not know that you have my heart and everything that goes with it? Oliver. *You are the only person who has ever really talked with me.*"

He shook his head. "I cannot fix it."

"But perhaps *we* can."

"We cannot, sweetheart, but thank you. It is more kindness than I deserve that you want to try."

Cass sagged back on to her heels. "Is there another woman who can help?" She felt the hot prickling sensation of tears behind her eyes and bit the inside of her own cheek as hard as she could to keep them from coming.

"Cassandra, *no*! Don't you understand? This is how I have cut my own throat! If I had not fallen in love with you I would be comfortably drunk or in an opium den right now, but you made me feel so much hope, so much happiness, excitement, I had to take the plunge to make you mine, and that lost you. I have not been drunk since then; I cannot find the numbness. The pain is no less agonizing for being self-inflicted, it is more so. Even if I had not given my heart to you, I could not subject another woman to the nightmare that is my family. But I *did* give my heart to you, and there *is* no other woman for me."

The way he looked at her, as if he were a man dying of thirst and she was the last glass of water in Britain, only intensified how much she wanted to kiss every inch of him, but Cass resisted the urge. "But you must tell me. How can I understand, how can I *begin* to repair my trust, if you don't tell me?"

The blunt sadness came over his expression again and he just shook his head. For long moments he sat there, but Cass did not turn away, and Oliver seemed unable to deny her forever.

"My parents—my father will cut off my brother's family and turn them out if I marry you."

"*What?* Why?" She had never imagined *this*.

"He believes I am a bastard and will not allow the possibility that a legitimate child of mine might inherit."

"*What* on *earth...*" Astonished into speechlessness, Cass sagged until she sat on the floor. Oliver leaned to follow her and keep his hands cradling her back.

She just kept shaking her head.

"What on earth could have given him such an idea?" She could not wrap her mind around it. The cruelty of it, the sheer desire to cause hurt.

"Not what. Who. Whom do you think could convince him of such a thing?"

"Not... *not* your mother. That is beyond absurd! What a senseless, vicious, heartless thing to do to her own family! To you *and* to your father!"

"It might be true," Oliver shrugged. He felt somehow lighter since he had finally shared his secret. It was good, it felt good, not to bear it alone.

"Oh, I doubt it. For her to pull out that convenient excuse only because you had finally *considered* marriage? Who would believe it for a moment?"

"I think my father believed it." It still hurt, thinking of the expression on his father's face, the straightness of his back as he had issued his ultimatum.

"I doubt it. I doubt it very much. Perhaps the moment she threw such a shocking idea at his head, but after..." Cass' head tilted a little. "When did she tell him this?"

"Either late the night before or very early that morning. I saw him just before I saw—"

Oliver shut his jaw with a snap.

"Before you saw Lady Gadbury—Oh, I see. You went and talked to her to see if she could help. As a friend of your mother's."

Oh, he loved that optimism in her. "You are the sweetest woman in the world. No, I went to talk to her in the hope that she would make me feel better. It seems to be a habit I have, expecting a handy woman to make me feel better. Heaven knows where I picked it up as it certainly was not from my mother."

"But... why did you not come to me?" Cass looked crushed. "Why could you not have talked to *me*?"

"Cassandra, you were the one thing in my life worth treasuring. I no more wanted to smear you with my family's angry mud than I would have wanted to drop you in the middle of the ocean. And I wanted you to have what *you* wanted. You were never looking for *me*; you were looking for a nice quiet earl who would not be troublesome to marry. And I shoved my way into your life and subjected you to them and to *that*. If I could rescue nothing else from the situation, I wanted you to have at least a chance for real love from someone who deserved you."

He made a noise of disbelief. "Not that anyone does. But I showed you too much favor in that house. I touched you too much, smiled at you too much. If I could not marry you, a link between your name and mine would have ruined your reputation in ways that would have destroyed your marriage chances. I have never had any liaison with an unmarried woman for a *reason*. Making you appear to be a merchant to the peerage was the smallest amount of damage I could do and still keep your reputation otherwise intact. I am... generally kind to women I have known, and if I were kind to you, the ladies of the *ton* would have shred you with their gossip. Being a merchant is one thing; being a lightskirt is quite another."

"I could horsewhip you myself." Contrary to her tone, her grip on his ears tightened, and she leaned towards him again. "It was so unfair. When we... I felt that you and I had... decided to solve problems together. It was devastating, finding I was alone without you."

"You had hope. I made sure you would have that."

"I had nothing. And I spent way too long shut up in that house trying to hate you and failing, and trying to decide if I could ever be happy again. And if you are wondering, I will tell you. The answer is still that I do not know. You have my whole heart and you took it with you and just disappeared."

"I am sorry. My poor darling. I'm glad you didn't cry."

"I wish I could have. You appear to have all my tears as well."

"My sweet love. I wish I could make things better. I wish I could make all this better."

"All I ever wanted was what you offered. Your help. Your conversation. Your company, your kisses, your body, your *astonishing* skills at lovemaking, your unbrushed hair and unshaven jaw, your dry wit, your huge heart. You offered those things to me. I promised to consider the offer!"

"You cannot be serious. My very existence is like a blight."

"Your very existence is all I want."

She could see his eyes traveling all over her. His hands still held her upright.

She settled back on her heels, forcing him to release her, searching his face.

She had to know that he understood that.

Oliver shook his head as if he did not believe her, or could not believe. But Cass would not leave, would not move, and would not take back a single word. She just looked at him, her face showing all the conviction she could not describe with words.

Slowly, he reached up with a hand that she could see was trembling, and he plucked out one of her hairpins.

"Miss Cullen." His voice had deepened, roughened; it contained both tears and laughter. "I have decided that there are certain things I want in a wife. I want a beautiful woman who is shockingly intelligent and does amazing things that no one else does. I want a woman who is far better to me than I deserve and who will never, ever leave me alone."

He had pulled out three, four more hairpins. Cass' eyes drifted closed at the feel of his hands freeing her hair, sliding up her throat, caressing each earlobe before cradling her head.

"Miss Cullen."

She opened her eyes again.

He was so close she could feel the warmth of his skin radiating against hers like fire. The slow, deep honey of his voice was sweet enough to drown in.

"Miss Cullen, I think it would be a wonderful idea if you were to marry me."

"Do you?" And then the magnitude of what he was saying hit her. "Do you *really*?"

"Yes, very much yes. I don't—"

"Dr. Burke." Cass' finger pressed against his lips to silence him. "No qualifiers. And you needn't tell me the downsides. I believe I have a good grasp of them."

Oliver stayed silent. He did, however, release her just enough so that he could move his hands. *I know.*

She nodded.

It would be fair of her, she thought in some distant part of her brain, to let him wonder. For at least as many weeks as she had so painfully wondered herself.

"Yes, Dr. Burke, I will marry you."

His eyes lit up and his smile burned away all of her pettier impulses.

"I will be interested to see you prove for the next fifty or sixty years that I have made the right decision."

"My lady, I would be grateful to be put to the test for so long."

Cass did not even notice the tears that finally ran down her face to soak into Oliver's shirt, into his collar. "I would like you to hold me for at least a year or two until I feel entirely better," she sniffled.

"I am delighted to agree," Oliver said softly. "I must check on my patient again. And I have let you sit on the floor too long. I would like for you to lie in this bed and rest, if you can."

"Will she be well?"

"I believe she will, but it is easy to check on her welfare from time to time, impossible to repair if she turns worse and no one notices."

"I do not want you to leave but as long as you intend to return, go."

CHAPTER 35

So much faith had Cass that her Oliver would return, that she went ahead and made herself comfortable, burrowing down into the quilts that had been stacked on the narrow, rough mattress.

So comfortable that she fell asleep.

When she woke, Oliver had just lifted the corner of the coverlets. The banked fire had burned low, letting the winter chill settle into the corners of the room. Oliver's feet were *freezing*.

Cass reached out to touch him and find out if the rest of him was as chilled, only to encounter the fabric of his shirt, untucked and billowing though it was, and that of his trousers.

"Why are you wearing so many clothes?" Cass wondered sleepily as she let her hands wander wherever they wished.

"Why are you wearing so *few*? My God, Cassandra." Oliver pulled her against him, soaking in her sweet warmth even as he gently scolded her. "Are you seducing me again?"

Cass just rolled her eyes. "The last time you accused me of that was unpleasant, to say the least. Would you truly rather annoy me than lie down here with me?"

"I want to lie down with you *desperately*." She felt the way his hands roamed her back but pulled her ever closer. She felt the same way. She could not get enough of the feel of him. After so many empty, cold days and nights she wanted all of him.

"It is so nice when we agree." She snuggled into the spaces in his arms, against his body, that seemed made only to fit *her*.

"Darling," and now his voice rasped with something rougher, "I know you know I am not a stony villain who takes everything a woman has to offer without offering anything in return. But I am not a *saint*. Exhausted as I am, I want you, I am hungry for you, and I am exceedingly conscious still of the fact that I should not have you."

"But you do have me," Cass pointed out with what she thought was simple clarity. "And I wish to have you."

"Cassandra," Oliver's deep voice vibrated into her, he pulled her so tightly against him, "Truly, I'm not a saint. I don't think I could make love slowly to you tonight, and as we know, you are not quiet."

Cass blinked her eyes open at that. Oliver looked smug, too smug for someone who claimed to still feel penitent. She wanted to take that smugness down a peg or two.

"I do not insist that it be slow or quiet," she said with a shrug of her shoulder.

She could not have described the noise he made, but she took it for some sort of agreement, shimmying out of her chemise. When she looked again, Oliver's face looked severe, different, and he had shed his clothes surprisingly quickly.

But he did not look smug.

"Let me lie against the wall so you do not feel weighed down, my love."

"It is fine, Oliver." Cass held out her arms to him. "Keep talking to me and I will be fine."

Muttering something that sounded like a curse Oliver slid into the bed next to her again.

His words ran along the lines of how good she felt, and how lucky he was, and Cass could only agree with him as the roughness of the hair sprinkling his chest rubbed against the sensitive skin of her breasts, her nipples pulling tight against him.

"I can't," she thought she heard him mumble before he pulled back. She made a noise to protest but Oliver only whispered, "Shh, I will not leave you," and slid down against her body.

She had already felt warm and heavy and ready for him, but the feel of his rough chin rubbing against the soft skin of her belly made her squirm and want to shout. She swallowed her own cry, partly because she did not want the sound to carry downstairs in the inn, partly because she did not want him to look so smug again. Catching a glimpse of his face as he slid up to grasp her nipple between his lips, Cass decided she had only been partly successful. He still looked quite smug.

She knew how Oliver affected her, but she was still surprised when he lay beside her again and touched her, and they both discovered how slick and ready she was. "I have missed you," she said into his hair without a trace of shame.

Groaning, Oliver slid his clever fingers inside her, swallowing her noise with his kiss.

When he let her free she could already feel her release gathering. "How many fingers *is* that?"

"Only two," and he grinned that boyish, open grin that she could not resist.

"It feels like a great many more," Cass managed to get out before he lashed at her nipple with his tongue and *pressed*, and her pleasure detonated.

Before she could even come down, she could feel the length of him, hot and pulsing, pressing into her belly. He was gritting his teeth.

"I want that." She was struggling to catch her breath, but she still wanted it, wanted more, wanted all of him.

Oliver looked as if something pained him. "In my medical experience, my being inside you at all has the remote chance of getting you with child," he gritted out through his teeth. "Until I can prove my sincerity to you with our wedding, you would be taking a terrible chance."

"I take chances," panted Cass, wiggling herself around until he was pressing towards the core of her.

Oliver's face sank into the crook of her neck. "The heat of you, I can't stand it." The movement of his hips back and forth seemed out of his control but he still restrained himself from plunging inside her.

"Sometimes you need to follow through with your original plan," Cass told him quite clearly, her breath coming just as quickly as his, as she did something with bracing her feet, and *pushed*.

The moan Oliver made didn't just resonate through her, it settled somewhere in the vicinity of her heart and she felt it stay there.

"This will work out because it has to work out," Cass told him, her hands, her arms wrapping around his ribs and pulling him closer. "I love you, I will *not* give you up, and I am going to marry you. Because whether or not it is a good idea, you make me so happy."

"It must be a good idea," Oliver managed to say. "You do have many, many good ideas."

She had never felt anything to quite compare to this before. Oliver was inside her, and it felt good, it felt hot and hard and slick and soft. And she knew it felt that way for *both* of them. She knew it from the way his touch spoke to her as he cradled her between his arms, unable to stop kissing her even as his body drove into her over and over again; she knew it from the hoarse words that poured out of him that were only for her; and she knew it from the way the motion was neither his nor hers, but theirs.

Even as she could feel her body gathering itself for another peak, Cass realized that *this* was what lovemaking felt like, this was what it felt like to be loved.

When she shattered against him, she could feel herself gripping him incredibly tightly, the waves of her pleasure passing into him until Oliver let out a gasping moan and drove himself deeply within her and she could actually feel him throb.

They lay together, looking into each other's eyes, catching their breath, and smiling.

"I feel made of joy," Cass whispered to her love.

"You *are* made of joy," said Oliver with great certainty back.

"You make me like this," she told him with her wide, sunny smile.

"That is my pleasure, Miss Cullen," and she could hear the smile in his voice as he nuzzled her again.

By the time he'd found a cloth with which to clean them up a little, Cass felt drowsy again, but much, much more peaceful in her soul.

The blast of heat when he returned to the bed made her snuggle against the warmth of his chest.

"So you think only women can reach that peak more than once during lovemaking," she yawned against him, unwilling to take her lips fully away from him for a moment but feeling herself falling asleep.

Oliver carefully tightened his grip on the love of his life. He could not *believe* the luck that had brought them to this place again despite every questionable decision he had made. He made a mental note to ask her to teach him how to say *luck*. "I believe that is true."

Quietly Cass just shook her head, feeling herself floating off to peaceful, happy sleep in his arms, the one place on earth she most wanted to be. "I believe you simply have not performed the correct experiments."

* * *

WHEN CASS BLINKED her eyes open, weak streaks of sunlight were struggling their way in through the tiny window and Oliver was sitting in the chair pulling his boots off again. He had some circles under his eyes, showing that his sleep had still been interrupted.

But he said, "Laurie will be well. She is quite warm, full of beef broth, and seems to be sleeping and waking normally."

"Wonderful," breathed Cass. "Are you coming back to bed?"

"Need you ask?" In seconds Oliver had shifted himself out of his half-buttoned clothes and back under the heavy quilts with her.

Cass shivered at the delicious sensation of his warm, solid body radiating heat against her, and then shivered again when the coarse hair on his legs rubbed against hers.

"Are you cold?" he murmured into her hair, before nibbling at the shell of her ear.

"Not in the slightest."

Before she knew what he was about he had tightened his arms around her and somehow slid *under* her. The feeling of all of him pressed so tightly against her was shockingly intimate and absolutely delightful. She wiggled against him experimentally just to see his eyes darken.

Which they did.

"This is a very unsatisfactory place to wait another day or so for Laurie to be ready to travel." He gently bit the spot behind the curve of her chin.

She swallowed. "Why is that?"

"Because I cannot make love to you as I would like, because all the men downstairs would hear you scream. I explained this last night," said Oliver in the tones of a man pointing out only what is reasonable and obvious.

"We must weather these ups and downs of life together," Cass sounded as resigned as she could before she gasped at the way his hands swept down her body at the same moment his tongue dipped into the space at the base of her throat.

"Truly, it will give us time to decide where to go when we leave and what to do." Oliver's hands had settled onto the slight swell of her hips and were pressing her against where he was growing hard. For her. Again.

She would never tire of that.

"I think there is only one answer to that," Cass murmured and wiggled against him again just to see what he would do.

* * *

"*I WANT that man thrown out into the ditch behind the stables!*"

Sir Michael's shout carried very well through the house, which was no doubt why Letty had gone to give him the news of their guests herself.

"*I want him horsewhipped and arrested and sent to the coldest, darkest gaol in the county!*"

Cass had already handed her cloak, dripping from snow, over to Sarah, but Oliver paused in the act of slipping his off. "Perhaps I had better hang on to mine."

Cass just waved him to silence. She could not hear anything, but she assumed from Oliver's face, and from knowing Sir Michael, that *someone's* welcome was not warm. Nonetheless, they were here and they needed to be here.

Looking like it was against his better judgement, Oliver gave up his cloak.

Helping Laurie off with hers, Oliver said, "Please don't stand, Laurie, not to wait for this. Do go warm up in the parlor. Can you walk all right?"

With a grateful smile and no trace of her usual French-styled disdain, the girl just nodded. She followed Sarah down the hall.

"*I don't care what Miss Cullen said, I—*"

Even after something cut off Sir Michael's shouting, it was many more long, uncomfortable minutes before Letty Grantley reappeared, her pale golden curls flying every which way but her expression calm.

Sir Michael Grantley rolled after her, red in the face and scowling madly.

Oliver had the distinct impression that Sir Michael fully intended to run him down.

But at the last moment he pulled up short, put his face far too close to Oliver's, and said, "So, she's forgiven you, has she?"

"She should not have, but yes."

Slightly mollified, but still glaring daggers, Sir Michael then turned to Miss Cullen. "Miss Cullen. What can we do for *you?*"

The emphasis made it staggeringly clear that what Oliver wanted was of no import whatsoever.

"We would like to beg of you a warm place to stop for a few days, sir, and perhaps you might help us chew over a bit of a problem we must solve."

"If it involves beating the tar out of this fellow here, I'm your man."

"Sir Michael." Cass stepped in front of Oliver and just shook her head. "Really, it absolutely does not."

"It should," put in Oliver calmly. "But apparently she doesn't want that."

Sir Michael looked back and forth between her, and Oliver, and her again until he let loose his breath. Oliver's lack of anger, and his seeming agreement, with Michael's own assessment of the situation seemed to take some of the air out of the baronet. "Well if it's anything more subtle, it's Anthony you want. You are lucky, he has been in London but is home again. We'll get him."

"I have already sent for him, sir," Letty put in smoothly. "Perhaps you'd like to return to your work. Your secretary is awaiting your direction."

"Oh no, I want to hear every word of *this*."

Without further ado Sir Michael rolled ahead of them all into the front parlor.

Letty just smiled. "He will be fine."

CHAPTER 36

The skies above Morland were grey and slung low as their carriages approached it, several weeks later.

"Perfectly fitting," Oliver grumbled. Cass only shrugged. It worried her to see the way his frown deepened as they drew closer to the manor, but if all went well they could soon be driving away again.

When they alighted, it was to see Anthony Hastings already descended from the other carriage, along with Geoffrey Eliot. Only Geoffrey Eliot could make the third man with them look small. The third man was a broad barrel of a fellow with cropped silvering hair and an expression that spoke of his disinterest in foolishness.

The estate's butler bustled out to meet them, followed by a phalanx of footmen, in very few minutes.

"Ah, Thompson." Oliver attempted to greet the man with a cheerfulness he did not feel. "Is Lady Gadbury still visiting, by any chance?"

"She has been here all winter, your lordship," said the butler, trying not to cast his head about like a confused young bullock faced with a bewildering herd of people he had not expected.

"I don't suppose Lady Sherrin is about as well. No? Well, Lady Gadbury will have to do. Ask her to join my little party wherever my father is—where is he, in fact?"

"Lord Rawleigh is in the green study, sir," and Thompson bowed as Oliver reached past him to tuck Cass' hand in the crook of his arm, and go in.

"It's a nice place," said the silver-haired man, looking about himself with the frankly impressed air of a man who lived in much humbler surroundings.

"It isn't," said Oliver tightly. "I wish I could offer you a more jovial visit, Mr. Leighton. But Morland is not a place for that."

Once inside, Oliver stopped as if something had just occurred to him. "Thompson, accompany Mr. Hastings on a small errand, would you? Bivens here can show me in to his lordship."

Finding no sympathy for his confusion in either Oliver's face or Anthony's, Thompson still looked like he was trying to think of a good reason not to agree as he and Anthony disappeared up a staircase.

The rest of the arrivals processed, in a grim silence, to the green study on the second floor of the main wing.

Lord Rawleigh was seated writing at his desk, gray hair brushed back smoothly and his pen scratching quietly.

The Earl started to his feet immediately as Oliver escorted Cass into his study, came around his desk in a way that looked anything but pleased. "What do you mean by this, sir?"

"I mean to ask you again, my lord, before these witnesses, if you are convinced of my bastardy. Before you answer—" Oliver cut off what the older man was about to say with the wave of his hand, "let me introduce you to William Leighton, a magistrate who is kindly lending me his advice."

"A magistrate? What?"

"The pleasure is mine, your lordship." William Leighton, the man with the bristling gray hair, bowed quite smoothly.

"This will not take a minute, sir, I am waiting only for a last friend of mine to join us."

"I am here, Dr. Burke, what *is* going on?" Lady Gadbury swept in wearing a becoming sky-blue gown and an unbecoming look of confusion.

"My apologies, my lady, I meant I was waiting on a friend of *mine*."

Oliver's eyes stayed on hers long enough that Lady Gadbury could be quite, quite sure of his meaning.

"Ah, here he is. Mr. Hastings. Thompson accompanied you to the room?"

"Indeed, sir." Anthony waited by the door, holding a large flat bundle under his arm.

"Very well. I do not intend to stay a minute longer than necessary, so let us make haste. Your lordship, when I was last here you accused me, I believe in some anger, of being a bastard."

Lord Rawleigh's lips were closed tight, but his eyes were full of an angry regret.

"Do you recall," Oliver pressed relentlessly, "accusing me of being a bastard?"

"I do," his father bit out.

Both Thompson and Lady Gadbury gasped.

No one else did.

"Then I would like to know the evidence for your claim. Think carefully, sir, before you answer."

Cass could feel Oliver's trembling, whether from nerves or anger she could not tell, but she squeezed his arm in what she hoped felt like a reassuring way. He turned to smile at her, and squeezed her hand back.

Then he said again, "Think carefully before you answer because your evidence would have to outweigh the more than thirty years in which you have never questioned my birth, including when I became the heir to your title."

He waved at Anthony, who brought forward his bundle.

Anthony unwrapped what appeared to be a sheet from a small painting, which had easily fit under his arm. To better show it to the assembled group, he propped it upright in a small chair.

It could have been a painting of Oliver himself. Which Oliver underlined by stepping closer, appearing to admire it. It was the same straight nose, strongly angular jaw, lush mouth and piercing eyes. Oliver considered it closely. "I do not wear a powdered wig, of course, though I do admire the rose-colored velvet suit. I believe I could do it justice, though I do prefer more modern taste in dress, as do you, sir."

Oliver turned.

"I wanted to remind you of this painting, which you must have seen many times over the years. I certainly have. I believe it is of your grandfather, sir, is it not?"

"It is."

The earl seemed transfixed, staring at the painting as if he were frozen in place. But the words were quite clear enough to hear.

"I only bring it to remind you of it, as you may have forgotten it. It may have been some time since you visited the fourth earl's gallery. Or it may be that you had forgotten it because it was moved from there. It was there when *I* last visited it. Mr. Hastings here, when he visited, also noticed this painting and its resemblance—it is rather well done, wouldn't you agree? Then he noticed later in the week-end that it had been removed from the gallery. He took it upon himself to uncover where it had gone. You found it where you expected, Mr. Hastings?"

"I did." Anthony sounded entirely calm.

"And Thompson, you saw Mr. Hastings retrieve it?"

"Yes sir, I did," stammered the butler.

"I am not sure, your lordship, if you would be entirely comfortable if I revealed in whose chambers the painting had been stored?"

"Well of course I did not—" The earl seemed to cut himself off as he realized who must have secreted the painting if he himself had not.

Oliver waited for him to go on. Lord Rawleigh remained silent.

"So let me ask you again—your lordship—did you have evidence for your claim? Sufficient evidence to disinherit me? Or was it only a burst of anger, and you misspoke? Because we have a magistrate here who stands ready to help you, if disinheriting me is truly your wish. Or..." And here Oliver's eyes became cold and cutting as glass, "perhaps this good man could help me swear out a claim of libel against whomever made that false assertion."

The earl's fists were both clenched till the knuckles showed white.

"Perhaps," Oliver added as if it had just occurred to him, "we should share with everyone where this painting was hidden?"

"Not at all," burst forth from Lord Rawleigh. "It was indeed as you say, a moment of temper. I do not truly believe you are not my son, Lord Howiston." And for one moment the man's eyes were old and desperately sad as he added, "I never really believed that."

"Really?" Oliver's voice was soft. "Because over the years I have sometimes wondered myself."

The two men, so alike in the way they held themselves and both wearing nearly identical coats, regarded each other for a moment longer.

"Well," Oliver cleared his throat, "we must be going. Your good health, sir."

Oliver turned to lead Cass out, but the old man strode forward quickly and grasped Oliver's hand before he had taken more than a step.

Oliver reared back in surprise.

"I hope Miss Cullen's presence here means that you... you still have a chance to marry as you would like. Marriage is... a weighty step."

Oliver studied his father's face. Cass could feel tears escaping but she didn't look at the Earl; she looked only Oliver's face, concentrating only on the surprise, then the relief she could read in the face of the man she loved.

"Thank you, sir. I am glad to hear it, as we are indeed already married. We were married just recently, in the neighboring county. It is a shame you could not attend. Good day to you, sir."

His father nodded, released his hand.

"Thompson, show our guests to the guest wing. I doubt anyone will be staying, just refreshing themselves from the travel. My wife and I will anticipate them by moving on."

Smiling at Cass with the smile he gave only to her, the one where his frown went away and his whole expression became sunny and light, Oliver carefully led his lady wife down the steps from the earl's desk and toward the door.

Pulling her close and patting her hand, as they exited Oliver tossed back over his shoulder, "Lady Gadbury, you will be reporting to the papers what Lady Howiston was wearing when you no doubt tell all of London about this fascinating afternoon, won't you?"

But he never looked back.

* * *

"Should we not at least visit your brother?" Cass murmured to Oliver as they approached again the front door of Morland.

Oliver shook his head. "There is no shortage of people in the house to tell him what has happened. I don't want to put him in any more difficult a position than his current one. Let him be able to say he had no idea what I intended to do; the ring of honesty can only help. As you saw from my dealings with my father, if one intends to survive in this family one must be eager to avoid confrontation with her ladyship at almost any cost. My father undoubtedly understands that she removed that painting and hid it in her rooms just to make sure that her assertion met no bald contradiction from the start. Just as it is easier for him if I avoid stating it outright, it will be easier for my brother if he can deny all prior knowledge of today's events."

They had discussed it, as part of the group at Roseford carefully planning this day. Cass was still not sure she agreed, but was willing to let Oliver handle people in his own family.

A footman approached them. "Lady Rawleigh would like to see you, Lord Howiston."

That they *had* planned for. Cass bit her lip, uncertain what Oliver would do despite the planning.

But it seemed to give Oliver no trouble at all to simply nod and say, "I am sorry that you will have to tell her that she will be disappointed."

It seemed to Cass that she was handed up into their carriage within moments. The horses still stood exactly where they had been.

After a few moments' conversation with the driver, Oliver joined her inside.

"You do not wish to even stay the night, Oliver?" Cass snuggled into her husband's side as their carriage gently rocked through the courtyard gate.

He folded both her hands in his own to warm them. "I have good reason to prefer spending the night in a coaching inn with you, my love, to spending one more night at Morland. In fact, I doubt I will pass through its doors again, at least until I inherit the damned place."

Cass turned and looked out the window at Morland's towers and carved stone crenellations. "It is too large a thing to be left unused forever, surely." The sense of relief Cass felt at having the confrontation over left her not only lighter, but clear-eyed. She could see more in Morland's outlines than she had seen before.

She briefly leaned over to bury her face against her husband's neck and kiss him there. She could feel the nearly silent noise he made and that made her feel lighter too. "Perhaps Morland will never be anyone's joyful home but it could be a place for something good."

"Like what?" Clearly the idea startled him.

"Something that would make you happy instead of sad." Cass looked out the window again, watched shadows start to form at the base of the towers as a few of the clouds above them cleared away. "Perhaps a hospital?"

His eyes sparkled again the way she liked to see them as he slid a hand behind her shoulders to pull her close and kiss her. Then he freed his hand again to say, *My very darling wife. You are a genius every day.*

Just sometimes clever, Cass responded but could not help adding with a pleased smile, *That might be one of my better ideas.*

EPILOGUE

Cass knew very little about flowers, but the ones that Mr. Adams brought into the library looked like a bright spring day in a vase.

Their lavender color against the yellow of the wallpaper in the room reminded her of the half-mourning dress she had worn for so long, and of the grandmother who had made it possible for her to have this very home.

Cass did hope her grandmother would not be disappointed. She thought perhaps that her grandmother had understood the pitfalls of aristocracy as well as the inescapability of real love.

There's a caller, in fact there's two, Peg appeared in the doorway to tell her, and Cass just nodded. She was not expecting anyone, and people still seldom came to the townhouse. Oliver was away but of course as a married woman Cass could now receive whatever guests came to call. She gave a brief thought to Lady Inglemawr, too, and hoped that wherever she was, she was well. Of all the letters that came to the house, she was still one day hoping to see one with an American direction.

Smoothing down the black front of her "drawing gown", as she thought of it, Cass slipped her pencil into her pocket before checking the twist of her hair as well. She thought she had done fairly well with it this morning, but her husband had definitely had his fingers in it before he had left the house. It was one thing for him to perpetually look ungroomed, but Cass felt it was quite another for herself.

I'll join them in the front parlor, thank you, Peg. Cass had repeatedly asked Peg if she ought to hire another maid since Selene's shocking departure and marriage. Peg kept saying no, but Cass thought that in a few weeks, when it was time to throw the windows open and clean for spring, more hands would be needed.

She would have to find people who would fit this place.

She was surprised to see her brother-in-law waiting for her in the front parlor, and the neighbor from the other end of the little crescent street whose name she had forgotten.

"Mr. Evelyn! You are too kind."

Victor, who had leaped to his feet when she had entered, bowed deeply over her hand. "It is too easy to be kind if all it entails is a visit to one's family."

"And Mrs.... Hipper, isn't it?" Cass smiled kindly at the other woman, who had also risen and given a little curtsey. "May I introduce my brother-in-law, Mr. Victor Evelyn?"

"Hibbert, Lady Howiston, yes indeed. I am pleased to meet you, Mr. Evelyn, and glad to see my neighbor. The weather is so much improved, I thought I would take the opportunity to visit."

Cass did not mention that their houses were not even two hundred yards apart on a small road that had been kept quite free of snow this winter. Cass only said gently, "Of course. You will forgive me if I sit next to you, I will have great trouble hearing you if I take this other chair. Mr. Evelyn?"

"I had hoped to find Dr. Burke at home, will he be here soon?" said Victor as they all seated themselves, showing plain eagerness to talk to his brother.

Cass had wondered why it had been so long since they had made their final visit to Morland before his brother had come, but since

JUDITH LYNNE

Victor was here now... "He will be home very soon, I believe. He is visiting the hospital where he hopes to engage some of the doctors in research."

Lady Hibbert looked startled. "I thought your husband was Lord Howiston, madam."

Cass just smiled. Letters still came to the house every day addressed to both Miss and Mister Cullen, as well as Dr. or Mrs. Burke. Very few came to Lady or Lord Howiston. She wondered how Lady Hibbert had found out about her title since it was so rarely used; she had not seen it in the papers this season, and neither she nor Oliver had any intention of attending any social function of the *ton*.

"You must be a friend of my husband's family," Cass said gently. "We have not yet resolved all of the problems of naming in the house."

Blinking, Lady Hibbert started to say something, then stopped, then finally said, "I see," in a way that made it very plain that she did not.

"My brother is doing research?"

"No, actually he hopes to create a sort of, well I suppose the easiest thing to call it is a club, of physicians and chemists who are studying medicines that produce unwakeable sleep. His idea is that it could produce far less suffering in the area of surgery, which as you know was his work abroad."

"Surgery!" Lady Hibbert turned slightly green. Cass wondered if she were the type inclined to vomit, or if she were the type inclined to faint.

"My apologies, Lady Hibbert, for conversation not appropriate to a lady."

The woman seemed to take a deep breath and steady herself to look carefully from Cass' dark glossy hair, with a few pinned curls in the back, down over Cass' long black linen gown, on top of which Cass had placed the single rope of her grandmother's pearls. Cass saw her eye them.

"I know, a lady does not wear pearls before evening," and Cass' tone seemed sincerely apologetic, "but they were my grandmother's and they remind me of her."

"Indeed. One should be at ease in one's home. I had not been at all sure if you were at home to callers, madam, so I will not keep you for long."

Cass knew it was evil of her, but she just waited to see if Lady Hibbert could come up with another excuse as to why she had come over to see the reclusive, rumored Lady Howiston.

She couldn't. In short order Lady Hibbert made her farewells, along with some vague mention of a musical evening for which Cass doubted she would ever receive an actual invitation, and she took her leave.

When she had gone, Victor sighed.

Cass wanted to sigh too. "I apologize, Mr. Evelyn, news of my marriage has started to leak as the social season has begun, and though no one really knows me, people are curious. Perhaps it is *because* no one knows me."

To herself Cass thought that she also suspected that the rumors would travel because many society women *did* know her *husband*. She was making plans for what she would say to any who were brazen enough to turn up.

"Do not overlook your sheer curiosity value, madam. You look like the true original you are, and I suspect at least a few ladies will be interested in coming to see."

That shocked her. "Do you really think so? That would be dreadful. I hope we are not subject to much of that. I have too much to do to entertain gawkers."

"I am grateful that you admitted me, then, as I truly wish to see Oliver."

"I am so glad! I had hoped to see you before this."

"I felt that my brother had perhaps lost confidence in me since he did not come to tell me of the situation with my father himself," said Victor quite somberly, "and perhaps I lost some confidence in myself. I wanted to wait until I could assure him that I can only agree with him that Morland is not a place for our home. I regret more than I can say that my family was used against him."

"You had no knowledge of it, sir. My husband will say the same."

"Nonetheless, I have found a place in the city and have already made arrangements to move my family here to join me."

"Never say so!" Cass leaned forward, her hands fluttering in her excitement. "What kind of a place? Oh, how exciting! Dr. Burke will be *so* pleased."

"I have no head for the work my brother can do, but I have some talent with maths." Victor looked gratified by her reaction. "With much investigation and some help, it turns out that there are financial houses that are happy to employ an unnecessary heir such as myself if only to smooth relationships with those who use their services. I believe I may be of some real use in dealing with their accounts, and I believe it will suit me well. I only wish I had pursued something like it sooner. I apologize to *you* that I did not pursue something like it sooner."

Cass hesitated, but went ahead and asked. "Your mother is fine with your son, Oliver's heir to the title, leaving the estate?"

"No, she is not," said Victor in a tone that made it clear that his mother's opinions would not have any bearing on the matter.

"Madam," said Adams, appearing at her elbow, "you asked to be notified when Dr. Burke approached the house."

"Thank you, Adams!"

Victor was slightly taken aback at the rush with which Cass told him, "Please do stay here—we will be back immediately—so delighted!" and darted out of the room.

Running down the stairs, Cass opened the front door enough to peek out and see her husband just opening the gate.

The late afternoon light glinted on his hair, which looked quite brushed smooth for once. In a few more hours his chin would show the stubborn shadow of beard once more, which Cass quite liked. But even now, as the sun slanted through the little crescent lane highlighting the cut of his clothes, she thought nothing had ever looked so beautiful. Of course, she knew the lines of his body and the curves of the muscles hidden beneath the wool and linen, and there was no doubt that increased his appeal. But it was the smile he gave her then, the smile that only she got to see, that she found most lovely as he bounded up the stairs to seize her around the waist.

They just barely made it inside before Oliver greeted his wife with a long, loving, and completely inappropriate-for-public-display kiss.

"Mm." Cass' eyes sparkled at him. "Is it the dress?"

"It is *absolutely* the dress." He bent his head to kiss her again.

Victor is here! Cass could not hide her excitement a moment longer; her hands flew.

Really? Oliver glanced up the stairs. Then he smiled again. *I have hoped to see him for a long while. He can wait a few more minutes; these kisses are more important.*

And one of the neighbors came to see what I looked like today. The lady at the other end of the crescent lane.

Oliver raised an eyebrow. *And what did you show her?*

Cass shrugged. *Just myself.*

Well, that *is more than enough for anyone,* Oliver said before pulling her against him again. And because his hands were occupied with holding her, he said into her ear, "You are a feast of plenty for me."

* * *

NOT AT ALL THE **End**

* * *

Cass and Oliver continue to appear in the future books of Lords and Undefeated Ladies

Read Book 3, **What a Duchess Does**, *in which Cass' cousin the maid takes a whirlwind trip to becoming a duchess*

And both Cass and Oliver appear in
The Caped Countess
The start of a whole new series of Regency action heroines in love!

S IGN *up for exclusive insider news (and free advance peeks!) at judith-lynne.com, or see About the Author and find me on social media.*

Keep these books coming - share a review at Amazon or Goodreads!

NEXT IN LORDS AND UNDEFEATED LADIES

The intriguing fairy tale romance
What a Duchess Does

* * *

"Miss de Gauer, I never had the impression that you were one of these young ladies who spent their afternoons sighing over imagined love affairs."

"I've never made a plan to sit down and sigh, true, but I am not entirely cold-blooded about the idea of marriage either."

The Duke snorted outright. "Very well; let us assume that I *am*. Why should I not offer you the vacant position of Duchess of Talbourne if it seems to me the best way to help you?"

The very idea made her want to shift nervously in her seat. She didn't. "Because it is not a *job*, Your Grace."

"It is very much a job, miss."

"It is not only the position; it is the job of being your *wife*."

"It need not tax you greatly."

Selene had rolled her hand into a fist; she began tapping her thumb against the other fingers, a habit when she was thinking, a habit her mother had tried to break.

Something about the *way* he offered her marriage didn't lighten the heavy worry in the pit of her stomach. In fact, it made it worse.

His Grace had the ability to take away Selene's grinding worries about her mother's health. But surely it was only a trade of that constant threat for this one? This tight feeling of dread about where this would all end, perhaps with him putting her aside as if she were a cup of tea?

She would need to become necessary.

"I do not lie fainting on couches dreaming of romance, but I have never before heard marriage described solely as work, either. If we suppose you need a duchess, we must assume there are thousands of women who could do the job better. Why marry *me*?"

* * *

She was very good at continuing to ask questions. That didn't worry Nicholas; he was very good at continuing not to answer them.

"I have grown tired of being invited to so many functions where boring girls are paraded in front of me like cattle. Men I must persuade, in my work in the House of Lords, make sly remarks about my widowhood and constantly ask about my mistresses, as if any duke must have many."

"And do you have mistresses?"

This was the Selene he knew, come out to play. Well, not amused, but not shying away from the shocking question, either. He had many reasons that he wasn't ready to share, including that he was out of excuses to make the hour-long trip to Lady Howiston's parlor.

"I do not."

"Surprising. Your duchess will apparently be able to enjoy your fidelity."

Was she pleased? He hoped she was pleased. She didn't look it. He wished she were.

But then she went on. "You *must* be lonely."

When he said nothing, she pressed him. "You *are* lonely, aren't you?"

The question threatened to crack something open inside of him which must remain closed.

"I have never used that word, Miss de Gauer. I am not proposing to inflict much of my company upon you, if that is what you are asking. I am an old man, and a plain and boring one. You need not fear that I expect you to wait in attendance upon me."

* * *

"On the contrary." Now Selene sat back, and she managed to smile. "If I am to do the job of a duchess, I would expect at the very least a little of my duke's company." She did not consider him old, doubted he was plain, and knew that he was far from boring.

He didn't seem to suspect the way he featured in her daydreams. And he did have a duke's disdain for romantic feelings.

Well, perhaps she would recover Lady Selene's disdain for romance too.

If she were to be married to the man for the rest of her life, it would at least be easier if he continued to like her. And she him.

She *needed* them to spend some time together.

* * *

"My company is no bargain for you, miss." Nicholas tried a glower, but of course she did not see it. He felt a flush of concern. His glower was an important weapon for keeping people at bay; he realized for the first time that of course he would never be able to use it on her.

She was undaunted. "No, I like the idea. Are you willing to play a game, sir?"

Nicholas stifled the urge to both laugh and groan. "This is not a parlor and you are not entertaining me while I wait."

"But you know I like games! And we ought to have one, for it will lighten what you describe as a heavy work, this marriage business. I propose…" Her thumb rubbed against her folded fingers, so he knew she was thinking. "I propose that we must spend at least a quarter of an hour together every evening, or the person who fails must pay a forfeit."

He could not stop his smile. Thank God no one on his staff was here to see it. His reputation as the iciest duke in Britain would be shattered. "And what sort of forfeit? I suppose you would play for a divorce? Annulment? You won't get out of the arrangement so easily, I promise you."

* * *

Selene hoped she managed to hide her reaction to the cutting chill that went through her when he mentioned such things so easily. That answered at least a few of her questions. Divorce and annulment were things that ruined lives, and would ruin hers, but he mentioned them as if they were nothing but game pieces on a playing board. If she did not please him, he would put her aside the way a pawn was eliminated from the board.

She did not shiver. If she accepted him, she would already have played away her future in exchange for her mother's life. It would be worth it. In Talbourne House her mother would have company every hour of the day and night, footmen to carry her wherever she might want to go, beef broth and sweetmeats whenever she liked.

Selene could risk going on as they were, but it risked her mother's life, and she was only trading away what the rest of the world no longer valued anyway.

Before she grew too despondent thinking about *that*, Selene remembered that she had been in the middle of a proposition.

"A forfeit of the other person's choice, of course. What do you say, Your Grace? Are you willing to play?"

* * *

Order *What a Duchess Does* at Amazon here!

AFTERWORD

I am not deaf, or Deaf, or hard of hearing, so first let me apologize if I have misrepresented what it is to be hearing-impaired in my writing. Please feel free to contact me at judithlynne.com and give me feedback. I want to receive it. I always want to do better.

British Sign Language is different from American Sign Language, as the latter developed from the French version of sign language. (The French also at one time had a system that forced its users to sign French *per se*, including every feature of the language as if it were spoken French, right down to the verb tense. Obviously this was unworkable and was abandoned.) Sign languages are languages in and of themselves, not transliterations of some spoken language (except in the odd French example I just mentioned), so every time my characters here are speaking in sign language, it is a translation of what the fictional character is signing, not a transcription, and I tried to have the language reflect that a little. The terms "manual method of instruction" versus the "oral method of instruction" were taken from materials of the time, when "sign language" was not a term that was used.

There were many inspirations for a book this long, including my ongoing reading on the British wars of the period which also led to my invention of Sir Michael, my hero in *Not Like a Lady* who is also an amputee.

One was an article by Mary E. Kitzel from 2017, "Creating a Deaf place: the development of the Asylum for Deaf and Dumb Poor Children in the early nineteenth century," in the *Journal of Cultural Geography*. The article describes the founding and development of the Asylum, which was indeed always pressed for space. The history of that asylum informed how I pictured and described Cass' imaginary Institute. Among the things I borrowed were details like the schoolmaster's tendency to hire graduates of the school who also spoke Sign Language, who made good instructors for the younger students, and that this helped develop and consolidate British Sign Language. There definitely were also both poor students and rich ones, and I like to think that if Sign Language was being shared throughout the school, there was also the opportunity for many new friendships.

The other was about Jane Groom, a Deaf woman who conducted extensive correspondence with people all over Britain in her work to support the emigration of Deaf people to colonies of their own in Canada. This was in Esmé Cleall's "Jane Groom and the Deaf Colonists: Empire, Emigration and the Agency of Disabled People in the late Nineteenth-Century British Empire" in a 2016 issue of the *History Workshop Journal*. Today it is impossible to applaud the exercise of colonization itself, as the lands Groom obtained were removed from Native American peoples to which they rightly belonged; Deaf culture and Deaf cultural activists have also moved us all far beyond Miss Groom's supposition that deafness was a stigmatized deficiency. I still admire Miss Groom's determination to create a place for Deaf people even in the face of opposition by hearing people. At a time when people who could not hear were expected *not* to be self-sufficient, she knew very well that they could be, and worked to make a place where that could happen. Though not a rich woman, she was influential in ways that the rest of us can only hope to achieve, and a wonderful inspiration for me, as I hope my heroines have dreams that include shaping the world to be as it should be rather than accepting it as it is.

COMING NEXT - NEW SERIES

Get ready for an entirely new series!

The Caped Countess
The first of the action-packed
Cloaks and Countesses

* * *

By day, Lady Donnatella seems like a duke's silly daughter. So she can save London lives by night.

When she stumbles into something larger than a street fight, everything she's balancing may come crashing down...

It's another lonely season for Tella, dancing and gaming madly while keeping marriage away. She cannot tell her family or friends that her true self is the one battling danger in the city's dark streets. Nor will anyone guess; she's perfected her disguise.

Then her night-time alter ego is seen—just when she can no longer

COMING NEXT - NEW SERIES

count on her best friend, or her beloved great-uncle. And the resulting fuss in the newspapers isn't making any of this easier. Nor is the reporter who saw her...

Henry Fitzwilliam, third son of a marquess, left London society to serve in the wars, and won't go back. He's devoted his life to telling the stories Britain needs to hear, and perhaps this Caped Count falls into that category. He can't be sure until he gets much, much closer.

Tella can handle a fight, but tracking a murderer makes for higher stakes. She might need someone at her back. Fitz might be the worst choice—or he might be more perfect than either of them suspects.

The Caped Countess
Available at Amazon now

ACKNOWLEDGMENTS

Words can't express my gratitude to the team that helped me get this book off the ground and into your hands:

First and foremost, thank you to everyone who bought *Not Like a Lady* and gave me faith that other people would enjoy seeing more of these characters; and extra ice cream sundae-type thanks to the wonderful people who took the time to review it.

To Selena who told me I wasn't crazy to have a deaf heroine, thank you profoundly and I will buy you a coffee-beer any time.

To Holly, Rhonda, Lisa, and Alicia, who helped with editing and encouragement, thanks don't cover how critical your work was in making this a *much* better book.

Thank you Melody Simmons for another gorgeous cover, one that really inspired me.

And as always thank you to my husband Marshall for his insights into story structure, his eagle eye for typos, and his inspiration, because he is the love of my life every day, and that, as the poet said, is going some.

ABOUT THE AUTHOR

Judith Lynne writes rule-breaking romances with love around every corner. Her characters tend to have deep convictions, electric pleasures, and, sometimes, weaponry.

She loves to write stories where characters are shaken by life, shaken down to their core, put out their hand…and love is there.

A history nerd with too many degrees, Judith Lynne lives in New Jersey with a truly adorable spouse, an apartment-sized domestic jungle, and a misgendered turtle. Also an award-winning science fiction author and screenwriter, she writes passionate Regency romances with a rich sense of place and time.

Please sign up for the first information on new books from Judith Lynne, as well as sneak peeks and exclusive content on your favorite characters, at judithlynne.com!

ALSO BY JUDITH LYNNE

Lords and Undefeated Ladies
Not Like a Lady
The Countess Invention
What a Duchess Does
Crown of Hearts
He Stole the Lady (January 2022)

And stay tuned for *Cloaks and Countesses*!
The Caped Countess
The Clandestine Countess (July 2022)

Manufactured by Amazon.ca
Bolton, ON